# Romance is DEAD

**Katie Bohn** is a communications specialist by day and a fiction writer by night. Located in Pennsylvania, USA, she writes about love and all the mysteries that go along with it. In her spare time, she enjoys spending time with her husband and son, as well as being bossed around by her cat.

# Romance
## is
# DEAD

## KATIE BOHN

QUERCUS

First published in Great Britain in 2025 by

**QUERCUS**

Quercus Editions Limited
Carmelite House
50 Victoria Embankment
London EC4Y 0DZ

An Hachette UK company

The authorized representative in the EEA is Hachette Ireland,
8 Castlecourt Centre, Dublin 15, D15 XTP3, Ireland (email: info@hbgi.ie)

A CIP catalogue record for this book is available
from the British Library

PB ISBN 978 1 52943 926 7
EBOOK ISBN 978 1 52943 927 4

1

Text designed and typeset by CC Book Production
Printed and bound in Great Britain by Clays Ltd, Elcograf S.p.A.

MIX
Paper | Supporting
responsible forestry
FSC® C104740
FSC
www.fsc.org

Papers used by Quercus are from well-managed forests and other responsible sources.

For my mom and grandma,
who would have wanted to read this.
(Well. Maybe not the spicy scenes.)

# Chapter One

If people knew how horror movies were made, they wouldn't be scared of them.

That actress running terrified through the woods? Bored and exhausted from reshooting the scene a dozen times.

That abandoned hospital those teens are trapped in? Actually a warehouse filled with carefully curated vintage medical equipment from a supplier in LA.

That bad guy chasing them? Just some dude named Todd who will be hotboxing and eating Doritos in his trailer once the director calls cut.

The point is, movies are very different behind the scenes. On-screen, stylists have made everyone look otherworldly gorgeous, editors have coaxed the story into perfect shape, and composers have crafted scores to depict just the right sense of impending doom. But in reality, actors are often tired, hungry, or uncomfortable.

Or, if they're anything like me on the first day of filming my last horror movie, all three.

Bursting out of my trailer into the early September air, I double-checked that the buttons of my candy-pink cardigan were straight as my stomach grumbled. Thanks to a misread call time, I'd arrived on set an hour late and there'd been no time to grab a snack from craft services. I'd never screwed up a shooting schedule before, but my subconscious must have been trying to protect me.

I was absolutely dreading making this movie.

Production assistants whizzed by as I wound through base camp, the community of trailers that would be our home while filming *House of Reckoning* on the outskirts of the Virginian mountains. Wardrobe assistants shuttled costumes to the actors' trailers and crew members hollered for people to get out of the way as they swung props and equipment into the backs of tiny golf carts that would transport the objects to set. Because the house we'd be filming in was located a half mile away in the middle of the woods, I'd need to find my own golf cart to get there.

And judging by the time, I needed to find it now.

I swept through camp, looking for the line of carts I'd been told would be waiting. Thankfully, there was one left. A young, gangly PA with shaggy, sand-colored hair and an eager smile on his face waved from the driver's seat.

"Need a lift?" he asked, reaching for the ignition.

"Yes." I gratefully hopped in next to him. "I do."

He steered us onto the dirt path that led through the woods, leaves that were just starting to turn orange rustling pleasantly on either side of us as we bumped along. The PA kept glancing at me out of the corner of his eye, opening his mouth but never saying anything. Finally, he broke the silence.

"Excuse me for asking, but you're Quinn Prescott, right?"

My stomach sank. After more than two decades of making movies, I was used to being recognized. But in the three months since my disastrous previous film, it usually came with either a snide comment or look of pity. I couldn't decide which was worse.

"Guilty." I braced myself for what was coming next.

The PA's face broke into a grin. "Wow, it's amazing to meet you! I've seen all your stuff. Your performance in *The Exorcism of Luna LeGrand*? Genius."

Some of the tightness eased from my chest. "Thanks."

"Gosh, I was so excited when I learned I'd be working on one of your movies. This sounds so lame, but can I get your autograph later?"

"Of course."

"Amazing, thank you. Seriously, you've got a fan for life. Anything you're in, I'll be watching!"

I didn't have the heart to tell him that after this, there wouldn't be any others.

"My name's Trevor, by the way. I'm so rude." He took one of his hands off the wheel and reached for a handshake.

"Nice to meet you." As I shook his hand, I noticed a brightly colored friendship bracelet on his wrist. "I like your bracelet."

"Thanks! My niece made it for me a few weeks ago at camp and I haven't taken it off since. She's the best, just the cutest kid."

My mind wandering as Trevor chatted away, I scanned the

landscape for any sign of the set. In the movie, four college students rent an Airbnb where they accidentally conjure the spirit of an evil witch, who then proceeds to slaughter them one by one. The setting and atmosphere would be one of the most important aspects of the movie.

At first, all I saw were trees as we wound through the woods. They leaned close, their branches brushing the cart like they might snatch us if they had the chance. Finally, a weathervane peeked above the treetops, twirling in the wind and spinning lazily as though by an invisible hand.

Then we rounded a corner, and the entire house lurched into view. With sides of gray stone and a roof of black shingles, the towering Gothic mansion looked straight out of a Hitchcock movie—complete with turrets, creeping vines, and shadowy windows. It had been nicely maintained, clearly loved, but still had the air of a house with secrets.

I shivered. It was perfect.

"Here we go." Trevor steered us to the far side of the driveway and threw the cart in park. "I hope—"

But I was already out of the cart and gone, waving in thanks over my shoulder. Weaving between a grip wheeling a camera rig and two prop assistants lugging a rolled-up carpet, I slipped through the front doors.

The foyer was spacious, paneled in dark shining wood and featuring a grand staircase. Briefly, I wondered how a gaggle of college students would be able to afford such a fancy Airbnb, but decided not to raise that particular plot hole with production. An archway to the right led to a dim dining room, but it was in the room to the left that we'd be filming. The parlor had been dressed like a college party was underway: a large sound system dominated one corner and a beer keg sat on one of the chairs.

I took a moment, soaking in the last first day on a set I'd ever have.

Had my decision to leave the movie industry last month been hasty? Yes. Had selling my LA apartment and putting all my belongings in storage until I figured out a new plan been even more impulsive? Also yes. I'd been making horror movies since I was eight—a bit part I'd nabbed solely because my dad had been playing the infamous horror villain Puzzle Face since the nineties—and in the years since, I'd worked my way up to become one of Hollywood's go-to scream queens. Horror was my thing, my passion. My happy place.

But then a year of horrible, no good, very bad events made me realize I needed to leave the industry—and LA—for good.

I'd just have to suffer through one last movie first.

As I stepped into the parlor, the room was abuzz—crackling with the special energy only found at the beginning of a new production. Like the first day of school, but better. The energy followed you everywhere, from your trailer to the set and back to your hotel room. It sizzled through the atmosphere, electric and full of anticipation, rife with the possibility that this could be it: the blockbuster that could catapult everyone to fame and superstardom.

The optimism made me want to puke, but it was impossible not to feel.

"Girl, what did you do to your makeup? I saw you less than an hour ago!"

A makeup brush appeared out of nowhere, bristles fluttering

dangerously close to my cornea. The hand wielding it belonged to Mara, who today was dressed in a floral-print dress with her chestnut hair styled in vintage victory rolls. Last month she'd been sporting high-end athleisure almost exclusively, but now she seemed to be favoring a 1940s pin-up aesthetic. Thankfully, her commitment to being my best friend was far more constant than her fashion du jour.

"Sorry." I waved my hand vaguely in the air. "I'm feeling a little off today."

Mara eyed me warily. "I bet. You're sure this is the last one?"

Saying nothing, I nodded.

We'd met ten years ago when we were both nineteen and working on the slasher *My Mom Married a Demon 2: Zaddy Zebub Returns*. We instantly clicked, bonding over being two of the only women on set and a mutual love of the TV show *Scream Queens*. I loved the campy horror; she loved the frothy fashion. We'd been inseparable ever since—and even more so over the last month, once I'd started crashing on her couch after selling my apartment.

"You don't want to spend more than a few weeks deciding whether to end a twenty-plus-year career?" Mara rustled around in the fanny pack that held her on-set supplies. "You don't think that's a little rash?"

"Shh!" I glanced around frantically, hoping no one had overheard. "I'd prefer to keep this under wraps for now. And yes, I'm sure. I told you—"

"I know, I know. I get it." She dabbed some fresh concealer under my eyes and started to blend. "By the way, did you hear your co-star had to drop out?"

"Wait, what?"

"I just found out. A motorcycle accident, apparently. He only broke his thumbs, but production thought he wouldn't be able to do his stunts, so they replaced him."

"With who?" Endless possibilities flashed through my mind. Could it be Adam Driver? Chris Hemsworth? Zac Efron?

"You know that reality show from a couple months ago? *Pleasure Island Paradise*?"

I rolled my eyes. "The one with that guy who's been all over the press for dating every supermodel in the continental US?"

Mara stared at me pointedly.

"Are you serious?"

"Dead. Sorry, girl." She sighed. "Looks like your luck hasn't turned around just yet."

My brain spun like an overloaded computer as I tried to comprehend this development. This could not be right. Teddy James was a vapid reality star, not an actor. He was nothing but an opportunistic fame-chaser. After *Pleasure Island* wrapped, the tabloids had spent the summer analyzing paparazzi shots and social media interactions to predict which starlet he was dating that week. The more famous the better. I'd only met Teddy once, but it had told me everything I needed to know: that he was a jerk, a player, and a fuck boy of the worst order.

This was not good.

My anxiety ten times higher, I glanced at my phone. I'd thought I was running late, but it still didn't look like we were ready to start.

"What are we waiting on?" I spotted our director, Natasha Vossey, pacing the length of the room, peering out the window each time she passed. I'd worked with her before and knew she hated starting even a minute late.

"Teddy," Mara said. "He's hot, but can he read a clock?"

Then, right on cue, the sound of the front door opening echoed through the room.

It was Teddy. Golden sunlight slanted through a nearby window, illuminating him like something from a Renaissance painting. His sun-kissed skin looked lit from within and his hair shone like burnished bronze as he moved leisurely into the room, no sense of urgency or remorse, clearly unconcerned that he'd kept everyone waiting. He slung a letterman jacket over his shoulder as he greeted the cast and crew, his biceps straining his white tee-shirt as he made sure every person in the room had noticed his arrival.

He was, unfortunately, even hotter than I remembered.

"There you are!" Natasha stormed across the set. She was a petite woman, but you hardly noticed when she was stomping toward you in a leather jacket and Doc Martens.

Teddy's eyes widened as she approached, and I silently cheered her on, hoping she'd give him the dressing-down he deserved.

Instead, she simply motioned toward the set. "Over there. Now. We're running behind and we haven't even started blocking, for Christ's sake!"

"Sorry. Yes, ma'am."

Natasha gave him a withering look. "Never call me that again." She spun around to take her place behind the camera, motioning for everyone else to get moving.

The whole room shifted. Actors moved toward the set, crew members headed toward the lighting rigs and sound systems, and PAs scurried to get out of the way. Meanwhile, I prayed Teddy wouldn't remember me. Our interaction earlier that summer had been so brief. So meaningless, so nothing. I hadn't even given him my name. Ideally, he wouldn't recognize me and we'd never have to address what happened. After all, my character did wear a wig. I could assume a fake identity and remain in the wig at all times.

That was it. The new plan.

Before I could leave, Teddy broke away from the wardrobe assistant who had been taking her time double-checking the fit of his tee-shirt and locked eyes with me. Something like recognition flashed across his face—a startled raising of his eyebrows and opening of his mouth. Panic flared in my chest, and even though my brain told my feet to flee, they remained rooted in place.

A second later, a body crashed into me—and my entire torso was suddenly soaked in boiling hot liquid.

I screamed and tore at my sweater. It was hot, way too hot. I tried to rip it over my head, but the wet material merely bunched on itself and I only got it half off. I was no longer being boiled alive, but I was stuck with my sweater wrapped around my head and my arms twisted helplessly in the fabric. Which meant I was now standing in front of the entire cast and crew in my jeans and a soaking-wet bra.

And the person with a front-row seat to this spectacle was Teddy.

## Chapter Two

Please don't let my nipples be showing, I prayed to whatever deity might happen to be listening. I'd love it if everyone on set couldn't see my nipples right now. Would be absolutely thrilled.

"Oh my God, oh my God, oh my God," a voice shrieked nearby. "I'm so sorry!"

I assumed the panicked voice came from whoever had just drenched me in boiling hot liquid. Straining to peek above the fabric bunched around my head, I spotted the culprit: Trevor, the PA who had driven me to set.

And right in front of me, now in direct eyeline with my bare, scalded chest, was Teddy.

"Trevor!" The urgent call came from another room. Probably someone wondering where their coffee was. They were about to be disappointed.

"Sorry," Trevor squeaked once more before scurrying away, the cup caddy dribbling as he went.

I craned my neck, still swaddled in my sweater, scanning the room for Mara. She'd just been here—where the heck could she have gone? I finally spotted her across the room, where she was helping a young, blonde woman who was desperately gesticulating to her face in an apparent eyeliner-related emergency. I silently cursed the wardrobe department. They'd been so determined for my character to look "sexy in a nerdy way" that the sweater they'd given me was at least a size too small. I'd struggled to pull it on before it was soaked in coffee; there was no way I'd get out of it by myself now. I was looking for the nearest wardrobe assistant, my arms still pinned in the air and my hands losing circulation quickly, when Teddy cleared his throat.

"Do you need some help?" His smile was smug and self-satisfied, like he assumed I'd been waiting on pins and needles for him specifically to rescue me.

Which, maybe I did need rescuing. But not by him.

"I've got this under control, thanks."

Teddy stared at me wryly. "Suit yourself." He started to walk away.

"Actually!" I swallowed, my pride slipping down my throat. "Some help would be great."

"I gotcha." Teddy said, taking another step closer. Without my neck having its full range of motion, I was stuck staring at whatever part of his body was at eye level, which turned out to be his collarbone. This close, he smelled of pine and something earthy—like the forest after it rains. It was . . . pleasant.

How annoying.

Teddy mimed rolling up his sleeves as he widened his stance. "You ready, hon?"

My skin crawled at being called "hon", but I nodded, at least as much as my limited range of motion allowed.

Carefully, he pulled the bottom edge of the sweater, his fingertips grazing my arms as he lifted the garment up and over my head. The touch sent pleasant tingles along my shoulders and down my spine, and I was transported back to the night we met—and the way his fingertips along my skin had set my entire body aflame.

*Stop it*, I reminded myself. *You know how that ended.*

With one final unceremonious yank, Teddy finally succeeded in pulling the sweater over my head. I shivered as my body was freed of its acrylic-and-wool-blend prison and immediately glanced down. Yes, my nipples were indeed visible beneath the wet, ivory fabric of my bra. Not only that, they were now hard and pointed. Great.

Teddy, however, seemed unfazed. "That's a new record—it usually takes longer than ten seconds after I meet a girl to help her undress." He grinned, my now-ruined sweater still in his hands.

I reached up to adjust my wig, which was now horribly askew, before snatching the top back. "I'll take that."

Teddy let the fabric slip through his hands. "You're welcome, by the way."

"Thanks," I said grudgingly.

"I'm Teddy." He reached out a hand, his expression belying no hint that we'd met before.

On the plus side, it looked like my plan to remain incognito was working. On the downside, it still stung that I was just that unmemorable.

"Quinn. Nice to meet you."

I took Teddy's palm with as little enthusiasm as I could muster. His skin was warm and dry, his grip firm but not aggressive. A perfectly normal handshake. But the moment our skin touched, tingles once again ignited the nerves from my fingers all the way up my arm and down into my stomach.

I jerked away, dropping his hand unceremoniously. "I, uh, didn't even know you were part of the cast until this morning."

"I was sort of a last-minute addition."

"Poor Drew. And his thumbs."

"You know what they say. One man's thumb injury is another man's treasure."

I cocked my head. "Do people say that?"

"Now they do." He smiled, his eyes crinkling and his gaze boring into mine like we were the only people in the room.

A strange warmth bloomed in my chest, and I found myself unable to break my eyes away from his. What were we doing? Bantering? Had I no self-control?

Thankfully, before we could continue, the assistant director loudly cleared her throat.

"Positions!" She cupped her hands around her mouth and repeated herself. "Positions, people!" She looked me up and down, a withering expression on her face. "And you. Get some clothes on."

I rarely got embarrassed on set. After years of filming scenes running around half naked while screaming and ugly crying, it took a lot for me to feel self-conscious. So while stripping off my top in front of everyone on day one wasn't ideal, it also wasn't the worst thing to have ever happened to me at work.

(That honor belonged to the time I accidentally ate the prop food for a picnic scene set in a graveyard. It was potato salad. It had been sitting in the sun for hours. I was immediately sick everywhere.)

And yet hours later, after we'd finished blocking the scene and wardrobe had fetched me a new sweater, I was still flustered. I didn't mind that I'd flashed half the cast and crew, but I was unnerved by how easily I'd been swept into conversing and joking with Teddy. One smoldering look, and I'd immediately dropped my defenses.

The heat from the spilled coffee must have momentarily overcooked my brain.

"Last looks!" the AD hollered, once we were in position to begin filming. "Finishing touches, let's go."

The makeup and wardrobe assistants waiting in the wings jumped into action, ready to make any last-minute tweaks to ensure we all were camera-ready. Mara scurried over, giving my face a quick study.

"You got this," Mara whispered as she gave my makeup a final touch-up. "Think about capybaras." It was an inside joke, something we'd come up with years ago as a way of saying good luck. And for the smallest second, it grounded me.

"Think about capybaras." I squeezed her hand and walked onto set.

In addition to Teddy and me, there were three other actors in the main cast. I already knew Brent, a surfer type with shaggy blond hair and sun-kissed skin, from our time filming *Killer Croc Attack* together a few years ago. He was playing the resident bad boy in the group of friends and was currently staring at his phone as the hair stylist touched up his slicked-back hair. I suspected the faint whiff of marijuana detectable on set was coming from him.

In contrast, Chloe—an actress a bit younger than me, with bright blue eyes and a tumble of long blonde waves—was chatting Mara's ear off as she touched up her lip stain. If I remembered correctly, this was her debut film. I resisted the urge to tell her to run, quickly, before the industry could ruin her life too.

A loud giggle pierced the air. It was Audrey, a pretty British woman who would be playing the film's villain: the witch. She had one hand over her mouth, trying to contain her laughter at something Teddy had just said. Because much of the witch's look would be added by special effects in post-production, she was decked out in a special bodysuit covered in inch-wide sensors that looked like ping-pong balls and would be used to align the digital costume and effects with her movements.

Teddy whispered something in her ear and she shook even harder, the sensors jiggling even more frantically.

Gross.

Deciding to ignore them, I closed my eyes and whispered my traditional prayer to the patron saint of scream queens herself, Ms. Jamie Lee Curtis.

"Oh, badass mother of final girls," I murmured, "watch over me while I carry the torch as yet another girl in the wrong place at the wrong time. May my screams be convincing, my acting adequate, and my legs strong enough to run for more than half of this movie. Am—"

"Am I standing in the right place?"

I opened my eyes in irritation. It was Teddy, who had apparently had enough of flirting with Audrey and was now posing his question to me.

"How should I know? Am I supposed to remember your marks?" I did have them memorized, actually, but that was beside the point.

"I just thought—"

"And they didn't tell us to hit our marks yet anyway."

"I was just asking a question. You don't have to be so uptight."

"Uptight? Are you serious? I—"

An older man who was moving very fast for his age brushed past us, knocking me off balance and interrupting our squabbling.

"Took me near a dozen flea markets before I found the perfect one," he said proudly, setting down an ornate lamp and rubbing a microscopic smudge off one of the stained-glass panels in the shade.

Ah. The props master.

"Couldn't just pick one up at Pier One?" Teddy grinned, clearly impressed with his own joke.

I winced. As a general rule, props masters were not only extremely particular about their props, but also took their jobs extremely seriously.

Indeed, the man did not find this amusing. Instead, he looked downright offended. "Why, so it can look like every other house in this country?" He adjusted the lamp once more before he left, grumbling as he went. "Young people. No respect for the art form. Always want instant gratification."

I waited until he was gone before turning back to Teddy. "Trying to piss off every member of the cast and crew before filming even starts?"

He frowned, clearly annoyed that at least one person on set hadn't been swayed by his charms. But before he could reply, the AD reappeared.

"Lock it up!" she shouted, sending the last makeup artist scurrying off set.

A moment later, Natasha took her place behind the camera. Everyone who was out of view of the cameras hushed and I took a deep breath, closing my eyes as I slipped into my character. It was showtime.

In the script, it's the group's first night in the house. Their plans consist of nothing but drinking and hooking up—they have no idea that all but one of them will be dead by Monday. The scene culminates with Teddy's character running backward to catch a football, saving it before it crashes into an expensive floor lamp. Over his shoulder, the witch emerges from the shadows for a brief moment. It's the audience's first glimpse of the bad guy and a hint that things will soon go terribly wrong.

Meanwhile, everyone but my character was supposed to be drunk. You know, because she's such a goody-goody. Yawn.

"Roll, camera!" And then, a moment later, "Action!"

Everyone sprang into motion.

Chloe stumbled around in the background, tripping over herself and slurring her words. I sat primly on an armchair, surveying the group with judgment. Meanwhile, Brent tossed around a football, looking for someone to join a game of catch.

"Hey, captain! Catch!" Brent shouted. He pulled back his arm, which was Teddy's cue to try and stop him.

But instead, Teddy froze—his expression growing more panicked by the second.

He'd forgotten his line.

"Cut!" Natasha popped up from behind the camera, glowering in Teddy's direction. "Let's try that again."

We started over. This time, he remembered to jump in front of the lamp, but still couldn't remember the words. The next time, he remembered the line but failed to catch the football before it sailed into the hall. I tried to hide my frustration. He might have been a late addition to the cast, but surely he'd had some time to prepare.

"Cut!"

Another take, and yet another line missed.

Again, and again.

"How about we take a break?" Natasha suggested. Her voice was even, but the pounding vein on her forehead suggested she was anything but calm.

When we returned, Brent once again delivered his line, winding his arm back to throw the ball. I held my breath, praying Teddy would finally nail the take.

"No!" Teddy shouted, jumping to his feet to intercept the ball. "Not in the house, there's priceless antiques in here!"

The air whooshed out of me in relief. He'd got it.

Brent released the football and it sailed across the room, heading straight for the lamp. As Teddy ran backward to catch it, the joy of remembering his line must have wiped everything else from his brain. Instead of stopping on his mark, he kept going. And going.

And then, he crashed right into the lamp. The priceless, twelve-flea-market lamp. It teetered back and forth dramatically, its wide base lurching first to one side and then the other, and a voice called out from somewhere off set.

"I got it!" Trevor the PA hurried over, grabbing for the lamp. But instead of getting a firm grip, he tripped over the base, sending both himself and the lamp careening toward the ground. On his way down, Trevor grappled for anything that could save him. Unfortunately, he only succeeded in pulling Teddy down too. Audrey poked her head around the corner to see what the commotion was, resulting in Trevor hitting her with his flailing arms and knocking several sensors off her special CGI suit.

By the time they all hit the floor, the set was deathly silent—except for the sound of the extremely expensive-looking glass lampshade shattering into a million pieces.

"Cut!" Natasha jumped out from behind the camera, hands braced behind her head. "Are you fucking kidding me, people!" For a moment, it looked like she was going to throttle Teddy, or Trevor, or both. Instead, she just marched off the set in dismay, slamming the front door as she went.

"I am so sorry!" Trevor said to no one in particular, looking at the wreckage in dismay.

Teddy remained where he'd landed on the floor, seemingly in shock.

"My lamp!" The props master, who had apparently stayed to watch the performance of his beloved lamp, charged onto set.

He made a beeline straight for Teddy and Trevor, who backed up in fright until he was pressed against the wall.

"You." He leaned in until he was mere inches from Trevor's face. "And you." His glare pivoted to Teddy. "Do you have any idea how long it took me to find that lamp?"

"Um." Trevor's voice trembled. "Hopefully not very long?"

"Two months! All for the two of you to break it in two seconds!" Spit spewed from his mouth as he yelled. "This industry is riddled with people like you. You don't give a damn about anyone else's time. Selfish. Selfish!"

"I'm so sorry," Trevor squeaked.

Teddy, meanwhile, said nothing, sitting on the floor with his head in his hands.

The props master straightened his shoulders. "You're not sorry. But you will be." Then he too stormed off, out the back door.

After an excruciatingly long moment of awkward eye contact, everyone else started to leave too. Brent murmured a few words to Trevor and Teddy before giving them claps on the shoulders and wandering off. Chloe and Audrey followed shortly after, throwing sympathetic looks behind them as they disappeared around the corner. Trevor looked like he was going to cry as he fled, but Teddy stayed on the floor, not bothering to move.

What a disaster.

I wanted to have empathy, but the irritation that had been building all day instead ignited into anger. Just like I'd predicted, Teddy was inexperienced and unprofessional. Worst-case scenarios ran through my head: production losing money due to filming running long, rumors of discord amongst the cast leaking out, and the movie being doomed before it even hit theaters.

I stalked over to him, the words bursting from my mouth as soon as I got close. "What the hell was that?"

He lifted his head "I really don't need another bag of shit right now. I think I got enough from Natasha and that props guy."

I ignored him. "Didn't you prepare at all?"

"Not enough, apparently."

"No, that's pretty obvious."

"I had, like, two weeks to prepare, you could cut me some slack."

"You couldn't learn the first scene at least?" I balled my fists and placed them on my hips. "If you keep wasting everyone's time, we're going to fall behind schedule."

His face clouded. "So it'll take a little longer. What's the big deal?"

"Are you serious?" I let out a humorless laugh. "If we fall behind, that means we're also going to go over budget, which means it's less likely that the film will, you know, earn money. And what do you think happens if this movie flops?"

"Hey, I already got my paycheck."

I narrowed my eyes. This was the Teddy I remembered from the party. "You don't care about anyone but yourself. What about Chloe? She's just getting started. What if her first film is a flop? And this could be a really big break for Brent and Audrey." I poked my finger in the middle of his broad, firm chest. "This is bigger than you. Don't be such an asshole."

"Asshole?" Teddy huffed out a laugh. "You're making a lot of snap judgments about someone you don't even know."

"I think I've seen all I need to see." Determined to leave on a high note, I spun around. I strode forward, intent on storming off set as quickly and efficiently as possible. Unfortunately, I'd forgotten about the toppled light fixture that still lay sprawled across the floor. My foot snagged on the hunk of metal, sending me falling painfully to my knees.

"There's a lamp there," Teddy offered helpfully as I staggered to my feet. "I hear it was expensive."

# Chapter Three

**Mara:** You back at the hotel? We're celebrating in my room!

**Mara:** Hello?? I know you're not busy!

**Mara:** BITCH. When are you getting here?

"I don't know what you expected." Mara collapsed into one of the armchairs in my trailer. "You ignored my texts—what am I supposed to do? Not come kidnap you?"

"Yes," I grumbled, sitting back down on my sofa. It was nine o'clock at night and I was still in my trailer, lounging in a pair of ratty old leggings and an oversized Rolling Stones tee-shirt. And, until thirty-seven seconds ago, I'd been blissfully alone. "That's exactly what you were supposed to do."

"Too bad. I'm not letting you mope all night."

"Good luck trying to stop me." I picked up my crochet project, a half-finished gray-and-white chevron blanket. An older co-star had taught me when I was seventeen, shortly after my parents had gotten divorced during my first time shooting on location away from home. The woman, a grandmotherly type playing a murderous fortune-teller, showed me how to stitch simple washcloths during downtime between scenes, something to take my mind off my angst and homesickness. Now, whenever I had a hard time turning off my thoughts, the rhythmic movements of a crochet pattern helped tune them out.

At home, I had a whole shelf filled with tiny, crocheted figures of Freddy Krueger, Pennywise, and other horror icons, but on set I preferred a mindless project like a scarf or a blanket.

"Oh, stop. Today wasn't that bad, was it?"

"It really was."

Even with my expectations for the industry on the floor, I still hadn't expected filming to start this poorly. This was my eighteenth movie. I was a pro! It was supposed to be an easy last job that I could check off my to-do list before figuring out what I wanted from the rest of my life. Destroyed property, cast and crew walk-outs, and cussing out my co-star had not been on my last-first-day bingo card. Although, I considered, maybe it was actually a blessing in disguise. Maybe I needed a sign that quitting was the right thing to do. If I hadn't been convinced before, I certainly was now.

"Well, I brought goodies." Mara reached into her bag and pulled out a packet of all red and pink Starbursts. "I figured you'd need cheering up at some point—I just didn't think it was going to be the first day."

I immediately perked up. "See, I told you I was happy you came over." I didn't want to know how many bags of candy the two of us had demolished over various disappointments, heartbreaks, and late-night shoots, but I was happy to add one to the tally.

"Mm-hmm." She eyed me warily as she tossed me the sweets. "How are you feeling? Lamp disaster aside."

"I don't know," I admitted, carefully unwrapping one of the candies. "It still doesn't feel real. That this is the last one."

"It doesn't have to be."

I sighed. "It does though."

My decision to quit making movies at the age of twenty-nine after a twenty-one-year career may have been hasty, but it wasn't without reason. The first strike was the reception of my most recent film, at the beginning of the summer. Maybe in retrospect, I should have known that a film called *Zombie vs. Vampire: Battle of the Undead* wasn't destined for greatness, but it was campy and fun and I loved it. Critics did not agree.

One reviewer called the movie "notable only for the towering heights of terribleness it achieves." Another said they were "worse off having viewed it than if their eyeballs had been removed." Several called out my performance in particular, with one claiming I must have "suffered zombification myself to agree to the film."

Ouch.

As the rotten cherry on top of the shit sundae, my agent called a week after the premiere to say she was dropping me. She was retiring the following year, but apparently couldn't bear to keep representing me until then.

As Mara and I sat around later that night slugging wine and mainlining Snickers in her apartment, I'd realized I was a year away from my thirties and not only was I at the lowest part of my career, but I was burnt out. I was tired. Tired of the cold scrutiny of auditions and the criticism of my performance in the roles I did manage to snag. Tired from making a movie almost every year since I was eight. Tired of the tabloids speculating about my body and blasting every detail of my personal life for the world to see. Just a week earlier, a TikTok from a Hollywood gossip account had gone viral for saying *House of Reckoning* would be a smash success—but only if they replaced me as the lead.

Still, my final decision to quit had been reserved for a month later, when I met Teddy for the first, awful time. That night had been enough to make me throw it all away for good.

"Things will get better. First days are always rough," Mara said. "And hey, at least you have a hot co-worker to stare at every day."

"Gross. You better not be talking about Teddy."

"You're still mad at him? You should have seen the way he filled out his sweatpants when he showed up first thing this morning."

"Please never talk about his sweatpants area around me ever again."

"Fine, but you should still give him a chance as a colleague. Or filming is going to be really miserable." Mara glanced at her phone and stood, tapping something on the screen. "Are you coming back for the party or what? You know it's tradition for the first night of filming."

"I'm sorry. I really just want to be alone tonight."

"Fine." Mara sighed heavily, grabbing her bag. "You'll have to make it up to me another time, though."

I blew her a kiss. "I promise."

As the door clattered shut behind her, I picked my blanket back up and tried to focus on stitching. But I couldn't stop my thoughts from straying back to Teddy. He was an annoying itch I couldn't scratch, an irritating noise that wouldn't let me focus. Who didn't know you had to have your lines memorized before filming began? Who couldn't hit a mark without destroying an expensive prop and injuring themselves?

Someone whose only experience was a reality show.

My eyes strayed to the TV. I'd never seen an episode of *Pleasure Island Paradise*, but now I was curious. Maybe I could check out an episode, just to see.

For science.

The premise was simple enough: eighteen singles arrive on an island with the ultimate goal of finding a partner and becoming engaged. Drunken antics, formulaic storylines, and dramatics ensue.

Two hours later, I was halfway through the third episode.

Some of the contestants had fallen in love. Some had gone through devastating breakups. All favored wearing as little clothing as possible. Teddy was no exception, prancing around in nothing but a puka shell necklace and tight swim trunks as he flirted with every woman on the cast. I wanted to scoff, to make fun of the show's ridiculousness. But honestly, it was pretty entertaining.

A sudden rapping on my trailer door yanked me out of my reality television reverie.

I jumped, giving a shrill yelp like the first hapless victim of a cheesy slasher. "Damn it, Mara." I paused the TV in the middle of a challenge involving the contestants licking whipped cream off each other's bodies and hurried to the door.

But it wasn't Mara waiting for me. Standing at the bottom of the metal steps was Teddy. No longer in his football captain costume, he'd changed into dark jeans and a gray Henley, the top button undone and sleeves pushed up past his elbows. He looked surprised, as though he hadn't expected me to answer.

"Um, hi." It was jarring to see him after watching him swim shirtless in the ocean a moment ago on the TV. "What's up?"

"I just wanted to apologize. For earlier."

"Oh." I hadn't expected that.

"I . . . Can I come in? It's getting chilly out here."

"Uh. Sure." I didn't love the idea of him sticking around long enough to come inside, but I also didn't want to miss an opportunity of being told I was right.

"Thanks." He hopped up the stairs, twisting sideways so he could fit his broad shoulders through the narrow doorway.

"Do you want a seltzer or something?" I was still annoyed with him, but if he was trying to be nice, I could at least offer a snack. "Or some . . . Cheetos?" I cringed inwardly. Holey leggings and cheese-covered extruded cornmeal—so classy.

Teddy waved away the offer. "I just wanted to say that I'm sorry for completely screwing up those shots. I know I got defensive, but . . . you were right. Everything you said."

I couldn't help but soften a bit. Music to my ears. "Thanks for saying that. In that case, I'm sorry for calling you cocky and selfish."

He tipped his head in appreciation. "You weren't one hundred percent wrong. I could probably do the bare minimum from now on and actually learn my lines." He chuckled. "Shouldn't be too hard, I suppose."

Cue the record scratch.

"Excuse me?"

"What?" He looked genuinely confused, as though he hadn't just been totally condescending. Again.

"You'll do 'the bare minimum'? Why are you doing this movie if you don't give a shit?"

He stared at me flatly, like the answer was obvious.

"Ah," I said. "Money. Or is it just the fame?"

Teddy wearily ran a hand through his hair, causing a stray lock to flop over his forehead. "You're awfully uptight about a movie you don't even care about. It's not exactly high art."

"I . . . Where'd you get the idea that I don't care?"

"Doesn't take a genius—you looked miserable all day."

I flinched. He wasn't wrong, but I hadn't realized it'd been so obvious. "I don't owe you smiles. I was just concentrating on my work. Something you might want to try."

"You know, I came here to apologize and you're just—"

"I dare you to finish that sentence." I crossed my arms in front of my chest. "I'm not one of your girls of the week that's going to fall over with gratitude just because you threw a half-assed apology my way."

He yawned, gazing lazily around my trailer. "Are you done?"

For the second time that day, I found myself toe to toe with Teddy, furious and fuming and trying to stop staring at the way his muscles were straining the sleeves of his shirt long enough to come up with a satisfying retort. But before I could, Teddy's eyes strayed to the TV, and a moment later, they lit up with delight. A satisfied grin spread across his face.

Irritated, I followed his gaze to see what was so amusing. And then—oh no. Oh, no.

No, no, no.

He was staring at the TV, which had been paused in the middle of *Pleasure Island Paradise*. But it hadn't stopped on, say, the ocean. Or the beach. Or even a nice view of the contestants talking.

No. It had paused on a close-up of a giant tongue about to lick whipped cream off a nipple that filled the entire screen. And it wasn't just any nipple. It was Teddy's nipple.

"Well, well, well," he said, leaning back to admire the scene. "I didn't know you were such a fan."

"Don't flatter yourself. I was ..." I frantically searched my brain for an excuse, but nothing came. "There was nothing else on."

"Nothing else on streaming? Isn't that famously full of more content than you could ever possibly watch?"

Cheeks burning, I grabbed the remote and turned off the TV. How much more humiliation could I endure for the day? And so much of it nipple-related.

"I'm going back to the hotel. You need to leave."

"I'll walk you out."

"I'll pass."

He made a show of peering out the window. "It's awfully dark out there. And we are headed to the same parking lot."

"I'll give you a head start."

Teddy burst out with a laugh. "Wow, you're stubborn."

I hesitated. Everything in me wanted to insist that I could walk my own self to my own car, thank you very much. But I had to admit he was right. There were no lights and we were in the middle of nowhere—it was freaking dark out there. Jason Vorhees himself could be lurking nearby in his hockey mask with a chainsaw.

"Go." I pulled on my Converse and hoodie and grabbed my bag. "I'm leaving so you need to go too."

"Ladies first."

I rolled my eyes as I exited the trailer, locking it securely behind us. I was in no mood for his patronizing attempts at chivalry.

The day had been warm, but the night air was brisk. The moon was a skinny sliver, offering almost no light to walk by. I lengthened my stride as I made my way through base camp, eager to put as much distance as possible between me and Teddy. But as we came to the long stretch of field that came before the road we had to cross to get to the parking area, I heard Teddy's footsteps getting closer and closer.

"Would you stop creeping up on me?" I wrapped my arms around myself, trying to ward off the chill.

"Why, you scared?" Teddy whispered in my ear.

"What? No. Of course not."

"Interesting. Then why are you pressed up against me?"

Looking down, I realized he was right. Somehow, we'd ended up so close that we were hip to hip.

I jerked away. "Sorry. I've always had trouble walking in a straight line."

"You might want to get that checked. Sounds like it could be a problem with your amygdala."

"I'm pretty sure it would be an inner ear issue."

Teddy shrugged. "Either way. Doesn't sound normal."

"It's totally normal, I just— Ah!"

I screeched to a halt, narrowly keeping myself from running into the deep ditch separating the field from the road. I windmilled my arms, suddenly off balance, reaching for something—anything—that would keep me from toppling over. Teddy gripped my arm, steadying us both as we moved back onto stable ground. I grappled with my phone, turning up the brightness as I tried to find a way across.

And then I screamed.

## Chapter Four

Finding a dead body in a movie is easy. You wait while the extra is oh-so-carefully arranged in a gruesome manner, listen for the AD to call "Action!" and then hit your mark and scream in a way you've artfully practiced in the mirror until the effect is perfect. Terrified, but in a sexy way.

In real life, it's different.

At first, it took me a few beats to register what I was seeing. The ditch was deep and dark, shrouded in shadow. By the time my brain registered there was a human at the bottom, I assumed they had simply fallen down and must be awfully hurt to be lying in there, completely motionless. My stubborn brain refused to believe that what I'd simulated more than a dozen times on screen was happening in real life.

But then I saw the blood. Gallons of it, black as ink where it had sunk between the rocks and into the earth.

That's when I screamed. And it wasn't a pretty, moonlight-bouncing-off-my-tits scream. It was ugly and hurt my throat, wrenched out of my lungs like the rattling buzz of a chainsaw. I staggered back, pulling Teddy along with me. We fell to the ground and I used my feet to push us away from the ditch. My scream died in my throat, my chest constricting until I couldn't catch my breath. Teddy wrapped an arm around my shoulders, yanking me close, and my lungs finally loosened.

"Call 911!"

"Right."

As Teddy fumbled through his pockets for his phone and hit the emergency call button, I crawled over to where the body— no, the person—was lying. Shock was rapidly being replaced by an all-encompassing dread. But I needed to get a closer look so we could relay information to the 911 operator.

I lifted my phone for light as I peered into the ditch, which ran along the road. The bright orange temporary fencing that would typically keep someone from falling in and hitting the rocks below had fallen away, leaving a gap. The person was curled inside, wearing jeans and a black tee-shirt, and my stomach sank when I finally made out their face.

Damn it, Trevor.

"Hang on, I'll check." Teddy pulled his head away from his phone. "Are there any visible injuries?"

"One second." Bracing myself for what I might see, I scanned his body. The blood seemed to stem from a gash on his forehead, likely inflicted by the rock he'd fallen on. His clothing was dark, and the light dim, but I didn't see any other obvious injuries.

I relayed the information to Teddy, who passed it along to the operator.

"A pulse, uh, I don't know. Quinn, is there a pulse?"

"Um . . ."

I eased myself gently down into the ditch and tugged down the neck of his shirt. It didn't look promising. I took a deep breath and pressed two fingers on his carotid artery. Nothing.

"No!" I yelled back up to Teddy. "Shit, no, he doesn't."

"No pulse," he repeated into his phone, sounding queasy.

As I scanned Trevor's body, looking for anything else that might be helpful to first responders, I noticed that his wrist was conspicuously bare—there was no sign of the friendship bracelet from his niece, the one he told me he never took off. The thought that he was here, alone and without his beloved token from his niece, made me impossibly sad.

Shortly after the paramedics arrived and, grim-faced, called the coroner, the police also pulled up on the side of the road, lights flashing. Two officers climbed out of the vehicle—a pudgy man who might have been in his fifties and a woman who looked like she could have been his twin. After a quick word with one of the paramedics, they ambled over to where we stood, the man shining his flashlight in our faces as he approached.

"You two the folks who found the body?" His mouth worked at a toothpick and he was still wearing sunglasses, even though it was well past midnight.

I bit back a smart comment about him being able to see better if his eyes weren't covered.

"Yes," I said, squinting and holding up a hand to shield myself from the blinding light. "That's us."

"Ah, sorry 'bout that." He lowered the flashlight and tucked it back into a holster on his belt.

"Honestly, Larry." The woman shook her head, rolling her eyes as she turned to us. "Can you tell us what happened, sweetie?"

Teddy and I recounted what we'd seen, each helping the other remember. Teddy hadn't noticed the pool of blood had already been coagulating when we found him, while I completely forgot to mention the time we left my trailer until Teddy chimed in. The two cops jotted down notes, nodding along as we told them everything, which—admittedly—wasn't much.

"Did you see anyone else in the immediate vicinity?" the woman cop asked.

Teddy and I looked at each other. "No," we agreed. "No one."

"And where were you two prior to finding the body?"

"I was in my trailer, since about . . ." I wracked my brain, trying to remember. "Seven, I think it was."

Teddy nodded. "Same. In my trailer, that is. Since eight."

"I see." The woman chewed on the end of her pen. "So you two were the only ones in the area where the body was found. Interesting."

"That we saw!" I clarified. "There could have been someone else, we just didn't see them. We only left my trailer, like, five minutes before we found him."

"I thought you were in separate trailers?"

"I paid a late visit to her trailer," Teddy explained. "I knew she'd be missing me and wouldn't want to wait until tomorrow to see me." He capped off the lie with a jaunty wink.

I bit my tongue to avoid cussing him out in front of the cops. This freakin' guy.

Nodding, the woman police officer held out the notebook and pen. "Your contact info, please."

Mouth dry, I jotted down my name and number before Teddy did the same.

"Thank you kindly." The man tipped his hat to us. "I think we have what we need here. Hey, Deb? You want to start taping off the scene?"

"Sure thing, Larry."

He flipped to a fresh page in his notebook. "Now, do either of you know how to get in touch with the person in charge of this whole show?"

I nodded bleakly, rattling off Natasha's contact information. By the time they told us we were allowed to leave, my adrenaline had worn off and I was exhausted.

Teddy and I finished walking to the parking lot in silence. Along the way, a swell of emotion built in my chest. I'd only known Trevor for a day, but it'd been enough to know he hadn't deserved to die alone. No one deserved that, and especially not someone as sweet as Trevor. If the day had been a disaster before, it was an absolute catastrophe now. And as we reached my car, I couldn't shake the feeling that all of it was Teddy's fault.

"Thanks for that, by the way," I spat. I knew it didn't make sense to blame Teddy for what happened to Trevor—not really— but I also couldn't deny that the entire day had been cursed since the moment he showed up on set.

Teddy blinked as he ground to a halt. "For what?"

"That!" I motioned wildly at the field behind us.

"Hang on. You can't seriously be blaming me for what just happened?"

"I was getting ready to leave when you showed up at my trailer! If you hadn't slowed me down, maybe I could have helped him!" My throat was growing thick, and I swallowed hard, desperate not to get emotional.

"First of all, we already established that you were in the middle of staring at my nipples on the TV when I got there, so your story isn't adding up."

"Whatever."

"Second of all, it didn't look like he moved much after hitting his head. There's nothing you could have done."

"You don't know that." I swiped at my eyes, which were filling with tears at an alarming pace. "Just leave me the hell alone from now on."

I yanked open the door to my car and climbed in, immediately locking it behind me. I twisted the keys in the ignition and turned on the radio, the thumping sounds of the Talking Heads filling the vehicle.

Psycho killer . . . Qu'est-ce que c'est? . . .

Gunning the gas, I peeled out of the parking lot, leaving Teddy standing alone in the dark.

# Chapter Five

Despite setting three alarms, I was still late to set the next morning.

It had been a rough night. Every time I was about to nod off, visions of Trevor's glassy eyes jerked me awake. If I wiped that image away, it was replaced by violent slow motions of him falling, his head crashing into the rock. I was able to snag a few hours of sleep, but it still felt like I'd been up all night by the time my alarm went off.

Hopping out of my car, my face was still puffy and my eyes full of grit. Mara was going to have her work cut out for her. I winced as I passed the spot where we'd found Trevor. Bright yellow police tape was still cordoning off the scene, evoking memories of sitting in the dark next to his body. I shook my head, desperate to clear it. I needed more caffeine. Stat.

As I wound through base camp on my way to craft services, there was a distinct lack of commotion. I hadn't been run over by any PAs distracted by their headsets. There was no sign of

Natasha or her AD looking for someone in a blind panic. And I'd expected to run into at least one hungover actor stumbling onto set late after celebrating the night before.

But everything was eerily still. Had the entire production been paused? Had no one thought to tell me?

A cup of coffee slid into view.

"I figured you might need this." Teddy fell in step next to me, also in sweats and a hoodie, making the two of us look like partners in crime. But while I looked like death warmed over, Teddy was—irritatingly—as handsome as ever. There were faint shadows under his eyes, and that stubborn curl of hair had flopped onto his forehead, but he still looked ready to walk onto a modeling shoot. I hated that after two fights and finding a dead body together, I was still as attracted to him as the night I met him.

"Oh my God, thank you." I grabbed the cup and took a long swallow, sighing in relief. I might have been tempted to toss it on the ground the night before, but now I couldn't afford to waste precious caffeine. "It feels like I got about seven minutes of sleep last night."

"I can tell."

I raised an eyebrow. "Excuse me?"

"You look tired."

"Thanks so much."

"I didn't say you looked bad." He cocked his head to one side, studying me. "You look . . . worn." He snapped his fingers. "I know. Like Jigsaw. In those *Saw* movies."

"Jigsaw," I repeated flatly. "I look like a seventy-year-old terminally ill man?"

"Yeah, kind of that vibe."

"Fantastic," I grumbled. Teddy threw back his head as he laughed, his eyes crinkled with delight.

I watched him as we continued our way through base camp. I'd been so angry with him the day before, so frustrated with how selfish he'd been by not preparing and wasting everyone's time. And his arrogance after his lame attempt at an apology. But I had to admit he'd helped me talk to the cops, and he had brought me coffee. And I did like the way his eyes twinkled when he laughed, even if it was because he'd compared me to a horror movie villain.

Shaking my head, I snapped myself out of it. No. The man just knew how to be charming, as evidenced by the fact that he seemed to be in active relationships with three separate Instagram models at the moment. And falling for that charm had bitten me in the ass earlier in the summer.

As we rounded a trailer a few steps later, I had my answer to why everything was so quiet. Everyone had gathered in the middle of base camp, and Natasha was facing the crowd as her voice boomed across the space.

". . . did not make it." Her voice was solemn. "His family has been notified."

Gasps and murmurs echoed through the crowd. As she waited for everyone to quiet down, Natasha spotted us.

"And actually, here are the two that found him." She out-stretched an arm, motioning to where Teddy and I stood at the edge of the throng.

Everyone craned their necks to stare. Two boom operators caught my eye, whispering behind their hands, while a group of lighting techs openly gawped. I squirmed, uncomfortable under the scrutiny. I took another sip of coffee, trying to shield myself with the cup.

"As I was saying," Natasha continued. "He was taken to the hospital, where it was determined he was already deceased by the time he was found. Police are willing to talk to anyone with information, but after carefully examining the scene, they are considering the death accidental at this time."

Something twinged in the pit of my stomach. Rationally, I knew it made sense that Trevor's death had been an accident. But something, some alarm bell buried deep in the back of my mind, made me feel like what happened the night before was more sinister. I just couldn't put my finger on what.

"Thankfully," Natasha said, "PAs are easy to find and we'll get a replacement in here soon." She straightened her shoulders and clapped her hands. "In the meantime, the show must go on. Filming will resume today as originally planned."

Before Natasha could stride away, the AD placed a hand on her shoulder and whispered something in her ear.

"Oh. Right. If anyone feels 'traumatized'"—Natasha put scare quotes around the word with her fingers, looking pointedly at Teddy and me—"counseling is available if you find it absolutely necessary. Back to work!"

I only made it a few yards before Mara caught up to me, grabbing my arm as we fell into step.

"Are you ok? Why didn't you call me last night?" She tightened her grip, her fingernails digging into my skin. "Oh my God, Quinn, you found a body! How awful."

I winced, as much from the pain as the guilt of not telling her. "I know, I'm sorry! It was so late when I got back."

"Who cares? You found a body."

"Stop saying it out loud! And Mara, you know damn well you're in bed every night by nine." On a previous movie, I'd had to fetch her from her trailer when she'd fallen asleep before what she referred to as a "late night shoot." It started at nine thirty.

"I'll have you know I was up until ten last night." She finally relaxed her talons, slipping her arm companionably into mine instead. "But even if I wasn't, you know you can always call me or bang on my door. Especially if you—"

"If I found a body. I know. And thank you." I took a sip of coffee with my free arm. "It's so wild, it all kind of feels like a dream at this point."

"More like a nightmare." Mara opened the door to the makeup trailer. "Come on, I'll even let you fall asleep in my chair."

Mara was able to spackle enough makeup on my face to make me look more like a fresh-faced college student and less like a zombie from *Night of the Living Dead*, but I had a harder time summoning the energy to focus on my scenes. I missed my mark twice and accidentally spoke other characters' lines for them. Teddy remembered more lines than the day before, but still made some truly bizarre acting choices. Why he thought it would be appropriate to give his character a Southern twang in the middle of one scene, for example, I had no idea.

The rest of the cast also seemed affected by the news about Trevor. Brent, for all his cool-guy bravado, kept missing his cues.

Audrey kept spacing out, falling out of character by the time the camera landed on her. And while Chloe's personality was usually as bouncy as her champagne-colored curls, she kept pausing between takes to dry her eyes.

When we finally wrapped for lunch, I was so exhausted that I almost skipped it in favor of taking a nap. Knowing I'd feel worse if I didn't eat, I picked up my meal from catering, double-checking that the top was marked with "No peanuts." Apparently, my parents learned about my peanut allergy when I was two and stole a peanut butter cookie from Drew Barrymore at the *Scream* premiere. My mom's yells of panic were initially attributed to the movie before someone finally realized I needed medical attention and whisked us off in a limo.

Choosing a seat under the tent where I could eat alone, I tossed the lid onto the table and dug in. I'd barely forced myself to eat three bites in when a shadow hovered overhead.

"Mind if I sit here?" It was Chloe, eyes bright and holding a salad identical to my own.

Hesitating, I finished chewing a cherry tomato to buy myself some time. Chloe seemed sweet, but she also seemed to spend a lot of time on set chatting and asking questions whenever the cameras were off. I was in the mood to sulk alone, not listen to a barrage of small talk. But her face was so hopeful that I couldn't help but acquiesce. I nodded and she sank onto the seat opposite me, smiling in relief.

"Thanks." She pushed her disposable fork through its plastic film wrapping. "I feel like the new kid at school trying to find a seat in the cafeteria."

I wanted to point out that there were several empty picnic tables, but that would be rude.

"It'll get better. That feeling never lasts long."

"I hope not." She speared a hunk of avocado. "Actually, there was another reason I wanted to come over here."

"Oh?"

"Not to be weird, I know we don't really know each other, but I wanted to check on you. Going through what you did last night?" She pressed her hands to her cheeks. "I can't imagine."

I stiffened. "That's nice of you, but I'm ok."

"It must have been awful."

"It wasn't great." I pushed some lettuce around with my fork, what little appetite I had evaporating as Trevor's bashed-in forehead came to mind.

"What happened? Natasha just said there was an accident."

"Honestly, I don't really feel like talking about it."

"Totally. No, of course you don't." Eyes falling, Chloe set down her fork. "I'm so sorry, I shouldn't have asked." She stared at her salad, looking dejected. Neither of us felt like eating anymore, apparently.

As we sat in silence for several beats, my heart twinged. I knew she hadn't meant any harm—I'm sure everyone else was curious about what happened, too. And it was clear she felt anxious on set and just wanted a friend, even if she was going about it a little awkwardly.

"How do you like filming so far?" I asked, forking up some lettuce. "This is your first movie, right?"

Looking a bit surprised, Chloe nodded. "I've had a few bit parts here and there, but this is my first major role."

"You're doing great so far."

"You don't have to say that. I ruined a whole take earlier by bursting into tears."

"And I missed my mark twice in a row. But the way you kept reaching for the ibuprofen over and over because your character was hungover? Genius, so funny." It was one of my favorite parts of making movies—the little choices actors made that really sold a scene.

"Really?"

"Really."

Chloe smiled, looking relaxed for the first time all day. "Thanks for saying that. It's all I've ever wanted to do—be an actor."

I bit my tongue. I didn't need to dash any dreams today.

"I am a little nervous, though," she admitted. "For tomorrow's shoot."

"Why's that?"

"The scene on the balcony? It's not a huge stunt, but I'm still worried I'm going to screw it up." Chloe laughed. "Or that I'll actually get pushed off and break my neck."

Picturing the scene we'd be filming the next day, my stomach plummeted. There it was: the lurking feeling that had been bothering me, telling me that Trevor's death might not have been so accidental after all.

"I have to go." I staggered to my feet, grabbing my half-finished salad.

"Are you alright?" Chloe's face crinkled in concern. "What happened?"

"Something in the salad isn't agreeing with me. Maybe the

avocado?" I pressed a hand to my stomach, trying to sell the story. "I'm sorry, we can chat again later!"

Leaving my food behind, I fled the tent. I needed to go back to the ditch where we'd found Trevor. Now.

## *Chapter Six*

It takes a lot to shake me up.

Maybe growing up with a constant reel of horror movies playing in the background had desensitized me. The kind of things that happened in the movies just didn't happen in real life—there was no evil clown waiting to lure you into that nearby storm drain. No matter how wild your little niece or nephew acted while you were on babysitting duty, they were almost certainly not the actual spawn of Satan.

And during my two decades in Hollywood, it became clear that you're much more likely to be hurt by someone close to you than a man who hunts you in your dreams. See also: the guy who dumped me as soon as our relationship made him famous enough to snag a role in the latest superhero movie, or the "friend" who swore she wouldn't audition for a part I particularly coveted but then did anyway. And got it.

I'd take Freddy any day over that kind of pain.

The point is, I wasn't the anxious type. But that scene Chloe had reminded me we'd be filming the next day? Her character is pushed off a balcony by the ghost of the witch, and even though Chloe's character survives with a minor knock to the head, it was eerily similar to Trevor's so-called accident. Maybe too similar.

After fleeing the lunch tent, I'd returned to the spot where we'd found Trevor. Just like I'd remembered, a swathe of the bright orange temporary fencing that ran along the ditch had collapsed where Trevor had tumbled in. But it wasn't torn, like Trevor had broken through when he accidentally ran into it, and it wasn't lying flat, like the wind had ripped it from its proper place. Instead, it had been cut, neatly rolled up, and set to the side. Like it had been intentionally removed.

Hours later, once filming had wrapped for the day and I was back at the hotel, I couldn't stop thinking about it.

"What do you think, Jacques?" I asked my stuffed crow, who stared at me balefully from my hotel room desk. A prop I'd salvaged from one of my movies, he was a real taxidermized bird that a crew member had found at a flea market. One of its legs pulled away to reveal a switchblade, and I always brought him to a new set for good luck. It didn't seem to be working this time. "Would someone want to hurt Trevor?"

Unsurprisingly, Jacques didn't answer.

Still, the question remained. It was entirely possible that his death had been an accident. Trevor had seemed like the sweetest, albeit clumsiest, cinnamon roll the few hours I'd known him. Although, I supposed, that was the thing—I didn't really know Trevor, did I? It seemed like a little too much of a coincidence that Trevor would meet his demise in an accident so eerily similar to one of the earliest scenes in the movie, and that'd he'd just so happen to fall into a ditch at the precise spot the fencing had been removed.

I joined Jacques at my desk and opened my laptop. It was time for some good old-fashioned Internet stalking.

Facebook ended up being a bust. Trevor's profile was private—the only thing visible was a photo with two people who looked like they might be his parents. He wasn't on TikTok, and even though he had a Twitter account, his most recent post was from three years ago—a retweet of Quentin Tarantino saying he wished he'd been the one to write and direct *Love Actually*. Upon closer inspection, it appeared to be a parody account.

Finally, I hit the jackpot when I pulled up Trevor's Instagram. His feed was full of photos of himself with celebs and crew members on previous film sets, the most recent posted just yesterday. It was a selfie in front of the set house, the camera angled to fit as much of the mansion in the frame as possible. It was posted at 7:36 p.m., just hours before we found his body.

I studied it closer, desperate for a clue. Trevor's face offered no insight—his eyes looked tired after a long day of shooting, but he was still wearing a big smile. He'd taken the photo alone, no one else in the frame. There was no sign at all that everything was about to go terribly wrong. But then I noticed the background. Behind Trevor, you could just make out the end of the props trailer, the end of it jutting into view.

Next to it, just poking into the frame, was a face.

I stood up from the desk, my heart pounding in my ears. It was like the face had appeared out of nowhere, even though clearly it had been there all along. I peered closer, trying to make out who it was. The face was small, and when I zoomed in, the resolution was grainy. All I could tell was that it was a man, glaring in Trevor's direction.

My stomach chilled. Who was it, and why did he look so angry at Trevor?

Antsy, I jumped to my feet. If his socials were anything to go by, all poor Trevor had wanted was to be a small part of making movies alongside his heroes. And the industry had chewed him up and spat him into a ditch. Whoever was responsible, I wasn't going to let them get away with it. And there was one person who could help me. Before I could talk myself out of it, I stormed out of my room, walked quickly down the hall, and rapped on the last door on the left.

A moment later, the handle rattled and the door flew open.

"Hey, it's Jigsaw." Teddy stood in the doorway, wearing nothing but a towel knotted around his hips and an amused expression. I'd already seen him half-naked, but seeing his chiseled chest and perfectly sculpted shoulders again in person made me irritated with just how familiar I was becoming with his naked form.

I pushed the thoughts from my mind. "I need to talk to you. I think Trevor was murdered." I whispered the last word, holding up my hand to shield it from anyone that might be passing by.

"What"—Teddy cocked an eyebrow—"the hell are you talking about?"

"I found something." I pulled out my phone, ready to show him the Instagram photo, but my anxious jitters sent the device flying out my hand instead. It landed unceremoniously at Teddy's feet.

"I got it." Teddy squatted down, his towel creeping up his thighs, threatening to expose what that banana hammock on his reality show had barely been able to conceal. As he went, the towel kept inching higher, like a curtain rising at the beginning of a very X-rated show.

I reached out an arm, unable to bear the thought of being caught staring at both his nipple and lower appendage within the same twenty-four hours. "Wait!"

But a moment later, the towel parted to reveal . . . a pair of swim trunks. Of course. The towel, the wet hair. He'd probably just gotten back from the pool. My anxiety was turning me into a sex pervert. Why couldn't I stop embarrassing myself in front of him?

I knew why, of course. The swimsuit, the water running down his pecs. It all reminded me of the night we'd met. When both of us had been wet and nearly naked, and his lips were very much all over me.

Back in July, Mara had dragged me to the wrap party for a film she had just finished working on. Unfortunately, her ex, Austin—who had unceremoniously dumped her very recently— was also going to be there, so Mara made me tag along for emotional backup.

It was a swanky, ritzy affair—filled with stuffy, pretentious industry types. And I did not want to be there any more than Mara did.

Mere weeks after my movie had flopped and my agent had dumped me, I was facing the task of finding new representation. I knew I should be networking and setting up meetings, but I couldn't muster the enthusiasm. Did I really want to convince someone to represent me just so I could continue taking the same old roles in the same old movies? So I could keep meeting people that would eventually let me down or betray me? So tabloids would continue to invade my privacy and spread lies about me?

I wasn't sure anymore.

A few hours after arriving and making sure Mara was ok I slunk away, tired of people consoling me about my latest flop by telling me how much they loved films I made five years ago. I snuck out the back door and into the grotto at the far end of the kidney-shaped pool, kicking off my shoes and dipping my feet into the cool water.

"There's pee in that pool."

I jumped. On the other side of the water, a man was perched on the steps, half hidden in shadows.

"Wait, really?"

"My buddy was in there earlier, so there's definitely a chance."

Good enough for me. I pulled out my feet. "Thanks for the heads-up."

"Sorry, that was a weird way to say hi." He stood, moving into the light.

I recognized him immediately. He'd been hot in the commercials for *Pleasure Island Paradise*, but in person he was downright breathtaking. His upper body, shirtless of course, was chiseled and muscled. His sandy brown hair was slicked back, emphasizing cheekbones that would put James Dean's to shame. But it was his eyes—piercing blue and sultry even in the low lighting—that wouldn't let me look away.

Suddenly, I felt just as hot as I had inside the house.

"I'm Teddy." He walked over and reached out a hand.

I took it, neglecting to mention I already knew who he was. "Are you here solely to warn people about the pee?"

"No, I just needed some fresh air."

A kindred spirit. "Same."

Perched on pool chairs, I was surprised at how easily the conversation came. We talked about the best local hiking spots (he was so enthusiastic he almost sold me on the exercise), gossiped about everyone at the party (the director was cheating on his wife with one of the guests but we couldn't decide who), and ranked the best pizza toppings (jalapeños and pineapple).

Eventually, Teddy stood. "I feel like a swim. Want to join?"

"Absolutely not. There's pee in there."

"I said there might be."

"Not a chance I'm willing to take."

"Actually," he leaned in conspiratorially, his breath tickling my ear, "I might have lied about that."

Tingles danced down my spine. "And why would you do that?"

"Maybe I wanted an excuse to talk to you. Pretty girls make me nervous."

I wanted to laugh. There was no way Teddy James had a problem talking to any girl.

"I don't have a suit."

"So?" He extended a hand to help me up. "Come on."

He'd looked so cute, so undeniably sexy, that I couldn't resist. I'd sworn off dating actors years ago, after a guy I'd been dating for over a year sold photos and gossip about us to a tabloid. The ensuing press coverage had been humiliating—no one looks flattering in a tankini after they've wolfed down nachos at the beach—and he dumped me two weeks later, after he'd been cast in the latest superhero franchise and gotten all he needed from the relationship.

But at that moment, feeling a spark of attraction for the first time in months, maybe throwing caution to the wind with a devastatingly handsome stranger was exactly what I needed.

Quickly, before I could psych myself out, I stripped down to my bra and undies and jumped into the pool. With a quick laugh of surprise, Teddy followed. We both slipped under the surface, kicking through the shallow depths until we were sufficiently cooled off. We resurfaced, out of breath and laughing. But as he looked at me, his smile faded.

"Hold still." Teddy slowly slid through the water toward me. "There's a bug in your hair."

"Uh-uh. You already got me with the pee thing. You think I'm going to believe you now?"

"I'm serious. Here, hang on."

Determined to call his bluff, I reached up to the top of my head. To my horror, something crunchy skittered across my hand.

"Oh God, what is it?" I slapped at my head. "Get it off!"

"I was trying to," Teddy laughed softly. He slid through the water, placing a calming hand on the back of my neck as he combed through my hair with his other hand. "Got it!" He threw my assailant across the patio. "Better?"

"Yes," I breathed, focused less on my galloping heart rate

and more on Teddy's hand, which was still wrapped around the back of my neck. He was close, close enough for me to count the water droplets dotting his cheekbones and make out the sapphire streaks in his cornflower-blue eyes.

"Come here," he whispered, his leg slotting between mine as he drew closer. My heart thudded as I let my hands travel up the damp skin of his arms and twine around his neck. His muscled chest pressed against my own, my soaking-wet bra the only thing between us. I held my breath in anticipation of the kiss, but when he finally dipped his head, it wasn't to press his lips to mine. Instead, they landed on my neck, just below my ear. He hummed as he applied suction, his teeth gently scraping the sensitive skin. I threw my head back, dangerously close to moaning as I pulled him closer.

Footsteps.

Teddy yanked himself away as a woman entered the grotto. She was gorgeous, with long wavy red hair and wearing a flirty sundress.

"Teddy, are you ready to go?" Her expression cooled as she spotted us, her lips pinching into a polite smile. "I've been waiting."

My cheeks flamed first with embarrassment, and then with anger. He'd flirted with me when he was already planning on taking a woman who looked like an honest-to-God mermaid home with him.

"Sure." Teddy hopped out of the pool, and the woman smirked as he slipped an arm around her waist. He looked down at me. "Hey, maybe we can—"

"It's cool," I said, cutting him off. "Have a good night."

As they left, the woman glanced at me over her shoulder as she whispered something in Teddy's ear. He shook his head, and ". . . not my type," was all I could make out in his reply.

# Chapter Seven

It hadn't bothered me that Teddy didn't think I was his type. Not really. He wasn't my type either—even if he did have a body like the ones that used to inspire statues. Naked ones. But pretending to forget the embarrassment of him bailing on me mid-kiss to sleep with another woman?

That was a tall order even for an Oscar winner. And I definitely wasn't that. I'd already been reeling from the industry chewing me up and spitting me out earlier in the summer, and my humiliation at the party had now given me the final push I needed to throw in the towel on making movies for good. At the time, I was already under contract for *House of Reckoning* with a sweet contract that would give me a cut of the box-office profits. I decided that once filming wrapped, I'd be done with Hollywood.

The day after the party, I'd called a realtor about selling my apartment, started packing my things into storage, and convinced Mara to let me crash on her couch until I'd figured out what I'd be doing with the rest of my life.

It remained unclear what that would be.

Now, Teddy eyed me suspiciously as I retrieved my phone from the ground. "Why exactly are you here?"

"Yeah, I . . . Can I come in?" If I was about to allege that whoever was in the background of Trevor's Instagram photo had murdered him, I should probably do it behind closed doors.

"As long as you're not here to yell at me again." He stood aside and pulled the door open farther. "I promise I'll put some clothes on."

*You don't have to do that.* The thought popped into my head as I stepped into his room, making my cheeks flush. Oblivious, Teddy followed me in and grabbed some clothes from a suitcase. "I'll be right back." He headed to the bathroom, clothes slung over his shoulder. "Make yourself at home."

I perched awkwardly on the chair next to his desk, trying to forget that Teddy was now very naked and just a few yards away. The room was a carbon copy of my own: one king-sized bed, a TV, and a tiny nook with a mini fridge they probably advertised as a "kitchenette." It was generally neat, with the exception of an overflowing suitcase in one corner. A book had been left on the desk, open and face down. I picked it up and peered at the cover. It was a mystery—*Tripwire* by Lee Child.

But even as I scanned the back cover, my mind strayed back to Teddy on the other side of the bathroom door. It bothered me how quickly I was slipping into the same thoughts I had the first time I met him—wanting to touch him, wanting him to touch me. Wanting to know what his mouth tasted like, even as I was here to talk about a potential murder on set.

I shook my head, knowing better than to go down that path.

KATIE BOHN | 60

Even if I didn't already know that Teddy wasn't interested in me, I'd dated celebrities before. I knew how it always went: a few short months of dating before they moved on to a hot new thing they met on a movie set or photo shoot, sometimes without breaking up with me first.

I didn't live by many rules, but not dating actors was a firm one.

The door to the bathroom opened and Teddy stepped out, now dressed in gray sweatpants and a sleeveless tee that showed off his biceps. He sat at the foot of the bed, running a hand through his still-damp hair as he lowered himself onto the mattress.

Yanking my eyes away, I grappled for conversation that didn't involve the size of his muscles. "You read?" I held up the book, still in my hands. "You actually know how?"

Teddy side-eyed me. "You know, I invited you in, trying to be nice."

"Ok, ok, sorry. Do you like reading?"

"Not really. My brother does, though."

"Oh?"

"He's a senior in college now, but when he was a freshman, he was really anxious moving away from home. I called him every night, trying to help him chill out a bit, but we ran out of things to talk about, so we started picking books to read together."

"Like a book club?"

"I guess. So what's up?"

Taking a deep breath, I quickly ran through the coincidence with the upcoming scene and the evidence that the fencing had been removed on purpose so someone could push Trevor into the ditch.

"And look at this." I pulled out my phone, successfully this time, and scrolled to Trevor's Instagram. "He took this photo an hour or two before he died. Look at the face in the background. They look pissed."

Teddy squinted at the screen. "Just because someone looks grumpy doesn't mean they killed someone. Look at how mad you were at me yesterday. And yet here I am. Unmurdered."

"So far."

"Very funny." Teddy's own phone dinged, and he picked it up. "Who said I was kidding?"

Teddy ignored me, tapping something into his phone.

"Hello?" I kicked his shin, irritated.

"What?"

"Did you hear anything I said?"

"Yes, you think a frowny face is evidence for murder." He tossed his phone to the side and ran a hand down his face. "I'm pretty sure I'm getting fired tomorrow, anyway. I don't need to worry about all this—I'll be gone in twenty-four hours." His mouth cracked into a crooked smile, but it faded just as fast.

"No offense, but did you prepare for this role at all?"

"I did." He buried his head in his hands. "I practiced all my lines and even had my brother run through the scenes with me to make sure I had them down. Then I got here and the cameras started rolling and I just . . . blanked."

"Yikes. That sucks."

"And once I started forgetting lines, it kept getting worse and worse." He rubbed his temples, his hands shaking. "But hey, at least I'll be out of your hair if I get fired."

His phone dinged again, but this time he didn't pick it up.

"Listen." I leaned forward and placed a hand on his shoulder, momentarily distracted by how solid it was. I decided to remove my hand. "Listen. You're not getting fired. I've seen actors do worse and not even come close to getting fired."

"Doubt it."

"No, really. One showed up to set drunk and puked on the AD."

"That was probably like . . . one of those guys in the Marvel movies."

I bit my lip, unable to lie.

"Oh my God." Teddy grimaced. "I'm so fucked."

"I promise it'll be fine."

"Easy for you to say—you're amazing. The way you change into a literal different person as soon as Natasha yells 'action' is mind-blowing."

Despite myself, my heart fluttered at the praise. I thought back to the episodes of his show I'd watched, trying to find something—anything—I could compliment about his performance.

"What about that scene when you rescued that girl's lunch from the crab? Totally made episode two."

One corner of Teddy's mouth tugged upward, a crack in his dour expression. "You know, I think that's the moment that landed me this gig."

"We should find the crab a part, too."

We both smiled then, even me, and I couldn't help but notice how nicely his eyes crinkled when he did that. But then his phone dinged for a third time, and he grabbed it off the mattress.

"Can't you leave that alone for ten minutes?" I spat.

Teddy swiveled the device to face me, beaming like a proud parent. "Kendall Jenner is DMing me."

"Oh my God." I rubbed the bridge of my nose. "I have an idea. Both of us need this movie to be a success, right? You're trying to make a name for yourself, and I barely get paid unless this movie is a hit at the box office. Preferably, this would happen without any additional murders."

"Preferably."

I took a deep breath. "If you help me figure out what really happened to Trevor, even if you don't believe me, I'll help you with your acting."

Teddy considered this for a long moment. "You really think you can help me?"

"Probably. At the very least, I can help you make better choices than pulling a Southern accent out of nowhere in the middle of a scene." I exhaled and waited a beat. "What do you say?"

Teddy looked thoughtful. "I'm in." He clapped his hands together before making finger guns, pew pew pew. "But I can't make any promises that I'll be too helpful with the detective stuff."

"That's ok. I already know where to start."

We needed to find the face in the photo.

# Chapter Eight

Teddy: We still on for this morning?

Teddy: Did you forget our rehearsal?

Teddy: I'll sacrifice you to the killer if you don't get up here.

Teddy: Just kidding, I wouldn't do that. But seriously.

It's not that I'd forgotten, per se.

I'd totally remembered that after we'd agreed to our pact the night before, we'd planned our first acting lesson for eight o'clock tonight. What I'd forgotten was that Teddy had texted me an hour later to reschedule for eight this morning instead so he could still call his brother tonight for their book club. This was a problem because it was currently 8:08 a.m. and Mara, Chloe, and I were at the hotel's restaurant, elbows deep in a giant breakfast spread. None of us had been able to make up our minds, so we'd ordered several dishes to share, including an irresponsible number of biscuits.

The meal was doubling as a therapy session for Mara, who'd

just gotten word that her ex-boyfriend Austin had sent an unexpected package to her apartment in LA. I tucked my phone beneath the table, trying to listen as I tapped out a reply.

"... just don't understand why he'd send everything back like that—it's so mean." Mara stabbed at a spear of asparagus covered in hollandaise sauce. "I certainly don't want this crap after he's had it for months."

My ears perked up as I continued to type. "Wait, what did he send back?"

I'd liked Austin the one time I'd met him—he'd clearly adored Mara and didn't mind giving her just as much sass as she gave him. But he'd lost all points with me when he dumped her without explanation on the last day of filming.

"A sweater I left in his trailer, and an old glasses case, and"—she hiccupped a little cry—"the stuffed hedgehog I bought him for our one-month anniversary."

My heart squeezed. No one loved and craved love as much as Mara did, and no one was as loyal. Once you were in her heart, you were there for good.

"He never deserved you," I said. "He doesn't even deserve your old glasses case. I'm glad he sent it back."

"Yeah, what a dick." Chloe reached across the table and squeezed Mara's wrist. "You'll find someone way better, I know it."

I gave Chloe a small smile of thanks, grateful she was there to help comfort Mara. We had started including Chloe at our table for breakfast every morning, and so far she was a welcome addition. She could still be a little shy and awkward at times, but she was sweet and clearly appreciated being included. We'd invited Audrey, too, but she had declined. Instead, she spent most mornings at a separate table, alone. She was currently in a booth in the far corner of the room, her eyes glued to the script as she mouthed her lines.

"Thank you, guys." Mara swallowed, putting on a brave face. "We were only together for two months—I don't understand why this is still bothering me."

"Hearts don't make sense sometimes." Chloe handed Mara a chocolate-chip scone. "Here. It'll help."

My phone dinged: Teddy, saying it was ok if I was a few minutes late. Clocking me once again reaching for my phone, Mara nudged me with her foot.

"Everything ok?"

"Yeah, sorry." I clicked it off and returned my attention, rightfully, to Mara. "Just . . . my dad."

This was only a half lie. My dad had texted me earlier, asking when I'd be coming to visit since he lived just a few hours away from the set.

"How's Mr. P?"

"Enjoying his retirement, maybe a little too much." My dad might have been in his sixties, but he had a far more exciting life than I did. A few weeks ago, he'd gone zip-lining with a local outdoors club for retirees. They'd smuggled beer in their thermoses and called it a Zip 'n Sip.

His lifestyle stressed me out.

"I want to be your dad when I grow up." Mara split apart the scone and spread on some butter. "Maybe I should move to a cabin in the mountains, where I can be bitter and single for the rest of my life and never have to think about Austin again."

"If you do, I'm coming with you." I stood, collecting my phone and wallet. "I need to go call him. Sorry to cut this short."

"You're not coming back?" Mara's eyes were wide, like a sad basset hound puppy. "It'll only take a minute, won't it?"

"Um . . ." I hadn't planned on telling anyone about helping Teddy, but now Mara and Chloe were both staring at me.

"Actually, I'm about to go give Teddy an acting lesson." My cheeks burned in embarrassment.

Mara and Chloe looked at each other knowingly.

"It's not like that!" I insisted. "You both saw him the other day. He desperately needs them if this movie is going to work."

"I did see, but I wasn't paying attention to his acting, I'll tell you that," Mara quipped. Chloe nodded in agreement, one hand over her mouth to stifle giggles.

I rolled my eyes. "Whatever. I'm not filming today, so I'll catch you both later."

"Ok." Mara heaved a sigh. "I guess Chloe and I will just have to finish this by ourselves."

"You'll be having a much better time than I will," I assured her, envisioning the morning ahead. "Trust me."

My stomach fluttered as I rapped on Teddy's door. It was still awkward not knowing if he remembered me from the party—either he did and was helping me save face by not bringing it up, or he had no memory of me at all. I couldn't decide which was more humiliating.

The door flew open, revealing Teddy dressed in joggers and a white tee-shirt that was a hair too snug, accentuating every muscle in his upper body. I swallowed, trying not to stare. I could see his pecs, for crying out loud. He could have a little modesty.

"Jigsaw!"

I smiled thinly, already tired of the nickname. "If I'm Jigsaw, who are you? Pinhead?"

Teddy grinned. "Wasn't he like . . . a sex demon?" He cocked his head to the side. "Seems about right."

"I . . . I didn't mean—"

"Get in here, I'm just screwing around." He opened the door wider and I followed him inside, already flustered. "Want something to drink? I've got Dr. Pepper and . . . Dr. Pepper."

"It's eight in the morning."

"Wrong." Teddy pulled two cans out of the fridge and handed me one. "You were supposed to be here at eight but you weren't. Which means we're officially in the Dr. Pepper time zone."

"Touché."

He cracked the tab on his can as he dropped onto the couch. "Did you have any epiphanies overnight about who the face in the photo could be?"

"Unfortunately not." I opened my own drink and took a long sip of the sweet bubbles. "It's just too blurry."

"Like a photo of Big Foot," Teddy added solemnly.

"We should make a list. Of who it could be." I grabbed a pen and pad of paper and scrawled "suspects" at the top.

"Sure, you can help yourself to my belongings."

I gave him a withering glare. "You were going to use these?"

"Yes." He crossed his arms. "Maybe I write poetry at night."

"Do you?"

"Workshopping pickup lines is an art form."

I decided to ignore him. "Ok, so the face in the photo is suspicious, but we don't know for sure that they're the killer. That means we can't exclude women from the official suspects." I started to list everyone I knew on set. "Natasha, Brent, Chloe, whoever's in the photo—"

"Mara," Teddy interjected.

"It was not Mara."

"How do you know? Was she in your trailer?"

"Not the whole night, but—"

"I thought you wanted to solve this?" He reached over and tapped the paper. "On the list."

I gritted my teeth. "Fine." Then, below Mara's name, I scrawled Teddy's.

"Hey!"

"You showed up at my trailer after the murder, which means you were at base camp but unaccounted for at the time of his death. Suspicious."

"This," Teddy said, pulling up Trevor's Instagram photo, "looks nothing like me. My jawline is way squarer!"

I shrugged, unmoved. "We also have to unofficially add the entire crew." Becoming overwhelmed, I rubbed my temples. "That's so many people."

"And my hairline is better, too."

"You're supposed to be helping me!"

Reluctantly, Teddy put down his phone. "It'll be fine. We'll figure out who the face in the photo is, talk to him, and go from there. One step at a time."

Shockingly, Teddy was making a lot of sense. I took a few sips of my soda, feeling the wisps of stress start to dissipate. He was right, we had to focus on finding the man in the photo. But in the meantime, I had a lesson to teach.

I stood and placed my half-empty can on the counter. "Should we get rehearsing?"

"Oh. Yeah." Teddy reached for the scripts that were resting on the desk. "The seance scene, right?"

I nodded, taking the stapled stack of paper and paging to the scene we'd be shooting the next morning. It was going to be a fun one.

Our characters, a few hours into their beer-fueled party, stumble upon an old Ouija board in one of the bedrooms. They use it in a game of truth or dare, holding a seance and giving the witch's spirit permission to enter the mortal world. It's the scene that kick-starts the rest of the movie—not a particularly serious scene, but an important one.

I held the script but didn't bother reviewing my lines. I already had them memorized. "Ready?"

We started at the top, with Teddy's character pulling the Ouija board out of the closet. He had to keep checking the script, and there were a few spots when I could sense nervousness creeping in. He wouldn't meet my eyes, shifting on his feet and running a hand along the back of his neck instead of fully committing to acting out the scene. I slowed us down, making sure he had his lines memorized before we continued.

As we practiced, I was surprised at how much I enjoyed coaching him. It was nice not to feel the pressure of performing myself, and to instead focus solely on what Teddy was doing. It was gratifying to watch him finally get out of his head and loosen up, to watch the lines between Teddy and his character start to blur. Was his cocky and sexually charged character strikingly similar to his own personality? Yes. But I wasn't going to point that out now.

Once Teddy had mastered the first half of the scene, we moved on to the next part, when it was time for the game to begin and my character would be dared to start the seance.

"Truth or dare?" Teddy asked, finally nailing the line with just enough flirty arrogance.

"Dare." I said, my voice filled with trepidation.

"I dare you ..." Teddy paused, glancing around the room as he pretended to search for an idea, "... to give me a lap dance."

I nearly choked. "Excuse me? That's not in the script!"

"Um, yes it is."

Flustered, I flipped through the pages. Sure enough, there was Teddy's line, just like he'd read it—the seance didn't begin for another few pages. My stomach dropped. They must have revised the script since the last time I read it. I had to admit it made sense for the story—it would launch our on-screen romance while pushing my character out of her goody-two-shoes comfort zone. But at that moment, I would've rather chewed foil than perch my ass anywhere near Teddy's lap.

"It's ok, we don't have to practice this part," Teddy laughed. "I don't expect you to have a lap dance memorized off the top of your head."

"Actually, I do."

The words flew out of my mouth before I realized I'd have been better keeping that information to myself.

Teddy's eyes widened in a way that was annoying and more

than a little insulting. "Damn, ok. I didn't figure you for the type."

I frowned, the memory of the night in the pool once again flaring up. Of course. I hadn't been the type to make out with in a swimming pool then, and I wasn't the type to do a lap dance now. It was infuriating. He didn't even know me.

"Well, I am." Grabbing my phone, I started scrolling through Spotify. "Are you sure you're comfortable with it?"

Teddy cocked an eyebrow. "Absolutely." He dragged the chair away from the desk and took a seat, motioning toward his lap. "Go for it."

I could tell he was calling my bluff, sure I wouldn't go through with it. But I wasn't going to let him win.

"Perfect." I found the song and got ready to queue it up. "Can't wait."

The truth was, I only knew the dance because I'd had to learn it for my movie *Dead Tide*: my character performed it for her boyfriend as their yacht sank into shark-infested waters. The song was "My Heart Will Go On".

Quickly, before I could change my mind, I pressed "play," set my phone on the desk, and got into position.

It wasn't until the tin whistles rang out that I realized how embarrassing this was going to be. But there was no way I could make up new choreography for a different song, and I wouldn't remember the moves unless I had the music, too. Besides, I'd already made a huge deal about knowing the dance.

I had no choice but to commit.

As Celine's breathy voice started to sing, I made my way

toward Teddy, keeping my steps in beat to the slow rhythm. I ran my hands up and down my body, keeping my face sexy and sultry. Or at least, my best attempt at sexy and sultry. Teddy, meanwhile, looked like he was trying his hardest not to laugh. The first round of the chorus kicked in, and I tried not to imagine Jack and Rose clinging to their doomed door as I bent my knees and slowly lowered myself to the floor. My calves screamed, but I refused to hurry. I stroked down the tops of my thighs as I went, maintaining eye contact with Teddy as the lyrics praised the ability of love to go on.

This time, Teddy couldn't hold back his snort of laughter.

"Stop," I hissed, trying not to giggle myself. "This is serious."

But who was I kidding? There was nothing serious about this. I could practically feel Celine's disappointment in us.

The drums kicked in, ratcheting the tempo up a bit. I flipped myself flat onto my stomach, kicking my legs up and down before moving back up onto my knees and undulating my body up and down. I prayed the effect was alluring, rather than making me look like a fish flopping for its life.

Teddy crossed his arms, widening the spread of his legs as he frowned. "The script specified a lap dance. Not a floor dance."

"I'm not finished yet!" I spat out a lock of hair that had gotten stuck in my mouth.

Right on cue, the music swelled to a new intensity. It was time for the finale.

I jumped to my feet, striding toward him with renewed purpose. Teddy leaned back in his chair as I approached, licking his lips as I moved like I was about to sit in his lap. But just as the climax of the song finally hit, I dramatically turned away from him instead. He moved his hands to my hips, but I slapped them away.

"No touching," I chided.

I flung out first one arm and then the other above my head, arching my back in an attempt to look graceful. But as my right arm swung away from my body, it collided with my phone on the desk and sent it clattering to the floor.

The song unceremoniously stopped, leaving us in total silence—and my butt poised mere inches above Teddy's lap.

I considered stopping right then and there. I'd done enough to prove I could do it, hadn't I? But now that the song was no longer rendering the situation completely ridiculous, I realized just how intimate our position was. I could hear him breathing, feel his thighs on either side of mine. Teddy didn't move a muscle, and instead whispered in my ear, "Keep going."

Against my better judgment, I did. I wanted to prove him wrong, to show him that whatever preconceived notions he had about the "type" of girl I was were misplaced. And maybe, the low rasp of his voice and the feeling of his legs pressed again mine were too compelling to ignore.

Bracing my hands on the seat of the chair, I took my time as I once again lowered myself to the floor before slowly rising up, making sure my ass brushed against his lap as I did. Teddy tensed behind me, his hands brushing the top of my butt as he wrapped them around my hips. I didn't slap away his hands this time—instead I pressed into them, savoring the pressure of each fingertip pressing through the fabric of my leggings.

Knowing I was playing with fire, I spun around. I draped one leg and then the other around his waist before sinking down, our bodies meshing perfectly. My arms fell around his shoulders, and when I finally looked into his eyes, they were hazy. Stormy. Wrapping one arm around my waist, keeping me firmly in place, Teddy snaked his other hand slowly up my side. Up, up it went, grazing the side of my breast before he brushed my bottom lip with his thumb.

His lips cracked into a smile. "Perfect," he murmured.

Any memory of how the dance was supposed to end flew from my mind. Teddy's face was mere inches from mine, and I was pretty sure he was moving closer. It would be so easy to close the tiny gap. To give in.

God, I wanted to give in.

Then, flashes from the last time we were this close: the sound of the woman's voice approaching, Teddy jumping out of the pool without a second glance at me, the way he'd breezily told her I wasn't his type anyway. Teddy was down to mess around with anyone in front of him, until someone better came along. And even if my body was screaming at me to kiss him, I wouldn't give him the satisfaction.

I couldn't do this.

"I should get going." I jumped off his lap, hurrying to make my exit. I ran a hand down my neck, hoping I wasn't as flushed as I felt.

Teddy staggered to his feet. "I'm sorry, I shouldn't have—"

"It's totally fine. You're overthinking it." I backed toward the door, trying desperately not to stare at the way his joggers had slipped down, revealing the muscled V that ran along the inside of his hips. "Tomorrow we'll get investigating, right? Don't forget, you need to hold up your side of the bargain."

## Chapter Nine

Thankfully, I had a perfectly valid excuse to leave the set and avoid seeing Teddy for the rest of the day. After spending some time reviewing my lines for tomorrow's scenes, I decided to pay a visit to someone special: Puzzle Face himself.

My dad's property was an hour and a half away from the hotel, nestled in the forest and surrounded by acres of land he'd purchased to ensure its seclusion. The drive was gorgeous—the road cresting over hills and winding through the trees. Unfortunately, it also gave my mind ample time to spin over what had happened in Teddy's room just hours earlier. Had I imagined the way he'd gripped my hips, trying to pull me closer? Or the heat in his eyes as I'd lowered myself onto his lap?

I didn't think so.

But it didn't matter, I reminded myself. Boys like Teddy couldn't be trusted. He had Kendall Jenner in his DMs for God's sake. And even if he was trustworthy, I wasn't interested. Any tension we felt hadn't been the result of anything real; we'd just been swept up in the magic of my dance skills.

Their powers were too great. It couldn't be helped.

By the time I pulled up to the cabin, it was after three in the afternoon, the sun streaming gold and hazy through the trees. The front door was always unlocked, but I rang the doorbell anyway. Once I'd walked in unannounced and found my dad and his girlfriend at the time in flagrante delicto in the middle of the living room. I'd never been able to look at him, or pineapple, the same again.

There was a slight rumble of footsteps before the door flew open.

"Squish!" My dad reached out and wrapped me in a hug. He was still the towering height that made him so foreboding on screen, but in recent years he'd grown a sizeable paunch that made his hugs extra comforting. "I was just thinking about you."

"Good to see you, Dad." I rested my head against his chest, savoring the feeling of peace and safety. Living in LA, I tried to fly out to see him once a month, but depending on my schedule, that sometimes fell to once every three months. It was nice to be located so close for once.

He patted my shoulder as I pulled away. "What the hell is going on at that movie set of yours?"

So much for my feeling of peace.

"How do you know about that?"

"Old buddy of mine is married to the camera operator. Said it was real weird. A kid just dying out of nowhere like that."

I would have to tread carefully. If my dad suspected a killer was on the loose, he was likely to barge onto set himself by the next morning. And I didn't want that.

I shrugged, playing it cool. "The police seem confident it was an accident. Just bad luck, I guess."

"I guess." He moved aside, motioning me into the cabin. "Come on in. I just pulled some bread out of the oven."

Stepping inside, a renewed calm immediately washed over me, scrubbing away the anxiety brought on by my dad bringing up Trevor not thirty seconds into my visit. The cabin always soothed me, my dad's energy radiating from every corner. The interior was more spacious than it looked from the outside, with a large living area and vaulted ceiling that let you peek into the second-floor loft. It was tidy but not overly so, the walls plastered with framed posters from my dad's movies, each featuring him in his iconic Puzzle Face mask and duster.

It might seem narcissistic, but I knew my dad was just genuinely proud of every movie he'd ever done.

My dad hadn't planned to star in a horror franchise. In 1989, he'd been working in a gas station in northern California when a customer approached him about auditioning for an indie film he was producing. It was a slasher called *Final Curtain* that was trying to mimic the success of iconic movies like *Halloween* and *Black Christmas*. My dad, figuring it could be a fun way to spend the summer, agreed.

Not only did he get the part, but the movie went on to be a surprise box office success. My dad still swore it made more than *Back to the Future Part II* and an accounting error was the only thing keeping it from being one of the top ten films of the year. They immediately wrote a sequel, despite Puzzle Face technically dying at the end of the first one. By then, my dad had fallen in love with the character, and as luck would have it, also fell in love with my mother.

(She worked in the restaurant across the street from the set. He said she made the best coconut cream pie, which I decided to interpret literally and not metaphorically.)

Little me came along three years later, and when I was old enough, I got to tag along to movie premieres and even scored that bit part in the very last Puzzle Face movie. Even after he retired, my dad and I still bonded over horror, checking out the newest releases and traveling to horror conventions together. Especially after he and my mom divorced, horror was a way we could connect and I could make sure he wasn't getting lonely.

Which, unfortunately, was also why I hadn't been able to tell him I was quitting the industry yet.

A scuffle of tiny feet followed by a flash of black and white skittered in from the kitchen.

"Daffy!" The skunk—one my dad had "rescued" shortly after moving into the cabin, although I'm not sure she was actually in danger to begin with—was named Daffodil, but we called her Daffy. Because it was cute, but also due to personality. "Daffy, come here, girl!"

The skunk ground to a halt in front of me, stamping her feet and backing up quickly, her claws scraping against the carpet.

"Do you remember me?"

She repeated the scooting gesture, clearly upset that a stranger was intruding upon her domain. Never mind that we'd met several times before.

"She's grumpy it's not dinner yet." My dad ambled into the

living room. "I have some peppers cut up in the fridge. You might be able to win her over with a snack."

I followed him into the kitchen, where he pulled out a Tupperware container of red bell pepper squares. I offered her a few and she nibbled them swiftly, appraising me over her little paws as she chomped noisily. When she was done, she promptly waddled over to her cat bed, where she curled up and went to sleep. It wasn't a peace offering, but at least she didn't square up to me again.

"Want a beer?" My dad still stood in front of the open fridge, his hand hovering over cans of lager.

"No thanks."

"What about a slice of sourdough? Should be cool by now."

I climbed onto one of the bar stools. "That, I will definitely have."

Beaming with pride, my dad sliced off a thick slice of the homemade loaf sitting on the stove. After swiping on a generous amount of butter, he set it on a plate and slid it across the island.

"Thank you." I took a big bite, savoring the tangy crumb. Bread baking was another thing my dad had picked up post-retirement—a hobby I was more than happy to benefit from.

"How's filming going?"

"It's ok."

He glanced at me as he pulled out supplies to make spaghetti sauce. "Just ok? There's a lot of buzz about it. The last one was a bit of a stumble—"

"Thanks, Dad."

"—and I think this one could be a real hit that will make people forget about that! Is all I was going to say." He carved a slice off the loaf for himself. "It'll make that crummy old agent of yours sorry she had the nerve to drop you." He gave me a roguish wink.

"Yeah . . ."

I knew he was trying to be helpful, but all it was accomplishing was reminding me about my failures—and about the fact that I hadn't told my dad I was quitting yet.

I felt awful not being honest with my dad. Horror was what bound our relationship, from him showing me *Poltergeist* when I was way too young, to the time we both geeked out over meeting Gunnar Hansen at a convention. (He even posed for a photo with us with the actual chainsaw from *Texas Chainsaw Massacre*.) My dad never pressured me to act, but he'd been so thrilled when I'd gotten my first big gig. He framed the tickets from the premiere and still had them on display in his spare bedroom.

I couldn't bear to picture the look on his face when I told him he'd never get to go to an opening night of one of my films ever again.

"Also, I've been meaning to talk to you." My dad popped the crust of his piece of bread into his mouth. "About an opportunity."

"Oh, yeah?"

"Well, more of a favor."

"Ok . . ." I had a bad feeling about this.

"One of my buddies, we go way back to the early Puzzle Face movies. He's finishing the script for a new project. It's a little experimental—a classic slasher but from the perspective of the killer, who's a woman. He asked if you might be interested."

I mumbled something indecipherable.

"I know, I know." He chuckled as he added onion and beef to the skillet. "It's probably not cool, teaming up with your old man's friend."

"It's not that . . ."

"But it sounds like a great project, and I think it'd mean a lot to him if you gave him a call."

I hesitated. The project did sound interesting, and it's something I would have jumped at in different circumstances. And I knew I would have to be honest with my dad. Eventually. But at that moment, I just . . . couldn't.

"Yeah." I feigned some enthusiasm. "Maybe I will."

"Great." My dad beamed. "And speaking of old friends and old memories . . .' He grabbed a can of tomatoes to start the marinara. "I was finally cleaning out the storage unit and found something I'd like you to see."

"Sounds great."

Once the sauce was simmering, my dad and I relocated to the living room, where he sank onto the sofa and pulled a faded photo album out from under the coffee table.

He wiped some dust from the cover as he cracked it open. "Your mom made this with photos she took on the set of the first Puzzle Face movie." On the first page was a photo of the two of them, my dad decked out in his costume as he wrapped an arm around my mom and kissed her neck. She was laughing, head thrown back, as she threw up a peace sign. Around the photo, she'd pasted cute decorative cutouts: a movie camera in one corner, a reel of unwound film in another.

"Mom made this?" It was hard to imagine my mother, so career-driven and analytical, creating something so sentimental.

"Oh yeah, she had a big scrapbooking phase for a while." He chuckled. "Didn't last long. I think this was the only one."

As we flipped through the pages, I tried to take in every detail, thirsty for glimpses of my parents when they were still happy. On one page she'd stuck a photo of my dad listening intently to the director next to a snap of my dad holding up bunny ears behind the same man when he wasn't looking. On another, there were photos of the two of them—my mom and dad curled up napping between scenes or eating together with the cast. I tried to ignore the pangs of sadness that my mother had thought it important to document her early relationship with my dad but not the early years of her only child. Baby photos of me existed, but not in anything even remotely resembling a baby book.

"Did you tell her you found this?"

My dad shook his head, a wisp of a rueful smile on his face. "Nah, I'll show her at Christmas."

There was no bad blood between my mom and dad, and my relationship with her wasn't too strained either. She flew down every year for the holidays, and we spent the week together, catching up and watching *A Christmas Story* on repeat as we baked cookies. But while my dad and I had formed a close, natural bond before my brain had even started to form memories, my mother and I struggled to find things we had in common. I was sad when they divorced, and it was a transition when she moved east to take the New York City real estate market by storm, but my dad had always been my rock, grounding me even when things were uncertain.

My mom and I texted on occasion and had a monthly phone

call, but that relationship was nothing like the one I had with my dad.

Finally reaching the end of the scrapbook, we turned to the last page, which featured a huge photo capturing the entire cast and crew. I peered from face to face, each of them beaming exhausted but happy grins. There was just one that hadn't bothered smiling, a glowering man standing all the way on the left side who looked strangely familiar.

I peered closer. There, staring back at me, was the face in Trevor's Instagram photo. It was the man who'd been so angry when Trevor and Teddy broke the lamp on the first day.

"I know him," I murmured, my pulse thumping. "That's our props master."

"Scott Rossi? He's still in the business?" My dad frowned, his whole face darkening. "Stay away from him, ok? He's not a nice guy."

"Why? What's he done?"

"He was the props assistant on this first movie. Real piece of work. Always in a bad mood, and I saw him punch an extra for ruining a prop once. It was just an old boom box, not even anything expensive. The guy's an asshole."

"Yikes."

"He ended up getting fired halfway through filming. Never forgave me, though, for turning him in to production. Best to just avoid him, if I were you."

My stomach sank, a dark picture of what could have happened to Trevor forming in my mind. "Got it. I will."

I hated lying to my dad.

Thankfully, there was no more talk of my career as we dec-imated the spaghetti and a pint of Cherry Garcia ice cream for dessert. Daffy even woke up in time for me to make her a special dessert of strawberries and the tiniest squirt of whipped cream. It made her like me for a whole forty-seven seconds. The sky had darkened by the time I put on my shoes to leave, and my dad walked me to my car even though it was a mere ten feet from the house.

He leaned through the open window of the passenger side door. "Thanks for visiting, Squish. It's always good to see you."

"Of course. It was good seeing you, too."

"Drive safe."

"I will."

"And listen . . ."

I tensed, knowing where this was going.

"Will you at least think about calling my buddy? Just to chat?"

I sighed. "Sure, Dad. I will."

But as I backed out of the driveway and took off down the road, getting in touch with my dad's friend was the last thing on my mind. Dots were starting to connect, and I was convinced I'd found our first lead.

Scott had a motive, and apparently a history of lashing out when people damaged his props. And now, we had photographic evidence that he was near Trevor shortly before his death. Did Trevor go to apologize, but Scott snapped and hurt him? Or could Scott have planned the entire thing—rolling back the fencing before following Trevor and pushing him into the ditch? He could have even moved some rocks, making sure Trevor didn't have a safe landing.

Either way, I would have to forget whatever happened between me and Teddy while rehearsing the lap dance scene. We needed to regroup, and then Teddy and I needed to talk to Scott.

# Chapter Ten

"Well, that can't be good."

The next morning, Brent and I were standing in the foyer of the house, fresh out of hair and makeup. It was early, the sun just creeping through the windows and suffusing the set with a warm glow. Scott and the rest of the props crew were bustling around, prepping for the day's shoot. And in the dining room to our right, a clean-up crew was scrubbing at the wall where someone had spray-painted graffiti overnight.

"Quick, what are the odds Natasha's already found some poor PA to fire?" Brent smirked, his black leather jacket and dark jeans a sharp contrast to his usual tees and athletic shorts.

Despite believing this was a very real possibility, I laughed. The odds game was a relic from a bad vampire movie Brent and I had starred in together two years ago, a way for us to kill time on long days of shooting. We bet on everything from how many takes our hungover co-stars would blow to how many times our fake fangs would fall out over the course of a day.

Brent usually won because he'd actually taken a statistics class in college while my guesses were based purely on vibes.

"I'd say . . . ninety-two percent," I wagered. "It's only day four and we're already dealing with the death of a crew member and vandalism? Please. She'd need to blow steam somehow."

"Ninety-two? This is a serious game, Quinn. I give it a solid twenty-three percent chance. Not impossible, but unlikely since Trevor dipped and we're already down one."

"Dipped? He didn't leave—he died!"

"Well, he definitely left this life."

"That's awful." I shoved his shoulder as he winked mischievously.

Things hadn't always been this cordial between me and Brent. We first met nearly ten years ago, both of us freshly in our twenties and starring in the same zombie movie. What started as on-set flirtation quickly led to late-night hookups. It ended how you'd expect: with Brent hitting on one of the extras and me getting unreasonably jealous.

I may have stolen his guitar and smashed it in front of the entire cast and crew.

All of this made it incredibly awkward when we found ourselves working together again a few years ago. Thankfully, we'd both gained a little more maturity by then, even if he'd needed it more than me. The odds game became a way for us to co-exist without expressing blatant contempt for each other. And eventually, with something resembling friendship.

Chloe and Audrey filed in behind us, the two of them letting out identical gasps when they spotted the mess in the dining room.

"What happened?" Chloe stood on her tiptoes, trying to get a better look around the crew, who were still blocking the graffiti.

"No idea," I said. "We just got here too."

"How did someone get in?" Audrey glanced around nervously, like the culprit might still be lurking on set. "I don't think they're going to be able to scrub that off—they'll have to repaint."

It did look bad. The crew had managed to lighten a few spots, but the pigment was still boldly visible. Tossing their brushes to the ground, they stepped away to take a break, finally revealing what had been painted on the wall.

My heart stuttered. Filling the wall was a symbol, a giant circle with a distorted cross cutting through the middle. Below, in jagged letters, were the words "Run, Rabbit."

"Ugh!" Chloe grimaced. "That's creepy."

"Fucked up," Brent muttered under his breath.

Audrey only nodded, her mouth opened in a little "o" as she stared at the wall.

While the others were creeped out, I was likely the only one who understood the full significance. The symbol was from a movie I'd filmed years ago called *Hearts Stop*. I played a nurse who's killed off early in the film, the villain whispering, "Run, rabbit," before murdering her in the halls of the hospital. The movie was a cult classic, amassing a dedicated niche following but not widely known by the public. Whoever did this was obviously familiar with the movie—and considering the significance of the phrase "run, rabbit" it was hard to interpret it as anything but a threat. To me.

Staring at it, goosebumps prickled up the back of my neck.

"You four!" Natasha strode across the dining room from the kitchen, bumping into the crew as she gesticulated vaguely. "Don't even look at it! We're proceeding as usual, there's no use gawking."

Brent rolled his eyes. "What the fuck's us looking at it going to do?"

Natasha looked like she was about to go from a seven to a nine on the rage scale, so I hurried to step in. "Where would you like us?"

"In there." She motioned to the parlor, where the set was ready for filming. "Call time won't be affected, so you all need to be ready."

"Do you know who did this?" Chloe murmured.

"How should I know?" Natasha raked a hand through her short, spiky hair. "Someone obviously got in here overnight. Crew swore they locked up, but clearly something was missed."

Intuition tingled at the back of my mind. We were only four days into filming and things were already going seriously wrong.

"Now go!" Natasha shooed us away. "Go wait over there until we're ready."

Twenty minutes later, Teddy had barely stepped foot in the house when I grabbed his arm and tanked him into the kitchen. I pushed him into the breakfast nook, where we'd be shielded in case anyone passed by.

"Damn, Jigsaw, you trying to get me alone?"

Ignoring him, I lowered my voice to a whisper. "Someone's trying to scare me off."

"What?"

"The spray paint." I motioned toward the dining room as I explained the significance of the symbol and phrase. "It's the killer. They're warning me to stop investigating, I know it." I chewed on one of my fingernails, the thought making me uneasy.

"How would they know we're investigating? We haven't even done anything yet."

"I don't know! But it's too much of a coincidence not to be intentional." I glanced behind us, making sure we were still alone. "Also, I found the man in Trevor's photo."

"Where?" Teddy peered around the kitchen, as though he expected him to be right there in the room with us.

"Oh my God." I pressed my eyes closed. "No, I mean I found out who he is." Quickly, I filled him in on the visit with my dad—the scrapbook, the photo, and my dad's history with him.

"Wait, your dad was Puzzle Face? *The* Puzzle Face?"

I nodded impatiently. "Yes, and he said that Scott is a real asshole. He was fired from a movie after attacking someone who ruined a prop. That sounds awfully familiar, don't you think?"

"You two sound so close. It's cool that you continued the family business." Teddy looked impressed, and a little wistful, which was not the reaction I'd been expecting.

"It's not really a family business, it's—Never mind." I took a deep breath, trying to push down my irritation that Teddy seemed more interested in my dad than the very real threat of a murderer. "Did you hear me? We have our first suspect!"

"Oh. Right." Teddy's eyes refocused. "So . . . what do we do now?"

"We need to talk to him. Or maybe look around the props trailer for clues? What do they do in all those mystery novels you read?"

"Something to make things worse, usually."

"Let's not do that. How about you meet me at my trailer later tonight, around ten? We can try to sneak into the props trailer. Depending on what we find, maybe we can track him down and talk to him."

"Got it." He gave two enthusiastic thumbs up.

"Actors to set!" Natasha's voice cut through the house. "Actors, let's go!"

We peered around the doorway before leaving the kitchen— the last thing I wanted was someone to see us sneaking around and start a rumor about me and Teddy.

The coast was clear.

Moving into the parlor, I passed the Ouija board sitting on the coffee table and my stomach lurched. I'd been so focused on telling Teddy about Scott that I'd forgotten which scene we were filming: the seance scene that culminated in me giving Teddy a lap dance. The one that had resulted in some not-so professional touching, and some very not professional thoughts, the day before.

You'd think I would have realized that rehearsing something meant we'd eventually have to film it, too, but I'd obviously blocked that out.

Natasha wanted to film the dance sequence first, which only spiked my anxiety further. As we ran through the choreography, I tried not to remember the way Teddy's breath had caught when

I straddled his lap, or the way I'd been so tempted to taste his mouth when we drew close.

There was no attraction between me and Teddy, I reminded myself. "My Heart Will Go On" is just a really sexy song. It would make anyone feel like making out.

As Teddy and I hit our marks and waited for Natasha to call action, I tried a new tactic. Every time we got close or had to touch, I would summon the grossest, worst images from my decades of watching horror films. I tried it as we waited for the cameras to roll, focusing on replaying the pea soup scene from *The Exorcist* in my head instead of noticing the way Teddy's mouth tugged up in a playful smile as we made eye contact. Was he thinking about our rehearsal, too?

Pea soup, pea soup.

"Action!"

I launched into the choreography, this time set to a far more appropriate pop song. When it came time to run my hand down Teddy's chest, I pictured Jeff Goldblum transforming into a bug in *The Fly* instead of noticing the way Teddy's pecs felt under my trailing fingers. When I straddled his lap, I imagined the scene from *Saw* when the main character had to use the titular tool to get himself out of his leg cuffs. And when Teddy's hands circled my hips, ever so gently slipping up the back of my shirt, I pulled out the big guns: anything that happened in *The Human Centipede*.

"Cut!" Natasha straightened up, pulling off her headphones. "We got it."

Thanking the gods above, I jumped off Teddy and rushed off set. I'd managed to film the scene in just one take, and hadn't fixated on Teddy's physique—or the way he'd been touching me—once. Nope, I definitely wasn't thinking about it at all.

Maybe horror was still good for something after all.

Thwack, thwack, thwack.

The knock at my trailer door came just after ten. I padded quickly across the floor, twisting the door's handle with an almost imperceptible click. Teddy stood at the bottom of the steps, hands clasped behind his back. But instead of blending into the night as we'd agreed upon, he wore charcoal gray joggers, black sneakers, and a bright orange tee-shirt, vibrantly visible even in the pitch black.

"What are you wearing?" I hissed.

He stared at me a moment before glancing down at his shirt. "What?"

I motioned to my own outfit—black shoes, black leggings, and a black crew-neck sweatshirt. I'd debated a black balaclava, but ultimately decided against it.

"We're supposed to be inconspicuous." I stared dubiously at his shirt, which was all but glowing in the dark.

"Well, I didn't have anything black. Besides the shoes."

"Oh my God, get in here."

As Teddy hopped up the stairs and followed me back inside, I retreated to the tiny bedroom to rifle through what few spare clothes I'd stashed away for emergencies.

Reaching the bottom of the drawer, the only thing I could find was an oversized black tee-shirt with the silhouette of a cat with a mohawk on it.

"Here." I tossed it to him as I entered the living area. "Try that."

He caught it, glancing at it with distaste. "There's no way that's gonna fit."

"You won't know until you try." I shrugged. "Should have come prepared instead of showing up looking like a fluorescent tangerine."

Sighing, Teddy gripped the bottom of his shirt and yanked it over his head, revealing rippling abs and chiseled pecs. I averted my eyes, trying not to look. But the moon was angling through the window just right, highlighting his broad shoulders and taut biceps as he roughly pulled my tee-shirt down over his torso. I imagined slipping my thumbs beneath the waistband of his joggers, pushing him back onto the sofa, and climbing onto his lap.

I shook my head, physically trying to clear it.

"What?" Teddy groaned. "I told you it wouldn't fit." He'd managed to get the shirt on, but the armholes were so strained I was shocked they hadn't ripped, and the hem hadn't made it down past his belly button.

I smothered a laugh with my hand. "You look great."

"I look ridiculous."

"No, that look was very popular when I was in middle school. You just need a belly button ring and you'll be set."

"I hate you."

"At least you and your hate will blend into the surroundings now."

He grinned, his eyes sparkling in the moonlight, and the trailer suddenly felt very small, and very dark, and we were very alone. Once again, images of us on the couch flashed in my head. This time, Teddy easing the straps of my bra down my arms, his head dipping to press his mouth against—

"Anyway." I cleared my throat. "Let me grab you something else. I think I have an old sweatshirt somewhere." I returned to the bedroom and rustled around until I found it, an oversized crewneck with a Boston Red Sox logo emblazoned on the front.

"Here you go."

Teddy eyed it skeptically. "This isn't from one of your exes, is it?"

"Yeah. You can keep it—honestly, I don't want it."

"I'd rather not, thanks." He held it by the tips of his fingers, looking even less enthused than he was about the tiny tee-shirt.

"Hurry up! We have to get going."

Mutinously, he glared at me before slipping it over his head.

We crept outside and tiptoed through base camp, the moon illuminating our path as we made our way toward the props trailer. It was a long walk—the trailer was located next to the set house, and at this time of night there was no PA in a golf cart to shuttle us. The air was chilly, a breeze ruffling my hair and cutting through my sweatshirt with ease.

Teddy and I didn't talk much along the way. Everyone was most likely back at the hotel, but you never knew—there could have been a late-night wardrobe emergency that needed attending to or a problem with logistics that had to be discussed.

Or there could be a murderer on the prowl, looking for their next victim.

As we finally made it to the trailer, a rare twinge of nerves snaked through my stomach. How would we explain ourselves if Scott caught us? And what, precisely, were we going to do once we got inside?

"Psst," I hissed, grabbing Teddy's arm. "Wait."

"What's up?"

"We should have a plan before we get inside."

"Ok, uh. I don't have one."

"You were supposed to help me with this! I help you not suck so much at acting and you help me catch a killer."

"We're not even sure this was a murder! Scott could just be a weird dude who's unreasonably passionate about lamps."

"We've been over this! We at least need to find out what he knows."

"Alright, uh ..." Teddy ran a hand through his hair as he glanced toward the trailer. "We're looking for clues, right? So let's poke around and see if we find anything interesting."

"I figured as much."

"I wasn't finished!"

"Ok, fine, finish."

"So we go inside, and then"—he looked at me dramatically—"we look for anything that could tie him to the crime."

I sighed. "You don't say?"

"A written confession would be great, but bloody clothes or a murder weapon would also work."

I rubbed my temples. This was going nowhere fast.

Motioning for Teddy to follow me, I approached the trailer. The door at the back end was locked, and a quick peek through the window didn't net much information. All we could see were piles of junk—smaller items like alcohol bottles, a radio, and a Ouija board were lined on rows of shelves, while bigger props like chairs and an oddly large number of bikes were piled on the floor.

Tiptoeing through the grass, we moved to the door at the other end of the structure. A light shone through the window above, and I could hear whispers of classical music.

"He's in there!" Excitement pumped through my blood and I hurried toward the door, eager to see what he was up to. I hadn't made it two steps when Teddy grabbed the back of my shirt, yanking me to a stop.

"Wait." Teddy gripped my arm, rooting me in place. "You could be sneaking up on a killer!"

"Weren't you just saying you didn't even think this was a murder? Let go."

Reluctantly, Teddy released my arm. "I just don't think we should be rushing into anything. We need to be careful."

"Fine. I'll carefully go spying." I continued, slower this time, as Teddy trailed after me, grumbling. Standing to the side of the door, I carefully peered through the window.

Just like we'd suspected, Scott was inside. He stood at a makeshift workstation that had been pushed into the corner, complete with a workbench and lamp with a flexible neck for precise positioning. A radio sat alongside a bottle of paint, glue, and various solvents. Scott was facing away from us, bent over the bench. I assumed he was working on some kind of prop, but he was blocking the view and it was impossible to see what, exactly, it was.

"It's him," I confirmed to Teddy, who was hunched out of sight of the window.

"What's he doing?"

"Working on something."

"On what?"

Irritation sparked. "You know, I think he's working on a murder right here as we speak." I peeked back through the window, hopeful that Scott would shift enough to allow me to see his project. He was still crouched over, his arm moving in small, precise movements, clearly working at something delicate.

*Come on*, I thought. *Get the hell out of the way!*

Seemingly satisfied, Scott eased back on the stool. He shifted to the side, cocking his head as he examined his work. Only as he moved to get a better look did he finally reveal what he'd been so absorbed in.

A severed human head sat on the bench, eyes staring and mouth agape.

Unable to stifle my scream, I hollered as I wheeled back, my heart hammering as I braced myself against the side of the trailer.

"What happened?" Teddy moved between me and the door, grabbing my hips with both of his hands as he moved me out of the way. The unexpected contact took me off guard, and for a moment I forgot that mere seconds ago I'd been staring at a head on a desk. His fingertips pressed into my skin, the touch firm and protective. Soothing. But it just as quickly came back to me—the terrible staring eyes and the way Scott had reached for his weapon.

"There's a head," I gulped. "On the bench."

Teddy's eyes widened. He released my hips, instead sliding an arm around my waist as he pulled me away from the trailer. "We're going. Now."

But we didn't have the chance. A second later, the door flew open. Scott stepped out, his eyes wild as he brandished a scythe high above his head, its blade glinting in the moonlight.

## Chapter Eleven

"What the hell are you doing here?" Scott set down the scythe and grabbed both of us by the ears, yanking us into the light pouring out from the door.

I craned my neck, frantically trying to get another look at the head. A shock of pain tore through the side of my head and I stopped, not wanting my ear to be added to the list of severed body parts in the immediate vicinity.

"Lay off, man." Teddy wrestled free. "We weren't trying to spy." He moved between me and Scott, succeeding in getting him to release me.

"Shut up," I said, my teeth gritted. "He wasn't even thinking that." Rubbing my ear, I was finally able to squint into the trailer and see that the head was, in fact, a prop.

Damn it, of course it was a prop. It looked eerily real—its eyes bright and glassy, the mouth gaping and bloodied—but the wig had slipped off, revealing an obviously plastic scalp with bolts holding the plates together.

"Bullshit you weren't spying." Scott looked at me, his eyes narrowing. "Hey, you're Quinn, right? Jim's little girl?"

I bristled. "I'm hardly little. But yeah, he's my dad."

"Figures." Scott rolled up the arms of his shirt, which had slipped down in our scuffle. "Any kid of his was bound to make trouble. What are you two doing here if you weren't trying to stick your nose where it don't belong?"

"Natasha asked us to stop by," I blurted.

Teddy's eyebrows jumped in alarm. "Yeah, uh . . . she wanted to make sure the . . . special prop would be ready for tomorrow."

My brain spun, trying to remember what scene we'd be filming tomorrow in case Scott asked us to be more specific. Thankfully, he didn't.

Instead, he beamed. "Sure will be!" He opened the door and motioned inside. "Want to see?"

I did not, actually, want to see. But Teddy and I complied, climbing into the trailer after him. Scott picked up the fake head lovingly, smoothing the blonde wig back into place.

"Now, I only have the one." He glanced at Teddy out of the corner of his eye. "So we can't afford to ruin it."

"Hey." Teddy held up his hands. "That was Trevor who broke the lamp, not me."

Scott grumbled something indecipherable.

"Speaking of Trevor," I said. "Did you happen to see him? The night he died?" Realizing this probably seemed out of the blue, I hurried to add, "I thought I heard him say he was stopping by."

"Yeah, he did. To drop off props and apologize about the lamp." Scott shook his head. "Real nice kid. A shame what happened to him."

Teddy and I exchanged a meaningful glance, which didn't go unnoticed by Scott.

"Why?" He set the head back down and crossed his arms. "What's going on?"

"The police think Trevor's death was an accident, but we're not so sure," Teddy said carefully. "We're just trying to figure out what really happened. Right?" He looked down at me, his eyes stern. Normally I would chafe at such a blatant attempt to keep me in line, but considering we were dealing with a potential murderer, I decided to comply.

And, coming from Teddy, I kind of liked it.

The realization took me off guard. When, precisely, had I stopped hating being in his presence? Was it when I was straddling him for the camera? When he'd pushed himself between me and Scott just minutes ago? I brushed the thought away.

Meanwhile, Scott looked taken aback. "Listen, I may not have liked that kid too much after he broke that lamp." He ran a hand over his head. "But hell, it wasn't worth killing over."

"Do you have an alibi?" I asked.

"As a matter of fact, not that I owe you two anything, but I do." He knelt to the floor and started rummaging through an old, worn backpack. "Here you go." He pulled something out and extended his hand. It was a receipt.

I studied the small piece of paper. Sure enough, it was from the date of the murder and timestamped at 10:07 p.m. Teddy and I had found Trevor shortly after that, so it seemed like Scott would have been far away at the time the murder took place. Still, that didn't mean he couldn't have killed Trevor before scurrying off to get a receipt for this very reason.

I squinted at the top of the slip of paper. "Why did you need to go to Jenny's Beauty Supply?"

Scott rolled his eyes toward Teddy, elbowing him playfully in the ribs. "Your girl here is a right pain in the ass."

Teddy opened his mouth, but before he could get a word out, Scott continued.

"Well, Ms. Nosy, after Trevor apologized, I drove around trying to find a replacement lamp, which I also have the receipt for, and then to the beauty supply store for liquid latex so I could finish our pal over there on the bench." He nodded toward the head, which was still staring at us bleakly. "Anyway, I didn't get back here until after midnight."

"Did you notice anything strange?" Teddy asked. "Anyone sneaking around?"

Scott hesitated. "I didn't think of it at the time, but . . ."

My ears perked up. "What?"

"The light was on in the attic before I left to find a new lamp. I thought it was weird, because who would need to be up there? Anyway, I was standing out there staring up at the window and I saw a face."

A chill tripped up my spine. "Who was it?"

"Beats me. I couldn't make them out. They were just sitting up there, staring down at me. Like they were waiting for something."

"Well, that was a bust." I hopped into my car, grabbing the seatbelt as I slipped the key in the ignition. After the long walk back from the props trailer, the adrenaline from confronting Scott had ebbed away and been replaced by something else—brutal disappointment.

"I wouldn't say that." Teddy climbed in and slammed the passenger-side door closed. "Now we know it's not Scott."

"You believe the story he told us?"

"It was a pretty solid alibi." He cocked his head to the side. "I don't remember the last time I saved a receipt. Hope I'm never suspected of murder."

I sighed as I switched on my music and pulled onto the road. The Smiths played through the speakers, Morrissey whining about being miserable. How appropriate. It was silly to have thought we'd solve the mystery on our first attempt, but it was still discouraging.

"We'll figure it out," Teddy said cheerfully.

"I guess."

Teddy elbowed me in the shoulder. "Come on, it could have been worse. What's up?"

"I just didn't picture my la—" I froze, catching myself. No one besides Mara knew this was going to be my last film, and I preferred to keep it that way. "I didn't picture the movie starting this way. Hunting down a murderer is my character's job."

"If it makes you feel better, I didn't picture my first movie going like this either."

This did make me smile. "It could be worse, I guess."

"Oh, yeah? How?"

"When Jack Nicholson was filming *The Shining*, they fed him cheese sandwiches for two weeks straight. He hated cheese sandwiches. They wanted to drive him literally crazy to better his performance. Stanley Kubrick was so mean to Shelley Duvall she lost her hair."

"Damn."

"While filming *Texas Chainsaw Massacre*, the cast had to spend over twenty-four hours in an abandoned house filled with dead animals and rotting food. In one-hundred degree weather. With no air-conditioning."

"Ok, that one might beat being in a real-life murder mystery. But barely."

I laughed. "At least we have air-conditioning."

We fell silent, but I could feel him watching me. I squirmed, uneasy under his stare.

Teddy twisted in his seat. "I promise we'll figure this out. And in the meantime, I won't let anyone hurt you. There's no getting past these guns." He rolled up the sleeve of my sweatshirt, which he was still wearing, and flexed his bicep in a convincing impression of Gaston from *Beauty and the Beast*.

I smirked, ignoring the fluttering in my stomach at the thought of him wanting to protect me. "That's awfully confident."

"What can I say? You can't argue with pure, muscular strength."

"Oh my God, gross." I reached over to smack his shoulder. His bicep was solid under my hand, and I fought the urge to remember the way those arms had gripped me in his hotel room, pulling me against him before I'd slammed on the brakes.

I flipped through the songs in my playlist, desperate for a distraction. Teddy started humming along, his mood shockingly light for someone who'd been questioning a man not a half an hour ago about whether he was a murderer. I was surprised—I didn't take him for someone who would be familiar with the Pixies.

"You know this song?"

"Sure do."

"You don't strike me as an eighties alternative rock guy."

"What kind of guy do I strike you as?"

"I don't know. Maybe . . . a Post Malone type guy."

He burst out with a laugh. "Not my style. My mom loves music, so I grew up listening to this stuff. She played R.E.M. on her big CD sound system every night when she was making dinner, and she took my brother and me to see Blondie when I was eleven. My first concert."

"You're really close to your brother, aren't you?"

Teddy nodded. "And my mom. She's amazing and did everything she could for us, but as a single parent with two jobs, she was gone a lot. So my brother and I got really close. Fought a lot, too, but we grew out of that."

I wanted to ask what had led to his mother raising them alone, but it seemed rude to pry.

"My dad used to play these guys as we drove around in his pickup to conventions and premieres."

"You rolled up to movie premieres in a pickup truck blasting eighties rock?"

"Sure did."

He grinned. "I love it." Teddy tapped his foot to the beat, unable to keep himself from drumming on the dash as the tempo increased. I watched him out of the corner of my eye, amused.

"I don't get you," I finally said.

"What do you mean?"

"You've been so worked up about performing that you were

blowing your lines and ruining takes." I shook my head ruefully. "But there might be a killer out there, possibly after us, and you're totally calm."

Teddy shrugged. "I guess."

"I feel like you need to get your priorities straight," I teased.

"Honestly, it's weird to see you anxious about something. You're so . . ."

"Bitchy?"

"I was going to say fierce."

"Oh." My cheeks tingled. The way he'd said it made it sound like a compliment.

"I don't feel like it lately," I said. "So if you have any tips, I'm all ears."

He paused. "For me, the worst part is the unknown. The waiting for something bad to happen. Wondering if everything will be ok or if disaster is about to strike. But once the bad thing happens?" He threw up his hands. "The anticipation is gone and I can focus on fixing it. I've usually rehearsed the worst-case scenario in my head anyway, so I already have a plan."

I took my eyes off the road for a second to look at him, a little surprised. I hadn't expected something so insightful from him. Teddy James was capable of depth after all. Who knew?

"That makes sense."

"Does it?" Teddy scrunched his face and ran a hand over his hair. "It's exhausting."

"At least you always have a game plan." And then, I don't know what made me say it. It popped out of my mouth before I could stop it. "I'm sure your girlfriends appreciate that. All that planning ahead."

Teddy chuckled, a low sound. "Not really. Girlfriends in the past haven't been very appreciative. Of the worrying. More like annoyed."

"I'm sorry. That's awful."

"Yeah, well. Relationships and I don't mix. And how could I party with all those girls from Instagram if I was tied down?"

Now there was the Teddy I knew.

Before I could reply, Teddy's arm shot out, twisting up the volume knob.

"Ooh, this is my favorite." He tapped out the beat on the tops of his thighs as the opening bars of "Bohemian Rhapsody" rang out.

"It's everyone's favorite."

"No way, it's a deep cut."

I snorted. "Are you serious?"

Teddy said nothing, just mouthed the opening lyrics in an exaggerated way as he stared at me, daring me to join in as he twisted the volume up even higher.

"You look ridiculous!" I shouted over Freddie Mercury singing about being a poor boy.

In reply, Teddy rolled down the window and started singing the words for real, his voice surprisingly strong and rich.

"Hey!" I reached for the button to roll the window back up. "It's late."

"And there's so many people around." He motioned outside, where nothing but dark fields flanked the car. He shot me a wicked look. "Lighten up a little!"

I was about to retort that I was in no way uptight when I noticed an irresistible glint in his eye. The song was really getting going now, the familiar plinks of the piano getting louder.

"Fine." I rolled down my own window, turned up the music even higher, and belted along with Freddie as he lamented to his mother about killing a man.

We sang along to the whole thing, my voice straining and breaking at the higher notes. But I didn't care—the wind was whipping my hair and Teddy was making wild conductor motions in the passenger seat and I was drumming along on the steering wheel, and for the first time in years I forgot about all the bullshit. I forgot about gossip magazines, and my failing career, and even the possible killer who was on the loose.

All I knew or cared about was the music, and the rasp in my throat as I took in great lungfuls of fresh air, and Teddy singing along with me, note for note.

When the song ended, Freddie's voice gently trailing off, Teddy reached out to lower the volume.

I swatted his hand away. "Let's see what's next!"

He grinned and leaned back in his seat, and then we sang along to the Pixies and Blondie and the Cure, not stopping even as we rolled into town and the chance of someone hearing us grew exponentially higher.

I finally turned it down as I pulled into the parking lot of the hotel, the two of us out of breath. I parked, disappointed that the drive was at an end. Compared to the energy in the car, the idea of going back to my lonely room was unappealing.

"Thanks for coming with me." I reached into the backseat for my bag. "If I'd been there alone with Scott, I probably would have gotten myself in trouble."

"No problem." He didn't say anything else, but he also wasn't moving to get out of the car. He just stared at me, a hint of a smile on his mouth.

"What?" I asked, suddenly suspicious.

"I remember you, you know."

My hand froze on its way to grab the keys. "What?"

"That night at the party. I kept waiting for you to mention it, but you never did."

There it was again—that stare, with his ocean-blue eyes focused so intently on me that I couldn't look away.

I threw my keys in my bag and fiddled with the zipper. "I don't know what you're talking about."

"Now who needs acting lessons?"

"You left with that woman, I figured you didn't remember . . . I mean, you obviously preferred—" My cheeks heated. I really didn't feel like reliving the humiliation all over again.

"Wait, you thought I was leaving to sleep with her?" For a moment, Teddy looked horrified. "She's a friend—she needed a ride home because her creepy ex was there and he wouldn't leave her alone."

"Oh." I didn't know what to say as I struggled to make sense of this new information.

"So you didn't leave because you didn't want to . . .?"

"No." Teddy's voice was resolute. "I really, really wanted to."

The walk up to the hotel was charged. Energy crackled between us, an invisible thread that seemed to connect us as we crossed the lot and climbed the steps. He placed his hand on the small of my back as he opened the door and guided me through, sending a warm flush straight to my belly. I was hyperaware of his movement as we made our way to the elevator, and neither of us said a word on the ride to the third floor.

We arrived at my room first. I fumbled through my bag, grasping desperately for my key card. It took me a moment to find it—I couldn't focus on locating the card with Teddy staring at me, not moving a single muscle toward his room down the hall.

Finally, I grabbed it.

Before sliding it in the lock, I lifted my gaze to Teddy's face. "Well. Goodnight."

For a moment, he said nothing. My eyes fell to his mouth, my center clenching as his tongue ran ever so lightly along his bottom lip. I imagined grabbing his shoulder and pulling him into my room after me, the two of us twining around each other before falling into bed.

As I stared, Teddy's lips dropped into a frown. "Are we saying goodnight already?" He reached out, cradling my neck in his hand as his thumb lingered on my cheekbone, the pressure soothing. I leaned into his hand, savoring his touch as he studied my face, looking at me like he was trying to memorize each freckle and feature.

"Quinn!"

A voice shattered the silence. We both jerked away, looking for the source. Chloe and Mara—arm in arm—were stumbling down the hall.

I swore under my breath. What on earth was Mara doing up this late? It was nearly three hours past her bedtime.

"We've been looking for you all night!" Chloe looked—and sounded—like she was more than a few drinks in, and Mara seemed not far behind. "Where have you been?"

"Seriously, you can't keep bailing on me like this." Mara stuck out her lip in an exaggerated pout. "I've barely seen you since filming began."

My heart sank. I really had been a terrible friend. I was about to apologize and make an excuse when I realized they had just seen Teddy and me outside my room and dangerously close to kissing—something Mara had surely picked up on.

Indeed, a smirk spread across her face. "Hey, were you guys about to—"

"No!" I yelped. I slipped my key card into the lock and yanked the door handle. "I was just going to bed. Alone."

"Are you sure?" Mara poked my shoulder. "You two look awfully cozy."

"Mara, please . . ."

Chloe's eyes flickered from Mara to me and back again. "Come on, if she says there's nothing going on, I'm sure there's nothing going on." She gave me a covert wink. "Right?"

"Right. Exactly." I breathed out in relief, making a note to thank Chloe later. "I'll see you guys in the morning."

Waving goodnight to Mara and Chloe, I slipped into my room and let go of the door. As it slowly fell back into place, I could see Teddy, his jaw tense, his eyes still smoldering as they bore into mine. I finished slamming the door closed before I could change my mind and pull him in after me.

# Chapter Twelve

I waited for the feeling to dissipate, for the desire I'd felt the night before to somehow dissolve by the time I woke up.

It didn't.

I caught myself replaying moments from the night before in my head as I showered and brushed my teeth—the way Teddy had called me fierce, like it was something he admired. The way I felt comfortable enough to sing in front of him, even though I have a terrible voice. The way a simple hand on the small of my back had almost driven me to yank him into my room, and how I couldn't stop wondering what would have happened if we hadn't been interrupted.

Driving to set, I imagined the whole thing—from Teddy stripping off my clothes and having his way with me over the arm of the sofa to us collapsing in a heap afterward. It was like I'd opened Pandora's box, except the only thing escaping were horny thoughts and fantasies.

I chided myself as I parked and made my way through base

camp. Not only did he have supermodels in his DMs, but he was very much involved with other people. Even if he wasn't the type for a relationship, I didn't want to be the one complicating things for other women. It was for the best that nothing had happened.

If nothing ever happened.

Craft services was bustling when I arrived. Our call time was too early to get breakfast at the hotel, so everyone was instead huddled around the long tables filled with bagels, cut fruit, and other breakfast essentials. I made a beeline for the coffee, intent on getting caffeine in my bloodstream ASAP. As I got closer, I noticed that Mara and Teddy were already there, which would have been fine if they hadn't been bent close, whispering conspiratorially over their cheese Danishes near the coffee station.

My stomach plunged. I recognized that look on her face—it was the same expression she'd worn the time she tried to set up my dad with Jennifer Coolidge at a premiere once. I had to get out of here. Nothing good came from Mara being in matchmaker mode.

But before I could sneak away, she spotted me and waved enthusiastically, alerting Teddy to my presence. He shook hair damp from the shower out of his eyes as he glanced at me and smiled.

My face immediately tomato-ed.

Trying to pull myself together, I threw my shoulders back and walked over to them in a very poor attempt to look unbothered.

"Morning." I gave a cursory wave to Teddy as I grabbed onto Mara's arm like a life raft. "I just have to borrow her for a sec."

"Wait, Teddy and I were—"

"Just for a minute!" Tightening my grip on her arm, I steered us to the other end of the breakfast tables.

"Ouch!" She pried my fingers off her wrist. "Good morning to you, too."

"What were you guys talking about?" I grabbed a plate and studied the spread. To my dismay, it was missing my favorite item—a giant blueberry muffin with deliciously buttery streusel on top. I grabbed one of the banana nut muffins instead, which didn't even compare. Trash.

"Just the type of makeup I'd be doing for his scene later." Mara raised an eyebrow as she grabbed a yogurt container. "Why are you all flushed, by the way?"

"Don't worry about it," I muttered as I finally succeeded in getting some coffee. "Let's go over there."

Mara glanced at Teddy. "But—"

"I think we should sit over here." I led us to a small table far away from where Teddy was now talking to Audrey. I'd never been able to get more than two words out of her, but she was already giggling at something Teddy had said, her hand pressed against his bicep.

"What's going on?" Mara asked as we sat down. "You look like you've run a marathon, which is something you would never do, and you're acting weird." She looked at me pointedly. "Does this have to do with the fact that Teddy was outside your room last night, looking like he was about to devour you like a snack?"

"I— What do you mean?" I raised my mug to my lips, nearly burning myself as I took a long sip.

"Please. I went to your room earlier last night to gossip and drink wine, two of your favorite activities, but you weren't there. Thank God Chloe was bored, too." Mara dipped her spoon into her bowl of yogurt and berries. "And I don't know what you and

Teddy were up to when we found you in the hall, but nothing innocent happens at that hour."

My mouth dried. The downside of having a best friend that knew you better than you knew yourself was that you couldn't get anything past them. I used to consider this an asset, but now that I was hiding both a possible murder investigation and a crush on my co-star that I was desperately trying to squash, I wasn't so sure.

"Um. Well."

Out of the corner of my eye, I could see someone approaching our table, thankfully giving me an excuse not to respond. But my relief dissipated when I realized it was Teddy.

"Sorry to interrupt. I thought you might want this." In his hand was a plate, holding one perfect blueberry muffin.

I couldn't help it. My eyes lit up.

"Oh my gosh, thank you." I took the muffin gratefully, narrowly avoiding an impression of Gollum in *Lord of the Rings*. "How did you know?"

Teddy smirked. "Please. You almost grabbed one out of a PA's hand the other day. Today there was only one left, so . . ."

"Thank you, that's really thoughtful." But inside, I was groaning. My fantasies were already out of control; I didn't need him fetching my favorite foods and making them even worse.

"Anytime." He winked. "Just wanted to give you that. I'll leave you two alone."

I watched as he crossed the room, a shimmering feeling in my chest.

Mara followed my gaze. "Teddy didn't give me any details about what you two were up to last night, by the way."

"Oh?" Relief poured through my body, although I wasn't sure

which I was happier about: that he hadn't told her about us investigating Scott or that he hadn't told her we'd almost slept together the night of the party.

"Nope. And I did ask." She poked me with her foot, teasing.

I didn't know how to respond, so I said nothing. Instead, I unwrapped the blueberry muffin and took a bite.

Studying my expression, Mara leaned back and took a sip of her tea, her face vaguely troubled. "Are you sure there's nothing going on?"

"I told you, there's—"

"I don't mean between you and Teddy."

"Oh."

"You've been weird ever since we got here. Avoiding me, not answering my texts. Being evasive." She fiddled with the handle of her mug. "You don't have to hide things from me. You can trust me. I thought you knew that."

Guilt swirled in my stomach. Everything she said was true: I had been avoiding her and lying about what I was up to. And it felt awful—before now, the only time I'd lied to her was when I supported her decision to grow out her bangs. They just suited her so well.

"I promise, I'm not keeping anything from you. And you know I trust you." I squeezed her wrist, hoping I looked genuine. "I'm just feeling off. I have no plan for what I'm doing once the film is done. It's a little unsettling."

In my defense, that was true.

Mara pursed her lips. "If you say so." She dropped her gaze to her yogurt, pushing a blueberry around with her spoon.

"How's the yogurt?"

"Fine."

My chest ached. I wanted to tell her everything. I wanted to tell her just how close Teddy and I had come to hooking up, and how badly I'd wanted it to happen. I wanted to tell her that I was becoming more convinced by the hour that Trevor's death hadn't been an accident, and that I needed to find out who killed him. I wanted to watch her listen and still tell me that everything was going to be ok.

But with a potentially dangerous person loose on set, I couldn't risk getting her involved in the investigation. And as for my feelings for Teddy . . . I could barely admit them to myself, let alone out loud to another person. Even Mara.

"I should get going." I balled up the now-empty muffin wrapper. "I'll see you at hair and makeup?"

"Of course." But she didn't meet my eyes as she said it.

I retreated to my trailer, eager for a few minutes alone. The day was already going downhill quick and I needed to regroup. Unlocking the door and stepping inside, I nearly fell as my foot slid on an envelope lying on the floor.

Picking it up, I slipped my thumb under the flap and pulled out the paper inside. It was covered in red type:

*While hid high in the attic above,*
*I watched until I could give you a shove.*
*Say nothing of which you know,*
*Or you'll be the one in death's throes.*
*Back in your very first role,*
*Did you know this would be the toll?*

*

"Jigsaw, we can't keep meeting like this." A corner of Teddy's mouth rose as he leaned against the door to the house's attic. "Just admit you're into me."

"Haha, funny. No. I found something in my trailer you need to take a look at."

After getting the note, I'd immediately texted Teddy, telling him we needed to talk. A hectic shooting schedule meant we weren't able to find time until lunch, and now that we were alone on the third floor of the house, I handed him the slip of paper. He scanned the words, his usually confident expression slipping as he reached the end.

"Is this for real?"

"I think so. Everyone else still thinks Trevor's death was an accident. It mentions the attic, where Scott said he saw someone hiding." I stared at the door we were about to enter. "It has to be from the killer."

He frowned. "It's not even good. It's like poetry I would have written for English class in high school."

"It is really bad, but we have to focus." I snatched the paper away and stuffed it in my pocket. "If the killer knows we're investigating, we're both in danger. You didn't tell anyone about this, right?"

"No." He cocked an eyebrow. "Did you?"

"No."

"What about Mara?"

"No!" As if I needed another reminder of my secrecy. "Let's go. We need to be back on set in less than half an hour."

Light from the windows above streamed down as we climbed the steps, illuminating dust motes floating in the stuffy air.

Reaching the top, we took a second to survey the area. It was huge—reaching from one end of the house all the way to the other. It had bare, dusty floorboards with exposed beams running overhead in the eaves. The entire space was filled with junk from previous occupants, save for a few paths that wound through the piles of stuff.

This was going to be harder than I had thought.

"Should we just ... start looking?" Teddy swiped a hand across his forehead, looking as overwhelmed as I felt.

"I guess so."

As we made our way down one side of the attic, I carefully studied all the belongings forgotten and left by previous occupants: a brightly colored tricycle sat next to a box of kids' clothes from the eighties, which was next to a sewing machine that looked like it could be a priceless antique from the jazz era.

"Hey, look at this." Teddy gestured to an old record player next to a stack of albums and handed me an old Fleetwood Mac LP. It looked like an original edition of the *Rumours* album.

"Oh my God." I wiped some of the dust off Stevie Nicks. "I've always wanted one of these."

"Well, now you've got it."

I smiled wryly. "If I had more questionable ethics, I'd definitely be sneaking this back to my hotel room with me."

"Lucky record." His eyes twinkled as he gazed at me. I wanted to swim in that moment, enjoy the comfortable feeling of his eyes on me in the solitude of the attic. The energy between us crackled like something once again was brewing.

Whatever it was, it felt dangerous.

I looked away, breaking the spell so we could continue to

sift through junk and peer into shadowy corners. There was only about a quarter of the space left, and so far we'd found nothing useful. We picked our way over old rakes and shovels and through old racks of clothing, but nothing stuck out as potential evidence. I was about to suggest we admit defeat when I rounded a looming bookcase and stopped short.

Someone had been here. And by the looks of it, recently.

On the other side of the bookcase was a window tucked into a little alcove. Empty beer cans lay on the floor, and an old sweatshirt had been draped over an old chaise lounge. The cans looked clean and new, and the sweatshirt was free of dust, unlike everything else up here. Had they been left by whoever had been up here the night of Trevor's murder?

"Oh my God," Teddy said, hurrying over.

"What?"

He picked up one of the cans. "Who still drinks Natty Light?" He shuddered. "Disgusting."

"Is that what you're focusing on right now?"

"I'm just saying, whoever was here had pretty terrible taste."

"Insightful." I walked over to the chaise and picked up the sweatshirt. Holding it by my fingertips, I shook it out so I could take a better look. It was maroon with giant gray letters on it: WSU.

Teddy squinted at it. "Washington State?"

I nodded, my mind whirring. The sweatshirt looked familiar, but I couldn't pinpoint from where. I closed my eyes, holding the image in my mind. I'd seen it several times before, but where? I closed my eyes and focused, the face I associated it with gradually coming into view. It was . . .

"Brent!" I remembered now. "It's Brent's. He's had it forever. He wore it the first day before he took it off for last looks."

"You watching Brent strip, Jigsaw?"

"I haven't done that since 2017, actually."

"You and Brent?" Teddy crossed his arms across his chest as his face lit up in delight. "And what was that like?"

"Not great."

"Really? Because judging by his beer preference he seems like a really cultured, interesting guy."

"Can we focus on what's important, please? This is proof he was up here. He could have been the person Scott saw shortly before Trevor was murdered."

I walked over to the window. The props trailer was obscured by some tree branches, but it would definitely be possible to see who was coming and going.

Chills crept up my spine. Brent could have been sitting up here, watching, until Trevor left—giving Brent the perfect opportunity to follow him and push him into the ditch, adrenaline spiking as he rushed after his victim. It was easy to imagine him forgetting his trash and belongings.

Suddenly, I didn't want to be holding the hoodie anymore.

## Chapter Thirteen

Most days, I picked up my costume from the wardrobe department with a smile. *How lucky I am*, I usually thought, *that my character lives in easy-fitting jeans and squishy cardigans. No lacy lingerie or skintight leather ensembles.*

That is, until I showed up to my trailer a few hours after our trip to the attic to find that my costume for the day was already waiting for me—and able to fit in a Ziplock bag. Not even a gallon size, but a quart size. The baggie had been daintily fixed to the hanger with a clothespin, along with a cheery note from the wardrobe supervisor that read "Let me know if you have any questions! xoxo Julian." Inside was an ivory-colored thong and two stickers barely the size of half-dollars.

Yeah, Julian, I had some questions.

Before I could change, my phone lit up with a photo of me and my dad, the two of us dressed up as Pennywise and little Georgie with his balloon from *It* at a horror convention a few years ago. I was Pennywise, naturally.

I answered the call, happy to delay my costume change. "Hey, Dad."

"Hey, Squish. I know you were just here, but I didn't want to mess with tradition."

"Wouldn't dream of it." Ever since he'd moved away from LA, we'd made it a point to talk on the phone every Friday. Sometimes I was busy—or, more often, he was—but we tried to chat for at least a few minutes every week.

"You wouldn't believe what Daffy did today. She knocked over the garbage can and dug through the bag to get to one tiny chicken wing bone!" He laughed. "That damn skunk. How's filming?"

I filled him in the best I could without bringing up the thong I was about to change into or the fact that a murderer was on the loose. It didn't leave much.

"Well hey, I was wondering . . ."

I sucked in a breath, knowing where he was going with this.

"Have you thought about that movie my buddy's making? No pressure," he hurried to add. "He's just excited to hear from you."

I bit my lip. I wanted to say that I wasn't going to be in his friend's movie by default because I was never going to be in any movies again. But that was a conversation for another time, when I didn't have a thong and pasties staring at me, waiting to be put on.

"I actually haven't. I'm sorry."

"It's ok, no problem." I didn't miss the hint of disappointment in his voice.

"I'm sorry, it's just been a little crazy here on set."

"Don't worry about it for a second."

"Ok." I fiddled with the corner of the plastic baggie. "I should get going. I have to go finish getting ready for this scene."

"Oop, well don't let me be the reason you incur the wrath of Natasha. Love you, kid."

"Love you too, Dad."

We hung up.

Left in the silence, I stared at my costume, trying to muster the will to put it on. As if I wasn't going to be uncomfortable enough in the two square inches of fabric, now I had the guilt of lying to my dad weighing on me and making it even worse. After five whole minutes, I finally sighed and unclipped the baggie from the hanger. The scene we'd be filming was in the water, and while I'd been expecting a pretty skimpy bikini, this was on a whole other level. Feeling more like I was unwrapping a deli sandwich than an outfit, I pulled open the zip top and picked out one of the stickers, studying the peel-off backings. I knew they were supposed to cover my nipples, but I was not confident they would succeed.

I retreated into the bathroom, even though I had the entire trailer to myself. I needed double the privacy. The thong exceeded my expectations—it was even more uncomfortable than I'd anticipated. But, somewhat surprisingly, the pasties succeeded in covering up everything they were supposed to.

Wardrobe had also provided me with a robe in some attempt to protect my modesty, so I slipped into the swathe of blue satin and stepped into my flip-flops before exiting my trailer. The scene would be filmed at a different location than usual: a boathouse at a lake nearby. And honestly, I was thankful to get a break from the usual set.

I couldn't tell if my nerves were getting the best of me or if it was just an old house, but odd noises had been rippling through set all day, sometimes loud enough to ruin takes. Footsteps scurrying across the floors above when no one should be up there. Clanging coming from somewhere deep in the bowels of the house. Creaks from somewhere up high, maybe the attic. Or the roof. One particularly loud bang rendered an entire shot unusable, and even Audrey—usually so unflappable—was becoming spooked. She became so nervous that at one point we had to take a break. Natasha had taken to loudly counting down from twenty during moments of stress, which I could only assume she'd picked up in therapy at some point.

Maybe a change of scenery would do us all good. Now, climbing into the waiting car, nerves squeezed my stomach for an entirely different reason—the feeling getting steadily worse each second of the ten-minute drive.

Under any other circumstance, the idea of filming a nude scene wouldn't have phased me. Not only had I done them before—a topless exorcism scene stood out in particular—but I happened to be comfortable with my body, thank you very much. I liked the slightly androgynous shape of it, with my small breasts and slim hips. And even if I wasn't, the water would cover up everything besides my head and shoulders once the cameras started rolling. But being that close to Teddy, the two of us nearly naked?

That made me nervous. I was supposed to be suppressing my attraction to him, not finding new ways to fan its flames.

The car crunched along the gravel leading down to the lake. The scene was idyllic. Docks, boats, a boardwalk; the sun had already dipped below the horizon, rendering the water a dusky violet as crickets chirped in the distance. Gentle waves lapped at the shore, cattails swaying in the breeze. It was the picture of a lakeside paradise.

My steps shaky, I exited the car. Cast and crew buzzed around the boathouse, preparing cameras and lights as makeup artists put the finishing touches on the actors. I scanned the swarms of people, spotting Chloe sitting on a lawn chair, tapping away on her phone. Brent was off to the side, smoking a cigarette. And Mara was touching up Audrey's makeup as a member of wardrobe fixed her special CGI suit, adjusting a few sensors that were out of place.

No Teddy. Not yet. I made my way over to Chloe, waving to get her attention. As she pocketed her phone and got to her feet, I noted—jealously—that her wardrobe for the day was a simple skirt and tee-shirt.

"Hey! You ready for tonight?"

"I guess so." My hand strayed to the belt of my robe, checking it was still secured. "I just wanted to say thanks. For last night."

"What do you mean?"

"Getting Mara off my case. About Teddy. I appreciated it."

"Oh gosh, no problem. I could tell you were uncomfortable."

"She's the best, she just gets a little excited when romance is involved. Or,"—I hurried to correct myself—"when she thinks it is."

"I get it. Who doesn't get excited at the opportunity to play Millionaire Matchmaker?"

"Exactly." I laughed, some of the tension easing in my

shoulders. On a set that was feeling more dangerous by the day, it was nice to have another ally. "Thanks again. I owe you."

"Well . . ." Chloe's voice trailed off. "A bunch of us are going out tonight after we wrap. Want to come?"

Inwardly, I groaned. The day already felt too long; all I wanted to do was retreat to my room and crochet a few rows on my blanket while watching bad reality TV. "I don't know."

"Oh, come on! The Bar is only, like, five minutes away from the hotel. If you have a terrible time, you can pop right back."

"What's it called? I'll Google it."

"That's what it's called. The Bar." She paused a beat. "I guess there's only one around here."

"Maybe . . ."

"You just said you owed me one," Chloe pointed out.

I sighed in exasperation. "Ok. Alright! I will."

"Yay! Although, Mara and Teddy will also be there. So if you need me to run interference again, I'd be happy to."

"I'll hold you to that."

Chloe's eyes strayed over my shoulder. "Speak of the Devil."

I followed her gaze and my stomach dropped. Teddy was here, and much like me, he was dressed in a pair of swimming trunks that left absolutely nothing to the imagination. You couldn't even call them trunks. It bordered on thong territory.

Before I could decide whether I should go say hi, Natasha popped out of the boathouse. "Come on, everyone!" She clapped her hands loudly. "Positions!"

Oh God, here we go.

The interior of the boathouse was dim, with just enough light to illuminate us on camera. The scene would be dark—so dark that audiences would complain about not being able to see anything. But it would also be effective, with one of the best jump scares in the whole movie. A motorboat was secured to the dock, which creaked ominously under our feet.

There were several crew members in the boathouse with us, but when Teddy looked into my eyes, somehow it felt like we were alone.

"After you." He motioned toward the water.

"That's rude." I stared at the dark depths, unable to see below the surface. "What if a lake monster is waiting for me down there?"

"Ladies first," he insisted.

"If you're scared, you can just admit it."

"Never." Teddy flexed his muscles, the corners of his eyes crinkling as he grinned at me in a way that made my stomach flip. I faced the water, ready to sacrifice myself headfirst to the lake monster if it meant I didn't have to examine that feeling any further.

Instead, I shrugged. "Prove it."

"Alright, I will." In one swift motion, Teddy jumped up and canonballed himself into the lake, spraying frigid water all over my very exposed skin.

I yelped. "Damn it, Teddy."

"You said prove it." He shook his head to get the sopping-wet hair out of his eyes. "It's kind of nice actually."

I rolled my eyes. Taking a deep breath, I eased my body into the dark lake, clinging to the deck to keep my shoulders out of the water. The icy cold bit at my skin, taking my breath away. I treaded water furiously, trying to warm up.

Natasha filed in, taking her spot behind the camera as she started to check its settings. The prop head, which Teddy and I were already familiar with, thanks to our spying, waited on its own chair off camera. Scott sat nearby, likely guarding it from careless cast or crew members. I smiled and gave him a wave; he grudgingly raised a hand a few inches from where it rested on his knee.

"Alright, folks." Natasha stood and clapped her hands once, loudly. "We're ready to go."

At the top of the scene, my character and Teddy's have just finished hooking up on the boat when the spirit of the witch appears. We're able to jump into the water and hide under the dock as Brent's and Chloe's characters rush in, too late to warn us.

The scene took just a few takes. The cameras and lighting were reset, and Teddy and I resumed our places under the dock so we'd still be visible in the background for the rest of the scene. I was thankful our parts had been quick, but it also meant that for the rest of the shoot, we would be hiding under the dock looking scared. Scared and naked. Scared and naked and wet and clinging to each other.

Next, the script called for a confrontation between Brent's and Chloe's characters and Audrey as the witch. Chloe escapes, using her cheerleading skills to jump and somersault out of the way, but poor Brent's character meets his gory, spectacular end when his head meets the business end of the boat propeller—switched on magically by the witch, of course.

Huddled in the water, I was happy to have a front-row seat to the rest of the scene. Brent might not always bring professionalism to set, but one thing he took very seriously was his character's death scenes, striking the perfect balance between camp and realism. Usually. He had come dangerously close to overdoing it in the one where a crocodile devoured him, starting at his feet. Just before the croc got to his head, Brent had kissed the beast goodbye on the nose.

How his character would have accomplished this with no blood pressure remained a mystery.

The take started smoothly. Chloe and Brent burst in, yelling for us loudly as they struggled to see in the dim light. Audrey appeared at the precise moment she was supposed to, and Chloe screamed at just the right annoyingly high pitch. Then, Brent's character was supposed to duck as a spell was cast his way.

Supposed to.

The first time he missed his cue, we figured it was a fluke. But then he missed it again . . . and again . . . and then a third time. His eyes looked unfocused and he wavered slightly as he waited between takes. I squinted at him as he blew take after take. Was he on drugs? It wasn't unusual for him to show up a little high, but this seemed a bit much, even for him.

Teddy leaned closer to me, his chest brushing against my shoulder. "Is this what it was like watching me on the first day?"

I muffled my laugh with my hand. "Kind of."

"At least we weren't operating in subzero temperatures that day."

"Subzero? That's dramatic."

"Let's just say I'm glad no one can see me from the waist down right about now."

My cheeks warmed at the implication and the image that

quickly formed in my mind. Thankfully, my train of thought was broken by the thudding of footsteps as Natasha emerged from behind the camera.

"Cut! Cut, cut, cut." Natasha tugged at her hair as she approached the dock, quietly fuming as she walked toward Brent.

"Everyone else, stay in your places. That means you." Natasha gestured at Teddy and me. "Brent, come here."

I groaned as Natasha dragged Brent off to the side to regroup. It would have been a great opportunity to dry off, warm up, and clear my head of any thoughts of Teddy's body. My toes were numb and my shivers were rapidly progressing to shakes. My teeth chattered.

"Are you ok?" Teddy's eyebrows were creased with concern.

"Just ... c–cold." I tried to keep my teeth from clanking together, but they rattled violently.

He hitched an eyebrow. "Your lips are turning blue."

"I'll be alright. This won't take m–much longer." But even as I said the words, I could see Natasha hunching down as she demonstrated something with her hands to Brent, the two of them deep in conversation and giving no hint they were almost done.

"Seriously. Come here." With one hand still gripping the dock, he reached out his other arm, inviting me closer.

I bit my lip. Any other time, I would have refused—my pride generally didn't let me accept help from anyone. But it really did feel like I was about ten seconds from hypothermia, and what was the point in starring in one more movie if it meant I ended up frozen at the bottom of a lake?

"Alright," I conceded, letting go of the deck and pushing myself through the water.

I slid through the water and he caught me easily, scooping an arm around my waist and pulling me close until I was notched neatly against his hip. Warmth immediately spread from his chest to mine, and my arms slipped instinctually around his waist as I huddled closer, my fingers brushing wet, smooth skin. He tightened his grip, making sure I was secure and supported.

"Better?" He looked down at me, the ever-present stubborn lock of hair damp and drooping over his forehead, sexy and endearing at the same time.

"Yes," I whispered, my breath catching in my throat. I started to slip and he hoisted me up, hitching me higher until my legs were wrapped around his waist.

"Is this ok?" He swallowed, adjusting his grip on my thigh. I could feel his heart pounding, our chests pressed together. My own was galloping behind my ribcage, and I was sure he could feel it, too.

I nodded, my gaze sliding down to his lips. They had a natural pout to them, his bottom lip slightly puffy. I imagined what it would be like to press my own lips to them, run the tip of my tongue along them, perhaps give them a nibble. I imagined what they would feel like against me: against my lips, my breasts, my—

Natasha barged back on set. "Alright, back to first marks, people!"

The words hit me like a jolt. I pulled away and Teddy released me, his hands returning to the dock as I slid back to my own spot. I quickly dunked my head under the water as I went, hoping the chill would clear my thoughts and chase away any lingering, lusty feelings.

"We're moving on," Natasha announced. "We're picking up with scene twenty-seven."

I raised my eyebrows. It was unusual for Natasha to drop a scene once we started filming—Brent must be in really bad shape. I craned my neck, looking for him. But he hadn't come back into the boathouse. Natasha must have decided to film the shot of Brent's severed head flying out of the water while he regrouped.

"Do we need to stay in here?" Teddy whispered, stealing a glance at Natasha, who was staring intensely at the camera. She also looked intensely angry.

"I'm not risking it. I don't want Natasha chopping off my head to replace the fake one." As cold as I was, I drifted slightly away from Teddy, not trusting myself to get too close to him again.

Setting up the shot went quickly. A crew member climbed onto the boat and Natasha moved her camera so she'd have just the right angle to film the head coming out of the water. One poor PA was on standby, tasked with the job of going underwater and launching the head into the air. They treaded water nearby, looking frigid. I gave them a sad thumbs up.

Once the camera was rolling, Natasha gave the signal and the PA ducked under the surface of the lake. A moment later, the crew member climbed onto the boat, which was still tethered to the dock. They would make sure the engine turned on but the propeller remained off, both to preserve the safety of the PA in the water and to keep the boat stationary.

This was not what happened.

As soon as it was turned on, the boat lurched forward with a loud rev of the engine. Natasha froze above us as the rope securing the boat to the dock strained and pulled taut.

"Stop! Turn it off!" Natasha hollered.

But the crew member on the boat was still fighting for his balance after the unexpected motion. His arms windmilled as he grappled for something, anything, to hold onto. The engine whined as it surged forward, fighting against its tether. But while the rope held fast, the dock didn't. The pole snapped in half as the boat, finally free, jetted out of the structure and onto the lake, dragging the splintered wood behind it.

Above us, the dock groaned. Before I could register what was happening, Teddy pushed first me and then the PA out of the way. A wave swept over us as the dock sagged into the water where we had been mere moments ago, tipping Natasha and her camera into the water. Natasha popped up a moment later, but her camera did not.

"What the fuck was that?" she sputtered as we all climbed out of the water.

"I don't know." I looked down—a towel had manifested around my shoulders. Next to me, Teddy was draping the PA in an identical one.

"What the fuck happened?" she repeated, this time directing it at the crew member, who had finally succeeded in getting the boat under control and was guiding it back. After resecuring it to a stable part of the dock, he came over to join us.

"The damnedest thing," he muttered. "Who the hell would do that?" He was talking to himself, still in shock.

"Who did what?" Natasha snarled. "That was thousands of dollars' worth of equipment!"

The crew member looked back to the boat, as though convincing himself this was really happening. "There was a brick on the foot throttle." He shook his head. "Someone had to have put it there."

My blood chilled. Someone had sabotaged the boat—someone who had likely known Teddy and I would be huddled underneath the dock when the boat yanked away one of its supports.

"Fuck." Natasha kicked a nearby duffle bag. "There's another shoot we'll be behind schedule with."

"Let's get out of here," Teddy muttered. He wrapped an arm around my waist, starting to steer me away from the boathouse. "It's not safe."

"We should at least look around, see if there are any clues." I twisted, looking back toward the water. "There might be something on the boat."

"No." Teddy's voice was firm. "We're going."

Before I could protest any further, he was pushing me toward the parking lot, a hand firm on my lower back.

## Chapter Fourteen

"You're banging him tonight, right?" Mara pulled down the passenger-side visor to check her lipstick in the mirror. "Like, should I be planning to find a different way home?"

I raised an eyebrow as I swung the car into a parking spot. "I honestly don't know what you're talking about."

Thanks to the disastrous shoot the day before, we'd postponed our outing to The Bar. No one had felt much like partying after an evening of frigid temperatures and runaway boats. Teddy had split off for a phone call with his brother, while Mara and I had spent the rest of the night watching a new rom-com she'd been dying to see. Now, after another full day of shoots today, we were all very ready for a night out.

"Come on, you were wet in more ways than one filming that scene yesterday, if you know what I mean. And the way he got all protective after the dock collapsed? Please."

"He's a colleague, may I remind you? A coworker?" I shifted into park. "That would be inappropriate."

"And that has stopped you when? I see the way you look at him." Mara reached for the door handle. "I recognize horny eyes when I see them."

"Those weren't horny eyes. Those were I'm-freezing-and-might-die-of-hypothermia eyes."

"If you say so," she said in a sing-song voice as she pulled open the door to The Bar.

They'd definitely been horny eyes. But I'd made my peace with the fact that I was desperately, annoyingly lustful for Teddy but couldn't do anything about it. And Mara should know better than anyone about my rule against dating actors—she'd been there when I'd come up with it over two years ago. Once this movie wrapped, I didn't want anything reminding me of what I was giving up. So for now, I'd just have to cohabit with my horniness. Be one with the horniness.

Inside, the bar was exactly what I'd expect from rural Virginia. From the scuffed black-and-white checked linoleum to the neon sign behind the bar, the place had none of the pretension I'd come to associate with all the hot spots back in LA.

As someone who greatly preferred a dingy dive to a crowded club, I thought it was perfect.

The bar stretched along the left side of the room, with customers perched on tall stools and sipping frothy pints of beer. I quickly realized we weren't the only ones from the production who'd had the idea to come out—members of the crew were dotted around the room, gathered at tables and shooting pool. Apparently, this place really was the only joint in town.

Mara and I made our way to the bar, and the bartender, a tiny brunette with painted red lips and heavily tattooed arms, made her way over. "Can I help you, ladies?" She eyed Mara, her lips curving into a smile. "How about we start with you, gorgeous?"

Mara immediately snapped to attention. She leaned over the bar top as she ordered, fiddling with her hair and murmuring something that made the bartender laugh. Typical. Mara always seemed to attract attention wherever she went, even if she wasn't looking for it. And maybe a hookup with a hot bartender was exactly what Mara needed to get over Austin.

Minutes later, the door once again swung open and Brent, Chloe, and Teddy appeared. Trailing behind them, to my pleasant surprise, was Audrey. Maybe she was finally warming up to us.

Teddy's eyes roamed the room as he stepped over the threshold. He paused when he spotted me, nodding in my direction as his mouth spread into a grin. Like I'd been the one he was looking for. My stomach swooped in pleasure, and I couldn't stop myself from smiling as I waved him over.

Out of the corner of my eye, I could see Mara staring at me, lips pursed.

As the six of us grabbed our drinks and made our way to a table near the back, the topic of conversation immediately returned to what everyone had been gossiping about all day: who had sabotaged the boat?

"Was it definitely on purpose?" Chloe asked, grabbing one of the battered chairs. "Couldn't it have been an accident?"

"I mean, a brick was weighing down the throttle." Audrey's British accent sounded extra posh against the country music playing in the background. "I'd say it had to be deliberate."

Sinking into the seat next to me, Teddy reached out an arm and rested it on the back of my chair. I froze. Had that been intentional? He shifted, moving his arm closer until it was tucked around my shoulders.

Yep. Definitely intentional.

"We're barely a week into filming." Mara shuddered. "A boat's been tampered with, the house was vandalized, and poor Trevor . . ."

Chloe's eyebrows jumped. "You think one person was responsible for all of that?"

Mara shrugged. "Maybe."

As everyone chatted, the only one silent was Brent, across the table from us.

Keeping my eye on him, I lowered my voice to a whisper and leaned toward Teddy. "I have an idea."

"Oh?"

I tipped my head toward Brent, who was already almost finished with his first drink. "We need to find out when he was in the attic and if he knows anything about Trevor. This could be a good opportunity."

Teddy nodded, one thumb rubbing my shoulder absentmindedly. "Why don't we make this interesting?"

I raised an eyebrow. "How so?"

"If I can get information out of Brent, you owe me a back rub. That shoot yesterday was very physically taxing."

"Waiting in the water was physically taxing?"

"Yes."

"How is that my fault?"

"It's not." Teddy shrugged. "Those are just the rules."

"Fine. And if I get the information?"

"I'll give you a back rub, obviously."

My heart thrummed. There was nothing I loved more than winning, especially if someone was trying to prove I couldn't. That was why my heart rate had spiked—the thrill of the competition, not because I was imagining what, exactly, it would feel like to have Teddy's hands rubbing my body.

"Deal. Better limber up those hands." I eyed Brent as he hopped to his feet, wavering for a second before heading back to the bar.

"I don't think so, Jigsaw. You'll be massaging this trapezius before you know it."

I considered, for a moment, that maybe losing wouldn't be so bad after all. But I quickly brushed the thought away.

"We'll see about that." Despite his bravado, Teddy hadn't noticed that Brent had left. His eyes hadn't left my face, and I intended to use that to my full advantage. Jumping up, I made a beeline for where Brent was waiting at the bar.

"Cheater!" Teddy called after me.

Muffling a grin, I rested my elbows on the bar top and focused my attention on Brent.

"Hey." I nudged his shoulder with mine. "Better day today?"

Brent huffed out a laugh. "No. Definitely not."

"Really? Natasha seemed in a better mood. I thought things were running a little smoother."

"Yeah, well." Brent's face darkened. "It was a different story with me."

Interesting. Natasha could be abrasive, but she was also quick to forgive. Did Natasha know something I didn't?

"Why don't I buy us a shot? Does tequila work?"

"Hell yeah, it does."

I waved over the bartender—whose name, according to the tag on her blouse, was Laurie—and ordered two shots of tequila, which arrived alongside a salt shaker and two lime wedges on napkins a few minutes later.

*Alright, look sexy*, I instructed myself. If I was going to get information out of Brent, my best chance was to flirt it out of him.

"Ready?" Brent nudged the salt shaker toward me. "Ladies first."

Grasping it in one hand, I slowly licked the skin between my thumb and index finger. His gaze followed my tongue, his eyes darkening as they lingered.

"Mmmm." I sprinkled the salt on my hand and passed him the shaker. "Ready?"

"Always." Brent salted his own hand and picked up the tiny glass, which he tipped toward me in cheers. "One, two, three, go!"

I licked the salt and threw back the shot. Thankfully, the brininess did its job of lessening the burn, but the tequila still scorched my throat. I sucked the lime wedge seductively, looking up at him through my lashes. The corner of Brent's mouth ticked up, the first sign of an emotion other than irritation I'd seen on him all night.

"Wow." I reached out and placed my hand on top of his. "I don't know about you, but I needed that."

"I need about three more."

"I can arrange that." I wasn't planning on drinking that much, but I was willing to foot Brent's bill if it meant I could get information out of him. "What happened today?"

"I've just had it, to be honest. Natasha won't get off my ass.

Weird shit's going on and somehow it's my fault?" He shook his head. "I didn't sign up for this."

"That sounds awful." I rubbed his arm soothingly. "Maybe I can help you take your mind off things later?"

I would do no such thing. But Brent didn't have to know that.

"Oh, yeah?" Brent's demeanor flipped. No longer slouched and glowering, he leaned in with a cocky smile. "I thought we were past all that."

"We don't have to be."

My eyes flitted toward Teddy. He glanced away as soon as I spotted him, but not quick enough for me to miss him clocking my hand on Brent's arm. And he didn't look happy about it. I pulled back, removing my hand. Why did I feel guilty? There was nothing wrong with me flirting with Brent. And it definitely didn't matter how Teddy felt about it.

"What's Natasha blaming you for?"

"The brick, obviously."

"Why would you have wanted to sabotage the boat?"

Brent shook the hair out of his eyes. "Exactly! She thinks because I've shown up high a few times that I'm responsible for everything that's been going on."

"That doesn't make any sense." I decided to go out on a limb. "Next thing you know, she'll be blaming Trevor's death on you too."

Brent's eyes narrowed. "What do you know about Trevor?"

"What do you know about Trevor?" We stared at each other silently, at a standoff. Then, Brent took a breath like he was about to speak.

"Hey, kids." Teddy pushed his way between me and Brent,

forcing us apart as he wrapped one arm around each of our shoulders. "Mind if I join you?"

Damn it, I was just getting to the good part.

"Kind of," I said through clenched teeth.

"'Atomic hot wing challenge,'" Teddy read out loud, squinting at a sign behind the bar. "'If you can't take the heat, get out of the bar.' That sounds fun. What do you guys say?"

"No thanks. We were actually in the middle of—"

"Brent? How about it? Loser buys the other a round."

Ah. So that's what he was up to—trying to steal Brent from me so he could win the bet. But before I could find a way to steer Brent away, he shrugged.

"Sure. I'm in."

"Alright." Teddy clapped his hands in triumph and waved over the bartender. "Two for the atomic hot wing challenge, please!"

Laurie made her way over and explained the rules. Those who accepted the challenge had to make their way through all ten of their hot wing flavors within fifteen minutes. No getting sick.

"Let the best man win." Brent held out a hand toward Teddy.

Ignoring the attempt at a handshake, Teddy turned instead to Laurie. "Ready. And thank you." She winked at him and headed back to the kitchen.

Ten minutes later, Laurie returned with three baskets of wings. The first three flavors were soft balls: Parmesan garlic, barbecue, and classic Buffalo. But despite the sauces being mild enough that I was pretty certain a seven-year-old would have no problem devouring them, it didn't stop the guys from gloating.

"So easy." Brent dropped the bones into the basket and licked his fingertips clean.

"Didn't feel a thing," Teddy said, glancing at me with a smirk on his face. "I could do this all night."

I rolled my eyes. I'd been trying to find a way to steer the conversation back to Trevor, but every time I did, Teddy would order more wings in an attempt to prove how non-spicy he thought they were. This, in turn, egged Brent on to do the same. His mouth was stuffed too full of mediocre chicken to be of any use.

The next three flavors kicked things up a notch. The guys didn't have a problem with the chipotle wings, but they slowed down after inhaling the extra spicy sriracha and Sichuan chili crisp varieties.

"Honestly, dude? I could eat like six of these apiece." Brent grabbed for a napkin to wipe his running nose. "A little kick to 'em, but good flavor."

"Definitely." Teddy turned his head to sneakily wipe away a tear that had beaded at the corner of his eye. "Barely even feel it."

The guys motioned toward Laurie, who was giggling and leaning against the bar to tuck a curl of hair behind Mara's ear. It took three tries to get her attention, and Mara glared at the boys in irritation when Laurie finally peeled herself away.

"So dumb," Mara muttered as she came to join us. "Couldn't you two just whip your dicks out and measure them instead of going through this whole rigamarole?"

Brent rolled and stretched his neck like he was gearing up for a swim meet instead of a wing-eating competition. "That wouldn't be fair, I have to give Teddy at least a shot, don't I?"

"Whatever you say, man."

Holy Habanero, Ghost Pepper, and Sting of the Scorpion were

next. This time, both of them struggled. Teddy sipped water after every bite and Brent ate a slice of bread between each wing. Both of their faces were turning an alarming shade of red.

"Y'all don't have to do this," Chloe said, frowning as they handed their baskets of bones to the bartender. She'd joined us around wing eight, when Teddy had swallowed his bite the wrong way and proceeded to cough so violently the entire bar had quietened. It was very dramatic.

"Yes we do," they shouted in unison.

Mara leaned back and caught my eye. "I feel like you're the one behind all this."

I shrugged helplessly. It didn't surprise me that Brent was pulling the macho man act, but I didn't understand why Teddy suddenly felt the need to convince us of his manliness. I kept remembering the way his face had changed when he'd caught me touching Brent's arm. Maybe he was jealous. But surely I was reading too much into it?

Laurie pushed through the swinging kitchen door, arms lined with wing baskets. "Alright, guys, here's the grand finale."

For the final act, they each had to eat three of the spiciest flavor: Don't Fear the Carolina Reaper. Whoever finished their third wing first won. While Brent's face remained neutral, albeit pretty red and sweaty, Teddy looked terrified as he took his basket. They both ate their first wings quickly, moving on to the second before the first one had a chance to fully kick in. But then Brent started coughing, dropping the half-eaten second wing into the basket as he sputtered for air.

"Went . . . up . . . my nose," he choked.

I patted his back in sympathy—if the tequila had done a

number on my sinuses earlier, I couldn't imagine what the hottest chili pepper in the world would feel like up there.

Clocking Brent's slower pace, Teddy seized the opportunity. He grabbed his third wing, shoved it in his mouth, and ripped away the meat quickly. Tossing aside the bone, he thrust his fists into the air as he swallowed.

"I . . .I did it!" Sweat was slicked across his forehead and a vein was bulging in his temple so big I thought he might be having a stroke.

"Are you ok?" I asked.

"Of course." He breathed through his mouth, clearly trying to cool his burning tongue. "That was no problem at all." He winced, placing his hands on his hips and bending over at the waist, trying to catch his breath.

Teddy managed to make it through his award ceremony, as Laurie took a Polaroid photo of him in his new tee-shirt that proudly proclaimed "I slayed the Reaper!" But the photo hadn't even had time to develop before he clutched his stomach and lurched toward the bathroom.

"I just need to pee!" he insisted as he disappeared around the corner. I was a bit worried he felt worse than he was letting on, but more eager to get Brent alone again. I'd been so close to getting information.

"Another drink?" I asked Brent, who seemed to be recovering slightly quicker than Teddy. "I'll meet you over there?" I motioned to an empty booth.

Brent smirked. "Nice."

"Give me just a minute."

After refreshing our drinks—a double tequila soda for Brent and a light beer for me—I made my way across the room.

Sliding across the vinyl seat, I pushed Brent's drink across the table. "Tough break in the competition. I know you can handle the heat."

"You bet." He winked as he took the glass and lifted it to his lips. "It's been a while, but I know you haven't forgotten."

I curved my lips coquettishly. "Maybe you can refresh my memory later?"

Barf.

"Hell yeah. You know it'll be better than whatever Teddy could do for you. Dude couldn't even handle some chicken wings, judging by the way he sprinted to the bathroom."

I was confident that wasn't the case, but I decided to change the subject. "Are you feeling any better?"

"I guess." He ran a hand down his face. "Just looking forward to this whole movie being over so I can go home, honestly."

I waited for him a take a long draw of his drink. "What were you saying earlier about Trevor?"

"I didn't say anything about Trevor."

"Ok." I took a sip of my drink, trying to look unbothered. "It's a pretty far-fetched theory anyway. Who would have wanted to hurt him? He was so nice."

Brent snorted. "Nice, my ass."

"What do you mean?"

"Trevor and I go way back. We worked together on a movie a couple years ago. He was a total dick. The type that didn't know how to mind his own business."

I thought it was more likely that Brent had just been up to

something he didn't want someone noticing, but I decided to go along with it. "I can see that."

"We were at a party one night, and I don't know what Trevor thought he saw, but everything that happened was consensual."

My stomach turned. "Jesus, Brent."

"Anyway. He ratted me out to production, and they fired me."

"And you're still pissed?"

"Hell yeah, I'm still pissed."

My heart skidded to a stop. What Brent had just revealed seemed an awful lot like a motive. I suddenly felt very hot, and a bead of sweat appeared at my temple.

Across from me, Brent narrowed his eyes. "Why do you look weird all of a sudden?"

"Nothing." I grabbed for my drink, desperate to cool down. "No reason."

Brent paled—or at least, his perma-tan lightened a shade. "You think I had something to do with his death. You do think it was murder!"

"No! No, I don't. Of course I don't." I stood, feigning a yawn. "Thanks for the drinks but I'd better go. Early call time and all."

Brent frowned. "You still want to come back to my room, though, right?"

"Wow, I don't think I can. I'm just so tired."

"Are you fucking kidding me, Quinn? This is bullshit."

"Thanks again!" I made a beeline for where Mara was congregated with Chloe and Audrey at the bar. Hopefully she wouldn't mind calling it an early night.

"Time to go," I whispered when I got close enough. "I . . .

don't feel well." I took some money out of my purse and laid it on the bar for their drinks.

"We can't leave yet," Mara whined. "Laurie doesn't get off until two."

"We'll come back another night. I'm sure your vagina will survive until then."

"Don't be a party pooper!" Chloe tipped the cowboy hat she was wearing at me. "The night's just getting started, partner!"

Next to her, Audrey giggled. "Yeah, you haven't even met our new friends yet." She gestured down the bar, where two men—one with a hat and one without—waved sheepishly.

"Sorry, guys." I grabbed Mara's arm. "Let's go. Please?"

"Fine." Mara stood and grabbed her purse. "But you owe me. Big time."

As the two of us hustled out of the bar, I couldn't shake the uneasy feeling creeping through my veins. It was strange that Brent would admit to having a grudge against Trevor if he'd actually murdered him. But he clearly still had ill will toward him, and we had evidence that he'd been the one Scott had spotted in the attic the night of Trevor's death.

Looking over my shoulder as we made our exit, the last thing I saw was Brent, glaring at me from his booth.

## Chapter Fifteen

"He could be telling the truth." Teddy looked skeptical, frowning from his seat on my hotel room couch as he popped a Tums into his mouth. "He's not exactly the sharpest knife in the drawer."

My hand paused halfway through the blanket row I was crocheting, the stitch slipping off the hook. "Are you kidding me? You're giving Brent, the one single-handedly responsible for you needing to spend the last hour curled up by the toilet, the benefit of the doubt?" After fleeing The Bar, I'd rushed to my room and texted Teddy in his room, letting him know we needed to regroup. Ten minutes of recounting my conversation with Brent later, this was not the reaction I'd been expecting.

Teddy shrugged, crunching on the chalky tablet. "He doesn't strike me as the criminal mastermind type. More of the sleazy dirtbag type."

That I couldn't completely argue with.

"Exactly. A sleazy dirtbag that got axed from a movie for

what sounded an awful lot like sexual assault. And Trevor was the one who got him fired."

"True."

"Plus, we found his sweatshirt in the attic, so we know he was up there. Plus, the motive."

"So, what, do we think he's the murderer?"

I bit my lip. "I'm not sure. But he's definitely suspicious."

"And what now?"

"We need harder evidence. We know he's lying and being shady, but that doesn't mean he's the killer. We know he was in the attic, where he could have watched Trevor leave the props trailer before following him. But we don't know for sure that he was in the attic that particular night. We need something that would specifically pin him to Trevor on the night he was killed."

"Or . . ."

"What?"

"Maybe you're fixating on Brent too much."

"Excuse me? I told you, he—"

Teddy held up his hand. "I'm just saying, are you sure your past isn't influencing your theory here? Maybe you're still a little salty he broke up with you?"

I gaped at him. "Absolutely not. I was the one who broke things off with him."

"If you say so."

"I do say so. In fact, I'm going to update the suspects list." I retrieved it from where I'd stashed it on top of the microwave. Next to Brent's name, I jotted "has motive, Trevor got him fired." Then, I took the liberty of crossing out Mara's name at the bottom.

"Hey! I saw that." Teddy came up behind me, looping one arm around my waist as he grappled for the list with the other. Succeeding in snatching the paper out of my hand, he dashed back to the couch as he tried to scribble out his own name.

"I don't think so." I dove for the list, straddling Teddy's lap as I yanked it out of his hand before he could cross himself out. "You still haven't given an alibi for before you came to my trailer."

"You know . . ." Teddy's hands settled on my hips. "I'm not going to dignify that with a response."

"Sounds like something someone guilty would say."

Out of breath, we stared at each other, our faces inches apart. Teddy ran his thumb under the hem of my shirt, rubbing the skin above my hip bone. It was a small gesture, intimate. *Too* intimate. Rattled, I hopped off his lap and reached for the list, now lying crumpled and half scribbled over on the floor.

"I still think we should try talking to Brent again. See if he offers up any more information." I moved to the opposite end of the sofa, putting as much space between us as possible. "Maybe you can take the lead on that, though. He gives me the creeps."

Looking momentarily thrown by my swift departure, Teddy recovered quickly. He raised an eyebrow, the corner of his mouth curling up in a smirk. "Oh, really? You guys looked awfully cozy earlier tonight."

My cheeks burned. "I was trying to get information out of him."

"Sure you were. Listen, I make bad decisions when I'm horny, too." Teddy was smiling gleefully now, his hands folded behind his head as he leaned back against the couch. Any illusions I'd had of him being jealous quickly fled my mind—he was having way too much fun teasing me.

"I'm not horny! Now or then or ever."

"Ever? Jigsaw, please. There's nothing wrong with being horny. I get horny all the time."

Obscene images flickered in my mind: Teddy, sweat beading at his brow. Teddy, breathing hard as he moved above me. Teddy, gripping his—

"Well, I'm not. And we're not here to talk about horniness, anyway—mine, yours, or anyone else's." I stood and grabbed a copy of the script that happened to be nearby, desperate to change the subject. "We should start rehearsing."

Teddy cocked an eyebrow. "Rehearse? Now? It's awfully late."

I glanced at the clock. He was right—it was after midnight. "Yes, well. We still need to prepare."

"Fine." He stood and stretched his arms over his head, his white tee riding up a few inches to reveal his abs. "If you insist."

We both flipped to the correct page of the script with the scene between Teddy's and Chloe's characters. In it, he confronts her after Brent's unfortunate demise via boat propeller. He suspects she knows something about how to banish the witch, and he tries to seduce her to get the information.

Once we were ready, I cleared my throat in my best Natasha impression. "Action!"

Immediately slipping into character, Teddy narrowed his eyes. "I thought I'd find you here." He took a step toward me. "Isn't it dangerous for you to be in here all alone?"

"What's it to you? Shouldn't you be with your girlfriend?"

"My girlfriend?"

"Yes!" I said indignantly. "I saw you two on the boat! Before the awful thing that happened. I saw what you two were doing."

"And? What did you think?" Teddy took another step closer.

"Nothing. I didn't think anything about it."

"Are you sure?"

"Yes." I made my voice wobble—this was where Chloe's character started to lose her resolve.

"What if I told you I was thinking about you . . . when I was with her?"

At this point, Teddy was supposed to back Chloe's character against the wall, using his sex appeal to pry for information. He advanced toward me slowly, his eyes burning into mine, gently guiding me backward until I was pressed against the hard wall. He wasn't touching me, but his face was mere inches away.

Oh no. My body was humming again, that thing it did whenever Teddy was too close. I swore I could feel his hand hovering somewhere near my hip, and my mind was running wild, imagining him running his fingers along the waistband of my jeans, slipping them down until he reached the top of my underwear, further still until—

"Line?" Teddy whispered.

"Uh." I glanced down at the script, scanning frantically for my line. "'I would tell you that you were lying.'"

"I'm not. I was picturing you the entire time I was with her." His voice fell to a whisper as he leaned closer. "Pretending it was you, wishing it was you."

"Oh?" I couldn't take my eyes off his lips, and the word came out as barely a squeak.

"Maybe it can be?" His voice was raspy, his lips so close I could feel his breath on my mouth.

"What are you suggesting?" I was supposed to say it coquettishly but it came out flat—I couldn't manage anything else. I couldn't tell if we were acting anymore, and I waited for him to say the next line, praying we could get this scene over with. Next, Teddy's character was supposed to push Chloe for information. But instead of saying his line, Teddy pressed his hips into mine—gently, just enough that I could feel the jut of his hipbones—and reached up a hand to curve gently around my neck.

"You and me," he said. "Here. Now."

The oxygen evaporated from my lungs. That definitely wasn't in the script, and therefore I had no idea how to respond. Another day, I would have assumed he'd forgotten his lines. But he was right: he was getting better. And something about the way he was looking at me—intensely, burning, intentional— made me think he knew exactly what he was doing. My heart hammered in my chest, so hard he surely could feel it. I waited for a clue, any hint about what he wanted me to do. But he only waited.

"And then what?" I finally whispered.

"And then." He slipped his hand higher until his fingers wound through the hair at the base of my neck. He tightened his grip at the roots and tugged ever so carefully, enough to apply delicious pressure and tilt my head backward. The movement sent a jolt of electricity straight from my scalp to between my legs. "I make you scream my name."

For perhaps the first time in my life, I was speechless. If I'd felt desire shooting our scene in the boathouse, I was filled with pure, unbridled lust now. His face was close, so close, and when his eyes dropped to my lips, I wasn't sure I could hold myself back from kissing him. And there had been a tiny hitch in his voice, a slight pant to his breathing that made me feel like I wasn't the only one feeling the energy crackling dangerously between us.

And then, Teddy broke out into a grin.

"Not horny, huh?" Teddy smiled as he let go of my hair and backed away, leaving me fighting to slow my heart rate against the wall. "I don't know, Quinn, you seem a little hard up."

Any feelings I'd had moments ago fled, replaced like a bucket of cold water by embarrassment and irritation.

"It's called acting, asshole." I ran a hand through my hair, shaking it out where he'd messed it up. "I know I'm supposed to be teaching you how, because you're so hopeless, but I figured you'd at least understand the concept by now."

"Sure, sure." Still smiling, he stretched his arms over his head, clearly pleased with himself. "Happens to the best of us, you know."

"Well, you were right before, it is late. It's time for you to go." I shooed him toward the door.

He went willingly, still chuckling as he went. "It's not something you should be ashamed of."

"Noted." I opened the door and motioned toward it. "Although I promise none of my horniness past, present, or future has anything to do with you."

"Keep telling yourself that, Jigsaw." He winked, and the cockiness of it made me bristle.

"Out."

"I'll see you in the morning." His voice was singsong, his eyes twinkling.

"Bye." I shut the door firmly behind him.

Still feeling foolish, I changed into pajamas, removed my makeup, and washed my face, replaying the series of events over and over again. It was ridiculous, thinking he'd been propositioning me for . . . what? Sex right there against the wall?

But climbing into bed, I couldn't help but imagine what he would have done if I'd taken him up on the offer.

Base camp was eerily quiet the next morning.

At first I assumed everyone was hungover, considering the entire cast and half the crew had been out drinking the night before. But then I noticed the PAs huddled in groups, whispering. The set dresser and wardrobe supervisor stared at me as they walked by, almost colliding with a golf cart as they gawked. Even the AD, usually joined with Natasha at the hip, was tucked behind a trailer having a quiet conversation with one of the camera operators as they kept an eye out for eavesdroppers.

By the time I climbed the steps into hair and makeup, dread was balling in my stomach. I pulled open the door, hoping Mara would be her usual sunny self, offering a reprieve from the weird vibes.

But instead, Mara also seemed off. Her face was tired; she hadn't done her makeup, and rather than one of the fun sundresses she'd been favoring, she was wearing a dark tee and leggings. She waved limply in greeting as I slid into her chair.

"Where'd you run off to last night?" Stealing a sideways

glance at me, she grabbed her tote and started pulling out foundation and concealer.

"I went back to my room. I told you, I was tired." This wasn't a lie. I was just conveniently leaving out the fact that Teddy had come over, too.

"Alright." Mara glanced out the window before she grabbed a bottle of primer and started dabbing it on my face. I waited for her to continue, but she didn't.

"What's going on?" I cracked open an eye, risking getting the milky liquid sponged into it. "Everyone's acting weird and now you are, too."

"I am not."

"Yes you are. You're not even wearing your false eyelashes." Mara sighed wearily. "It's been a long morning."

"Why?"

"Chloe and Audrey were both here early, having panic attacks." She put down the primer and grabbed some foundation. "Have you heard what they're saying about Trevor?"

"Who's 'they'?"

She gestured out the window with the brush. "Everyone. A rumor's got out that he was murdered."

"That's ridiculous."

She stared at me in the mirror, like the answer was obvious. "Really, because it sounds like everyone heard it from you."

"What?" The room seemed to tilt beneath me and I grabbed onto the armrest. "Where the hell are they getting that?" This was not good. Worse than not good. If everyone was gossiping about Trevor being murdered—and worst of all, saying that I was to blame for the gossip—it would surely get back to the killer.

It probably already had.

Mara propped a hand on her hip. "If there's something you're not telling me—"

"There's not."

Her mouth set into a hard line. "You could tell me."

"I know. But there's not. I swear."

"Fine." Mara grabbed some setting powder and picked up a clean brush. "I believe you."

But I could tell she didn't.

By the time I made it to set, the feeling in the pit of my stomach had only gotten worse. My brain flashed through different explanations—had someone overheard Brent and I talking the night before? Had Teddy let something slip? Had I blacked out after my rehearsal with Teddy and actually spread the rumor myself?

Walking into the house, it was clear we had a serious problem. Audrey was talking to Teddy, eyes wide and brow furrowed, and Brent was slouched in the corner, sunglasses on and staring at his phone. No one was smiling or laughing—least of all Natasha, who was behind her camera with an expression that could only be described as livid.

I slid up to Chloe, who was standing alone by the wall, biting her fingernails. "What's going on?"

"Natasha's pissed."

"I see that."

Chloe glanced at me out of the corner of her eye. "Are you really surprised?"

"Kind of, actually."

Chloe gave me a curious look, and I decided to press further.

"What are people saying?"

"Do you really not know?"

"No!" Now I was getting frustrated. How had everyone on this production heard a rumor that hadn't existed six hours ago?

"Ok, well . . ." Chloe leaned closer, lowering her voice. "After you and Mara left last night, Brent was really upset. He kept taking shots and got super drunk, and then he started saying you'd accused him of killing Trevor."

"He what?"

"He told literally everyone at the bar. Us, the crew, complete strangers." She gave me a look of pity. "Sorry."

"Great."

Before I could ask any follow-up questions, Natasha strode to the middle of the room, clapping her hands loudly once and then twice. "Listen up, everyone. We need to have a little chat."

I tried to catch Teddy's eye as we all gathered around. Spotting me, he maneuvered through the crowd to stand by me.

"We're totally fucked," I whispered. I was still less than pleased about his teasing the night before, but the possibility of the killer—Brent or otherwise—knowing we were onto them trumped my annoyance.

Teddy glared at Brent. "I knew I hated that guy." He reached down and squeezed my wrist. "We'll figure it out."

I appreciated the reassurance, but I was starting to think that wasn't a possibility.

"It's been brought to my attention," Natasha began, "that a certain rumor has begun floating around set."

Standing on the other side of me, Chloe bit her lip. Audrey

peered around the crowd as Brent stood skulking at the back of the group. Crew members hovered nearby, obviously trying to eavesdrop. Scott studied us from across the room, a curious expression on his face.

"Let me be clear." Natasha made stern eye contact with each of us in turn. "These rumors will not be tolerated. The police were very confident in their findings that what happened to Trevor was an accident. It was tragic enough, without someone"—she paused as her eyes landed on me—"spreading insidious untruths."

Teddy raised his hand like he was in school and trying to get a teacher's attention.

Natasha waited, but when he didn't speak, she rolled her eyes. "Yes, Teddy. What is it?"

"I don't think they're trying to be malicious. The person saying these things." He looked down at me, a beatific smile on his face. He may be trying to do me a favor, but the extra attention couldn't be helping my case.

I stomped on the side of his foot. "Shut up."

"What?" He leaned down and lowered his voice. "I'm helping."

"Are you?" I covered my face with my hands. If everyone didn't already know Natasha meant me, Teddy had just confirmed it.

"Regardless," Natasha continued, "I don't want to hear anyone speak a word about this again. Not a single one." She glanced at Teddy. "Malicious intentions or not. Now let's get to work."

As we filed onto set, I understood why Natasha wanted to squash rumors. As director, she didn't want anything to distract us from what we were here to do: finish the movie on time and within the budget. But as I got into place to start blocking the scene, something nagged at me.

If there was a possibility that someone had been murdered on her set, shouldn't she want to find the truth?

And if not, why?

## Chapter Sixteen

Despite the rough start to the day, filming began smoothly. I had the afternoon off, but I still reported to set after lunch to watch Chloe and Teddy do the scene he and I had rehearsed the night before. I should have spent the time mulling over what we'd learned about Brent, or trying to squash the newly sprouted rumors, or—quite frankly—taking a nap. But instead, I tagged along, eager to watch from the sidelines.

"I thought I'd find you here." Teddy sauntered across the living room, all smirk and swagger as his boots fell heavily on the floorboards. "Isn't it dangerous to be here all alone?"

Chloe watched him approach from where she stood near the fireplace. She looked gorgeous—her blonde hair hung in long, loose waves, her lips were painted red, and her body looked insane in pajama shorts and a snug tee-shirt.

"What's it to you?" she purred. "Shouldn't you be with your girlfriend?" The question was less indignant and more of a challenge. An invitation.

No matter how alluring Chloe looked, I couldn't take my eyes off Teddy. His tight white tee-shirt showed every ripple of muscle as he made his way across the room, and even when he wasn't speaking, he commanded attention. He was magnetic. When had he gotten so good?

As they ran through the scene, it was strange hearing Chloe say the lines I had practiced with him just hours ago. It shouldn't have been—I'd rehearsed other scenes with him before. But this one was different. Teddy had played the tension between us off as a joke, but a part of me still wondered if it had been real. The scene felt like it somehow belonged to us.

Now, Teddy tweaked his delivery to match Chloe's tone, becoming even more coy and seductive. "What if I told you I was thinking about you when I was with her?"

From where I stood, I had a clear view of how close the two of them were. I bit my lip as Teddy pressed her against the wall, his hand hovering at her waist. He slowly drew closer, tilting his head to catch the light before whispering into Chloe's ear.

"I was picturing you the entire time I was with her," he rasped. "Pretending it was you, wishing it was you."

Searing, white-hot jealousy snaked through my veins. I knew it wasn't rational. They were just lines; it was just a scene. It was all pretend—words written in a script for people who weren't real. Teddy and Chloe were just doing their jobs. But when I heard him say those words, *I was wishing it was you*, all I could think about was him wishing that I had been Chloe last night, picturing her when he had pressed me against the wall of my hotel room, pulling my hair until the space between my legs ached.

I should have left then, sparing myself from watching the rest of the scene. But I couldn't tear myself away from what was coming next.

"What are you suggesting?" Chloe whispered, arching her back against the wall as she pressed herself against Teddy's chest.

My breath caught in my lungs. This was where we had gone off script, where Teddy had changed his line and made me question whether he'd been acting or we'd slipped into reality.

Teddy leaned in close to Chloe, their lips almost touching. "You and me. Here. Now."

Suddenly needing air, I stood as quietly as I could and fled for the exit.

Gasping, I burst out of the back door and braced my hands against the side of the house. The bricks were rough under my fingers, but I pressed harder, trying to calm my racing heart. The porch was quiet, withered flowers in faded planters hanging overhead and swaying gently in the breeze. Bugs buzzed in the trees, an ever-present hum. I squeezed my eyes shut, trying not to let tears leak out.

I'd thought maybe he'd been speaking to me when he told me he'd wanted me right then, right there. That maybe he'd been using his character as a cover for what he really wanted to say to me. But he hadn't—he'd just been riffing, improvising. It was ridiculous, how much it hurt to hear him use the same words with Chloe.

Had I really thought he'd been using his character to confess real feelings to me? That didn't happen in real life. Least of all from someone like Teddy. But I had believed it. The moment had felt special, like something just for me. A sign that maybe he was feeling the same energy growing between us. That I wasn't the only one going crazy trying to tamp down feelings that were becoming harder and harder to ignore.

I guess I had my answer now. No, it hadn't been special, and he wasn't, and it was just me. The realization made me so very sad. And not just sad, but also stupid.

I knew his type—I'd met them a thousand times. The careless player who didn't mind playing with a person's feelings if it meant they could have a bit of fun; the arrogant actor who cares more about stoking his own ego than making a genuine connection. I knew better. I shouldn't want him. I didn't want to want him.

But I did.

I don't know how long I had been standing there—trying and failing to stop the cracking sensation ripping through my chest—when the back door flew open. I jumped, bringing my hands to my eyes and trying to wipe away the few tears that had managed to escape. I assumed it was Natasha, coming to scold me for ruining the scene or distracting her actors or irritating her purely with my presence before fleeing the set.

"I'm sorry." I wiped my eye with the heel of my hand and pulled it away. "I didn't mean—"

But it was Teddy standing a few feet away. Not Natasha, not even Chloe. Teddy. He stood with his hands in his pockets, staring at me as the screen door clattered shut behind him.

I groaned, debating running away for a moment before

ultimately deciding against it. He'd already seen what a mess I was; there was no hiding it now.

"What happened?" Teddy looked truly flabbergasted, taking in my red eyes and my tear-stained cheeks. "What's wrong?"

"Nothing." I wiped at my cheeks with the sleeve of my shirt. "Just, you know, allergies."

"Unless you have the most violent allergies known to man, I don't think so." He took a step toward me, his forehead creasing with worry. "Seriously, what's going on?"

"Um . . ." My brain spun, trying to come up with an excuse for my current state, but it came up short. "I thought . . . that line you improvised . . ."

"What line?"

I choked out a laugh. He didn't even know what I was talking about. "Never mind." I tried to push past him, debating quitting the movie right then and there. A threat on my life wasn't good enough to scare me off the film, but the thought of facing this humiliation every day for the rest of filming might be.

Teddy grabbed me by the shoulders, halting me in my tracks. "What line are you talking about?" His eyes bore into mine, startlingly blue in the afternoon light.

"It doesn't matter." I shrugged out of his grip. "Let me go, this is embarrassing enough."

Letting his hands slip from my shoulders, he raked them through his hair. "I don't understand what about that scene could possibly . . ." A dawning realization crossed his face. "Are you jealous?"

I squeezed my eyes shut. As distraught as I'd been mere moments ago, I still didn't want to admit he was right. But I was in no position to lie when tears still clung to my eyelashes. "Yes, ok fine, maybe I am! Which I know is stupid and you can laugh at me if you want. Again, like last night. And then can we please, for the love of God, forget about this?" I reached for the handle of the screen door.

Teddy slammed a hand against the frame, blocking my path. "Why do you think I gave you such a hard time last night?" His voice was quiet, deathly calm.

"What do you mean?"

"When I teased you about trying to hook up with Brent?"

I shrugged. "I have no idea—you give me a hard time about everything. I figured it was business as usual."

"No. It was because I hated it."

"What?"

"Seeing you with him. Talking to him all night, sticking by his side. Flirting." He gritted his teeth. "I. Hated. It. But I couldn't do anything about it—that was your choice to make. So I joked about it instead. Because that's how I could cope."

The confession took me off guard, and I struggled to compute. "You were jealous too?"

Teddy moved closer, backing me slowly against the wall. I was grateful for the support, my knees suddenly weak. This time, I didn't notice the scraping prickliness of the bricks, focusing instead on the way Teddy's arm was snaking around my waist.

"Yes. I was jealous." He leaned in until I could feel his breath in my ear, sending shivers of pleasure down my spine. "And for the record, I was hitting on you. And if you had said yes, I would have fucked you right there against the wall."

The air whooshed out of my lungs, leaving me unable to reply.

But I didn't need to, because then Teddy reached up to cradle the back of my head, cushioning it from the bricks before he pressed his mouth to mine.

The kiss was gentle at first, like a question. But then we both surged forward, rough and urgent, like we didn't know how starved we'd been until we had a taste. Teddy pinned me against the wall, engulfing my senses—the taste of his mouth like peppermint, the sound of small groans as I raked my fingers through his hair, pulling him closer. The feel of his body pressing against mine as he dipped his mouth to my neck, his hand gripping my hip hard enough that I hoped it left a bruise. He was everywhere, and it was everything—relief from an aching need that had been building for only God knew how long. I didn't want it to end, content to stay there pressed against the wall forever if it meant I never had to give up this feeling.

I deepened the kiss, my arms twining around his neck, and he matched my intensity, gripping my hips to his.

"Teddy?" The voice came from inside the house. But not deep inside the house—it was close.

I pulled back, gasping. "I think that was Natasha."

"Shit." Teddy's eyes were hazy and he blinked to clear them. His lips were puffy. *I did that*, I thought. But then, Natasha called again.

"Go!" I ran a hand across my collarbone, trying to catch my breath. "She's looking for you."

Teddy grabbed for the screen door, thought better of it, and turned to press his lips to mine once before loping inside. I was left alone on the porch, grinning like a fool. I brought my fingers to my lips, caressing them where Teddy's mouth had been just moments before. I could still smell his woodsy scent.

I closed my eyes, trying to relive the kiss before the spell broke. If I hadn't been before, now I was well and truly fucked.

## Chapter Seventeen

I played our kiss on replay for the rest of the day.

After Natasha called Teddy back to set, I'd made a beeline for the hotel. Motoring down the back roads, I'd cranked up the radio, desperate for a distraction—only for "Bohemian Rhapsody" to come galloping out of the speakers. It took me right back to the night we'd questioned Scott in the props trailer, except this time, I knew exactly what it would have felt like to end that night with a kiss.

Pulling into a parking spot at the hotel, I remembered the way he'd murmured my name as we caught our breath. As I retreated to my room and changed into sweats, I relived the precise way his thumb had traced my cheekbone, desperate yet tender. And as I'd tried to distract myself by crocheting row after row of my blanket, I pictured the way he'd leaned in for one more before hurrying inside.

God, it'd been perfect. Better than I'd imagined. It had been knee-quaking, stomach-melting, toe-curlingly good.

Every time I replayed it in my mind, I imagined what could have happened if the kiss hadn't been on the back porch, but somewhere private. If Teddy's hand hadn't stopped on my waistband, but dipped lower. If we'd been alone and I was able to have all of him and not just a taste.

But the fantasies eventually gave way to different images—memories of the last time I'd trusted an actor with my heart. Memories of opening my phone to embarrassing photos, of tabloid headlines speculating on whether the paunch on my belly was a bad angle or pregnancy. Phone calls from my dad asking if there was a wedding that I hadn't told him about.

I couldn't let myself go through that again, not when I'd dealt with the fallout of my failed movie just months ago. It didn't matter how good the kiss was.

By the time a knock came at my door at precisely seven o'clock, my head was swimming from so much back and forth between blissful fantasies and traumatic memories. I padded to the peephole, peering through. It was Mara, holding what appeared to be a brown paper bag of takeout and an extra-large bottle of wine.

Shoot. I'd forgotten we'd made plans the night before—my penance for cutting our time at the bar short. This was going to significantly interfere with my intention to spend the evening hiding from the world.

Another insistent knock. "Come on," she called out. "I'm starving."

I swung the door open. "You didn't have to bring food."

"I know you haven't eaten." She pushed her way into the room. "So yes, I did."

As the scent of fresh French fries permeated the room, I happily closed the door and followed Mara to the kitchenette. Despite my plans to lie low for the evening, it wasn't Mara I'd been trying to hide from. Teddy had texted me as soon as he'd finished filming, suggesting we meet to rehearse later. Panicking, I'd told him I was having dinner at my dad's cabin, thereby banishing myself to my room for the night. Knowing he was just down the hall, I couldn't help but wonder what would be happening right now if I'd agreed.

"Today was interesting." Mara started unpacking the bag, setting brown-paper-wrapped sandwiches and cardboard cones of fries on the table. "Are you ok?"

No, but she didn't need to know that.

"What do you mean?" I asked, rustling through the cabinet for some plates.

Mara's hand froze in mid-air, holding a dip container of garlic aioli. "Everyone thinking you spread the rumor about Trevor's murder? Natasha putting the fear of God in everyone? The general air of doom and misery?"

"Oh! Yeah." I'd been so wrapped up fantasizing about Teddy's mouth that I'd forgotten about the drama du jour. "Yeah, it was a hard day." I succeeded in finding the plates and grabbed some forks, hoping Mara wouldn't notice my stumble.

She did. Of course she did.

"Hang on, what did you think I was talking about?"

My cheeks burned.

Mara tucked a fist onto her hip. "Quinnberly Marie." She tried one of her fries. "Ugh, this is cold." She moved toward the microwave.

The microwave that had our list of suspects resting on top of it.

"Wait!"

Mara quirked an eyebrow. "Do you not want me to warm up the fries? I mean, I know they're not as good reheated, but . . ."

"Um." My mind spun, trying to think of something—anything—that would get her away from seeing that list.

"Teddy kissed me today," I finally blurted. I might not want to talk about it, but I wanted her discovering our investigation even less.

It worked.

Mara screeched at such a high decibel, I was sure someone would call the police, convinced another murder had taken place. Abandoning the French fries on the table, she dragged me over to the couch, plunking both of us down on the cushions.

"Oh my God, oh my God! You have to tell me everything."

"Don't get excited, it didn't mean anything." But as I detailed the whole thing, from our rehearsal the night before to him following me out onto the back porch, I couldn't help the grin that grew wider and wider on my face.

"You guys are totally in love."

"We're definitely not in love. And it's definitely not happening again."

"And why not?" She looked offended at the mere suggestion.

"Be serious. Why would I want any ties to LA? I'm leaving. And even if I wasn't, you know I don't date actors. Look what's happened to me in the past. Look what happened to you!"

At this, Mara looked down, picking at her fingernails.

I reached over and squeezed her knee. "Sorry, I shouldn't have brought him up."

"It's fine."

"Are you ok?"

She shrugged. "I texted him to say I didn't want my stuff back and he should pick it up off my porch. He never replied."

"God, what an asshole."

"Whatever. I'm feeling slightly less terrible every day."

"Don't you see my point? We've both seen firsthand why getting involved with actors is a terrible idea. Why would I put myself through that again?"

"You're overthinking this." Mara stood to pour some wine. "The fact that he's a player could actually be an asset."

"I have no idea where you're going with this."

"Think about it." Getting excited, she handed me a glass and curled back up on the couch. "Both of you are obviously attracted to one another, are only going to be here for a limited amount of time, and then you never see each other again. Sounds like a prime opportunity for a friends-with-benefits situation."

I opened my mouth to counter, but she cut me off.

"I get why you don't want something serious. But why not collect as many orgasms as possible before filming wraps? You know, gotta catch 'em all, like a way sexier game of Pokémon?"

I cocked an eyebrow, skeptical. "Does that ever work?"

"Absolutely. Just look at Natalie Portman and Ashton Kutcher."

"That was a movie. And they ended up together at the end!"

Mara waved her hand in dismissal. "There's no reason it couldn't work."

"Those sound like famous last words."

"Trust me. Now let's eat, I'm starving."

Happy to change the subject, I dug into my turkey and avocado sandwich, fully intending not to follow her advice. Mara fell in love quicker than anyone I knew and I had a sneaking suspicion she was trying to cast me and Teddy in her own private rom-com.

But as the night wore on, my mind kept trailing back to the idea. If Teddy and I were both willing, and there was a built-in expiration date, would there be any harm in a little indulging?

Getting ready to go to set the next morning, I was thinking less about whether Teddy and I should kiss again, and more about how I was supposed to act when I saw him. Sweet? Flirty? Indifferent, like it hadn't happened at all?

Yes, maybe that one.

As I gathered my wallet and got ready to leave, I noticed something lying on the floor in front of the door. I froze. How long had it been there? I wracked my brain, trying to remember Mara leaving the night before. No, it definitely hadn't been there.

My stomach sinking, I picked it up. Sure enough, the size and shape of the envelope were all too familiar. I slipped a finger under the flap and pulled out the note inside:

*You've been sneaking around, you've been playing the spy,*
*So now it's time for you to say goodbye.*
*You've had your fun, but it's no lie,*
*If you don't quit, prepare to die.*

Mouth dry, I dropped the paper like I'd been burned.

Whoever was behind these notes had probably heard the rumors yesterday and believed that I wasn't just investigating, but also now telling others that a murder had been committed. And they'd be willing to kill me too if I didn't shut up.

It should have scared me. It should have made me back off. But all it did was make me mad.

I glanced at the clock. I wasn't due on set for an hour, but if I remembered the schedule correctly, Teddy was already there and preparing to shoot. But he needed to know about this now. Pulling up his number on my phone, I quickly called him. No answer. Either he was deliberately ignoring me or he was already filming. Sending a text and dashing out the door, I prayed it was the latter.

I sped to base camp faster than was probably advisable. Hopping out of my car and jogging toward set, I hoped I could find Teddy quickly. It's not that I thought he was actively spreading details of our investigation to anyone who would listen, but with him, you never really could tell. I was rounding a row of trailers when something solid collided with my shoulder, stopping me in my tracks. The solid something lifted his head, clearly as startled as I was.

It was Brent, who—dressed in basketball shorts, a tee, and sunglasses—was clearly just arriving too.

"Shit, sorry, my bad." Seeing it was me, his tone changed. "Oh. It's you."

I bristled at the edge in his voice. "Yeah. Me." I turned to walk away. I was in a hurry and Brent was clearly in a horrible mood.

"I know you were spreading rumors about me." It was a statement, not a question.

"I don't know what you're talking about."

"Cut the shit. You corner me at the bar to ask me about Trevor, and the next day people are saying I killed him just by coincidence?" His voice lowered to a mutter. "I'm not that dumb."

"From what I heard, you were spreading those rumors yourself. Do you even remember that night? Exactly how many shots did you have?"

"Just lay off, ok? You don't know what you're talking about."

"And you do?"

"Trust me. When it comes to Trevor, you've got the wrong idea."

My blood chilled and I took a step closer, lowering my voice. "What do you know? You can tell me—I swear I'm not the one spreading gossip." He shook his head, but I continued to press. "We're talking about someone's life, Brent. If you don't want to tell me, you should tell the police."

"Just stop, ok? Mind your own business."

"Whatever." This was obviously going nowhere. I spun on my heel, intent on storming away.

Behind me, Brent's voice called out. "They're serious, you know. About what will happen if you don't stop."

My skin crawled as I continued on my mission to find Teddy. I considered the possibility that Brent was lying. He was obviously mad at me, thinking I'd been spreading rumors. He could be trying to throw me off or scare me. But I couldn't shake the eerie feeling that Brent was telling the truth. And unless I was reading him completely wrong, he wasn't angry that someone was on his trail. He looked scared. Like he knew something he shouldn't.

And how had he known that the killer had threatened me?

## Chapter Eighteen

The set was swarming when I arrived, the rush between scenes when everyone is either coming or going and the crew is scrambling to prepare for the next shoot.

I slid into the house, doing my best to avoid detection. I needed to talk to Teddy—now—and the last thing I wanted was to be waylaid by another conversation that would take up more precious time. I passed the parlor, where Chloe and Audrey were bent over one of their phones, laughing, and the now blessedly repaired dining room, where Natasha was watching back footage she'd just shot.

No sign of Teddy.

Footsteps and voices echoed from the second floor. I took the steps two at a time, finally finding Teddy in the middle of the upstairs hall, talking to—of all people—Scott. I hovered for a moment, trying to gauge how critical the conversation was.

"... goin' about this the wrong way." Scott chewed on a

toothpick as he crossed his arms and leaned against a door frame. "You can't lay out all your cards like that, man."

"So what do you suggest?" Teddy was leaning in, an eager pupil, the shirt he was wearing ripped and bloody from the scene he'd just shot.

"It's like this." Scott widened his stance, holding out his hands like he was about to describe a football strategy. "You make her think you hate her."

Teddy's eyebrows flew up in alarm. "Are you sure about that?"

"Chicks love that shit. Makes them want what they can't have."

"I don't know." Teddy looked doubtful. "I'm pretty sure she already thought that and she did not dig it."

Oh God, were they talking about me?

Scott pulled the toothpick out of his mouth and pointed it at Teddy. "I'm telling you, it works every time." He placed it back in his mouth. "Most of the time, anyway."

"I'll think about it."

I had to put a stop to this. I stepped out of the shadows. "What are you two talking about?"

Both of them startled, looking as guilty as two schoolboys caught cheating on a test.

Scott recovered first. "Football. Just going over the game from last night, right?" He gave Teddy a not-at-all-subtle wink.

"Uh, yeah. Definitely." He forced a chuckle. "Love those Eagles."

I narrowed my eyes. Damn it. If only I knew whether that was a real team or not.

"I need to skedaddle." Scott gave us a wave as he walked toward the stairs. Before descending, he turned. "And remember"—he gave Teddy a long, weighted look—"what we talked about."

"Bye, Scott!" Teddy said loudly as he waved the older man away. He drew closer, one corner of his mouth curving up in a smile as he flipped a hand towel over his shoulder, looking a little too charming for someone covered in fake gore.

When he got close enough, he reached out to touch my elbow. "I missed you last night."

For a moment, my heart stuttered, and I considered ripping his shirt the rest of the way off. But I forced myself to push it from my mind. There were more important things at hand. Or at least, equally important.

"I need to talk to you." I pressed my eyes closed, blocking out the intensity of his lake-blue gaze.

"What's up?"

A lighting tech shuffled past, bumping into us as he moved down the hall. This wouldn't do—we needed privacy. I glanced around frantically, my eyes landing on a narrow door to our left. I yanked it open, pulling Teddy in after me. As I closed the door after us, I realized it was a very small closet.

Dust plumed around us from the sudden disturbance. We both sneezed as I grappled above my head, searching for a light. Succeeding in finding a string, I pulled it and a weak glow filled the space enough for me to see that we were now squeezed in amongst dusty clothing and neglected cleaning supplies. Teddy was crammed against a stack of brooms and I was straddling one of his legs, pushing a stiff denim jacket out from between us.

It was at this moment that I remembered the last time I'd seen him had been moments after our kiss on the porch. Seeing him up close again, his lips mere inches from mine, made it temporarily hard to catch my breath. Teddy's arm snuck around my waist and pulled me close, his eyes falling to my lips.

"It's nice to see you, too," he teased, maneuvering his arm free from where it was pinned against the wall so he could cup my cheek in his hand. "I thought you were blowing me off last night."

He leaned in, the space between our lips rapidly closing. I stiffened. As easy as it would be to kiss Teddy again, I knew that if I gave in to that, I would forget all about the note and the killer that was quickly closing in on us. And if I was honest, the question of what was brewing between us was almost scarier than a killer being on my ass.

I leaned away, pressing one hand gently on his chest.

"Oh." Teddy stopped, his smile disintegrating. "No?"

"Sorry, I—"

"No, it's ok." He cleared his throat, pulling away to place some distance between us, even if the close quarters only allowed for a few inches. "I just thought—"

"Did you check your phone?" I blurted. "I tried to text you."

"No, we were filming all morning." He shifted and twisted, trying to reach into his pockets. Finally, contorting his body like something out of *The Exorcist*, he managed to retrieve his device. He tapped the screen, scrolling until he finally froze. "Another one?"

"Here." I wriggled until I was able to pull the note from my pocket. "And things get even weirder." I quickly filled him in on my run-in with Brent.

Teddy's face clouded. "I knew he was a bad dude."

"Did you? Weren't you the one who suggested we give him the benefit of the doubt?"

"I don't remember that," Teddy said stubbornly.

"Regardless. He definitely knows something, whether he killed Trevor or he knows who did. We need to talk to him again."

"I'll do it. I don't want you anywhere near him."

Something inside me bristled. "I'm not a child—I can do it myself."

Teddy stared at me blankly. "You just told me he might literally be the one who sent you death threats and killed Trevor. You're not talking to him alone." His voice was firm. "And I also think it's time we called the police."

"Police, fine, but I at least want to be there when you talk to Brent."

"Oh, come on." Teddy rolled his eyes. "You're being ridiculous."

"I just want to make sure we're asking him the right questions!"

"You know, you need to trust people more."

"What?" The accusation took me aback. I trusted people just fine. When they gave me a reason.

"You asked me to join this investigation so I could help, but this whole time, you've barely given yourself a break." He softened, reaching up to tuck a strand of hair behind my ear. "You're exhausted, not to mention in real danger. I'm going to talk to Brent. I can let you know what I learn."

Despite myself, I leaned into his touch. His hand hovered on my cheek and I savored the feeling, my body loosening and relaxing as I took a deep breath.

"I . . . Fine." Pulling away, I checked the time on my phone. "Look, I need to get to hair and makeup. You can talk to Brent as long as I can be there when you talk to the police."

"Of course."

"Now let's get out of here—my knee is cramping."

Pouring out of the closet, some of my panic started to ebb. We had a plan, and hopefully getting the police on board would help. And even if I preferred to talk to Brent myself, I had to grudgingly admit that Teddy would probably do just fine.

"We got this, I promise," Teddy whispered, squeezing my elbow before he disappeared down the stairs. His breath in my ear sent tingles down my spine. I watched him walk away, trying to remember why I'd stopped the kiss in the closet, and imagining what would have happened if I hadn't.

"Can someone tell me," Natasha said, slowly rising from her place behind the camera, "if I look like someone's genitals?"

No one moved.

We were in the middle of shooting a scene in which the witch's spirit is lurking in the background—creepy and dread-inducing like those scenes in *Halloween* when Mike Myers is standing in the bushes in the middle of the day.

We'd gone through several takes, and then several more, botching them all. No, we hadn't botched them. Brent had. Something was wrong with him—he looked haggard, even more than when I'd seen him just a few hours earlier. He'd had a hard time focusing, screwing up his blocking and not listening to Natasha's directions. And between takes, he'd started hitting on Audrey, even though she was clearly uninterested.

It was worse than when he'd screwed up the scene in the boathouse.

Meanwhile, I was struggling not to have a tantrum of my own.

Every second on set was excruciating. I kept analyzing everyone's face, wondering if they'd been the one to slip the envelope under my door. Brent or Chloe? Natasha or Audrey? Or maybe a member of the crew, whose name I didn't even know? It felt like Teddy and I were on the cusp of uncovering the truth, but it was possible we were nowhere close. I wanted, needed, this scene to be over as soon as possible.

Unfortunately, Brent seemed bound and determined to drag it out as long as possible.

Natasha stared at us expectantly, and when no one replied, Chloe stepped up. "Um, no?"

"Then why are you all fucking me on this!" Natasha ripped off her beanie and threw it to the ground, her short blonde hair sticking up in clumpy spikes. She marched toward Brent, one long finger pointing straight at his chest.

"You." She stopped a few feet away from him, her outreached arm shaking. "You need to get your shit together. What did I tell you?"

I prayed Brent would listen and not continue to try Natasha's patience. But to my horror, Brent laughed. And shrugged his shoulders. And rolled his eyes. I swore smoke eked out of Natasha's ears. If we'd been in *Carrie*, Natasha would have been Sissy Spacek and Brent would have been the dude she electrocuted with her mind.

Instead, Natasha did the opposite. She became eerily, scarily calm. Closing the gap between them, she stepped forward and pressed a sharp fingertip into Brent's chest.

"Get off my set." Her voice was so low I could barely make it out.

Brent kept smirking. "What, are you firing me?"

"We're breaking for lunch, and when we get back, I'm giving you one more chance. If you fuck up again, you're done." Then she stormed off the set.

No one moved. Even Brent, seemingly taken off guard, was quiet. But a moment later, the spell lifted and he shrugged his shoulders yet again, like he was trying to shrug off the entire encounter.

"Good. I can't stand being in this freak show house, anyway." Holding up both middle fingers and waving them to the rest of the cast, he left, hopping into one of the golf carts and waiting with his arms crossed for one of the PAs to escort him to base camp.

As everyone else filed off set, Teddy and I fell in step together.

"Are we calling the police now or later?" he whispered in my ear as we hopped into one of the waiting carts.

"Later. We don't have a lot of time, and I'm not sure how long they'll want to talk to us." I paused. "Plus, I'm starving."

The situation was dire, but so was the grumbling in my stomach.

Arriving at the lunch tent, I lined up for my entrée, walking along the table and looking for the container with my name on it. But as soon as I located it, a hand appeared out of nowhere, snatching it from right out in front of me.

Grinning at me from the other side of the table was, of course,

Brent. Not bothering to take the food to his seat, he ripped open the top of the container, dug in his fork, and shoveled a big scoop into his mouth.

"Delicious," he said around the mouthful of food.

I grimaced in disgust. Brent was clearly going to have it out for me as long as he thought I'd spread the rumor about him. My mood darkened as I looked for something else to eat—I was in the crosshairs of a killer, and I couldn't even eat my Chinese chicken salad in peace.

I'd made it to the other end of the table when I heard it. A choked gurgle, like someone hacking up a loogie. I bit back a snide comment. I was already annoyed about my stolen lunch; I didn't need people doing gross, immature things around the food. But when I turned around, all I saw was Brent's face, stricken and red, his eyes bulging. Then, clutching his throat, he collapsed on the ground.

I rushed over, picking up the still-full container that had originally been meant for me. "NO PEANUTS" was scrawled across the lid in Sharpie, a special order to accommodate my allergy. I ripped off the lid and peered closely, careful not to touch it. Sure enough, the salad was covered in crushed peanuts.

Someone had added peanuts to my food, knowing it would be a death sentence. But unfortunately for him, Brent was allergic, too.

## Chapter Nineteen

Once Brent collapsed, all hell broke loose.

A nearby props assistant called 911, Chloe started shrieking at an alarming decibel level, and Mara knelt down to check his vitals. I rushed to the first aid kit, frantically trying to locate an EpiPen, but it was missing. By the time Natasha heard the commotion and made her way over, it was almost certainly already too late—but that didn't stop her from yelling at Brent to "get the fuck up".

Feeling helpless, I stared at Brent's horribly still face, frozen in an expression of terror as he lay on the grass. I was allergic to peanuts, and it had been my lunch, and it was supposed to be me. I, very easily, could have been the one unconscious on the ground. And it hadn't escaped me that my lunch had been tampered with the day I'd received another note.

Had the killer run out of patience mere hours after warning me?

Standing under the food tent, surrounded by screaming cast

and crew and mere feet away from someone I was pretty sure was dying, I started to hyperventilate. I gasped for air but it didn't feel like it was coming fast enough—my lungs felt tight and I was growing light-headed. Had I somehow ingested the peanuts, too? Was I minutes away from my own death?

"Hey, look at me." Teddy grabbed my shoulders and eased me into a chair on the opposite side of the tent. "Focus on me. I want you to breathe in for four seconds, hold it, let it out for four seconds, and hold it again."

"Hold my breath?" I swatted his hands away. "It feels like I'm having a heart attack—I need more air, not less." I bent at my waist, gulping for oxygen.

"You're having a panic attack—you need to get your breath under control."

"How would you know? You're not a doctor."

"Because I've been having them since I was seven years old." He kneeled on the ground, looking up at me patiently. "Trust me, it'll help."

For a moment, I was distracted from my heart hammering in my throat. Then the pieces started clicking into place: Teddy forgetting his line because he was so nervous the first day, the way he'd learned to anticipate and plan for worst-case scenarios, the way he'd helped his brother when he struggled with anxiety. But before I could ponder it further, a fresh wave of panic swept over me and the pressure returned to my chest.

"Ok, fine," I gasped. "What am I supposed to do?"

Staring into his steady blue eyes, I attempted to follow his directions. He knelt on the grass, breathing along with me, until my panic attack finally subsided. I squeezed Teddy's hand gratefully as the ambulance blared onto the scene and the paramedics swarmed Brent's very still body.

He was gone.

As soon as the paramedics pulled away, Teddy and I locked eyes.

Police. Now.

"We're driving." Teddy held my hand as he helped me out of the folding chair. "I don't want you anywhere near this set right now."

"Ok." I was still too in shock to argue. "Let me just grab my wallet." But I'd lost track of it in the chaos—knocked off the table or kicked under a chair. "Damn it, where is it?"

"Quinn!" Mara rushed over, her hair falling out of its vintage twist. "Quinn, that was supposed to be yours!" She clutched me against her and I felt a surge of affection for her so strong it nearly took my breath away.

"I know." I pulled away, still shaky. "Teddy and I were just leaving. Will you be at the hotel later?"

"Wait, where are you going?" She glanced from Teddy to me, eyes wide.

"I just . . . need to lie down. I'm really shaken up."

Mara nodded. "Yes, yes, of course. Go. I'll see you later."

"I'll call you!" I promised, yelling over my shoulder as we made a beeline for the parking lot. Teddy led me to his car, a worn Ford SUV that looked at least a decade old. He unlocked the doors and I hopped in, the interior neat and tidy except for a stray McDonald's wrapper that lay crumpled on the floor.

"What are we telling the police? We need a plan." Teddy stretched out his right arm and braced it against my headrest as he looked over his shoulder to back out of the spot. His biceps strained at his tee-shirt, and a vein bulged on his forearm.

I swallowed, suddenly distracted. Why was that motion so hot? It made me wonder about a certain other bulging appendage—

"Jigsaw?"

"Oh. Right." I closed my eyes, trying to concentrate on where to start. "The notes, obviously. They were clearly threats. I have the one I got this morning and a photo of the first one on my phone."

Teddy's jaw tensed. "But it wasn't just a threat. They actually tried to kill you. Literally ten minutes ago."

I shivered, the thought still chilling me. "We can't prove that though, can we? People make mistakes about food allergies all the time."

"We need to tell them that you got the note and your food was messed with on the same day." Teddy steered us onto the highway, pushing the gas until we were going ten miles over the speed limit. Thankfully, the GPS said it was only twelve minutes to the station.

"Ok. Agreed." Still, something was bugging me. "It's just an awful coincidence that Brent steals my food the same day it was tampered with, and that he has the same food allergy as me."

"What are you suggesting?"

"I mean," I twisted in my seat to face him, "what if someone originally meant it for me, but got fed up with Brent and gave him the idea to steal my food so he would eat it instead?"

Teddy frowned, skeptical. "Isn't the simplest explanation the likeliest one? Isn't that, like, Myrtle's Law?"

"Merv's Law," I corrected.

"Whatever."

(Later, I would Google it. We were both wrong.)

"I know it's a long shot, but think about it. This morning, Brent said whoever was leaving me notes was serious. He knew who killed Trevor, I just know it. But he didn't go to the police. Whoever it was must have been blackmailing him."

"I can see that."

"And that would explain why he's been so off. If he knew there was a killer on the loose and they were threatening him, no wonder he was in bad shape. He was getting high more than usual to cope."

"Not bad enough shape to keep his hands to himself the other night," Teddy grumbled.

"Would you stay on topic?" Suddenly, something clicked and I gripped his arm. "What if it was Natasha? What did she say before we all broke for lunch? 'What did I tell you?' She must have been threatening him before today. Maybe earlier this morning she put peanuts in my food to stop me from investigating, but after Brent pissed her off so badly, she decided to off him instead?"

"Fuck." Teddy ran a hand down his chin. "You could be right."

"You were on set this morning. Could she have snuck away to mess with my food?"

"She definitely disappeared between wrapping the first scene and when we came back for the second one." Teddy tightened his grip on the wheel. "If she did kill Trevor and knew you were investigating, that would be a very big motive."

Suddenly, it all clicked into place. "Trevor pissed off Natasha the first day by ruining my costume and then rushing onto set to help you knock over the lamp. She found out I was poking around investigating, so she decided to get rid of me, until Brent irritated her enough to change her plans."

"You could be right." Teddy glanced at me. "Do we have proof of that, though?"

"No," I admitted.

"So, all we're reporting is the notes?"

Bile rose in my throat in disappointment. "Just the notes."

Larry the cop wasn't thrilled I'd waited so long to come in.

"You've been hanging onto these for how long?" He squinted as he took my phone to peer at the photos. The three of us were in Larry's office, a space with terribly unflattering fluorescent lighting and piles of paper that should probably have been securely filed away somewhere. I'd already told him about the note I'd received that morning and had moved on to the one I received the day after Trevor's death.

I squirmed in my seat. "Um, a few days?"

"And why didn't you report it then?"

"They told me not to. I was worried for my—for our—safety."

Larry sighed heavily as he handed me back my phone. "We'll need copies of those photos for our records."

"Absolutely."

"And you need to tell us if you receive any more of these."

"I will."

"Promise?"

"I promise."

"Good." Larry leaned back in his chair, resting his hands on his ample belly. "Now, I can't guarantee we'll be able to find the perpetrator of these notes. We don't have much to go on. But since they allege that a crime has been committed, we'll be heading out to that set of yours to talk to a few folks."

"Ok." My voice was shaky. I reminded myself that this was what I wanted—for the police to believe that Trevor's death had been intentional. But now the killer would know I'd ratted them out to law enforcement. My skin crawled, feeling like the killer was in the room with us. Watching. Like they already knew what I'd done.

Next to me, Teddy reached out and put a reassuring hand on my back, his thumb moving slowly up and down. My heart rate relaxed. I took a deep breath—slowly in and then out, reminding myself that this was the right thing to do. The police had to know what was going on. And hopefully, they'd be able to help.

Because I really didn't want to think about what would happen if I'd just put myself in harm's way for nothing.

## Chapter Twenty

Teddy and I were quiet on the drive back to the hotel. I rested my head against the window, watching the little town's shops roll by. It was hard to believe it'd only been a few hours since Brent had laid on the grass, gasping for air.

Unbidden, the images started rolling back.

Brent, grinning at me before the smile died from his face. Chloe, her face contorting in horror as Brent collapsed on the ground. The paramedics, their expressions falling as they checked for a pulse. Then it was back: the feeling of not being able to get enough air, like my heart was going to burst.

I gripped the armrest, my knuckles turning white. "I can't go back to the hotel."

"You ok?" Teddy took his eyes off the road for a second to glance at me.

"Yeah, I . . ." I ran a hand along my collarbone. "This is just a lot." I took a deep breath in, held out, pushed it out, held it again. Just like Teddy had taught me. Several cycles and I started to feel better. But only just.

Worry flickered in Teddy's eyes but he said nothing as he let me breathe. We motored along and after a few minutes of scanning the road, he pressed on the brake and flicked on his turn signal.

"Here we are."

"Where's 'here'?" I craned my neck to see out the window.

"You'll see."

Moments later, Teddy and I were standing in the middle of the parking lot, staring up at a sign reading "Mothman Mini Golf." A giant cutout of the cryptid crouched on top of the sign, only one of its eyes glowing red.

"Mini golf?" I stared at the sign skeptically. Upon closer inspection, one of the i's in "mini" was missing.

"Yep!" Teddy said brightly. "My treat." He marched confidently toward the entrance, where an admissions stand squatted near a barrel of putters and a rack of golf balls.

Not having much of a choice, I followed.

The course looked like it'd seen better days. The man at the entrance was grumpy, handing us clubs that were slightly rusted and pencils for our scorecard that were sharpened down to nubs. The sidewalk leading to the first hole was cracked and bumpy, roots from nearby trees running underneath and making the walking surface uneven. But the shade was nice, and a breeze rustled the leaves overhead pleasantly.

And, more importantly, my heart started to slow from a frenzied gallop to a brisk jog.

"I have to warn you," Teddy said as we approached the first

hole, themed after the cryptid MVP himself: Bigfoot. "I am very good at mini golf."

"Please." I held my club over my head with two hands as I stretched side to side. "I'm basically an expert. I could go pro."

This wasn't true. I couldn't remember the last time I'd played mini golf. But it felt like something that could be true, if I tried hard enough.

Teddy raised an eyebrow. "I didn't know there was a pro mini-golf circuit." He stepped aside, holding out an arm in deference. "After you."

Slightly regretting my showboating, I placed my ball on the tee and studied the green. It was a straight shot leading to a giant replica of Bigfoot's head. You had to get the ball through his mouth to the other side, where the hole presumably waited. I squared up to the tee, swung my arms back, and tapped the ball gently.

It promptly barreled toward Bigfoot's head, missed the mouth, and ricocheted off one of its cheeks.

"Pro, huh?" Teddy placed his own ball on the tee. "Is that some kind of pro strategy that I'm unfamiliar with?"

"Yes."

Unfortunately, Teddy completed the first hole with ease, getting the ball through the Sasquatch's mouth and into the hole with two strokes. Meanwhile, it took me four tries.

"Who's the pro now?" Teddy marked the numbers on the little scorecard, the mini pencil laughably tiny in his hand.

"Really? You're keeping score?"

"Absolutely, Jigsaw. And no cheating. I saw the way you tried to sneak an extra stroke in there when I wasn't looking."

"You would know about extra strokes."

He smirked. "That doesn't even make sense."

I grumbled something indecipherable as we moved on to the next hole, this one featuring the Loch Ness Monster. Players needed to jump their ball over a little canal and then dodge the mechanical neck of the monster, which swung its head over the hole.

"Thank you, by the way." I gave him a look of gratitude before lining up to take my first shot. "For teaching me that breathing trick. It really helped." My ball shot off the tee and rolled into the water.

"No problem." Teddy tossed his club into the air before catching it handily. "Box breathing. I'm a frequent flier."

"Does that happen to you a lot?"

"Panic attacks? Not all the time. I got them more often when I was a teenager, before my mom got me into therapy." Teddy tapped the ball, making it over the water on the first try. "It's a good technique for a lot of situations, though. Anxiety attacks. Or when you're just worrying a lot. Or when you're already losing mini golf after two holes."

Biting back a grin, I smacked him playfully on the arm, determined to refocus and claim victory. But once again, Teddy got it in after two tries, while it took me three. At least it was an improvement.

Although I did mentally cross professional golfer off my list of next career possibilities.

After another three holes—themed around the chupacabra, Jersey Devil, and thunderbird, respectively—we caught up to a family of five at the sixth hole. The two women looked harried and exhausted as their three kids all tried to putt their balls at the same time. Once the older two finished, the parents tried to get the youngest—a little boy who looked around the age of four—to hurry up. However, he would not be deterred from his preferred strategy, which included holding the putter with one hand on the grip and the other approximately two inches above the foot.

It wasn't effective.

Sensing it would be a while, Teddy leaned against a nearby tree. "If you had to date a cartoon character, who would it be?"

I nearly choked on my spit. "What?"

"It's Popeye, isn't it?"

"Um, no." I thought for a moment. "Hmm. Probably Robin Hood."

"I said animated. Didn't that guy from *The Princess Bride* play Robin Hood?"

"I meant the fox!"

Teddy gaped at me. "A sexy fox, Jigsaw? How am I supposed to live up to that?"

I ignored the implication. "What about you?"

"Velma. Definitely."

"From *Scooby-Doo*? No, you're definitely a Jessica Rabbit type."

"No way. That orange turtleneck really does it for me."

The family finished and we moved up to the yeti-themed hole.

"So I should wear mine the next time we hang out?"

If he was being flirty, why shouldn't I?

Teddy lined up his shot, keeping his eye on the green. "Nope, you're not going to distract me just because I'm beating you."

A moment of concentration, and then a smooth hit. He beat me once again.

As we moved forward and waited for the family ahead of us, I noticed the littlest one studying Teddy. He leaned on his tiny club, his big brown eyes never leaving him as the rest of the family took their turns.

I nudged Teddy, gesturing to the little boy. Teddy grinned and gave him a wave. It must have given the boy a boost of confidence, because he took a step toward us, holding out his little club.

"Can you teach me?" The little boy peered up at Teddy, his eyes wide and hopeful.

Teddy didn't miss a beat. "Sure, if it's ok with your parents." They nodded, looking relieved that he'd be occupied for a few moments.

"Alright, little guy, get over here."

Teddy was at ease as he stood behind him and got them both into position. His body dwarfed the little boy's, but he was gentle as he moved the boy's tiny arms slowly into the swing. Watching them, my breath caught and my chest swelled with affection. It was hard for me to remember how I'd ever thought of Teddy as arrogant and selfish. The Teddy I'd come to know was so thoughtful, so willing to help others. And he had such a confident way of existing in the world. Even when he was anxious, he seemed so sure of who he was. I wished that I had a little bit of that ease, instead of feeling constantly odd and out of place.

But then, I realized I didn't feel like that around Teddy. Teddy made me feel at home, like I belonged. Like I fit.

"Thanks, Eddie!" the boy yelled when they finished their impromptu lesson. The family headed to the next hole, where the boy promptly returned to his previous form.

"Good job, Eddie," I teased as I joined him on the green.

"Careful. Do I need to show you how to stroke properly?"

I opened my mouth to say no, that I didn't need his help for any kind of stroke, actually. But then I paused. The anxiety I'd felt after my brush with death had been replaced by something else—a recklessness that made me want to say screw it and do what I wanted. If a killer already had a target on my back, why not?

"Actually, I think I do need some help. Stroking properly." I looked up at him, eyes round with innocence. "If you're up for it?"

Teddy's eyes widened in surprise and his throat bobbed. He caught himself, his mouth then twisting into a smirk. "I'm always up for it." He moved behind me, pressing his body against my back as his arms encircled mine. "Just don't expect me to take it easy on you once I show you my tricks." His voice was low in my ear, his breath sending tingles down my spine.

"Promise." My stomach swooped as he tightened his arms around me and placed his hands over mine. Our kiss had been soul-rocking, but somehow this felt even more intimate.

"Ready?" Holding my arms snugly, he swung them back and brought them forward to tap the ball. It skipped prettily down the green, landing just a few inches away from the hole.

"Perfect," I breathed, only half talking about the shot.

Teddy held me a few beats longer, neither one of us wanting to move. I leaned into him, my back pressed against the muscle of his chest. The way he held me felt like nothing could hurt me, not just because he was there but because I felt peaceful. Secure. Like everything would be ok.

Finally, Teddy shook himself away, his fist contracting as we moved apart. "That was, uh, good. Good job."

"All because of you . . . Eddie."

He pressed his eyes closed. "Please never call me that again."

My lips cracked into a smile as we continued down the path. We'd have to go back to the hotel, and our murder mystery, eventually. But in the meantime, I was happy to exist right there, at a rundown mini-golf course that had an obsession with cryptids.

Perfect.

## Chapter Twenty-one

"I'm not sad he died," a voice whispered behind me. "He was an asshole."

"Exactly," said another. "He felt me up during one of his costume fittings. What a creep."

"Well, everything happens for a reason," said the first voice. "Maybe he shouldn't have fucked up his karma so badly."

It was the next morning and I was sitting in one of the hotel's conference rooms along with half the cast and crew as the other half slowly trickled in. Some were talking amongst themselves while others sat quietly as they drank their coffee. Everyone looked anxious. Teddy was sitting next to me, tapping his feet nervously. I glanced at the time—5:58 a.m. Two minutes to go.

Waking up that morning, I'd felt more at peace than I had in months. Getting off set with Teddy the day before had been a balm, even with the horrible events of the day swirling in the background. Returning to the hotel and dropping me off at my room, Teddy hadn't attempted a replay of our kiss on the back porch. I'd been disappointed until I remembered me turning him down in the closet—maybe it wasn't a surprise he hadn't tried again. But I could still feel him pressed up against my back, and the way he'd cradled my wrists gently as he helped me practice my swing.

Lying in bed, my room still dark, I'd wanted to swim in that moment just a bit longer, not ready to let the memory go.

But then my phone had dinged with an email from Natasha, the subject line blaring "Outrageous and unfounded claims!" She was asking everyone to meet at six that morning for an "update on the state of production."

That didn't sound good.

Now, as the clock rolled over to 5:59, Natasha's eyes were steely, her mouth slightly pinched. If she'd been angry with Brent for coming to set high, I could only assume she was absolutely apoplectic that he'd gone ahead and died too. Next to me, Teddy rubbed my arm with a crooked knuckle—not obvious enough for anyone to see, but enough to signal he was there.

As the clock ticked over to 6:00 a.m. on the dot, Natasha rose from her seat and stepped to the front of the room.

"Thank you all for coming this morning on such short notice. I'm sure by now everyone is aware of what occurred on set yesterday afternoon." Natasha's voice was somber, and she paused as the crowd murmured. "An autopsy is being performed, even though the cause of death is strongly suspected to be from anaphylactic shock. In the meantime, the police will be performing a brief investigation to ensure there is no evidence of foul play. It appears a member of our team has been receiving threatening notes, something the police are taking very seriously."

My stomach plunged. The killer would already know I'd tattled on them purely by virtue of the police being on set, but I hadn't realized Natasha was going to rat me out in front of everyone. I glanced around surreptitiously, trying to gauge people's reactions.

Audrey was clutching a hand to her chest, looking very much like I had during my panic attack. Chloe looked uneasy, her eyes shifting as though she, too, was unsettled there was still a killer on the loose. Mara's face was blank, giving no clue to her feelings. Our old friend Scott Rossi was scowling in the back row, likely resentful that he'd been questioned about Trevor for a second time.

"Obviously," Natasha continued, "this whole charade will affect our schedule. Filming will not take place today so the police can conduct their interviews. We're also still ironing out changes to the shooting schedule now that Brent is no longer here." She frowned. "And unfortunately, these events have caught the attention of the studio. Representatives will be arriving tomorrow to conduct their own investigation. Everyone must be on their best behavior."

"Excuse me." A voice rang out from somewhere behind me. "Sorry, I have a question."

"Yes?" Natasha's voice was crisp.

"Just to clarify, a murder has taken place?" It was a camera operator, a woman maybe a year or two older than me. "They just don't know who did it?"

Natasha gathered herself before answering. "I don't believe I'm qualified to answer that question. They believe it's possible a crime could have taken place."

"Which means they probably have evidence one was committed?" the woman pressed.

Natasha waved a hand. "I don't—"

"Cops don't waste their time if they're not sure a crime happened," another voice yelled.

And yet another: "And what about Trevor? They said that one was an accident too."

Voices started to rise, everyone pitching in with their personal and first-hand knowledge of the legal system.

"On *CSI*, I saw—"

"Well, in my 'Introduction to Criminal Justice' class—"

"My aunt almost became a cop and she—"

"Enough!" Natasha raised her voice. "I'm simply going by what the professionals have told me. You'll all receive an email tomorrow with the updated schedule. Let me know if you have any questions." She stepped back from the podium, making it clear the meeting was over.

As people stood and started to trickle out, dread dripped through my body. I'd known the killer would eventually find out that I'd gone to the police, but now it was real.

And they might be in the room with me right now.

Less than an hour later, Teddy and I were called into our interviews first, summoned one by one to the same conference room where Natasha had briefed us. My session was quick—I simply confirmed what I'd already told the police, which seemed to satisfy the two detectives conducting the interviews. Teddy was next, and he gave me a little fist bump before slipping into the room and closing the door behind him.

Anxious, I waited nearby in the hotel lobby. I could have returned to my room, which would have been much more comfortable than the lumpy armchair I found pushed against the wall. But after the way he'd been there for me the day before, I found myself not wanting to be further away from Teddy than I needed to be. His presence was comforting, grounding. I should be distancing myself, but I somehow couldn't force myself to.

Trying to occupy my mind, I scrolled through the news, which for me meant checking the tabloid sites—nosy for gossip while praying my name wouldn't show up. Minutes into my scrolling, a text popped up on my screen, obscuring a headline teasing a new dating reality show:

Dad: Alright Squish, I've given it almost twenty-four hours.
Are you alright?

Whoops. I hadn't called my dad to tell him about what happened to Brent, mostly because I forgot, but also because I didn't want to. It would only make him worry, and the last thing I needed was Puzzle Face himself storming onto set asking questions.

Quinn: How'd you even hear about that?
Dad: I can't give away my secrets! I've got eyes and ears everywhere.
Quinn: There's an active investigation, Dad.
Dad: Ok, ok. Well, you'll never believe who sent me a Facebook friend request the other day.

I waited for seven minutes, wondering what this could possibly have to do with Brent, but the answer never came.

**Quinn:** Who?
**Dad:** Scott Rossi! We got to talking and he said I'd raised an impressive young woman for a daughter, by the way. Anyway, he told me about what happened to that young man. You ok?

Huh. Who would have thought our buddy Scott had a secret soft side?

**Quinn:** I'm fine! I thought you and Scott hated each other?
**Dad:** Old age is making us soft, I guess! Told him all about your career, how proud I am of you. He has a little girl, too, though she's not as successful as you 😊

A churning started in my stomach—a suspicion of just where this conversation was going. Sure enough, ten seconds later, another message came through.

**Dad:** Don't want to pressure you, but do you have any thoughts about that movie I pitched you?

I squeezed my eyes shut. The reality was I'd forgotten about it completely. The reality was I was never making another movie again. The reality was I'd have to tell my dad all of this someday, but today couldn't be the day.

**Quinn:** I'm late for my call time! I'll call you later.

The guilt felt awful, but I also couldn't deny the relief I felt shutting down the conversation. Was the future eventually going to catch up with me? Yes. But that was future Quinn's problem.

A few minutes later, the door to the conference room cracked open and Teddy emerged.

I jumped to my feet. "How'd it go? You didn't tell them too much, right? Just what we already told them yesterday?"

"Nope, I told them all about our investigation and everything we've been up to."

"You what?" I felt the blood drain from my face. "Why would you do that?"

Teddy rolled his eyes. "Relax, Jigsaw. It went fine. You can trust me, you know. We've talked about this."

"Jerk." I thwacked him on the shoulder and he pretended to wince, screwing up his face and rubbing the muscle.

Footsteps padded down the hall behind us, yanking both of our attentions. Natasha, entering the conference room for her own interview. Wordlessly, we both eyed the room next door.

"You think it's soundproof?" Teddy asked. "We probably couldn't hear anything."

"Only one way to find out."

We scurried into the room, locking the door behind us. Feeling very much like a cartoon character, I crept across the floor and pressed my ear to the shared wall. After just a few moments, I heard familiar voices.

I motioned frantically and Teddy joined me, pressing his own head against the striped wallpaper.

"Would you say you've been feeling a lot of pressure lately, Ms. Vossey?"

"Not particularly." Natasha's voice was casual, with a defiant edge.

There was a faint rustling of papers. "So this hasn't been on your mind at all?"

Teddy and I glanced at each other in alarm. What had they shown her?

"No." Natasha's voice was firm. "That happened two years ago and was a total accident."

I pressed my ear harder to the wall, but despite my cartilage audibly crunching, it failed to make Natasha or the police any easier to hear.

"Of course. It did cost the production company millions of dollars, though, didn't it?"

"I fail to see what this has to do with my current project."

"Nothing at all." A table creaked, like someone had leaned forward on it. "Just . . . that you might be feeling a little pressure for this production to go off without a hitch."

"I try my best to do that on all my movies. Are we about done here?"

"One more question." More paper-flipping. "Is it true that you argued with both Trevor Hill and Brent Milburn on the mornings of their deaths?"

Natasha was quiet for a long beat, so long I thought she might have stormed out. But then there was a sharp intake of breath.

"Yes. But if you asked around, I think you'd find that I argued with almost everyone on those days."

Natasha, I had to admit, had a point.

As they continued their conversation, Teddy and I pulled out our phones. A quick Google search found that Natasha's last three movies hadn't just done miserably at the box office; they'd also been universally panned by reviewers. Worse, we found that two years ago, a stunt woman had been paralyzed on one of Natasha's sets after a stunt went horribly wrong. The woman had sued the production and won, netting herself—and costing the company—millions.

I felt a pang of empathy. I knew firsthand how terrible it was being the subject of scathing press. "Poor Natasha. No wonder she wants this movie to be a success so badly."

"'Poor Natasha'?" Teddy side-eyed me. "Her carelessness ended up with a woman paralyzed."

"True."

My mind whirred, trying to put the pieces together. It was possible Natasha's increasingly erratic moods were simply caused by anxiety about her career. Not only had her reputation as a director been tanking but she was actively losing people millions of dollars. If she didn't have a hit soon, it was very likely no one would hire again.

But it was also possible that she was careless on her sets, and that she didn't mind hurting or killing someone to try to get her career back on track.

# Chapter Twenty-two

## SUSPECTS LIST

Scott—Has motive, was near Trevor shortly before death
Natasha—Has motive, is desperate
Brent—Has motive, Trevor got him fired
Chloe
Audrey
Mara
Teddy

As promised, the new shooting schedule arrived in my inbox the next morning.

I scrolled through the email as I walked across base camp, a piping-hot caramel apple latte in my other hand to help fend off the chilly September air. It was painfully early, still dark, and I scanned the call sheet as I sipped my coffee, anxious to know what scene we were on. With Natasha as our current number-one suspect, being on set would either allow me to keep an eye on her and an ear out for clues, or put me right in her crosshairs.

Then I saw what scene we'd be shooting.

I started to get a bad feeling as soon as I saw "INT KITCHEN" as the scene's location. My fear intensified as I spotted the phrase "closed set." And then . . . Oh, no. Oh, no, no, no. I stared at the scene description, trying to convince myself that if I looked long enough, the words would change. Of course, they didn't.

Today, Teddy and I would be filming our sex scene. And I knew what would be waiting for me as soon as I stepped inside my trailer.

"Hello, old friend." I gingerly removed my costume from the hanger inside the door. Once again, I'd be decked out in pasties and a thong, this time with the addition of a thick modesty patch on the crotch—to create more of a barrier between Teddy and myself, I assumed.

Sexy.

My stomach fluttered as I got changed and was shuttled to set. I had known the time would come for this scene eventually, of course. But it had always seemed far away, too far in the future to worry about. Now, I was worrying.

In the days since our kiss, it had felt like Teddy and I had put it behind us—that it had been a mutual moment of madness that both of us were keen to forget. But I thought about it now, the way he'd drawn my lip into his mouth to gently suck it. How his hands had gripped my hips as he pulled me against him. How I wasn't able to stop imagining it. Teddy and I had found a delicate equilibrium in the days since: friendly, but not romantic. Being thrown back into physical contact could throw that balance completely out of whack.

And what then?

Nerves fluttered in my stomach. Filming sex scenes always felt absolutely ridiculous—it was hard to feel sexy when a camera was six inches from your butt and you had to keep arching a certain way so the light hit your chest correctly. A necessary evil that I didn't love but felt comfortable doing. But with Teddy? I felt like a newbie getting ready to shoot my first love scene.

Should I kiss him with tongue? How much? What should I do with my hands? Would it be weird if I moaned on camera the same way I had when he'd nibbled my neck below my ear?

I was overanalyzing everything by the time I arrived on set, which was much quieter than usual. Only those who were absolutely needed were there—Natasha, of course, and as few sound and lighting crew as possible. No other cast. It was a small relief knowing I wouldn't embarrass myself in front of nosy PAs, at least.

The scene would take place in the kitchen, clearly the sexiest of all rooms. After all, who didn't fantasize about being railed in a space filled entirely with hard surfaces? The cameras and lighting had been set up by the time I wound my way to the back of the house, all trained on the counter where our characters first kiss. In the script, we're in the middle of rummaging through the cabinets looking for ingredients for a potion to defeat the witch when lust overtakes us and we go at it right on the kitchen table.

I did not expect it to be comfortable.

The table and chairs in the dining room had been pushed out

of the way to make way for equipment, and Natasha nodded at me from her place behind the camera as I entered. Teddy was over by one of the windows, talking to a woman I'd never seen before. The intimacy coordinator, I assumed—a pretty Black woman with box braids pulled up in a bun and dressed in leggings and a maroon tunic.

Teddy, in contrast, had apparently rejected the use of a robe. At first glance he looked stark naked, until you looked close enough to see that he was decked out in a modesty thong (talk about an oxymoron), similar to mine, but with the addition of a sock-like apparatus. And I didn't know how short-term memory loss works, but I'd apparently forgotten how toned his body was since we'd filmed our scene in the boathouse. He wasn't just muscular; he was absolutely ripped.

I gulped, forcing my gaze to remain above his waist and not dip down to the sock-covered area. It was a large sock.

The woman, who somehow seemed impervious to the charms of the naked man in front of her, smiled pleasantly as I approached. "You must be Quinn. I'm Gabby."

"That's me." I took her hand, which was reaching out for a handshake.

"I'll be helping you two prepare for and choreograph your scene today. My job is to make sure you're both comfortable at all times, so please don't hesitate to say if something doesn't feel right."

I looked down at my robe, which I knew I would have to remove at some point. "This underwear definitely doesn't feel right, but I guess you're not talking about that."

Gabby laughed. "I can't do anything about that, I'm afraid.

Why don't we head into the kitchen?" She swept her arm toward the next room, and Teddy and I filed in obediently.

As we moved through the dining room, I repeated the breathing exercise Teddy had taught me. It slowed my breathing marginally, but my hands were still shaking. I'd never been this nervous before a scene before. It was unnerving.

"Hey." Teddy placed a hand on the small of my back as we crossed the threshold of the kitchen. "This'll be a snap. There aren't even any boats around to put us all in mortal danger."

My erratic heart rate sure made me feel like I was in danger, but I nodded anyway.

Getting down to business, the three of us discussed what the scene would entail. Our characters would make out against the counter, and once we got that shot, Teddy and I would disrobe and move to the kitchen table. The part on the table would be brief—the script only calls for a few moments before the cameras cut to Chloe being stalked, and eventually killed, by the witch.

Hopefully we'd be able to get the shot before I got a stress fracture from being banged against the tabletop.

"Above all," Gabby said, "we want this to be an environment of consent."

"Definitely." Teddy glanced at me with determination in his eyes. "I want her to be comfortable at all times."

*I'd consent to you having your way with me against this counter right now.*

The thought popped into my head out of nowhere, and I could feel my cheeks redden. We hadn't even started filming, and my mind was already running itself into the gutter. How would I control myself once he was actually on top of me? I mentally shook myself, chasing away the image before it could materialize.

Gabby, meanwhile, was nodding at Teddy in approval. "We can play around and experiment with different shots and angles if we want, but if one of you wants to go off script, you must ask and get consent first from your partner." She looked first at Teddy and then at me, her expression knowing, as though she could tell I was already having impure thoughts. "Understand?"

Teddy and I both assured her we did.

"Alright, then." Gabby nodded at Natasha. "I think we're ready!"

We slipped into our costumes for the scene, making sure not to stretch out or tear the modesty garments, and took our places at the counter. As the cameras started rolling, I hiked myself up on the Formica and starting rummaging through the cabinets—my character hunting for cream of tartar, naturally a key ingredient in a protection charm.

"It's not here," I said with an exaggerated pout as I spun around to sit on the countertop. "What do we do now?"

Teddy bit his lip, rubbing his hands as he looked me up and down. "I have an idea."

It was all that I could do not to laugh. This dialogue. I managed not to break and instead cocked my head to the side. "Oh?"

Teddy nodded, licking his lips before moving in for the kiss. For a moment, my stomach hitched. Our mouths met, feather-light, and it was so similar to how our kiss on the back porch began before we quickly lost ourselves. But then a moment passed, and then another, and our stage kiss was nothing like our frantic make-out session. It was forced, completely void of passion. I nearly sighed from relief.

We got the shot on the first take, and Natasha beamed as she called cut. As soon as the cameras stopped rolling, Teddy held out his fist for a fist bump. He winked as our knuckles collided.

"Wonderful!" Gabby said as she ushered herself onto the set. "You two clearly have chemistry."

Did we? The kiss we'd just filmed utterly lacked in chemistry as far as I could tell. And maybe that was for the best—clearly whatever had happened between us on the back porch had been nothing but temporary insanity. I mentally patted myself on the back as the crew adjusted the cameras and lighting for the next part of the scene. I'd been all worked up over nothing.

When the set was ready, Teddy and I were given the signal to disrobe. I averted my gaze, focusing on removing my own clothes in the least awkward way possible. I wasn't sure which was going to be more embarrassing: stepping out of my pants to reveal my padded thong or pulling off my shirt to reveal my stickered boobs. Deciding not to overthink it, I yanked them both off quickly, before reaching up to make sure I hadn't knocked my wig out of place.

Sensing eyes on me, I finally let myself look in Teddy's direction. He was staring, his eyes glazed and mouth slightly ajar, and not at my face. I wanted to say something, tease him about letting his eyes wander. But I couldn't make myself open my mouth—I liked feeling his eyes on me, like he was devouring me with his gaze. Like he was hungry.

"Ready?" Gabby laid a hand on my shoulder and I jumped.

Teddy's eyes snapped away from my body and he turned away, both of our cheeks flushing.

"Yes." I cleared my throat. "Sure am!"

"Fantastic. Let's head back into the kitchen."

Trying to forget the way Teddy had been looking at me, I forced myself into work mode as we approached the table. Gabby walked us through the choreography, and Teddy and I gave feedback as necessary. Luckily, since it was such a short scene, it was fairly straightforward. After our make-out sesh on the counter, the camera would cut to us pounding away on the table for a few moments before it cut away again. Therefore, the only thing we needed to do was pound away.

"The movements are simple, but we also want to make sure everyone is as comfortable as possible," Gabby said. "That's why we have . . ."—she reached into a duffle bag that lay out of view of the cameras—"this little guy."

She removed her hand from the bag, clutching a half-inflated volleyball. Teddy and I started at it blankly, not comprehending.

Teddy leaned in close to my ear. "Is there a volleyball subplot I forgot about?"

I snickered, but managed to turn it into a cough.

"Look!" Gabby positioned herself near the edge of the table, placing the ball between herself and the wooden edge. "All of the movement, none of the contact." She pushed her hips against the ball, which had enough give to let her thrust without hitting the hard surface.

"Talk about a subplot," Teddy whispered.

I bit my lip, trying not to laugh. But then Teddy caught my eye, one eyebrow raised, and an ugly snort escaped from my nose. I clapped a hand over my mouth, realizing we were veering dangerously close to being unprofessional.

Thankfully, Gabby didn't notice.

"Ready?" She clapped her hands together. "Let's begin!"

Teddy and I tried to get serious, but unfortunately, climbing onto the table and placing the ball between us didn't help the situation. We tried one, two, three, then four and five takes, and neither of us could stop laughing. The sight of Teddy bouncing above me, face scrunched in concentration, as he thrust against a volleyball that was deflating more and more by the second was too much for me to take. I buried my face into his neck to try to muffle my laughter but failed, and Teddy collapsed on top of me, not even trying to hide his own amusement. We clutched each other, laughing, as Gabby watched with growing restlessness.

Finally, she clapped her hands, pausing us. "Why don't we try something different? Let's scrap the volleyball." Apparently catching herself, she paused. "If that's alright with both of you, of course."

Teddy looked down at me, a serious look on his face. "Quinn, do you consent to removing the volleyball?"

"Yes, Teddy." I bit my lip, trying my hardest not to laugh, the image of him furiously bouncing against the ball still strong in my mind. "I consent."

"Great." He leaned back on his heels and tossed the ball to the side. "It was rubbing me the wrong way, anyway. Literally." He looked at me, held my gaze a beat too long, his eyes smoldering. My giggles died on my lips and I struggled to suss out his meaning. Was he still just making a joke about the awkwardness of our previous takes? Or was he, too, thinking about how much closer our bodies would now be, minus one very big barrier?

We got back into position, Gabby hovering nearby as we arranged ourselves and made sure our modesty patches weren't visible to the camera.

"Here, let's change the angle." Gabby gestured for us to move a few inches to the right. "This way, your bodies will look much closer together than they are. Give you a bit more wiggle room, so to speak!" She ran through the movements with us once more now that the ball was out of the picture.

At least, of the volleyball variety.

When Natasha called action, it took us a moment to begin. I hadn't realized how much space the floppy piece of sports equipment had been creating between us, and I was a little taken aback by how intimate the shot now felt—Teddy's muscular legs tucked between my thighs, his chest pressed against my own.

"You ok?" Teddy whispered, his face hovering inches away. He looked different too. Like he was nervous.

I nodded. My eyes dropped to his lips and anticipation fluttered in my stomach, as though we hadn't just spent the last hour making out on the counter and grinding against the tabletop.

"Good." He shifted above me, bringing up his arm so he could cradle the side of my face in his palm. "You look super-hot, by the way."

I breathed a laugh, some of the tension escaping. "You look pretty good yourself."

Natasha called action, and then we started to move.

Just like he had in the takes before, Teddy gently lowered

his mouth to mine to begin the scene. But this time, it wasn't Teddy's character kissing my character. It was Teddy kissing me, his lips sinking into mine with an urgency that hadn't been there before. It was his hand caressing my cheek, his thumb running along my cheekbone, a bit rougher now. Then it was his hips pressing into mine, hungry, like he was using all his energy to restrain himself. And now it was me kissing him back, wrapping my arms around his shoulders to pull him closer, like I couldn't get enough. Like the cameras weren't there at all.

This time, it wasn't funny.

Logically, I knew that Natasha was still rolling, and that Gabby was watching us from somewhere nearby. But everything had become hazy, and the only thing I was paying attention to was Teddy's mouth, working against mine like a fever, and his hands—one tangled in my hair as the other gripped my hip. It was enough to tell me that whatever has passed between us on the back porch hadn't been a fluke. It'd been real. It *was* real.

Then he started to thrust, his hips snapping toward mine, and an aching heat surged through my body. Teddy seemed to agree, breaking his mouth away briefly to swear under his breath. His lower body wasn't close enough to actually press against me with every thrust, but I could still sense his long, thick hardness just out of reach.

I arched my back, desperate to be closer. Desperate for friction, for relief. But then I pulled back, stopping myself because this wasn't real, this was all fake, and Natasha was about to call—

"Cut!" She popped up from behind the camera, looking breathlessly pleased. "Wow, that was great. You guys were really—"

"Excellent! We're done?" Barely sticking around to hear Natasha confirm it was a wrap, I hopped off the table, grabbed my robe, and hurried off, suddenly desperate to get as far away as I could.

## Chapter Twenty-three

Every nerve ending in my body was on fire as I hurried up the stairs and down the hall. I slipped the wig off my head, wringing it in my hands as my feet hurried along the floorboards. It took me a moment to realize where I was headed—a spare room on the other side of the house that had been converted into a makeshift hair, makeup, and wardrobe space. Almost no one had used it since filming started, and I was pretty sure everyone had forgotten it was there. It would be a quiet, private space to catch my breath after whatever the hell had just happened between me and Teddy.

And what had happened had been unbearable—finally having him but not having all of him. His lips had been on my mouth, but never dropped down to my chest. His hands had dragged delicious pressure down my arms and up my ribcage, but never dipped below my waist. And the thrusting, God, the thrusting. Feeling him right there without any of the relief had been torture.

Thank goodness Natasha had gotten the take she needed, because I don't know how I could have lasted another second on that table.

Footsteps echoed behind me. I glanced over my shoulder—Teddy, following me, his breath ragged. Shit. I knew what could happen if we ended up in that room alone together. I should tell him that I needed some time alone and that he should, under no circumstances, continue following me.

But I didn't.

A few more steps and I was at the door. Without hesitating, I yanked the doorknob and walked inside. As I stood, chest heaving, I heard him cross the threshold behind me, close the door, and lock it with a click.

I didn't move a muscle, waiting to see what he would do. Wordlessly, he padded slowly across the floor. I waited, my skin on fire, every sense heightened. Then he was right behind me, the front of him pressing against the back of me, his hands gripping my hips.

"Tell me to leave," he whispered, his lips right below my ear, his breath sending tingles tripping up my spine. "I will."

For one brief, fleeting moment I considered it. I could stop it, tell him to get out, and listen as he left. But the words wouldn't leave my throat. I stood there, savoring the feel of his hands on my hips, his fingertips gripping me hard through my robe like it was taking everything in him to hold himself still. I pushed back slowly, pressing my ass against his groin. He gasped, a groan escaping his throat as he pulled me against him harder.

"Fuck." He swallowed. "You feel so fucking good and we still have our clothes on."

I almost did it, almost told him to get out before we could go any further. But I'd run out of excuses.

Spinning around, I crushed my lips to his. His mouth met mine with urgency, his arms wrapping around my waist and lifting me with ease until my legs wrapped around him and I was perched on his hips. I let my robe fall open, eager to have my bare skin against his. I was done ignoring whatever this was between us—I wanted him as close as possible.

"I've been fantasizing about this," Teddy said against my mouth as he sank onto the sofa with me still in his lap.

"Me too." He was in nothing but a pair of boxers he'd changed into, and I ground myself shamelessly against him, taking satisfaction in the groans I elicited from him.

"Hang on." Teddy broke the kiss to press his mouth against the base of my neck, giving my skin a gentle nip. "Let's get this out of the way." He ripped my robe from my shoulders, tossing it across the room, where it pooled on the floor. I didn't mind. I pressed our bare torsos together, letting my head fall back, and he trailed kisses along my collarbone. I could feel him erect beneath me, and I imagined what it would feel like to have him lay me down and push into me. Hopefully hard, almost rough—gentle strokes wouldn't be enough for the aching need between my legs that was growing more intense by the moment.

"Wait." Teddy pulled away, breathing hard. "I want to look at you." Gently, he pushed me forward, his eyes trailing down my body. Taking me in. Like I was a feast for his eyes. His hands ran up my belly and splayed across my chest, his thumbs curving under my breasts. I could tell my nipples were hard under the pasties, begging for attention, and I moaned as I let my head tip back.

"These are also in my way," he said, studying the circles of silicone, his eyes hazy with lust. One fingertip played with its edge, loosening the adhesive a touch.

I waited for him to continue, but he said nothing—just kept rubbing the perimeter of the material. Taking his time, enjoying teasing me. I made little noises of discontent, dying for him to get on with it and give me some relief. My breasts ached, needing him to massage them, to play with my nipples, which I swear could have cut glass.

But he didn't. He kept circling his thumbs before backing away to run a trail along the underside of my breast, then pressing closer, without ever giving me the attention I was begging for.

"Then take them off," I finally said through gritted teeth.

Teddy raised an eyebrow. "So impatient." He pulled me closer, pressing his lips, featherlight, to my collarbone. "Should I take them off slowly? Or quickly?" His hands trailed back down my ass, gripping me roughly for a second as his mouth moved to a spot behind my ear that made my eyes cross. "God, you're so beautiful. I can't keep my mouth off of you."

"Rip them off. Now."

Without another word, he obliged, finally—gripping the edges and tearing them off in two swift motions. The delicate skin stung, especially given how overstimulated and sensitive every square inch of my body was feeling. But no sooner had the material been ripped away than Teddy's mouth met the hard, sensitive point, his thumb massaging the other, and my head fell back with the sheer force of relief. God, his mouth was amazing, soft and wet and firm and moving on my breasts in a way that made me ache for it on other parts of my body.

I whimpered as I once again ground against him, feeling like I might explode.

"Do you have a condom?" Teddy's voice was husky in my ear, his lips moving against my neck as he spoke.

I pulled away, the lust lifting just enough that I could reply. "Seriously?" I motioned to the grand total of five square inches of fabric covering my body. "Where exactly would I be hiding it?"

He groaned, pressing his forehead between my breasts. "I figured—I just didn't want to believe it."

"My trailer?" I tried to imagine pulling myself together enough to slip past crew members without them thinking I was in the middle of some kind of cardiac event.

Teddy shook his head. "Too far away."

"Unfair." I rubbed myself into his lap again, savoring his hard thickness. "But you're right. Shit." I pulled back, trying to catch my breath and calm my heart rate. "You're right. We need to stop."

"Stop? I don't think so." Teddy gripped me by the hips and swung me off his lap, turning me around and depositing me onto the sofa cushion. He kneeled on the ground, staring up at me with lust-glazed eyes. "Can I?" His thumb worked under the strap of my thong.

The way he was looking at me, like I was a work of his art he was lucky to be experiencing, made my inner thighs clench.

"Yes," I gasped, unable to get the words out fast enough. "Yes please."

"Thank God."

Just as quickly as he'd removed my pasties, he tore off the thong—sending it sailing somewhere across the room. Where, precisely, I did not care. Because a moment later, my thighs were pressed along the sides of his face, and his mouth was on me, and everything beyond the precise sensations of his tongue became suddenly, wholly irrelevant.

Dear God. Men had gone down on me before, but not like this, like I was dessert he was both savoring and eager to finish at the same time. He ran his tongue up me slowly before centering on my clit, his tongue swirling and flicking. The sensation was utterly, deliciously divine. Each warm, wet stroke sent me dangerously, dizzyingly close to the edge.

"Teddy," I moaned, reaching a hand down to twine through his hair, to feel his head between my legs. "There. Don't . . . don't stop. Shit." My pleasure was tightening, twisting into a peak that was rapidly mounting. "I'm close." My voice was hoarse. "Close. Fuck."

*Not yet*, I thought. I didn't want this to end. I gasped, slapping a hand down on the couch next to me and squeezing the fabric.

"Hey." Teddy let go of my thigh and grappled for my hand. "Stay with me," he murmured, squeezing it. And then, instead of licking me, he took my clit in his mouth and sucked, gently, once and then twice.

That did me in. I came, so hard and so long I saw stars. The waves of pleasure pulsed through me and didn't stop, pounding for what seemed like an eternity. I must have let go of his hand at some point because when I finally started to come down, I was holding my own head in my hands and Teddy was climbing onto the sofa next to me.

"Holy shit," I breathed, pushing myself up so I could rest my head on his chest. "That was incredible."

Grinning, he wrapped an arm around my shoulder, pulling me close. "And to think you said we should stop."

I let my eyes droop closed, my entire body exhausted and boneless. "I'm not wrong very often. But that was definitely the worst idea I ever had."

## Chapter Twenty-four

Holy shit. I did that. We did that. Teddy had laid me down, made me come with his mouth, and asked for nothing in return. And that suction maneuver he'd done with his tongue? I was absolutely ruined for any person I'd be with in the future.

I hadn't been able to bask in my post-orgasmic bliss for long. After coming back down to earth, I'd remembered that filming wasn't over for the day—and soon people would notice we were missing. Especially with Natasha eager to make up the day that we'd lost to police questioning the cast and crew.

The following twenty-four hours were filled with back-to-back shoots, but I still couldn't turn off the horny replay in my head.

My suspicions had been correct—Teddy was more skillful with his tongue than any mortal had the right to be.

"Look up." Mara was staring at me expectantly, eyelash curler in hand. I hadn't even noticed that she'd spun me around and that I was no longer facing the mirror in the makeup trailer. I obeyed, holding as still as possible.

Mara was mad at me. The night before, I'd forgotten—again—that we'd made plans, this time to get coffee and dessert at the hotel's restaurant. I'd been so exhausted from the day's filming and so distracted from replaying my hook up with Teddy that it had completely slipped my mind until I got her text asking me where I was—eight hours later, when I woke up this morning.

I'd spent the day trying everything to get back in her good graces: peace offerings of onion rings and wine, a new romance novel based on thinly disguised Reylo fan fiction, and two separate bouquets of flowers delivered to her trailer. Nothing had worked. She'd dumped the wine down the drain, trashed the onion rings, and shredded the flowers right in front of me. (Although she did keep the book.)

There was only one option left: sex gossip.

"I guess you don't want to hear what happened between me and Teddy yesterday." I sighed tragically.

Mara swiped extra mascara onto my lashes. "Nope. I'm good."

"I see." I obediently kept my eyes trained on the ceiling. "Too bad. I don't have anyone else to tell about the best orgasm of my life."

Mara's eye twitched. She pressed the curler to the base of my lashes, helping the falsies stick to my real ones. "Unfortunate."

"A real talented tongue on that one."

Finally, Mara's resolve crumbled. She threw down the eyelash curler and leaned in close. "Tell me everything."

So I did.

"Oh my God, finally." She retrieved the eyelash curler from the floor and cleaned it before returning to my lashes. "Have you guys talked about it? What did he say?"

"No."

"Quinn! You need to talk to him."

"Why?" I asked stubbornly, blinking as she released one set of lashes and started on the other. "Weren't you the one encouraging a friends-with-benefits situation?"

"Yes, but—"

"He told me himself he's not a relationship guy, and I'm not in the market for anything serious, either. So what is there to talk about?"

"Healthy communication never hurt anyone." Done with my lashes, Mara moved on to dusting a hint of highlighter on my cheeks. "As long as you're ok with it not being anything more."

I sighed, ready to give her the same spiel I'd been telling myself all day. No matter how earth-shattering the orgasm had been, I was in no position to get involved with anyone. No matter how magical his hands and mouth felt against several different parts of my body.

"I'm just saying," Mara continued, "that friends with benefits rarely works without someone catching feelings."

"You were the one who told me to do it! The whole Ashton Kutcher and Natalie Portman thing!"

Mara stared at me blankly. "Quinn, that's a movie."

"Oh my God." I rubbed my temples.

"I'm just saying, you should see how it goes." She held up her hands in surrender. "That's all."

"Absolutely not."

"You don't have feelings for him?"

"I . . ." I wanted to say no. But there was something else stopping me, an inkling that if I went any further with Teddy—if whatever was brewing between us continued to develop—that I wouldn't be able to put a stop to it. Because I hadn't just spent the last twenty-four hours thinking about the amazing ways he'd made my body feel. I was also remembering the way he'd reached for me as I was about to tip over into ecstasy—the way he'd gripped my hand like he was holding on for dear life and whispered, "Stay with me." The way we'd sung together in the car. The way he'd taught me how to breathe and stop the panic that took over my body the day Brent died. I'd felt so secure, so taken care of. So safe.

I thought hooking up with him would get it out of my system, but deep down I suspected it had done the opposite.

"No." Even I had to admit it sounded unconvincing.

Mara stared at me closely as she reached for the setting spray. "Alright. But you can't run away from love forever."

Chloe and I were killing it.

Everything cluttering my head had cleared as soon as the cameras started rolling. The two of us nailed shot after shot, and even Natasha couldn't find anything to nitpick—which was really something considering the mood she'd been in since the representatives from the production company had shown up to start their investigation.

In the scene, our characters are searching for an old book that holds the secret to defeating the witch once and for all. It had all my favorite components: snappy dialogue, creepy atmosphere, intense lighting, and some good old-fashioned gore.

"What's that?" The cameras pulled in tight as Chloe pointed to the ceiling, trembling.

Slowly, making sure Natasha had enough time to get the shot, I tilted my head up toward the dark ceiling of the library, my eyes creeping up the shelves as candlelight sent shadows flickering across the dusty books. For a moment, I acted like I saw nothing. But then, a crew member perched high above on a ladder dripped something from a syringe and it landed squarely on my cheek. A single drop of blood. Next to me, Chloe had the same red liquid dribbling onto her hair.

And then, the ceiling caved in—sending a dead body plummeting onto the floor.

Not really, of course.

The set crew had rigged a false ceiling that could hold a fake dead Brent along with copious amounts of corn-syrup-based blood that would come spilling out. And it worked, magnificently. All the camera caught was the illusion of the ceiling collapsing under the weight of a corpse, miraculously on the first take.

I waited a beat as the camera lingered on the body. And then I filled my lungs and screamed, loud enough to make my throat ache in protest. Loud enough to fill the room with its shuddering vibration.

"Cut!" Natasha popped up from behind the camera. She looked tired, worn, but vaguely pleased. "We got it."

Grinning, Chloe held up her fist. "Nailed it."

Catching my breath, I bumped my fist into hers. "You were fantastic. You're bringing such an interesting edge to your character."

"You think so?"

"Definitely." I reached for a towel provided by one of the

PAs and wiped the fake blood off my face. "I loved the way you play up her ditziness, but at the same time you can tell there's a deeper side to her. So layered."

She beamed. "Thanks! I was trying to channel your performance in *School of the Lost*, when you played the demon cheerleader."

I was surprised she knew that one. It was the second movie I'd ever starred in, and while reviews had been good, it hadn't exactly been a blockbuster at the box office. Although maybe I shouldn't have been surprised—over the past week, Chloe had consistently proven she was a true lover of horror, and talented to boot. If this movie succeeded, she might be the perfect person to take my place in Hollywood.

"You know what, I can see that." I ran the towel down my neck, knowing I would need an extra-long shower later to remove all the prop blood. "We should get coffee before you film your last scene. I'd love to stay in touch."

"Definitely! I'll text you." She smiled and bounced away, likely eager to get out of her bloody costume.

Pushing through the house, saying goodnight to the crew as I squeezed past camera operators and boom handlers, it occurred to me that this might be the last time I had this feeling after a scene. The last time I was filled with adrenaline after a director told me I'd nailed it. The last time I felt that particular brand of satisfaction after portraying a certain emotion just right.

The last time I felt like I was doing my character's story justice.

It gripped me with a sudden pang of sadness. Instead of feeling relieved that my career was coming to an end, I was starting to feel regret. It was hard to imagine that I'd never be on another movie set, that I'd never get to workshop another scene with a cast mate. I wouldn't miss the fame, but I'd miss the storytelling. And even if I thought Chloe would do a great job taking over the roles I used to take—and even though she totally deserved it—it was hard not to feel a pang of longing, of something edging into jealousy, when I imagined it.

I pushed the thought away. It was late, after midnight. I was tired. After I got back to the hotel, I could get a nice shower and climb into bed. I had tomorrow off, so I'd even be able to sleep in. Heaven.

Winding my way through the parlor, I stopped short when I found Teddy waiting for me at the bottom of the stairs. He looked like something straight out of a movie—staring at me through the throngs of cast and crew members filing in and out of the front door, waiting patiently with his hands in his jeans pockets and a small smile on his lips.

Butterflies swarmed in my stomach. What was he doing here?

He gestured to my hairline as I approached. "You still have some . . ."

Oh God, I was still half covered in blood. I looked like Carrie after the pig's blood incident—hopefully with less crazy eyes.

"They're not trying to squeeze in another scene tonight, are they?"

Teddy shrugged. "I just wanted to watch. You mentioned being excited about shooting it—how could I pass it up?"

My cheeks burned. "I said that a long time ago."

"I remembered."

There it was again, that fizzy, bubbling feeling telling me this is something special.

"Quinn!" Julian, the head of the wardrobe department, was hurrying toward us, nearly running into a PA who was wheeling a cart of props through the foyer in the process.

"What's up?"

"I need you to think hard. We're missing one of your wigs."

I stared at him blankly, trying to figure out what he was talking about. "Sorry, what?" A hand strayed to my head, where a wig covered in fake blood was most definitely secured.

"One of your wigs!" He waved his arms in frustration. "The things you wear on your head? We noticed earlier today that one of them is missing."

I wracked my brain, trying to remember how on earth I could have lost one of them. I hadn't shot anything earlier that day, and yesterday . . .

Oh.

My cheeks reddened as I remembered exactly where my wig was. I'd taken it with me after Teddy and I filmed our sex scene on the table, and once Teddy had followed me to the spare room, I'd thrown it . . . somewhere.

"Uh, I think I know where it might be. Can you give me a minute?" I shot a look to Teddy, who wrinkled his brow in confusion.

"Of course. Just make sure you find it." Julian marched off, his eyes already searching for someone or something else as he hurried away.

I immediately grabbed Teddy's arm. "You're helping me find it."

"Jeez, you could ask nicely."

"Considering you played a pretty big role in distracting me yesterday . . ." I stared at him pointedly.

"You had it with you?"

"You don't remember seeing it in my hand?"

"I definitely wasn't looking at your hands."

"Alright, well." I headed for the stairs. "Let's go."

We tiptoed up the stairs, down the hall, and into the spare room, which was thankfully as empty as it was the day before. I closed the door behind us, leaving it open a crack, and turned on the light.

The room was just as we'd left it, and there were only so many places I could have thrown the pile of synthetic hair. As I glanced around, I tried not to lose myself in memories—how he'd come up behind me, gripping my hips with need. Or how he'd splayed me on the sofa before burying his face between my legs. The way he'd moaned when he did it.

I shook my head, wiping away the images. Teddy was already peering around, clearly unaffected by what had happened here between us.

"You start on that side, and I'll take this one," I said, moving toward the far corner. It was unlikely that I would have tossed it behind the TV that had inexplicably been parked there, but you never knew. Maybe my arm was extra powerful when I was horny.

"Roger," Teddy said. He moseyed over to a clothes rack, eyeing the garments that hung from the rail.

"I guarantee it's not hanging there."

He raised an eyebrow. "Have you looked already?"

"No, but I know for a fact I did not take the time to hang it up." I bent to peer behind an armchair that looked like it was from the 1970s.

"And why's that?"

I didn't have to see his face to know he was smirking, so I promptly ignored him. If I wedged myself completely behind the chair, I could claim plausible deniability. And if I found the wig, even better. But all I found was dust bunnies.

"We haven't talked about it, you know." He said it softly, all the joking and teasing out of his voice.

I froze, still wedged behind the armchair. He wanted to talk about this now? I finished scooting out from behind the chair, praying I'd misheard. He was still next to the clothes rack, fiddling with a hanger.

"Do we need to?" I kept my voice light. Casual. Not at all panicky.

"I don't know. I guess not. I had a good time, though."

My heart clenched. I'd had a good time, too. Of course I had. But talking about it made it real, and if it was real, then it would have consequences. Frantically searching for a way to change the subject, I noticed a small piece of wood stuck in his hair.

"Do you have a wood chip on your head?"

Teddy's hand swiped over his hair, quickly finding the offending splinter. "Oh. Yeah."

I waited for him to elaborate. He did not. "Why?"

"I went to a woodworking class today."

"A woodworking class? They have those?"

"Sure they do." Teddy turned his attention to a large chest

that looked like it'd crossed the ocean in the days of the *Titanic*. "Haven't you ever felt the urge to make something out of wood?"

Sidestepping the obvious innuendo, I moved to the sofa. "Can't say that I have. Is this an urge you feel regularly?"

"It's relaxing. And it takes my mind off things. You can't be anxious about making a phone call when you're trying to make sure you don't saw your finger off."

I laughed. "That's true. What did you make today?"

"Just a picture frame. They were only offering a beginner's class."

"So you're an expert, then?" I teased.

"I wouldn't say that." He smiled, obviously pleased. "But I have been doing it since I was, like, six."

"Six? I didn't know woodworking tools were approved to be used by children."

"Oh, they're definitely not. My grandpa kept catching me sneaking into his shed to play with his tools and decided it'd be easier to teach me how to use them safely than to teach me how to leave them alone." He chuckled. "My mom hated it. She was so pissed when she came to pick me up and found me using a saw that was almost as big as I was."

"I bet."

Teddy shrugged. "She eventually changed her tune. I made her a set of built-in bookshelves last summer."

"That's really cool. I had no idea you were talented like that." I was genuinely impressed. And I also understood. Crocheting wasn't the same as woodworking, but it helped me relax and it was always satisfying to complete a project.

"You just thought I was talented in other ways, huh?" There was that wicked grin again. "And hey, look what I found." Straightening from where he'd been bent over the chest, he stood—with my very disheveled-looking wig in hand.

"Oh my God, thank you." I rushed over, reaching out to grab it. But at the last second, he stretched his arm straight above his head, sending the hairpiece very much out of my reach. I tried to jump and grab it, but to no avail.

"Hey!" I braced myself against his shoulder for leverage as I tried one more time, but he just stretched his arm even further.

"Tell me if you had a good time the other day. Here, with me."

"No, it's irrelevant."

"Or you'll have to go tell Julian you couldn't find your wig." He crooked a finger and used it to tip my head up towards his. "And do you want to have to do that?"

I stared at him, trying to suss out if he was serious. He was smiling but he also didn't budge, his eyes boring into mine like a dare.

"Why do you want to know so bad?"

"That might have been my best performance. I need the feedback."

"Oh, come on. Your best ever?"

"Definitely. I don't pull out those moves for just anyone."

He'd lowered his arm, the wig very much within reach, but I'd once again forgotten about it. Not just anyone. I hated to read into those words, but they were already making my heart squeeze.

"I had an ok time," I finally admitted. I wanted to tell him that

I'd had a fantastic time, an other-worldly good time, actually. But of course, I couldn't.

"Just ok?" Teddy dropped the wig on the floor, placing his hands on my hips instead, drawing me closer ever so slowly.

My whole body hummed, feeling like it was fizzing and melting at the same time. I looped my arms around his neck automatically, allowing our bodies to press together. The cocky expression on Teddy's face was gone, his eyes darkening as he looked down at me. Maybe Mara was right. Would it be such a bad thing to give in and enjoy myself? Shooting would only take a few more weeks, and after that I'd be gone. Hasta la vista, baby.

In the meantime . . .

Feeling reckless, I closed the space between us, pressing my lips to his. I was done resisting, done pretending like I didn't want this. He immediately deepened the kiss, grabbing my ass and lifting me so my legs looped around his waist. I twined a hand in his shirt, trying to pull him closer than was actually possible. I was alarmed at how desperate I was, how desperate my entire body was, for his touch. He rolled my hips, rocking me against him, and I groaned into his mouth.

Footsteps.

Panting, we wrenched apart, glancing at each other wide-eyed. Rushing toward the door, I flicked off the light, shrouding us in darkness. Teddy crept up next to me, our shoulders pressing together as we leaned toward the door to listen.

It took me a moment to focus, trying to clear my brain from its sexually aroused fog. But once I calmed my breathing enough to listen properly, I immediately recognized the voice. It was

Audrey, speaking in a hushed tone, like she was trying to avoid being overheard. She paced the hallway, feet rumbling up and down, up and down the floorboards.

" . . . don't need to worry, Mum," she said in her posh British accent. "Everything's going fine." A pause. "Yes, I saw the article."

I winced. The local paper had run a letter to the editor written by a member of the catering company claiming Brent's death wasn't an accident. Which, no shit. It had put Natasha in such a bad mood that she'd snapped at a PA earlier that morning for asking her if she needed a cup of coffee.

"It's a relief he's gone, honestly. He was fit, but he was a bit of a wanker. He even . . ." Her voice became inaudible as she wandered away.

"'Fit'?" I mouthed to Teddy.

"It's British for hot," he whispered.

"I didn't know you spoke British."

He shrugged. "I've hung out with a couple girls from that *Love Island* show. A lot of them are Brits."

I frowned. I didn't want to think about Teddy hanging out with hot British women. Or, sorry, fit British women. If the past twenty-four hours had taught me anything, it was that Teddy had a pretty loose definition of the phrase "hanging out." But before jealousy could fully rear its non-fit head, Audrey's voice drifted back into earshot.

" . . . no, nobody suspects anything, not . . . Oh, sorry." She cleared her throat, and when she spoke again, her accent was gone—she now sounded decidedly un-British and instead straight out of the American Midwest. "Is that better? It's become such a habit. What was I saying? . . . Oh, yeah. The director is so damn worried about falling behind schedule, she wouldn't notice—"

My head snapped toward Teddy, whose own eyes had grown wide. Where had her accent gone? Had she been faking it this whole time? And what was the person on the other end worried people would suspect? I pressed myself closer to the wall, straining to hear better.

"No, I know. I know. No one's going to find out though, I promise." Her steps picked up again, this time heading our way. She was now dangerously close to our hiding spot, so close that if she stopped she would surely hear us breathe. I peeked through the crack in the door, unable to resist.

"That's an idea," Audrey continued. "Anywho, I've got to get going."

I strained my eyes in the dim light, holding my breath as Audrey got closer. She reached up to swipe the hair out of her face as she passed, and there on her wrist, I saw Trevor's friendship bracelet. The one his niece had made him.

The one that had been missing when he died.

"Please stop worrying. I'm keeping it under wraps." Audrey gave a little laugh. "Mmm hmm. Bye-bye."

My heart pounding, I listened to her descend the steps to the floor below. The conversation had been barely five minutes, but we'd learned a lot.

Audrey had been faking her accent.

There was something Audrey had to worry about people being suspicious of.

And Audrey possessed a missing piece of Trevor's property, something he wouldn't have let go of willingly.

I backed away from the door, shooting Teddy a look. His mouth was a grim line and his forehead was furrowed, suggesting he'd also seen what I had. Suddenly, I didn't want to be anywhere near Audrey.

## Chapter Twenty-five

Something was definitely wrong with Audrey.

It was the next morning, and we had started filming one of the longest sequences in the movie. The three college students who remained—me, Teddy, and Chloe—were preparing to make their first attempt to defeat the witch. They'd ultimately fail, of course, and Chloe's poor character would meet her demise via a spell that mummified her from the inside out. It was pretty gnarly and would mark the end of act two, with only two of the main cast left.

It was a complex scene, but the plan was to start with a few simple shots: my character fetching the potion from where we'd hidden it under the sink, Teddy rigging together a makeshift shelter from the kitchen table and chairs, and Chloe pouring salt around the perimeter to create a circle of protection in preparation for Audrey, as the witch, to arrive and wage her attack.

Even before we started filming, no one seemed to want to be there. Teddy was distracted, screwing up the blocking twice by grabbing the wrong set of chairs. Chloe's energy was muted, with none of the verve she usually brought to set. Even the crew were dragging their feet, needing multiple reminders of the time as they prepped the set.

Natasha, especially, looked haggard from her long meetings with reps from the production company late at night. Dark circles ringed her eyes, and her usually perky hair was lying flat and greasy. Her energy seemed sapped—the only time she spoke was to snap at people.

I didn't blame anyone for feeling off. In the days since Brent's death, the vibes on set had only gotten stranger. Darker. Members of the cast and crew alike were constantly on edge, suspicious. The strange noises in the house had grown more frequent: odd groans and scurrying in the walls. Things had gone missing from my trailer—a chunky gold ring here, a marked-up script there—enough for me to notice but not be sure whether they were taken or just misplaced.

I couldn't shake the feeling that someone was lurking around, unseen and undetected. And even though the police still hadn't found hard evidence to the contrary, no one believed Brent's death had been an accident, and more and more were starting to whisper about Trevor, too.

So, everything considered, I understood why Natasha was out of sorts. But my empathy dissipated once cameras started rolling.

First, she accused me of closing the kitchen cabinet too aggressively after retrieving the potion. Then she made Chloe reshoot her portion of the scene, claiming the salt circle wasn't smooth enough. She completely unloaded on Teddy, yelling at him for not stacking the chairs on the table in the precise way she wanted. And Audrey couldn't even creep in the background without reprimand. Apparently, she needed to "lurk with more energy."

By the time we wrapped, we were all in rotten moods, and I felt bad that Chloe and Audrey had to come back after lunch while the rest of us had the afternoon off.

Relieved to get out of the house and away from its oppressive vibe, Mara and I set up a picnic on the lawn, inviting the others to join us. Nobody wanted to eat at the designated tables, with the image of Brent collapsing and asphyxiating to death still potent in our minds. The weather was gorgeous—sunny but crisp with a slight breeze rustling the leaves—and we stayed even after Chloe and Audrey returned to set to continue filming their scene.

We sipped warm apple cider out of our thermoses, decompressing after the stressful morning. Teddy hooked one arm around my bent leg, anchoring me tight against him as he lazily rubbed my calf. The gesture was subtle but intimate, making me feel safe and noticed in a supremely cozy way.

Unfortunately, Mara noticed, too. She immediately clocked our entwined limbs, a smirk slowly spreading across her face.

"Wow, you sure ate your food fast, Teddy," she said, despite the fact that we'd all finished our lunches at least fifteen minutes ago. "Do you . . . like eating?"

I narrowed my eyes, knowing exactly where she was going with this.

Teddy, however, was nonplussed. "Sure, I guess so."

"Interesting. What would you say . . . is your favorite thing to eat?"

This was getting ridiculous.

"You mean my favorite food?" Teddy asked.

"Sure, something like that." Mara winked exaggeratedly. "I was thinking maybe it was—"

Before she could finish her thought, a barrage of shouting came from the house, loud enough to make us stop and listen. I was thanking the powers that be for the interruption when the yelling continued, getting louder until the front door banged open. It was Chloe, tearing out the front door. Audrey came next, grabbing at Chloe's sweater and yanking at the fabric, trying to pull Chloe back into the house. Chloe fought back, prying at Audrey's fingers as she scrambled to get away. They nearly sent Scott, who was just trying to transport a crate of props into the house, tumbling over the railing as they grappled on the porch.

"Hey!" Teddy yelled, as Mara and I stared.

Audrey started at the sound. Seeing us, she immediately let go of Chloe and hurried back into the house. Now alone, Chloe collapsed onto the porch swing, her arms wrapped around herself as she started to cry.

"What the fuck just happened?" Mara stared at Teddy and me, looking as shocked as I felt.

I said nothing, unable to move as I listened to the sad sounds of Chloe whimpering across the lawn. This sudden display of violence, combined with the phone call the night before, didn't make sense with the Audrey I'd known, who was always calm and polite and agreeable, even if she wasn't terribly outgoing.

*No one's going to find out though, I promise*, she'd said on the phone.

"Poor thing," Mara said, tutting to herself. "I'm going to go see if she's ok." She put down her cider and stood to leave. As soon as she was out of earshot, I turned to Teddy.

"We have to figure out what's going on with Audrey."

He nodded. "When?"

I shivered, a feeling creeping in that if we didn't figure out what was going on, there would be another victim. Soon.

"Tonight."

"I think he's coming," Teddy whispered.

Trying not to be obvious, I tilted my head a few degrees so I could see the entrance of the hotel's bar. But instead of a grizzled older man, it was a visibly younger guy, of a completely different body type, who happened to be wearing a similar ball cap. "Nope, not him. You see him every day—how do you not know who we're looking for?"

"He's not the one I'm usually looking at." Teddy raised an eyebrow and grinned at me suggestively.

I rolled my eyes, even though I was secretly pleased. "You're ridiculous."

After filming wrapped, Teddy and I had beat a hasty retreat back to the hotel. We knew that most nights, Scott visited the bar for a single pint of beer before he retired for the evening. As props master, Scott was constantly on set, shuttling props back and forth and consulting with the crew about what was needed the following day. He was so omnipresent that he blended into the background—and he seemed to like it that way.

If anyone had overheard anything about what happened between Audrey and Chloe, it'd be him.

"Move over, I need a better view." I switched to the opposite side of the booth, sliding in next to Teddy so I could watch for Scott. Clearly, Teddy wasn't going to be very helpful.

"I was wondering why you were all the way over there." He snaked an arm around my back, tucking me in close. "This is much better."

Usually, I'd be paranoid about someone seeing us, but the booth was hidden away in a far corner and the place was vacant, the bartender focused on wiping down glasses across the room. I closed my eyes, resting my head against his firm shoulder as I let myself be held. He rubbed a thumb along my hip, the small gesture wiping away the stress of the day as our breathing synched. It was nice, letting my guard down even for just a moment.

"I've wanted to get my hands on you all day," Teddy whispered in my ear. His hand snuck down the waistband of my leggings, fingertips stroking the soft skin of my leg. A quiet sigh escaped my lips, and I buried my head in his shoulder to muffle the sound. It was ridiculous, how quickly the slightest touch from him made my heart start to race. "Why'd you wait so long?" I murmured.

"Because I'm a stupid, stupid man." Teddy shifted his hand, his fingers now grazing the crease of my inner thigh. The rest of the room seemed to dissolve as his touch dragged up and down, slowly. My blood simmered; every atom of my attention focused on the strokes creeping ever so slightly higher.

Across the room, Scott entered the bar.

I jumped, jolting to attention. I smacked Teddy's arm and pointed, and when he saw the older man, he groaned.

"Great timing, Scott," he grumbled, removing his hand from my pants.

"Truly."

"Come to my room after this." Teddy leaned in, his teeth lightly grazing my earlobe. "We can pick up where we left off."

"Definitely. Yes." I grinned, already counting down to the moment we finished with Scott and could escape to his room. But a moment later, Teddy cursed under his breath.

"Shit. My brother." He ran a hand down his face. "I have to call him later."

My heart sank. "Oh. Really?"

"Usually I'd reschedule, but I think something happened today. He was upset when he texted me earlier." Teddy closed his eyes, his face falling. "Damn it, I'm so sorry."

"It's ok, really." I rubbed his arm, trying to hide my disappointment. "Another time."

"Scott really owes me now."

"Well, hopefully he'll repay us with information. Let's go."

At first pretending not to see him, Teddy and I chose seats down the bar. We placed our orders with the bartender—a beer for Teddy and a Jack and ginger for me—and slowly nursed our drinks as we discreetly kept an eye on Scott. His face long and tired, he kept his eyes down as he sipped a draft beer.

"He won't look at me," I whispered, keeping my voice just low enough for Teddy to hear. "What else am I supposed to do?"

"Here, let me take care of it."

"No!"

He stared at me pointedly, and I let out a pained sigh. I'd forgotten—I was supposed to be "trusting him" or whatever.

"Fine," I conceded. "Just don't screw it up."

Teddy shifted in his chair. "Hey, Scott!" he boomed, his voice unnaturally loud.

I winced, but Scott didn't seem fazed. He looked up, slightly surprised, and raised his glass to us.

"An eventful day today, huh?" Teddy tried. Remembering the way Audrey attacked Chloe, I thought that was putting it mildly.

Scott raised a bushy eyebrow. "You two still doing your little investigation?"

"Um." I hadn't expected Scott to peg us quite so quickly. "Kind of."

"Never been on a set with so many problems." Scott shifted in his seat. "All these kids and their dramas."

"What do you mean?" I tried to sound casual as I sipped my own drink.

"Oh, no." Scott twisted his empty glass by its base. "I'm not getting into all that."

My heart sank. I tried to catch Teddy's eye, disappointed. But he didn't return my look. Instead, his eyes were sparkling as he stared at Scott's empty glass.

"Hey, Scott," he called out. "Let me buy you a drink?"

Scott rubbed at a chip in the bar top, considering. "I shouldn't."

"Just one?"

Finally, he relented. "What are you buying?"

Teddy grinned. "You like Long Island iced teas?"

An hour later, the three of us were congregated at the end of the bar and far drunker than we should have been, especially considering we had to be up in less than five hours. Scott was on his third iced tea while Teddy and I had been careful to stick to just one. Still, the potent concoction combined with my first drink had me way tipsier than I would have liked.

" . . . don't appreciate how much work goes into making props." Scott dabbed a napkin at his temple, which had sprung a sweat. "Take that game of pool we filmed yesterday. Did you notice how quiet the balls were? The real ones make too much noise and make the sound guys grumpy."

"I did! How did you do it?"

I muffled a grin. I could almost guarantee Teddy had not, in fact, noticed how quiet the balls were.

"The secret was using racquetballs—they're soft and don't clack around. Then we just had to paint 'em and apply a layer of gloss, and you can't notice the difference until you pick them up."

"That's amazing! I never would have thought of that."

I listened to them talk, amused and more than happy to let Teddy take the lead. He'd known just the right way to get Scott to open up, and had even coaxed an honest-to-God giggle out of him when he'd complimented his skills at mixing fake blood.

" . . . just going to be a shame if it's all for nothing." Scott's face clouded. "Everyone's too busy keeping secrets instead of making sure the production doesn't get shut down."

My ears perked up. "Who's keeping secrets?"

"Everyone! Natasha's lying about the studio reps." He gestured to Teddy and me. "You two are sneaking around. Trevor knew something about Audrey, some big secret, but I don't know what."

Teddy and I locked eyes.

"What's going on with the studio?" I pressed.

"Hell if I know. But I don't think the visit is going well, despite what Natasha is saying." He took a long draw of his drink. "I think they're considering pulling the plug."

Alarm flared through my body. They couldn't cancel it—I wouldn't get paid. And I hadn't decided where I'd be living once I moved off Mara's couch, let alone what my backup plan for employment would be. I couldn't be broke on top of that.

"Why would they want to cancel the film?" Teddy asked.

"I don't know, but I hope for Natasha's sake they make a decision soon. The stress is bound to kill her. I thought she was having a stroke that first night, even before you two found Trevor."

"You saw her that night? I thought you were driving around looking for a new lamp?"

"Exactly. I didn't get back here until after midnight. She was at the bar, raving about how bad the day went. A member of the crew said she was here all night."

The implication hit my body like a shock wave. If Natasha had spent the whole evening at the bar, that meant she'd been nowhere near the crime scene. We could cross her off our list. She wasn't the killer.

"You said Trevor knew something about Audrey?" Teddy pressed, draining his glass.

"You two need to mind your own business." But even though Scott side-eyed us, I could tell he was secretly pleased. "I don't know what the big secret was. I just heard her on the phone, something about Trevor being onto her."

Another secretive phone call.

"Did she say anything else?" Teddy hiccupped. "On the phone."

KATIE BOHN | 260

"No." Scott drained his glass and stretched his arms over his head. "And I need to go to bed. I'm too old for this."

"One more?" Teddy teased.

"Hell no. If I feel like shit tomorrow, I'm coming after both of you." He got up and placed a tip on the bar top, wavering slightly.

"He's definitely going to feel awful when he wakes up," I said as he disappeared into the lobby. "Did he really need the third one?"

Teddy shrugged as he reached for the bill. "I'll make sure to bring ibuprofen for him."

"And maybe some Gatorade."

Teddy signed the bill and pushed it back toward the bartender. "At least we learned something. Worth it."

Yes, we had. Just not enough. I was willing to bet that Trevor had also figured out that Audrey wasn't being truthful about her identity.

Who was she? And was she willing to kill, to keep it a secret?

## Chapter Twenty-six

My dreams that night were full of shadows.

I was on set in the house, except I was alone. I moved from one room to another, each one filled with more fantastical set dressings than the one before. The dining room was made to look like a vintage circus, the second-floor bedroom set to resemble a Victorian greenhouse. I was alone, except for the creeping presence of something that hid in the dark corners. Something I couldn't see but that I was certain was coming after me. After blood.

My blood.

Waking with a start, it took me a minute to calm my racing heart. It had felt so real, like something had actually been after me. And then I realized with a start that it was true. A person who'd already proved capable of murder was after me.

I glanced at the time on my phone—time to get up. Chloe and I had made plans to grab coffee before she checked out of the hotel and headed to the airport. And considering her last day on set had included her being berated by the director and attacked by another cast mate, I doubted she wanted to stick around longer than she had to.

After quickly pulling on leggings and a sweatshirt with Candyman on it, I brushed my teeth and slipped out of my room. Starting down the hall, I heard the crying as soon as I rounded the corner. It was soft but unmistakable—and coming from Chloe's room.

Carefully, I pushed open the door and peered inside. Chloe sat on the bed, knees pulled to her chest as she cried into her arms. An open suitcase lay next to her, like she'd been in the process of filling it before collapsing into tears. Her makeup smeared and hair pulled up in a messy bun, she jumped when she noticed me.

"Oh!" She wiped her eyes. "I didn't know you were here already."

"Are you ok?" Mentally, I kicked myself. Of course she wasn't.

"Sorry, I was getting ready for our coffee date and it suddenly all hit me. This just wasn't how I pictured this movie going."

I laughed humorlessly. "Me either. Murder mysteries are supposed to stay in the script, not jump into real life."

"It's not just that." Chloe rubbed her eyes, smearing tears across her cheek. "This was supposed to be my big break and I did a shit job."

"What are you talking about? You absolutely didn't." I was being honest. Even before our scene together in the library, I'd been impressed by her acting chops.

"Natasha reamed me out yesterday."

I rolled my eyes. "Natasha reams everyone out. I think you did a great job. Yesterday and all the days."

"Yeah?"

I nodded. "It's not you. I know Natasha and I've never seen her act like this. I mean, did you hear how she went after Brent?"

At the mention of our former cast mate, Chloe burst into fresh tears. She was full-on wailing now, burying her head in her arms and heaving with sobs. It took me off guard. Brent's death had shaken me, too, but I wasn't about to cry over it.

"I didn't know you and Brent were so close."

Chloe lifted her head. "Well, according to him we weren't."

"What does that mean?"

She hesitated, hiccupping as she tried to slow her crying.

"It's ok, you don't have to tell me," I hurried to add.

Chloe took a deep, shaky breath. "I did something stupid. Really stupid."

"Oh?"

"I shouldn't have done it," she continued, "but . . . Brent and I were sleeping together."

"Oh," was all I could manage. "Since when?"

"The first night. On set, too, up in the attic." She laughed. "I know what you're thinking: wow, she moves fast."

"I didn't think that."

Instead, I was thinking that now we knew exactly why we'd found Brent's sweatshirt up there. That must explain why he had lied about being in the house that night—because he didn't want people knowing about him and Chloe.

What a dick.

"He broke up with me, you know," Chloe continued. "Two days

before he died. He said he wanted to 'keep his options open.'"
She made exaggerated air quotes with her fingers, twisting her
expression into one of mockery. "He was full of shit."

My heart tugged. If anyone understood the perils of trying
to date in this industry, I did. "Any guy who pulls a line like
that isn't worth it." Out of comforting words, I sat with her and
rubbed her back as she cried it out. When her sobs slowly died
down, she finally pulled away.

"I'm sorry, I don't know why I can't stop crying." She sniffled.
"Actors, you know?"

I nodded. "I do."

Chloe laughed weakly. "I think this might have put me off
acting for good."

"Don't say that. The movie's going to be huge, and you're
one of the stars."

I knew it was hypocritical—me, of all people, urging someone
not to give up. But I also understood the desperation to be
successful, the way the industry could work its hooks into you.
Since Scott told us that the production might be shut down, I'd
caught myself no less than three times having panicky thoughts
about the fallout: would people think it was my fault? Would
my reputation be irreparably damaged? Would anyone want to
hire me again?

I had to keep reminding myself that it didn't matter.

"Maybe." Chloe looked doubtful. "It just seems so cutthroat.
Like no one in this industry can be trusted."

"Like who?"

"Brent for one, Audrey for two." She ticked the names off on her fingers. "And if you want a real shock, check out the name Eerie Poodle when you get the chance."

Eerie Poodle? I made a note to look it up later. "Audrey coming after you like that did surprise me. What happened?"

Even though we were alone in her room, Chloe lowered her voice and leaned in close. "Do you know what I caught her throwing away right after Brent died? A bag of peanuts. That's why she came after me yesterday. Because I told her I'd seen."

"Did you tell the police?"

She shook her head, a silent no. "I was afraid." Her voice was barely audible. "I didn't want her to know I told anyone."

Before we could continue, my phone buzzed. I checked the screen—a text from Mara. It was a link to one of Austin's Instagram posts, a photo of him and his new girlfriend, who happened to be one of the biggest up-and-coming actresses in the biz. They were both topless in his palatial bedroom, the woman curved against Austin's chest as his tattooed arms held her close. Ugh, poor Mara. I closed the message, making a mental note to reply later.

Chloe noticed me checking the device. "Is that your man?" She grinned at my puzzled look. "Come on, I see the way you and Teddy look at each other."

My stomach sank. We'd been that obvious? "There's nothing going on between us."

"If you say so. Probably for the best. I wouldn't want my boyfriend going on another dating reality show either."

"What do you mean?" This was news to me. But then, I guess we hadn't talked about our plans for after the film. Why would we?

"He's filming that show over the winter, isn't he?" Chloe looked at me carefully. "That's what he told me when we had lunch the other day. *Love by the Stars*, I think it's called. Something about matching people up by their zodiac signs."

"Oh." I said, my throat weirdly thick. "Good for him."

I shouldn't have been surprised. That was the type of person Teddy was: a hot guy who enjoyed being famous for being hot on TV. I knew that whatever was happening between us had a firm expiration date. I knew that.

So why was my heart sinking?

"Thanks for trying to cheer me up." Chloe stood, dabbing at her eyes and reaching for her clothes to finish packing. "Now let's grab that coffee. I have to leave for the airport in an hour."

As we stepped into the hall, I pulled out my phone. I was dying to know who this "Eerie Poodle" was that Chloe had referenced. Google pointed me to the user's TikTok, a gossip account focused on spreading rumors about celebrities—one that I immediately recognized from my own experiences with media onslaught. I clicked on the profile photo, curious to see the face of whoever got their kicks from putting other people down.

It was a young man, tipping a bowler hat down to protect his face. And there on his wrist was a friendship bracelet, one that was starting to look very familiar.

## Chapter Twenty-seven

"What a prick. What a little snake." I was pacing my room, still fired up that evening from what I had learned about Trevor earlier in the day. "He had the audacity to pretend to be a fan when I met him."

"What a pathetic way to make a living." Teddy leaned forward on the sofa, resting his arms on his knees as he clenched his fists. "If he wasn't already dead, I'd sure as hell make him sorry he ever said a bad word about you."

Teddy had been even angrier than me when I cornered him on set to tell him about Trevor's double identity. Come to think of it, it was the only time I could remember ever seeing him angry.

"I'd say."

"It does make me more convinced Audrey did it, though," Teddy mused.

"True."

We'd spent the day analyzing every comment Audrey made and we even eavesdropped on another of her phone calls, but all we learned was that she was suffering from a persistent foot fungus and that her mother was on her fourth divorce.

"We know she's not actually British, which suggests she's hiding her identity," I pondered. "Trevor loved spreading gossip, so if he figured out who she really is, that might be motive."

"And Brent?"

"Now that, I'm not sure of." My phone dinged with an email— the next day's call sheet had arrived. "He was definitely harassing her on set less than an hour before he died. Maybe after getting away with killing Trevor, she'd gotten bolder?"

"Maybe." Teddy sounded distracted.

"Are you ok?"

He frowned at his phone, leg jiggling. "I don't know if I can do this. The scene tomorrow."

"Really? Which one is it?" I grabbed a copy of the script from the desk. It was the scene in which Teddy and I try to fend off another attack from the witch. It's a lot of action, and would require careful blocking, but nothing particularly difficult.

"I don't understand. What's the problem?"

Teddy snatched the pages away from me and stabbed at the offending line with his finger. "Look, right here. My character 'grabs a loose leg off a chair and hits an incoming spell so it veers away and ricochets off the wall.'"

I tried to understand, truly I did, but something wasn't clicking.

"Teddy, I'm still not getting it. It sounds like you have to hit the thing like a baseball. They'll have you hit a ball and CGI the effect in later."

"That's the thing!" He took a deep breath. "I'm scared of playing baseball."

I stared at him blankly. "What?"

"I know, it's dumb." He raked a hand through his hair, grabbing at it in agitation. "I had a bad experience in Little League when I was eight, and I haven't been able to hold a baseball bat since. There's no way I'll be able to hit that ball."

Wild theories ran through my head. Had he accidentally killed someone? Had someone nearly killed him? At . . . Little League?

"What kind of bad experience?"

"It was the third night of practice." His eyes glazed over as he spoke. "I'd been striking out, literally, every night before that. When it was finally my turn, I hit the ball on my first try. I was so excited when it went flying through the air. But then it went sailing straight into the coach's balls."

"Oh no."

"And all the kids started laughing, because nothing is funnier than someone getting hit in the balls when you're eight, right? But the coach was in a lot of pain! And I felt so bad. And no matter how much my dad helped me practice, I couldn't hit another ball the rest of the season."

The corner of my mouth twitched. "Baseball or testicle ball?"

"Both." Teddy's face cracked into a brief smile before crumpling again. "It's so lame. But now that it's in my head, I can't turn it off. I can't focus on practicing my lines, because all I can think about is either not being able to hit the ball on cue or that I do hit it but then I hurt someone again."

"Listen." I nudged his thigh with my foot. "There's a baseball diamond in town. If we head out now, maybe the lights will be on and we can practice."

"Yeah?"

"Sure. As long as you don't hit me in the, er, balls."

A wicked look spread across Teddy's face as he surely bit back a snarky comment. "Deal." He hopped off the bed and reached out his hand to help me up. "Let's go."

The field was only five minutes away, a little diamond tucked behind an elementary school on the edge of town. A single light was on above home plate, illuminating the bases and casting deep shadows into both the outfield and the dugouts. Tiptoeing onto the field, knowing we shouldn't be there, made me feel like I was back in high school—sneaking out after my parents were asleep and feeling that rush of freedom with an undercurrent of risk.

Although the risk here was, admittedly, pretty low. A slap on the wrist by local police was nothing compared to Puzzle Face himself looming in the doorway as you made your way back home at two in the morning.

"If we get caught, I'm letting you go down for this," Teddy said, like he was reading my thoughts. "I'm not ruining my pristine record for a game of catch."

"Pristine record?" I hopped into one of the dugouts, looking for a spare ball. "Lame."

"Just means I haven't gotten caught." He bent down and peered at me through the fence separating the field from the dugout, one eyebrow raised. "You're saying you do have a record?"

"Well, no."

"Lame."

"Touché." Grinning, I knelt in the dirt and ran my hand under the bench until my fingers brushed something round and smooth. "Found one!"

"I see a bat over there." Teddy jogged toward home plate as I headed to the pitcher's mound.

"I don't want to brag, but I'm pretty amazing at baseball." I scuffed the plate with my foot, making a show out of getting into position.

"Oh, yeah? How's that?"

"Tony Todd taught me when I was a kid. He guest-starred in one of the Puzzle Face movies."

"Wait, the guy who played Candyman?"

"The one and only."

Teddy shook his head as he choked up on the bat. "We had very different childhoods."

I grinned. "Alright, slugger." I wound my arm back, waiting. "You ready?"

Teddy tapped the bat on home plate. "Let 'er rip."

I wound my arm back and lobbed the ball gently toward home plate. It sailed perfectly toward Teddy, who . . . missed it completely.

"Aw, come on," I cracked. "I lined that up for you perfectly." But Teddy's mouth remained a grim line and he tightened his grip on the bat as he stared at his shoes. Even from where I stood, far away, I could sense his shoulders tightening and his jaw clenching. Maybe it wasn't time for jokes.

I grabbed the ball once again and tossed it as gently as I could. Once again, Teddy missed.

"Third time's a charm." This time, Teddy's bat made direct contact with the ball. It wasn't the strongest hit, but it went a few yards before skidding toward third plate.

"Woohoo!" I threw my hands in the air and cheered, jumping up and down in celebration. "You did it! Watch out, Hank Aaron! That's a baseball player, right?"

"Shh, you're gonna get us kicked out." But his face still broke out into a grin, and he jauntily sent the bat twirling into the air before catching it again.

We practiced for another twenty minutes, with Teddy steadily improving until we were confident that even if he wasn't ready to try out for any baseball teams, he'd at least be able to handle the scene the next day. He even hit the last ball so far that it sailed into the outfield. Ready to call it a night, I jogged off to retrieve it.

After plucking the ball out of the grass, I tipped my head to the sky. The night was startlingly bright—the moon big and beaming, the stars sparkling across the atmosphere. I never got to experience moments like this. LA didn't have these kinds of views for one, but I was also always so busy flitting either to and from sets and studios or on the way to one event or another. It was nice, enjoying the quiet like that. I sprawled onto the grass, taking it in. Maybe I could move to an area like this, where I could see the stars every night.

Footsteps swished in the grass behind me.

"You disappeared." Teddy stopped at my side, tilting his head to take in the sight. "Damn, that's a beautiful view." And then, he lay down next to me, tucking his arms behind his head.

"It is beautiful."

"Too pretty not to memorialize." He outstretched his arm, his phone camera facing us. "If that's ok?"

I hesitated. The idea of snapping a cozy photo of the two of us felt strangely intimate—it didn't feel like friends with benefits, it felt like something more. But Teddy's face was so hopeful, and deep down, I was curious to see what we looked like together.

"Ok," I relented.

Teddy inched closer and wrapped an arm around my shoulders. I nestled into the crook of his neck, inhaling his woodsy scent. He tapped the screen and the flash momentarily blinded us.

"Let me see!"

"So eager," he teased. He tipped the screen my way and there we were, overblown by the bright light. Usually, I didn't like myself in photos, but I liked this one. A small smile curved my lips and my eyes were closed like I was in bliss, my head nestled on his shoulder. Teddy had also avoided looking at the camera, gazing at me instead.

It was beautiful, I had to admit. We were beautiful.

As Teddy made sure the photo was saved, I nudged him with my elbow. "You're welcome, by the way. Childhood trauma conquered."

He chuckled, a low rumbling sound, but didn't say anything.

My brow crinkled. "You ok? You were great out there. You'll be fine tomorrow."

"It's not that."

"What's up?"

"I guess . . ." Teddy hesitated, visibly uncomfortable. "I wish my dad could have seen that, is all. He would have gotten a kick out of it."

I rolled onto my side. "He'll see the movie, won't he? And you can show him before it comes out. Maybe rustle up a game of backyard baseball. Or tee-ball, if you get nervous again." It was supposed to be a joke, but he didn't laugh. "Sorry, that was dumb. I didn't mean—"

Teddy shook his head. "No, it's just . . . My dad died. Like a week after the baseball thing happened."

"Oh my God." My stomach bottomed out as I regretted the dumb joke about tee-ball even more. I reached out to touch his arm, rubbing the firm muscle under the fabric of his hoodie. "I never would have tried to joke about that if—"

"How could you know? I don't talk about it much. Not because it's too painful, but because people tend to be weird about it. They either don't know what to say, so they say nothing, or they make a huge deal of it, and I wind up telling them that it's ok." He ran a hand down his face. "It's exhausting. So, I just don't bring it up."

I wanted to kick myself. Now the whole thing made a little more sense—of course losing his father would make the memories of his disastrous little league season all the more painful. Of course he would freeze up, having to think about all that trauma.

"I'm sorry. I probably fall under the camp of people who react badly."

"Not at all." Teddy turned to look at me, his face so close I could count his eyelashes. "I told you because I wanted to. I trust you."

Something stirred deep in my chest, a desire to assure him I was worthy of that trust. "How did it happen?"

He tilted his head to the sky, moonlight gleaming off his blue eyes. "A heart attack, out of nowhere, when he was at work. My mother picked me up from school during lunch. I remember I was in the middle of this awful bowl of chili. I could tell she'd been crying, but she wouldn't tell me why until we got home. Then we went to my grandmother's, and it's all a blur after that."

"That's terrible."

"You want to know the fucked-up thing? Sometimes I wonder if my mom and I would be as close as we are if he hadn't died. Not like I'm glad that it happened. It's just . . ."

"Something you think about," I finished.

"Yeah. Even when she had to juggle, like, three jobs she'd always make sure to be home to read me and my brother a bedtime story. Or if she couldn't, she'd stop by school the next day to have lunch with us. Looking back, it must have been so fucking hard. But somehow she made it seem easy. She always made us feel loved." His jaw tightened. "All I want is to make life easy for her now."

"She sounds amazing." My chest squeezed with aching affection. Teddy was so good. At that moment, I thought he was maybe the best person I'd ever met. "Were you close with your dad before he died?"

"He was my hero." Teddy laughed softly. "I'm sure all boys think that about their dads though."

"No, I think there are a lot of crummy dads out there. You were lucky." I pushed myself up on my elbow. "My dad, for example, is a murderer." I immediately cringed—there I was, making jokes again, and a bad one at that. But Teddy burst out with a laugh, and some of the tension ebbed from his body.

"That must have been so fun, seeing all that as a kid." He wrapped an arm around my shoulders and I rolled over to rest my head on his chest.

"Most of the time. I don't think my mom liked it. She was pretty eager to move away and have a more normal life, away from the industry." I traced his collarbone under his shirt. Maybe I was more like my mom than I thought. "But it's hard to beat going to movie premieres when you're seven or Mike Myers coming to your fifth birthday party."

"That must have been kickass."

"Yeah . . . it kind of makes me sad now, though," I admitted. "Thinking about those things."

"Why?"

"It's gone, isn't it? That magical sheen that makes everything sparkle when you're a kid, that makes it seem so perfect even when it isn't." To my horror, my voice was thickening and catching in the back of my throat. "Once you grow up, that's gone. And it makes you sad knowing that either things weren't as magical as they seemed at the time, or that you'll never feel that happy again."

"You're not happy?"

I hesitated. "Maybe. But growing up means everything looks a little grayer, don't you think?"

"No. Not everything." Teddy's voice was resolute. He picked up my hand, twirling our fingers together. "I see color in you."

We both fell quiet then, and something about the moment

was too real, cut too deep. I wanted to tell him that to me, he was technicolor. But I couldn't.

He rubbed his thumb along my shoulder. "Why does your childhood look grayer now?"

The familiar feeling of resistance starting to rise, the urge to clamp my mouth shut or change the subject. But then it did something strange. It started to crumble. To weaken.

"I'm quitting horror movies," I blurted. "After this one, obviously. But then I'm not going to make any more."

Teddy was quiet for a long moment, his fingers slowing on my shoulder while he processed. "I thought you loved them?"

"It's so many things. Like the tabloids spreading rumors and publishing my personal business. Or putting every fiber of yourself into an audition only for a director to say you're doing it wrong, even though you spent two months analyzing your character's background and motivation. For every high there's a dozen lows, and the constant rejection is so draining. Not to mention I don't even have an agent anymore."

"She obviously screwed up."

I smiled, grateful. "Thanks. But the reviews are demoralizing, too. You don't believe the good ones that say you did a good job. But the bad ones? Those you believe. And it's hard not to internalize someone saying my 'angular features are better suited for character parts than a leading lady.'"

"What does that even mean?"

"That I'm not classically pretty enough to lead a film."

"I . . . Sorry, what?"

I shrugged, not sure what else to say.

"That's complete bullshit." He huffed out a laugh. "You're gorgeous."

I squeezed his arm. "And to make it all worse, I haven't even told my dad."

"Seriously? Aren't you two super-close?"

I sighed. "It just never seems like the right time. Every time we talk, he'll bring up my career, or ask me what I'm planning to do next, or tell me how proud he is of my work. And how am I supposed to tell him then?"

"Ah yes, the dreaded proud parent," Teddy teased. "Do you think he'll be mad or something?"

"Not mad, exactly. Just disappointed, you know? Horror movies are our thing. They always have been. How can I tell him I'm quitting the thing that's always brought us together?"

"I get that."

"And what if he gets upset and then our entire relationship changes?" The anxiety was swelling again, the thought of ruining things, of things never being the same.

"Did you get mad when he retired from making movies?"

"No, of course not."

"Well, there you go. It's not like you can't still watch horror movies, right?"

I grinned. "You can pry the next *Conjuring* sequel out of my cold, dead hands."

Teddy used his thumb and forefinger to tip my chin up until I was looking at him. "He'll understand. I know he will."

I squeezed my eyes shut, my heart clenching painfully as I hoped he was right. The words were a balm, soothing an ache that had been in my chest for months. So many people in the industry looked at you but didn't see you. It was starting to feel like Teddy saw me.

When I opened them, Teddy's gaze had fallen to my lips. I didn't hesitate before I closed the space between us, pressing my mouth to his. He wrapped an arm around my waist and hauled me up, twisting until I was on top of him. I pressed my hands to either side of his face, deepening the kiss. It felt different this time—kissing not just for the pleasure of it, but because I wanted to be as close to him as possible, like I couldn't stand a millimeter of space between us. I wanted him, all of him, to envelop me completely.

It was intense. Probably too intense. Teddy was filming his last scene tomorrow. And then he would leave, and I would never see him again. He would go off to film his next dating show, and I would be . . . well, whatever I ended up deciding to do. Which was exactly the plan, I reminded myself. Exactly what was supposed to happen. What needed to happen. But I couldn't chase away the feeling of being cheated. Like I hadn't had enough time. I'd had no idea about his father—what else didn't I know about him? Probably a million things.

I pulled back, breaking the kiss. "Tell me something I don't know about you."

"What?" Teddy laughed, cupping my cheek in his hand as he brushed hair out of my eyes.

"Tell me something I don't know about you," I repeated, rolling over to snuggle under his arm. "I want to know everything."

"I got spat on by a llama once. Does that count?"

"Definitely. Tell me another."

I knew it was late. I knew my alarm would wake me up way

too soon once I finally went to sleep. I knew delving further into Teddy's world wasn't going to make saying goodbye any easier. But I didn't care. I wanted to soak it up, soak him up, when I still had the chance.

So we stayed. I learned he didn't lose his virginity until he was twenty-one, and he learned that I slept with my baby blanket until it disintegrated two years ago. We didn't leave until the horizon started to lighten with a hint of the morning sun, driving back to the hotel with hands entwined. We had two hours before we had to be in hair and makeup, and I knew taking a nap would only make me more exhausted and that filming would be grueling.

But as we said goodbye and I collapsed into my hotel bed, I knew it was worth it. He'd been worth it.

## Chapter Twenty-eight

Lungs burning, I burst out the back door of the house. Teddy was two steps behind me, our feet clattering down the porch steps and onto the grassy yard. The night sky was bright, the full moon and a smattering of stars illuminating our way as we tore down the lawn. Dew was already forming on the grass, but thankfully our feet didn't slip as we sprinted toward the tree towering in the distance, mist swirling at its base.

"Cut!"

Thank God. I ground to a halt, bending over to grip my knees and catch my breath. We'd finally reached the point in the script where Teddy's character is killed off by the witch, and we'd been working on the scene since the sun went down a few hours ago. It was a key scene, but did it have to involve so much running?

Teddy stopped next to me, annoyingly not as out of breath as I was. "Damn, Jigsaw, you were booking it." He ran a hand through his hair, sweat gathering on his forehead. "It's like you're excited about my death or something."

"Of course not." I clasped a hand to my chest, as though mortally offended. "What on earth would make you think that?"

"Hmm, I can't imagine." He fisted his hand under his chin. "You were so kind to me on my first day. So welcoming. So forgiving."

"Listen, buddy, I take destruction of private property very seriously."

"Unless it's a wig you don't mind almost losing."

"Shh!" I hurried to cover his mouth with my hand. Laughing beneath my palm, Teddy wrapped an arm around my waist and pulled me close, making me giggle, too.

I knew we looked cozy, but I couldn't bring myself to push him away. Knowing it was our last day on set together, my heart had been doing something funny all day—a weird ache punctuated by moments of intense pride. It was hard to believe Teddy was the same actor who had flubbed his lines and sent a lamp careening onto the floor that first day. Now, he was so confident, so self-assured. And he was good. It was a shame that he was going to waste his talent on another reality show when I knew he could do something so much more.

I tried not to think about how much I would miss him.

"You two."

A sharp voice pierced my train of thought. I pulled away from Teddy, guilty, like we'd been doing something much more illicit than sharing a hug. It was Natasha, staring at us with one eyebrow raised.

"Yes?" I asked, inching away from Teddy.

"Everyone's moved over there." She gestured further down the backyard, where crew members were setting up the cameras and lighting near the giant, gnarled tree that stood in the middle of the long, sloping lawn.

"We were just talking," Teddy explained.

"Talk down there." Natasha rifled through her clipboard. "Once everything's set up, we need to run through blocking one more time and start filming as soon as possible if we're fitting in this shot tonight."

"Yes, ma'am," we both murmured.

"Don't call me ma'am." Without another glance, she hurried off to talk to a boom operator who was looking lost.

Feeling bad about stressing Natasha out more than she already was, I tugged on the arm of Teddy's shirt and we made our way to where everyone else was prepping for the next scene. Spotting me, Mara came over to freshen up my makeup as Teddy peeled off to get a hair touch up.

Avoiding eye contact, Mara said nothing as she took some concealer out of her fanny pack and started dotting my face with the cream.

"I'm really sorry," I whispered. "I know I've been screwing up lately, but—"

"I don't want to hear it again, honestly." She capped the concealer and grabbed some powder. "Let's just not talk, ok?"

My heart sank. Mara had never been this angry with me before. And I deserved it.

After learning the truth about the gossip account Trevor had been running on TikTok, I'd completely forgotten to respond to the text from Mara about Austin's Instagram post. I hadn't remembered until I showed up to hair and makeup earlier that morning to find Mara giving me the silent treatment. She wouldn't tell me what was wrong, but it wasn't hard to figure out: she'd found out that Austin was dating someone new, thanks to his post, and I hadn't been there for her when she needed me.

Worse, I'd actively ignored her.

"I'll make it up to you," I tried. "Once the movie wraps and things go back to normal, I promise."

"You know . . ." Mara met my eyes for the first time all day. "When I told you to explore things with Teddy, I didn't realize you would end up ditching me for your fuck buddy."

I gaped at her. "That is definitely not what—"

"Then what is it?"

"I . . . It's been . . ." I fumbled for an excuse, but without telling her the truth about what had been going on—hunting down a killer was depleting my energy and giving me brain fog—I came up short.

"Really, Quinn?" Mara's face was disappointed, but not surprised. "Then I have nothing to say to you." With a final spritz of setting spray, she left. Left standing alone and dejected, I stared up at the tree that would be the centerpiece of the next scene.

It was a mammoth thing, its trunk several feet thick with gargantuan branches reaching up and into the sky. It was the centerpiece of the next shot, which was a dramatic one: Teddy and I would try various methods to destroy the tree, which we'd learned was the source of the witch's powers. I'd end up falling when the branches cracked, but Teddy would make it to the top—where the witch would use her magic to secure a vine around his neck before pushing him off and hanging him.

RIP Teddy's character.

The camera crew would shoot a variety of shots to get the effect of me falling and edit them together. I'd be wearing a harness, of course, which could be edited out in post-production.

" . . . shots of Quinn standing on the branch as it breaks first," Natasha was explaining as we caught up with the group. "The harness will drop her just a few feet."

Ah, the harness. I'd worn one on the set of a different film and was not eager to relive the experience. I looked sympathetically at Teddy, who surely had it worse than me in that department. He only grimaced in response.

"Are you sure those branches are secure?" I stared up into the tangled limbs of the tree. Most of them looked thick and sturdy, but what if I stepped on the wrong spot?

"Of course." Natasha reached for one of the ropes attached to the thick branch I'd be climbing. "Look."

She gave it a hard tug. I expected the rope to catch sharply, for there to be no give as she yanked on the branch.

What I was not expecting was an ear-shattering crack, followed by screams and people diving out of the way. Confused about what was happening, I tilted my head up. The gigantic limb wasn't just bending, it was in total free fall. At least a foot thick and probably ten feet long, it was hurtling toward the ground at a rapid speed. It felt like an eternity, but it was likely just a millisecond before someone grabbed me and yanked me out of the way, just in time to miss it crashing to the ground.

Teddy, of course.

He pulled me to his chest as we both toppled onto the ground. I was so busy staring at the massive branch that had narrowly missed smashing me into bits that it took me a few seconds to understand he was saying "Are you ok?" over and over again as he ran his hands over my head and down my back, apparently looking for some hidden critical injury.

"I'm ok," I said, my voice shaky.

Audrey, however, did not appear to be.

While she had also avoided the bulk of the giant limb, one of its smaller offshoots had struck her ankle as she dove out of the way. She clutched it, howling in pain as everyone else stared in shock. Finally, it was Mara who leapt into action, calling an ambulance before kneeling down to examine the injured joint.

Natasha stood at the base of the tree, closing her eyes like she could rewind time if she concentrated hard enough.

"Hey, look at me," Teddy said, shaking my shoulder. "Look at me. Are you sure you're ok?" He looked frantic, like he couldn't believe that I'd survived the ordeal unscathed.

"Yes," I assured him. "I'm ok."

He nodded, pulling me to his chest and refusing to let me go.

It took the paramedics forever to show up. Audrey wouldn't stop whimpering, Natasha was panicking—pacing up and down the lawn, loudly wondering what was taking them so long—and Mara kept asking everyone if she could get them anything, as though she was a hostess at the worst party in the history of parties.

Meanwhile, I spent the wait staring at the limb, lying cracked and ruined on the ground. I couldn't stop thinking about how on earth the set designers would be able to fix it. Or if they'd be able to fix it. I think I fixated on these questions to avoid thinking about how close I'd come to being crushed to death. If it weren't for Teddy, I wouldn't be alive.

The ambulance finally arrived, pulling onto the back lawn with its lights still flashing despite there being no vehicles within a ten-mile radius. The driver, a burly man with red hair and a graying beard, hopped out.

"We're going to have to start giving you guys frequent flier miles." He chuckled. "Who are we looking at? I heard we have an ankle injury."

I glared at him. "Probably the woman over there clutching her foot and crying."

"Copy that." The two of them unloaded a stretcher and laid it on the ground next to Audrey before taking a look at her ankle.

"Looks like it's broken, I'm afraid." The medics helped Audrey onto the stretcher. "We'll have to take her in for X-rays and fit her with a cast once the swelling goes down. She'll be feeling good as new in no time."

"Nothing ever takes 'no time,'" Natasha snapped. "How long, exactly, until she's back here filming?"

The medics hoisted Audrey up to prepare to load her into the ambulance.

"I don't really know," the medic with red hair said. "But usually it takes six to eight weeks to heal from a break like this."

Natasha cursed under her breath, but it was nothing compared to Audrey's reaction. She sat bolt upright, throwing the medics off balance as they struggled to carry her into the ambulance.

"Excuse me?" she said, her accent slipping as she gripped the sides of the stretcher. "Are you serious? Are you fucking kidding me?"

Mara and Natasha froze, staring at Audrey as they registered the sudden shift in her voice. Audrey's eyes widened as she caught herself, but not before one of the medics noticed as well. He was a young, sandy-haired man who looked like he'd be at home in any college frat house if he wasn't at work, and his face lit up at her words.

"Hey! Are you Addie Abrams?" He squinted down at her, nearly dropping the stretcher in the process. "Man, you don't look like her, but you sure do sound like her."

I gasped. So that's where I knew Audrey from. Suddenly, I knew exactly why she'd looked familiar to me on the first day of filming.

A few years ago, I'd been asked to star in *Found Footage*, a film spoofing the uber-popular horror genre. I turned it down, and thank God for that. It wanted to be the next Scary Movie franchise, but instead it had bombed—hard. They'd found debut actress Addie Abrams to fill the leading role, but even though she'd clearly given it her all, the movie was a total failure. The press were particularly hard on Addie, making fun of everything from her weight to the shape of her nose to the way she said the word "bag."

It was awful.

A few months after the movie premiered, I'd seen a few gossip items about her being seen leaving a plastic surgeon's office covered in bandages. Clearly, the media coverage had got to her. I'd hoped she would rebound from the fiasco, but then . . . nothing. I never saw her name again.

Now I knew why. She must have changed her appearance, given herself a new name, and adopted an accent in an attempt to start over in Hollywood. Which seemed like an extreme reaction. But the poor girl had been through so much. That must be what she had been hiding this whole time.

A secret that would be a very good motive for murder if it meant keeping her true identity under wraps.

Watching the ambulance disappear down the path and into the trees, new questions wormed their way through my mind. We'd solved the mystery of what Audrey was hiding, but had our killer just been whisked off to safety?

Teddy insisted on driving me back to the hotel. We were quiet on the drive, adrenaline ebbing from the shock of the accident and Audrey's departure under the wail of sirens. I didn't even realize I'd fallen asleep until Teddy gently shook me awake.

As we rode the elevator to our floor and stepped into the hall, Teddy reached for my elbow, pulling me to a stop before I could go any farther.

"Stay in my room tonight."

I opened my mouth to protest.

He held up a hand. "Not like that. Just . . . I'd feel a lot better if you were with me and I knew you were safe."

"Teddy . . ." Deep down, I knew he had a point. And I knew he meant it when he said his intentions were purely safety-related. But in truth, I couldn't trust myself to keep it purely safety-related. And with Teddy leaving tomorrow, I couldn't risk my emotions getting deeper than they already were. Just thinking about him leaving made me miss him.

"I'll sleep on the couch," he offered, pressing on. "I'll sleep on the floor." He nudged my arm. "I'll sleep in the bathtub, if it makes you feel better."

"As much as I'd like to see you try to squeeze into the bathtub, I think I'll be ok."

A muscle in Teddy's jaw popped and he bit the inside of his cheek. "Fine. But I'm checking the room from top to bottom before I leave you alone."

"Deal."

My limbs were heavy as we trudged down the hall, the fact sinking in that there was someone still out to get me, likely angry that their attempt with the sabotaged tree limb had failed. I went through the evidence we had so far, unable to shake the feeling we were missing something. Scott had an alibi for Trevor's murder, and he had no reason to want to hurt Brent. Natasha had alibis for both Trevor and Brent's murders. Mara was a nonstarter. It had to be Audrey—but if she'd sabotaged the tree, wouldn't she have known to get out of the way?

Who was left? The entire crew, but I didn't know any of them well enough to even begin parsing whether they had a motive or means for murder.

We were running out of time.

"You sure you're ok?" Teddy asked as we arrived at my door.

"Yeah. Just tired." I forced a smile, not wanting to worry him, and slid my key card into the lock. "I'll be fine." I pushed open the door.

And immediately froze.

The entire room had been ransacked. Someone had been here.

## Chapter Twenty-nine

Tentatively, we stepped into the room.

All the sheets had been ripped off my bed, left in heaping piles on the floor. My clothes had been torn out of the dresser and strewn about. The drawers of the nightstands had been pulled out and dumped on the floor, even though nothing had been in them. Even one of the framed prints on the wall had been knocked askew.

And on the wall, scrawled in red, were the words, "I'm still coming for you."

I stared around the wreckage, trying to process. So far, the danger had felt near but still separate, something out there but not so close I could smell it. Now it had been here, in my personal space. We could have just missed them. They could still be here.

I should have been terrified. But mostly, I felt angry.

"Let's go." Teddy wrapped an arm around my waist, guiding me back toward the door. "I don't want you in here."

For once, I didn't argue. We retreated to Teddy's room, where he secured both the deadbolt and the security chain. I slid into the bathroom to splash some cold water on my face in an attempt to bring down my adrenaline. It didn't help. My heart was still racing, but now my mascara was smeared. When I came out, running fingertips under my eyes to remove the smudges, Teddy was pacing.

"Damnit." He slammed a hand against the wall as he passed. "I should have figured this out by now. You could have been in there when they broke in!"

I walked over to put a calming touch on his shoulder. "It's ok. I wasn't in there, so it's fine." Even as I said the words, I knew they wouldn't help.

Teddy shrugged me off. "It's not fine!" Balling his hands into fists, he continued his pacing. "I should have worked harder. I should have believed you sooner. I shouldn't have doubted you." He ran a hand through his hair and down his neck. "I can't believe I fucked this up."

I glanced around the room, trying to find a way to distract him. It was mostly tidy, with the odd pair of joggers lying in a corner. I spotted a picture frame on the dining table, the one he'd made in his woodworking class, I assumed. Next to it, I saw a tool I didn't recognize, a pen with a long needle and power cord attached to a plug into the wall.

"What's this?"

Teddy's cheeks reddened. "You're not supposed to see that yet."

My curiosity piqued, I moved closer. The frame was small, just large enough to fit a standard eight-by-ten photo. The wood was expertly cut and polished, and along the perimeter were tiny etchings. Decorative flowers and leaves, a miniscule portrait of me, my dad in his Puzzle Face costume, and even a little skunk in one corner.

"Is this Daffy?" Amazed at the detail, I ran my finger along the dark lines of the sketches. "Did you do this?"

"That tool is a wood burner." Teddy came up behind me, wrapping his arms around my waist as he rested his chin on my shoulder. "It's not finished yet. I was hoping to get it done before I leave tomorrow."

*Leave.* In the chaos of the accident with the tree and the break-in, I'd completely forgotten he was leaving tomorrow. My chest clenched with an almost unbearable ache and I fought to catch my breath.

"It's beautiful. I can't imagine how much time and effort this must have taken."

"You mean a lot to me, Quinn."

Heat flooded my body, making me lightheaded. The logical side of my brain was telling me to get out. Danger, red alert: talking about feelings was treacherous territory and I needed to shut this down immediately.

"Don't do that that," I protested, my voice barely a breath. "You can't tell me that when you're leaving tomorrow."

"You do." Teddy's voice was starting to rasp. He spun me around, his hands smoothing up my back. "I care about you. I crave you when you're not around. And I don't want this to end tomorrow." He ran a hand down my arm, pulling my wrist to his lips and placing his mouth on the tender skin.

I closed my eyes, trying to push away the feelings that were threatening to erupt. I'd fought so hard to push them away, but I couldn't anymore. I didn't want it to end either. Was that crazy? People did long-distance relationships all the time. Not that this was a relationship. Long-distance sex arrangement.

I pushed him back onto the bed and sank onto his lap, wrapping my legs around his waist. I smoothed the hair off his forehead, unable to look him in the eye as I whispered in his ear, "You mean a lot to me, too."

When his lips pressed against mine, they weren't rough and urgent like the times before. They were tender, filled with restraint as they telegraphed that this time was different, this was about something deeper. Something thrummed deep within me—a desire not just for pleasure, but for connection. I wanted to get closer, climb inside him, where he could keep me safe and never let me go.

And I definitely couldn't get close enough with all those pesky clothes on.

I raked my hands under his shirt and up his back, tracing my fingernails along the thick cords of his muscles as I tried to pull it over his head as quickly as possible.

"Hang on," Teddy rasped, breaking the kiss to reach back with one hand and rip the shirt off his back. Without pausing, he moved on to slipping both hands under my top, unsnapping my bra with ease before pulling both it and my tee over my head.

"That's better," I breathed.

His eyes darkened as he took in my bare torso. "Fuck, you're gorgeous."

Teddy dipped his head, pressing his mouth and swirling his tongue first around one nipple and then the next. I arched my back, desperate for more pressure. I was a woman possessed. Starving. When he returned his mouth to mine, he rocked his hips against me, the long hardness of him pressing against my center, the friction delicious even through our clothes.

The contact provided relief—but only for a moment. I needed more.

"You have a condom this time, right?" I whispered against his mouth, my lips never completely leaving his.

"Yes."

"Get it."

Teddy pulled back to look at me, one hand swiping the hair out of my face. "You sure?"

"God, yes, I'm sure!"

He tutted as he pulled away and moved to the top of the bed, rummaging through the drawer of the nightstand before pulling out a foil-covered square. "So bossy."

I followed him, lying down next to him and waiting impatiently. "I am not."

"Oh, you are." He swung a leg over me until he was straddling me and leaned down, resting his elbows on the pillow so his arms were framing my face. "But you're gorgeous when you're bossy."

Staring up at him, our bodies slotted together so perfectly, I felt a wholeness I'd never experienced before in my life. My chest swelled with it. I wanted to live in it forever.

Then, he leaned down to kiss me again and time blurred. Our kisses became frantic as we pulled at what remained of our clothes. He dipped his hand between my legs, moaning against my mouth when he felt how wet I was. He rubbed me in tight, languid circles, making me cry out when I realized how close I already was to coming.

"Mmm." Teddy kissed my cheek, his hand stopping. "I'm sorry, I have to." Then he moved down, his mouth replacing where his hand had been.

I threw my head back, swearing as his tongue flicked like velvet against me in a way that made me see stars. A tongue that magical should be illegal. It was lethal. I writhed on the bed, so close to tipping over the edge that if he did that suction thing again—

Of course, that's exactly what he did.

I came, violently, gripping his head between my thighs as wave after wave of pleasure racked through my body. When I finally stilled, I was wrung out. In the most delicious, perfect way.

Teddy appeared at the pillow next to me, his face grinning and flushed. "We can be done now. I couldn't resist."

"No, no." I wrapped my arms around him, pulling him closer. "I'm not done."

"Are you sure?" He reached for the still-wrapped condom where it had fallen onto the comforter.

"Yes. Fuck yes, please. Please." I had never begged a man before in my life. But with Teddy? I would beg for this.

Teddy opened the condom and rolled it on with the finesse of an expert before positioning himself between my spread thighs. He dipped one hand between us and then with a single, smooth thrust he was inside.

Oh. Oh my God.

I gasped as he pushed all the way inside, stretching me—the

perfect length, perhaps a touch too wide. I angled my hips, helping us fit together.

"Fuck, Quinn." Teddy tipped his head down until our foreheads met. "You feel so damn good. Fucking perfect."

I moaned in response, tipping my hips up and urging him on. And he responded, thrusting once, twice, three times—slowly, like he was savoring every second of me.

"Faster." I nipped at his lip. "Please."

He obliged, increasing his tempo as we came together faster and faster. It was amazing. Transcendent. I knew sex could be good, but I didn't know it could be like this.

After a minute, he started to slow.

"You feel too good," Teddy whispered, his voice rough in my ear. "I'm not going to last."

Pleasure hummed in my chest. "Good. I want you to come for me."

He groaned, pressing his hips harder into mine, burying himself as deep as he could go. "You feel so good. We feel so good."

Then he was moving in me again, his fingers working where our bodies met. It was alarming how quickly my orgasm built again, winding tighter and tighter until I knew I was about to come again.

"Teddy," I cried, burying my fingers in his hair. "Teddy." His name ended in a whimper.

He thrusted harder. "Quinn. Come with me."

I cried out, gripping the broad planes of his shoulders as I came apart for the second time that night. He followed a minute later, a final few quick thrusts before he collapsed on top of me, breathing hard. We stayed that way, sweaty and entwined, until we caught our breath. He rubbed my back, his fingertips drawing circles on shoulder blades.

We were quiet for a long time, catching our breath as his fingertips drew circles on my shoulders and back.

"I should go," I murmured into his neck, my eyes closed and body boneless. An old feeling was creeping back—that no matter what we had just done with our bodies, actually falling asleep together was too intimate. That this was a place my heart wasn't willing to go.

"Why?" he whispered back.

"I don't know." I knew that staying the night meant all those confessions we had made were real. That we felt about each other in a way that could no longer be ignored. And that no matter how mind-blowing the sex was, it was still scary. But I was too blissed out to formulate the words.

"Your room is trashed, remember?" He pressed his lips, featherlight, to the top of my head. "Probably by a murderer? Did you forget?"

Shit. I had forgotten.

"Mmm, good point." I replied, relieved I could stop searching for an excuse. His bed was so soft, and he was so comfy, and deep down I didn't want to leave anyway.

So I didn't. We didn't even turn off the light before we both fell asleep.

## *Chapter Thirty*

Waking up next to Teddy was a disorienting experience. Not just because I was used to sleeping alone, but because when I realized we'd spent the entire night with his arm tucked around my waist, my first instinct wasn't to jump out of bed and run away screaming.

Instead, I rolled over to face him—carefully—so his arm wouldn't slip out of place.

He was still asleep, his chest rising and falling with his rhythmic breaths, his mouth hanging open ever so slightly. I made a mental note to tease him about this later, something about him looking like a big-mouthed bass while he slept. But he didn't, really. He looked peaceful, strong. Like one of the most beautiful things I'd ever seen. It was still terrifying, admitting to myself what he meant to me. But maybe I could believe what he'd told me the night before. That I meant something to him.

I wanted to believe him. And I think I did.

With a stretch and a yawn, Teddy rumbled awake. Without

opening his eyes, he wrapped both arms around me and pulled me onto his chest.

"Morning," he whispered, his voice raspy with sleep. "You stayed."

"Correct. I didn't wake up and flee in the middle of the night."

He smiled and pressed a kiss to my shoulder. "Good. I'm glad."

"Me too."

"You know . . ." Teddy rubbed a hand up and down my back, his thumb straying to the curve of my breast. "We could do what we did last night again. A repeat performance, if you will. We're already dressed for it."

"You haven't even opened your eyes yet." I poked him gently in the rib. "What if you're horrified by what I look like first thing in the morning?"

Teddy made a show of opening his eyes and studying my bed head and bare face. "Nope, checks out. Still gorgeous. Maybe more."

"You don't want Mara to come fix me up first?"

"I definitely don't"—he lowered his head to my neck, sucking the spot below my ear that made me sigh—"want her here right now." His hand dipped to the crease of my thigh, running his fingers, featherlight, along the delicate skin.

"Yeah, ok." I pulled his mouth up to mine, unable to resist any longer as I wrapped my arms around his neck.

While the night before had been frantic and desperate, this time it was lazy and luxurious. We took our time, using our hands and mouths to find the spots we liked best. And when I came, he looked at me in wonder, like it was an act of worship.

When we were finished, we dozed off again for another hour, before I grabbed my phone with a gasp.

"Oh my God." I clicked on the screen, my heart sinking when I saw the time. Then I saw I had a mass text, sent to all the cast members from Natasha. "Oh my God," I repeated, louder this time.

"What?" Teddy's voice was groggy, his eyes still closed.

I ran my eyes over the message one more time, making sure I wasn't misreading. "The production has been . . . cancelled. Or postponed, I guess. Officially. But Natasha doesn't sound optimistic."

"Wait, seriously?" He grabbed his own phone, reading the text for himself. "Holy shit."

"Yeah."

"Maybe it's for the best." He ran a hand down his face. "It wasn't exactly going well."

I couldn't say anything, the breath squeezed out of my lungs as it registered that my very last movie wasn't going to happen. My career was over, and while I'd been telling myself that was what I wanted for months, suddenly I didn't feel ready.

Noticing the stricken look on my face, Teddy rolled over to face me. "Are you ok? I thought you'd be happy about this."

For a long moment, I didn't say anything. I don't want to talk about this, I thought, the feeling of my old walls once again rising up. I don't want to think about this, let alone talk about it.

But did I not want to talk about it? Or did I just not know the answer to the question?

"I'm sorry," Teddy reached out to rub my back. "We don't have to talk about it."

"No, it's . . ." I struggled to find the words. "I don't know how I feel about it. I don't feel like I thought I would, anyway."

"I thought you were excited to be done?"

"I thought so too." My voice was quiet and I refused to meet his eyes, focusing instead on a tiny knot in the comforter's stitching.

"You don't have to tell me if you don't want to, but . . . do you even want to quit making movies? Horror movies?"

Almost imperceptibly, I shook my head. "No. Yes? I don't know."

I could tell he wanted to press, to ask me what that meant. But he didn't. And I was grateful, because even if I had realized I wasn't done with horror stories, I still didn't know how exactly I fit in. I didn't want to be an actress, but I didn't know how to be anything else. I still didn't know where I fit.

"Oh, Quinn." Teddy pulled me against his chest, and I wrapped my arms around his waist. "I know we haven't talked about what this is between the two of us, but I promise, I'm not going anywhere until you tell me to. I'll be here while you figure it out, if you want me to be. No matter what you decide to do."

I wasn't ready to talk about what we were. All I knew was that I was happier when I was with him, and that I wanted to learn everything about how to make him feel the same way, and that he made me feel more ok with myself than I could remember . . . ever. I didn't know what I wanted to do with the rest of my life. But I think I wanted it to be with him.

Not that I was ready to tell him that.

I squeezed his hand, sitting up on the mattress. "Thank you." I leaned in to kiss him, trying to telegraph with my touch all the things my heart was feeling but wasn't ready to say. "I'm going to get dressed and go get us some coffee."

"I don't like coffee."

"I'm sorry, what?" I pulled away, ready to take it all back.

He shrugged, smiling sheepishly. "It makes me jittery."

"That's why decaf exists!"

"Why would I force myself to drink bitter-ass bean juice if it's not even going to make me feel anything?"

"Oh my God." I rolled my eyes as I climbed out of bed, looking for my clothes. "What do you want then?"

He looked pointedly at my naked torso.

I threw a pillow at him.

"Ok, fine. Just get me a tea or something."

"Do you actually like tea?"

"No."

"You're hopeless."

After a quick shower in Teddy's room and a sprint into my ransacked room to change into clean clothes, I stopped at the small coffee shop two blocks from the hotel, ordering a chai tea for Teddy and a latte for me.

As I waited, the bell above the door tinkled with another customer. It was Mara, decked out in a rose-pink vintage dress and large, dark sunglasses. Without acknowledging me, she approached the counter and placed her order. Walking across the room, she decided to wait as far away from me as possible.

Ah. So the news about the production hadn't done anything to endear me to her. I moved closer, until I was just within earshot.

"Did you see Natasha's email?" I tried.

"Yes." She remained focused on the counter, not even looking at me.

"Crazy, huh?"

"Yep."

"How do you feel about it?"

"I'm going to stop you." Mara removed her sunglasses, finally looking at me. "I know this year hasn't been great for you, but I let you crash on my floor, I've done everything I could to be there for you, and now you've ditched me for some guy—who you allegedly don't even like—and I still feel like you're hiding something from me."

"It's not that I don't want to tell you, it's just—"

Mara held up a hand, stopping me. "I love you, but I can't be friends with you if you're not honest with me. You know," her voice wavered, "I've really needed you lately. And you haven't been there."

"I'm so sorry. I didn't know."

"But I tried to tell you, didn't I?" The barista called her name, and Mara walked over to retrieve her drink. "When we get back to LA, you have a week to get out of my apartment. And don't expect me to help you move your creepy *Babadook* sculpture. Bye, Quinn."

Then she replaced her sunglasses and was gone.

I watched her go, guilt eating into my stomach. Getting swept up in Teddy and the mystery might have cost me one of the people I loved the most. I had lied to her, and worse, I hadn't been there for her when she needed me. When she'd always been there for me. But I told myself that once we got back home, I could explain and everything would go back to normal. Once she understood why I couldn't be honest—that I was trying to protect her—she would forgive me.

Wouldn't she?

As I continued to wait, I distracted myself by scrolling through the usual tabloid sites. I supposed that now there was no point in staying up to date with industry gossip, but old habits and all. I was about to put my phone away when I came across a story that made me freeze. It was an article from TMZ with the headline "Scream Queen Quinn Prescott Cozies Up with Reality Hunk Co-star."

Trembling, I clicked it open. There at the top was a dark photo of me and Teddy at the baseball field, me straddling him as we made out in the grass. Someone had hidden nearby, spying, and taken a fucking picture. Next to it was another snapshot, this one with me smiling as Teddy stared at me adoringly. I recognized it instantly.

It was the selfie that Teddy had taken of us in the baseball field.

I'm pretty sure I blacked out, my rage bending the physics of time and memory, because the next thing I remember, I was stomping back into Teddy's room and throwing my phone at the back of his head. It missed, crashing into the wall instead and falling behind the nightstand.

"What the hell?" He lifted his head, a crease from the pillow leaving a red streak across one cheek.

"Read it."

"Your phone?"

"Yes." My voice was clipped. "Read it."

Stretching out an arm, he fished it out from behind the

stand. He pressed the power button and looked up blankly. "I need your password."

Ugh. I reached over and tapped it in before once again retreating away to a safe distance, crossing my arms over my chest. I waited for the screen to turn on and for its contents to register.

Teddy's eyes widened. "Oh, shit."

"What the fuck, Teddy? Why would you do this?" All the things he'd said, last night and this morning, scrolled through my head like ticker tape. All lines, all things he'd known would make me trust him. And I'd swallowed them down like a sucker, while all along he was just trying to boost his career. Willing to sell us out for more fame and a couple extra bucks.

"I told you how much I hate being scrutinized in the tabloids, how all I wanted was to be done with this entire God-forsaken industry, and you still did this."

"Wait, you think I sent them the photo?" He sat up, crawling out from under the sheets. "You think I did this?"

"Who the hell else could? It was on your phone! And did you call up your paparazzi friends to let them know we'd be at the field? Is that why you kissed me?"

"What? No! Even if I knew any paparazzi, I doubt they'd just be hanging around rural Virginia."

"What about the selfie?" I tipped my chin up defiantly.

"I did not send that photo to anyone, I swear. Let alone to some pathetic gossip website."

"Why should I believe that? You didn't mind when they published those pictures of you and all those models." I knew it was a low blow as soon as I said it. But I couldn't take it back once it left my mouth, and it wasn't a lie anyway.

"Wow." He ran a hand down his jaw. "That's what you think of me, huh?"

"Who else could have done it? I'm willing to believe you didn't have anything to do with the first photo, but I'd love to hear about this magic technology that lets people summon pictures from your phone like magic."

Teddy sat up, eyes darting like he was running through the possibilities. "I honestly don't know. My photos don't automatically upload anywhere else—it all lives on my phone."

I laughed. "So you're not even going to pretend you were hacked? You're not exactly helping your case, you know."

"No, because I'm not going to lie to you." He shrugged helplessly. "I didn't do it."

Tears burned in my eyes. I'd been so stupid. I'd known this whole time, had told myself on day one of this production, that I couldn't get involved with anyone. Anyone, but especially not Teddy. Guys like Teddy are only out for themselves. To promote themselves, to do anything for more fame. They use people when they're useful and throw them away later.

I'd known it was a bad idea, and I'd done it anyway.

"Look at me," Teddy said. "I told you last night how much you meant to me. Why the fuck would I ruin that to make a few bucks from the fucking paparazzi?" He ran a hand through his hair, that curl in the front flopping over his forehead, and my heart ached with such force I could have collapsed. But I didn't. I locked my knees, holding my ground.

"Are you planning to be on *Love by the Stars*?" I jutted my chin toward the ceiling.

For a moment, he paused—his mouth half open as his mind recalibrated. "How do you know about that?"

"Answer the question."

"Yeah, but how did—"

"It doesn't matter. Don't give me all this crap about how much I mean to you when you were planning to go make out with whichever girl those producers tell you to as soon as the movie wraps." I turned to leave, not wanting to hear whatever bullshit excuse he was going to come up with next.

He reached out for my arm, grabbing me lightly by the elbow. "Hang on. Quinn, you've been the one telling me from day one that you don't want a relationship. Forgive me for not immediately backing out of a contract for a girl that obviously doesn't want me."

I yanked my arm away. "It doesn't matter! You want to be famous and will do anything to get it. This movie wasn't enough, your reality shows weren't enough, so now you decided to sell me out, for what? How much money did they pay you?"

"Nothing, because it wasn't me," Teddy said, his teeth gritted. "I don't know what else to say. Apparently, I've done nothing to earn your trust."

"Apparently."

"Please don't do this. Please listen to me."

"What did you say an hour ago? That you're not going anywhere until I want you to? Well." I reached for the doorknob. "That's now. I want you to leave me alone."

And then, without waiting for a reply, I spun around and marched out of the room.

## Chapter Thirty-one

Still fuming, I stormed to my room.

My throat was cramping and my eyes burning, unmistakable signs that if I let them, tears would spill over and I'd be crying harder than Florence Pugh in the *Midsommar* poster. And I wouldn't—couldn't—let that happen. Teddy might not be there to witness me falling apart, but I was. I'd have to admit that I'd been foolish enough to get my heart broken by someone I'd known all along wasn't fit to be trusted. And I wasn't ready to face that.

So instead, I channeled my rage into pushing the desk in front of the door. I only planned to be in my room for a half hour max, but with a killer out there with a key to my room, I wasn't taking any chances. I grabbed my phone and tapped out a text, letting my dad know I'd be at his place in a few hours. Then I yanked my suitcase out of the closet and started chucking in my belongings, made easier by the fact that everything was spilled onto the floor.

Scooping up clothes and balls of yarn, I started to laugh. This movie was supposed to be my horror send-off, a way for me to say goodbye to my fans and get some extra money while I figured out what I wanted to do with my life. Now it was canceled, I was in the crosshairs of a killer, and the whole world would know I'd been played by Hollywood's biggest fuck boy. He'd seemed so genuine, so genuinely good, so genuinely into me. Had it all been a lie? The stories about his brother, his mother? His father? Had it all been a ploy to gain my sympathies and build this fake relationship he could milk for publicity?

The worst part of it was that I had been genuine. My feelings had been real—they were real—and I'd been foolish enough to tell him.

Doing a final sweep of the room, I did a mental inventory of my things, trying to decipher if the intruder had taken anything. So far, everything had been accounted for. But as I zipped up my luggage, it finally clicked. The only thing that was missing was Jacques, my stuffed raven. This—realizing I'd lost the only relic from my career that meant anything to me—was finally enough to make me break down into tears. I sank onto the bed, letting my body heave with it, not caring who might hear me, hoping that if I cried long enough, the poison would seep out and it wouldn't hurt anymore.

A knock pounded at the door.

I jumped, my heart hammering. I wiped my tears and grabbed a lamp to use as a makeshift weapon before creeping to the door. It was already unplugged and lying on the floor anyway. Moving the desk out of the way and opening the door, I swung back the heavy brass base. The shade flopped unceremoniously to the carpet.

But when I swung open the door, there was no one there, just a package wrapped in brown paper and waiting on the carpet. Leaving the lamp in the hall, I took the package into my room, my insides sinking. Sure enough, when I peeled away the paper, it was Teddy's picture frame, still unfinished. Instead of a photo, it displayed a note—the handwriting messy and cramped:

Quinn,

I made this for you, so it's your choice whether to keep it or not. It was meant to hold the photo of us, but I figured that wasn't a good idea. There's only the one.

I'll miss our rehearsals.

—Teddy

Staring at the frame, my throat thickened. Teddy could have thrown it in the trash, or taken it with him to keep for himself. But he didn't. He'd wrapped it and written me a note and left it for me.

It was too much. I needed to get out of there. Stuffing the frame under my arm and grabbing my luggage, I ran out the door.

My dad was trimming a branch in a pot when I arrived at the cabin.

Not a branch that was attached to a tree.

Not even a branch that was attached to a shrub.

A branch that had been planted in a tiny pot, that my hulking father was now lovingly hunched over as he trimmed it with a pair of nail trimmers.

"Um, whatcha doing?"

He turned, looking shocked, as though he hadn't heard anyone pull up. "Squish!" He dropped the clippers at the base of the pot and hurried over to wrap me in a hug. "I'm happy to see you."

"It's good to see you too." I disentangled myself from the hug. "What's with the twig?"

"It's my new thing." He beamed. "It's a bonsai tree."

I studied it with skepticism. Any bonsai tree I'd ever seen had looked like the miniature of a grown-up tree, complete with twisting limbs and gnarled roots peeking out from the soil. The tree in the pot looked like something yanked off a bush.

"Hmm," was all I could muster.

"You gotta start somewhere." My dad plucked the nail trimmers from the dirt. "Let's go inside. I was just about to start dinner."

Happy to drown my sorrows in whatever he had planned, I followed, immediately hit by the smell of freshly baked bread and the now-familiar scuffle of claws on carpet.

"Really, Daffy?"

The skunk refused to be deterred. She stomped at me again, scraping herself backward as she dared me to take her on.

"Peppers in the fridge?"

"Melon today."

We filed into the kitchen, where I fished out the container of melon and gave a cube to Daffy as an offer of peace. She immediately grabbed it, her teeth chomping noisily.

"What do you have going?" I gave Daffy another piece of melon. "It smells amazing."

"Focaccia." He pulled open the oven a crack and peeked inside. "For sandwiches. And I'm going to try fresh-cut French fries in my new air fryer." He gestured proudly to a boxy appliance on the counter.

I shook my head. "I can't keep track of all your new hobbies."

"Retirement is treating me kindly." He eyed me carefully. "I'm sorry to hear about the movie, by the way. How are you holding up?"

"Not great."

"Hmm." My dad fished around in the drawer for a potato peeler as he waited for me to elaborate. When I didn't, to his credit, he proceeded with caution. "Do you want to talk about it?"

I sighed, giving Daffy the rest of the melon as I considered it. I didn't even know where to start. With the half-assed, failed murder investigation I'd convinced myself I could do? The mounting feeling that by quitting horror movies I was fucking up my life more instead of improving it? The fact that my best friend wasn't speaking to me? Or the sex scandal with a man I was no longer speaking to that was now sweeping the media?

Out of all of them, the scandal somehow seemed safest.

"I'm sure you saw the article."

He nodded, keeping his eyes trained on the russet potato he'd started peeling. "The photos were pretty innocent, though. You looked happy. What's the problem?"

"The problem is that he leaked them to the press!"

My dad frowned, the peeler sending potato scraps flying into a waiting bowl. "That's not good."

"No, it's not."

"What'd he have to say for himself?"

"He said he didn't do it."

My dad's hand paused mid-peel. "Then, forgive me, Squish, but how do you know he did?"

"It was on his phone, who else would have done it?"

"How the hell should I know! Couldn't it have gone up in the fog or something?"

"Do you mean the cloud?"

"Yes, that!"

"No, he said his phone doesn't upload photos anywhere else." I frowned, irritated my dad was giving Teddy the benefit of the doubt instead of trusting me. "Therefore, he was the only one who had access."

"Hmm." The potatoes all peeled, he moved on to carefully slicing them into fries. "Couldn't someone have taken his phone? And sent the photos themselves?"

My mouth snapped shut. I was embarrassed to admit I hadn't thought of that. Was that really possible? No, I decided.

"People have passwords on their phones, Dad. People can't just grab your phone and access your stuff." I scraped a nail against the counter, picking at a speck of dried focaccia dough. "It's pretty obvious he sold it for the money or attention, likely both."

"If you say so." He filled a bowl with ice water to soak the fries. "Listen, I trust your judgment." He hesitated, drying his hands on a tea towel.

I raised an eyebrow. "But what?"

"In this business, it's impossible to guarantee that no one will ever use you for your connections, or want something from you, or only want to get close to you because of some version of you they've cooked up in their head. But . . ." He fiddled with the towel, straightening it where it hung off the oven handle. "If you never give anyone a chance, you'll be awfully lonely."

"That's not true. I have Mara, I know I can trust her." But even as I said it, I knew it might no longer be true.

"Sure. And how many others?"

I tipped up my chin. "Maybe I don't need others." I knew I was being stubborn, but there was a part of me that believed it, too.

"Ok. You know you better than me." He walked around the counter and wrapped an arm around my shoulders. "I just want you to be happy."

I nodded. I wanted me to be happy, too. Why couldn't I figure out how to be?

## Chapter Thirty-two

I spent the night on the couch, so miserable that even Daffy took pity on me. She curled up by my feet until she woke up at the ungodly hour of five in the morning, tickling and nudging my arm with her paws until I got up and fetched her some fruit from the fridge.

She rejected the apples, but the blueberries she deemed acceptable.

Pouring myself a cup of coffee, my brain slowly started to come online in the quiet kitchen, the sunlight diffusing the room with a warm glow. The more awake I grew, the more the anger and resentment that had filled my body the day before was gradually replaced by an empty ache.

It had only been a day, but I already felt Teddy's absence like a physical thing—my chest vacant and hollow. I didn't know you could miss a person like this, like a piece of myself had been ripped away. I wanted to tell him about the baby bonsai tree my dad was growing, and the dream I'd had last night about

Natasha turning into a lemon. But just as I reached for my phone I remembered, with the inevitably blank home screen telling me that he also hadn't called or texted.

I'd told him not to.

I didn't have a choice, I reminded myself as I rooted around the fridge for breakfast supplies. I pulled out eggs, a knob of cheese, and some ham for omelettes. I absolutely could not be with someone I couldn't trust. Placing the food on the counter, I moved on to searching the cupboards for a pan.

Teddy had lied to me.

He'd used me.

And despite whatever he claimed to feel for me, he'd still been planning to throw it all away for a chance at fifteen more minutes of fame on another dating show.

I was better off now, no matter how much it hurt.

Woken by the smell of freshly brewed coffee, my dad eventually joined me in the kitchen. I made us breakfast and afterwards he gave me free reign to spend the day moping around the cabin. I watched an old Puzzle Face movie, finished crocheting my blanket, and even took a hike on a nearby trail, hoping the fresh air would bring me peace and clarity.

It did not.

Instead, not only did I manage to get hot, sweaty, and supremely uncomfortable despite the pleasant autumn weather, but I also had plenty of time to ruminate on the fact that the only thing I'd succeeded at in the past few weeks in addition to getting my heart broken and botching my friendship with Mara was failing to get justice for Trevor and Brent. They hadn't been perfect, but they hadn't deserved the fate they'd been dealt, and they still had people in their lives that deserved answers and closure.

I'd failed them, even worse than I'd failed myself.

Trying to distract myself from yet another post-mortem of my entanglement with Teddy, I ran my mind down our list of suspects for the last time as I picked my way along the rocky path.

Scott and Natasha were out—they both had alibis for the night of Trevor's murder. It was obvious Natasha had been annoyed with Brent, to put it mildly, but if she was already stressed about the production being slowed down, it wouldn't make sense for her to kill him and make it worse.

Chloe certainly would have had motive to kill Brent after the way he had treated her. I was living it right now, the rage and despair that came with a man betraying you when you thought he cared about you. But why would she want to hurt Trevor? And she was already gone by the time the killer broke into my room and tampered with the tree.

Audrey would have had motive to get rid of Trevor if he'd figured out her identity and was threatening to expose her on his TikTok account. But other than Brent being obnoxious and hitting on her, there was no reason for her wanting to get rid of him.

It didn't make sense. Something had to be missing.

After I got back to the cabin and showered, my dad and I ordered pizza for dinner. It was lukewarm by the time we drove all the way out to the restaurant and back, but neither of us had felt like cooking. After, we both grabbed some hard apple cider from the fridge and headed out back to the porch.

The late September evening was lovely as we stepped outside, the air cool and the sky orange-tinted from the sinking sun. The breeze rustled the leaves of the towering oaks as I sank into one of the Adirondack chairs, pulling my knees to my chest and wrapping my sweater tightly around myself.

We sat in silence for a few minutes, enjoying the sounds of the day slowly slipping away. I wondered how long I was going to feel like a rotten piece of trash left on the side of the highway. Probably for the foreseeable future. At least I was already one day down.

Finally, my dad broke the silence.

"You still upset about that Teddy guy? Or are you bummed about the movie this time?" He let out a long whistle. "You've had a run of bad luck, Squish."

He had no idea.

"I don't know. All of it."

"Listen." He balanced his cider on the arm of his chair and leaned forward, resting his arms on the tops of his thighs. "I know a thing or two about getting your heart broke. It's awful, and I know nothing I can say will change that. But if you let me, I can try to help with the next steps in your career. Have you been putting any feelers out for a new agent?"

"Not exactly." I squirmed in my seat, taking a long gulp from my bottle. *Tell him*, a voice in my head whispered. *Not yet*, my heart whispered back.

"And my buddy's still interested in you starring in that project of his, you know. Not just interested, to be honest, his heart's dead set on it. If you're on board, that is."

"I'm thinking about it," I hedged. I was being a coward—no wonder my life had fallen apart.

My dad sighed, his lips settling into a hard line. "I wish you could see what I see. I know it's easy to be critical of your own work, but you're so good at it. You absolutely shine on camera. You're the best thing in every film you've ever made."

Oh God, he was making this so much worse. Ok, I had to do it. Like ripping off a band-aid.

"Dad, I—"

"No, I'm serious. If you could just—"

"I'm quitting. Acting. I'm quitting acting."

As soon as the words left my mouth, relief loosened my shoulders and unclenched my stomach. I'd done it.

"Oh." My dad leaned back in his chair, temporarily at a loss for words. "You mean . . . for good?"

I swallowed, my mouth dry. "Yeah."

"I see." He rubbed his beard, taking a moment to absorb this new information. "When did you decide this?"

"In July."

He whistled, long and slow. "Why didn't you tell me?"

So I told him everything—how I'd been afraid of disappointing him, afraid that our relationship would change. Afraid that by admitting it out loud, I was giving up some integral part of my identity that I wouldn't get back. My dad listened, silent, his face growing more and more concerned by the second. When I stopped, he waited to make sure I was done before speaking.

"Squish, have I ever done or said anything to make you think I'd be disappointed if you stopped making movies?"

Wordlessly, I shook my head.

"Good lord, I hope not. Listen, I meant what I said about being proud of your work. But I don't love you because you're a horror actress. I love you because you're you. Nothing could ever change that. And hey . . ." He elbowed me gently on the arm. "If you quit, that's just another thing we have in common."

Tears burned my eyes, threatening to spill over. "I don't know who I am if I'm not acting."

"I know. But I also know you'll figure it out." My dad reached out to squeeze my hand. "And I know whatever it is, you'll be great at it."

Grateful, I squeezed his hand back. We once again lapsed into silence, crickets starting to wake up and chirp in the trees around us. Mentally, I chided myself for waiting so long to tell my dad. Of course it had gone fine. Just like Teddy had said it would. My heart squeezed, wishing I could reach out and tell him. Was this how it was going to be from now on? Innumerable moments that I wanted to share with him but couldn't?

"Oh!" My dad stood suddenly. "I have something for you. Let me go get it." He retreated into the cabin, leaving me thoroughly confused. Moments later he reappeared, carrying what looked like a picture frame.

"I found this a couple months ago while going through some things in storage." He handed me the frame, which was heavier than I expected. "Been waiting for the right time to give it to you. Now feels right. A nice bookend, if you will."

Wiping the dust off the glass, it took me a moment to place where it had come from. It was a group photo of people I didn't recognize, and judging from some of the fashions, it seemed to be from some time in the nineties. Why we ever thought neon color blocking was a good idea, I'll never know.

Then it came to me: it was a cast photo from my very first

movie, the one I'd been in with my dad when I was eight. The director had gathered the entire cast together on the very last day.

"Oh my gosh," I gasped. "I totally forgot about this."

As I scanned the faces, I remembered the first note I'd received after Trevor's death:

*Back in your very first role,*
*Did you know this would be the toll?*

My first movie . . . Everyone was right here in this photo. Pulse quickening, I started examining the faces closer, jumping from one to the next in search of one I recognized. Was the answer right in front of me? I found little me, grinning with my dishwater blonde hair pulled into pigtails. And there, right next to me, was a very familiar face.

I was staring at the killer we'd been looking for.

"Squish? Are you ok?"

Frozen, I couldn't reply. My heart raced as I tried to catch up with this new information. Should I call them to confront them? Go back to the hotel and look for them? Call the police?

Call the police. Yes. That's what I needed to do.

Pulling out my phone, I was ready to make the call when I noticed I had a text. It was from Teddy. Heart jumping into my throat, I clicked it open:

**Teddy: You have until midnight to get to set. If you call the cops,**
**he's dead.**

Below it, there was a photo. It was Teddy, tied to a chair with his wrists and ankles bound. I squinted, trying to make sense of it. The chair was on a dusty floor, and a pile of junk was behind it. Was this a joke? But then I noticed his eyes, wide and scared.

Not a joke.

I needed a new plan. Calling the cops was out the window— there was no way I was going to risk it. I needed to get to set. Now.

## Chapter Thirty-three

"You've got a lot of 'splaining to do." Mara climbed into my car, raising an eyebrow as she pulled on her seatbelt. "Starting with where we're going and followed by why you've been lying to me for weeks."

I adjusted my grip on the steering wheel, swallowing. "I know. I'm so sorry. It's kind of a long story."

"Well, let's get going. You can tell me as we drive."

As I pulled out of the hotel parking lot and headed to set, I did.

"Ok, so, after Trevor died, I was pretty sure his death was actually a murder, so I convinced Teddy to help me figure out who killed him. We thought it was Brent, but then he was murdered too, and then I started getting notes from the killer—"

Mara's mouth gaped as she took in these revelations. "You what? What kind of notes?"

"They were so weird, like little threatening poems. They'd figured out we were investigating, so then they—the killer, I mean—started coming after me."

"God, no wonder you've been weird lately."

"I wanted to tell you." I tightened my grip on the wheel. "But I couldn't risk the killer coming after you, too."

Mara reached out and rubbed my shoulder. "It's ok. But why not target Teddy? He was investigating, too."

"Apparently they did." My mouth set into a grim line. "I got a text from his phone a couple hours ago with a photo of him, tied up in the attic of the set." My voice started to crack. "I think they're going to hurt him."

"So you are in love with him!" Mara said triumphantly. Her anger at me had already melted away, replaced by satisfaction that she'd been correct all along.

"That's what you're choosing to focus on right now?" The stress and anxiety that had been building all day was making my head ache, and I took one hand off the wheel to rub my temple.

"You wouldn't be risking your life to save someone you didn't love," she pointed out. "Listen, do you actually want to be with this man or do you feel bad that you hurt him? Because you should probably figure that out. You don't want to send mixed messages as you're saving someone's life."

I wanted to say that she was wrong, and that I wasn't hopelessly in love with Teddy. That the thought of never speaking to him again wasn't tearing up my entire existence. I wanted to say that I felt bad that I'd been a jerk about the photo, and that's the only reason why I was rushing to be at his side. And that part was true. I did feel bad for being a jerk. Really, really bad. But I didn't feel bad just because I knew I'd made a mistake, or several mistakes. I felt bad because the thought of being without him, and a thousand of the little things that make him him, made something inside me feel like it was dying.

I loved the way he never said a bad word about anybody.

I loved the way that lock of hair always flopped down over his forehead.

I loved the way he thought "Bohemian Rhapsody" was a deep cut.

I loved the way he made me feel like I was enough—for him, for the world. For myself.

Somehow, at a time when I'd sworn off love in any shape or form, I'd found the person I couldn't imagine being without. The person I would change my plans for. The person I'd rather die than hurt. And I was pretty sure that despite all my resolutions to not, under any circumstance, fall for anyone on set, I was falling very much in love with Teddy.

It was terrifying. I still wanted to push it away—to stick to my rules. No more horror movies. No more dating actors. And a voice that whispered, *He lied to you and used you.*

But no matter how many rules you make, you can't guarantee that a relationship will work out, or that someone won't break your heart. You can't guarantee that your career won't implode, or that you won't fail.

All you can do is decide whether it's worth the risk.

I still didn't know how TMZ had gotten the photos of Teddy and me. I was still skeptical that it could be anyone but him. But maybe I needed to hear him out. Maybe I needed to trust.

I sighed, resigned to my fate. "I want to be with him. For real."

Mara squealed in delight. And despite the fact that I could be walking to my death in less than an hour's time, something like hope bubbled in my stomach. It felt good not just to finally open my heart to someone, but also to be honest with myself about it.

What didn't feel good was knowing that even if I thought I'd been doing the right thing, Mara had still suffered in the process.

"I'm really sorry I wasn't there for you. When the Austin stuff happened."

"You've clearly been busy. Getting hunted by a literal killer." She played it off with a little puff of a laugh, but judging by the way her body seemed to deflate, it was clear she was still hurt.

"I'll make it up to you?"

Mara smiled wryly. "You definitely will. You're officially on dinner duty for the foreseeable future when we get back to LA."

"So I'm not kicked out?"

"Never!"

I exhaled, the relief at being back in her good graces making me momentarily forget what we were on our way to do. But then the road grew narrow, tree branches brushing against the side of the vehicle, and my chest grew tight. We were almost there.

I steered us straight to the house, turning off the headlights as we approached, creeping along to be as quiet as possible. I parked out of sight, not wanting to risk anyone seeing Mara in the car.

"Are you sure I can't come with you?" she whispered as I turned off the ignition.

After hearing why, exactly, we were going to set late at night, Mara had immediately wanted to call the police. Which, I had to admit, was a logical course of action. But I believed the threat in the text. There was no way I was calling the cops or letting Mara come inside the house with me. I needed to make sure

Teddy was ok, to see him for myself. Instead, Mara would give me a few minutes to get into the house and hopefully convince the killer that I hadn't gone to the authorities. Only then would Mara call the police. Or, if she heard screaming, sooner.

I really hoped it wouldn't be sooner.

"It seems like a bad idea to go in alone." Mara chewed her lower lip. "We're dealing with a serial killer here."

"Technically you're only a serial killer if you've killed three or more people in unrelated situations."

"No, it's definitely two."

"Well, it's doesn't matter!" I hissed, unbuckling my seatbelt. "They've already proved they're capable of murder—they'll definitely kill him if I don't do what they say." My voice wavered, threatening to break. Screw feeling bad about blaming him for the photo leak; this level of guilt was way worse. I opened the door, ready to get out.

"Quinn?"

"Yeah?"

"Go kick some ass. I'll call in your backup."

It was a cold and clear night, the full moon shining down on me as I hopped out of the car and onto the grass. Walking through the trees toward the house, my nerves suddenly dissipated.

This was happening. There was no turning back now.

I stared up at the house, hoping for a clue as to where the killer would be waiting for me. But there was nothing— no lights, no sound, no indication of what I was supposed to do next. Taking a deep breath, I climbed the porch steps and wrenched open the door. The hinges groaned in protest, and I winced. The house was dead silent—they had to have heard. They had to know I was here. I waited on the threshold, convinced that at any moment I would be ambushed, hacked into pieces by some terrible, unseen weapon.

But nothing came. There was no hint of movement, no hint that anyone was here at all. If I didn't know better, I'd think I was alone. But I did know better, and I needed to get moving if I was going to find Teddy before they hurt him.

I was creeping through the dining room when a loud bang echoed from somewhere above. I tipped my head up, straining my ears. I couldn't tell where exactly it had come from, but it was my only clue.

Frantically, I looked around for something to arm myself with. The bat Teddy had used in the scene we rehearsed at the baseball field—my heart squeezed at the memory of our night there—was lying nearby. I grabbed it and methodically made my way through the house, going through the second floor and then the third, rounding every corner with the bat held high, ready to meet the killer at any moment. But room after room was empty, and soon I was staring at the door leading up to the attic, the only place left that I hadn't checked.

Gulping, I yanked open the door. As soon as I did, I noticed a flickering in the room above. Light. Candles. And then, a hushed noise—like someone telling another person to be quiet. Taking a deep breath, I climbed the stairs.

The first thing I saw when I reached the top was Teddy. He was sitting in an old ratty chair, his hands tied behind the back. His eyes went wide, but he didn't yell out.

The second thing I saw was the person we'd been looking for all along. The person who had been in the photo my dad had shown me.

It was Chloe.

# Chapter Thirty-four

Everything slowed down as I rushed to Teddy's side.

"Teddy!" I knelt on the floorboards, running my hands down his arms as I scanned his body for injuries. "I'm so sorry it took me so long to get here. I—"

Chloe kicked out her leg, knocking me off balance and sending the bat tumbling out of my hand. It rolled across the floorboards before spinning at a stop near her feet.

"Well, that was easy." She knelt down to pick it up. "I expected you to at least put up some kind of a fight."

I wanted to tackle her—small, non-threatening Chloe, with her sweet, heart-shaped face and cherubic blonde waves. I wanted to pull her hair and smack her and maybe push her down the stairs while I was at it. But if the past month had taught me anything, it was that maybe I needed to stop reacting so quickly. So I bit my tongue, hard, and instead rose slowly to my feet.

"I'm here to help you, Chloe. We can figure this out." I gestured to Teddy. "We can all figure this out."

I glanced down at him, hoping he would chime in. But he said nothing, his face tense and trained on Chloe. As though he was trying to anticipate what she would do next.

As though she'd already given him more than enough reasons to be frightened.

Chloe ignored me. "Who did you think it was?" She bent down and started rummaging through a duffle bag. "Like, you obviously didn't know it was me until, like, now."

"What? Why does that matter?"

"Oh, I was just curious." She laughed, a high, trill sound. "I was shocked you didn't figure it out right away. I left all those notes. At first I just wanted to scare you off from calling the police, which seemed to work. But if I was going to psychoanalyze myself, I'd say maybe I wanted to be found. I've been dying to talk to you about this."

I'd known it was Chloe since seeing her in the photo, but it wasn't until that moment—hearing her say it—that it sunk in. "You pretended to be my friend. Why bother? I never suspected you."

Chloe stood, holding something she'd fished from the duffle. "As much as I'd like to start my big villain monologue where I tell you why I did it, we're going to need to relocate first."

My heart accelerated. "Why is that?"

"You'll see." Chloe was positively vibrating with glee. "You'll see very soon."

"Why the hell should we follow you anywhere?"

"This is why." Chloe held out the object in her hand: a gun, small but powerful-looking. "You're going to help him out of that chair and do exactly what I say."

My blood chilled. It was possible that it was a prop gun—there was all manner of fake weapons in the prop trailer. But it was also entirely possible that it was real, and after killing two people on set, Chloe wasn't someone I wanted to test.

I rushed to help Teddy out of the chair.

"I'm so sorry," I whispered, my voice squeaking as I bent over to grab his arms and help him stand up. "I should have believed you. I shouldn't have pushed you away."

"It's ok." His voice was low, his eyes never leaving Chloe as he got to his feet. "We'll figure this out."

I really wanted to believe him.

"Alright, you two." Chloe pointed the gun at both of us. "March."

Teddy and I leaned on each other as we slowly made our way across the attic and down the stairs. I ached to hold him close and explain all the ways I was sorry, to ask him if we could forget everything and start over. But there would be time for that later. I needed to believe that.

"How the hell did this happen?" I whispered. "I mean, you. Here. With her." I glanced over my shoulder, trying to judge if Chloe could hear.

She was smirking.

"Go ahead!" she sang out. "Tell her."

Teddy took a shuddering breath. "After you left, I was worried about you. We already knew the killer wasn't just after you, but also had a key to your hotel room."

"Those receptionists are so helpful," Chloe said.

Teddy ignored her. "So I went down to the desk and explained that they'd given a key to someone they shouldn't have and that person had broken in and if they didn't want us to sue them, they'd tell us who they gave the key to."

"Could we really sue them for that?"

"Doesn't matter. They were able to give me a description and the only person it matched was Chloe. Which confused me at first, because she'd finished filming. She was gone. But then I remembered—"

"What Brent said," I breathed.

Teddy nodded. "He told you we shouldn't be looking in the hotel, and then made a comment later that day that he didn't want to be in this 'freak show' house. It made me wonder if we'd been right all along, that something in the house was the key to everything."

"Me!" Chloe cried out happily.

"Exactly." Teddy's voice was grim. "I figured if Chloe's scenes were over but she was still sneaking around, sabotaging the tree and breaking into your room to wait for you, she had to have a different place to stay. And maybe it was here in the house. So I came over this morning, ready to look for her."

"But he couldn't bring himself to hurt a delicate little woman like me," Chloe said, her voice babyish. "My mother swore all those self-defense lessons she signed me up for would come in handy, and I guess she was right."

"Fuck you," I spat.

"Enough." Chloe pressed the gun into my back as she steered us into the kitchen. "We're almost there."

"Where now?" I glanced around at the cabinets and counters, at a loss for where we were going.

"Down. Into the basement."

"There's a basement?"

Chloe sighed heavily. "Over there. Through the pantry."

With Chloe staying close behind us, Teddy and I opened the pantry door and flicked on the light. I frowned—all I could see were shelves and shelves of products that looked far past their expiration date. But as I peered closer, I noticed a gap on the back wall where the space seemed to make a turn. Getting closer, I saw that around the corner, there was more space. And at the end of that space there was a door.

My heart sank. Mara would have called the cops by now, but how on earth would they find us? Not only would they not know to look in the pantry, but the door was so hidden it was nearly impossible to see unless you knew it was there.

Even if the police did get there in time, they wouldn't know where to look.

Chloe stomped her feet behind us. "Get moving!"

Careful not to trip, Teddy and I gingerly stepped down the stairs. There was no light to illuminate the stairwell, so I prayed the whole way down that this wouldn't end with me falling and breaking my neck. How anticlimactic would that be.

Reaching the bottom, Chloe stepped onto the ground next to us. "Here we are. Home sweet home." She flicked on the light switch, and I gasped.

On the walls of the basement, which looked like it hadn't been renovated or updated since the 1800s, were posters of me— my movie posters. There I was, running through the woods and looking behind me, the poster for my first starring role. Another showed me possessed by a demon, my head thrown back as my eyes glowed red. There was even a poster for *Escape from Camp*

*Nowhere*, a direct-to-streaming film that hadn't done particularly well. I didn't even know there had been posters for that one.

Creepiest of all, a mattress was pushed up against one wall, complete with rumpled sheets and a pillow that looked recently used.

"You've been living down here?" Memories of the strange sounds echoing through the house filtered back. The thought made me gag.

"Sometimes. Especially since I checked out of the hotel," Chloe said cheerily. "Now get moving. Those chairs over there are for you."

Following her directions, we sat on what looked like two old dining chairs. Keeping the gun trained on us, she deftly tied me to a chair with one-handed knots and then finished tying Teddy up on the other. I immediately strained my wrists and ankles, testing the knots: they were tight.

Chloe placed the gun on a nearby shelf and sat down in an old velvet armchair across from us, stretching out her legs and folding her arms behind her head. "Now. I bet you want to know all about how I did it."

I rolled my eyes. Every fiber of my being wanted to tell her no, actually, I didn't want to hear it. I didn't want to give her the satisfaction of laying out her story piece by piece, bragging about how clever she was and how she avoided being caught the entire time. But the truth was I did want to know. Desperately.

"I guess I'll start with a question. Quinn, do you remember the day we met?"

I nodded curtly. "The first day of *Ghost of Puzzle Face*, apparently."

"That's right!" Chloe looked genuinely delighted. "I was an extra, even though I was only six at the time. It was the best experience of my life." She sighed wistfully. "There I was, playing hooky from school so I could be in a real movie. And there you were. You were amazing. I knew I wanted to be just like you when I grew up."

"I'm not that much older than you," I grumbled.

Chloe ignored me. "You were my hero. So imagine my excitement when I was cast in the lead of *House of Reckoning*, which was already generating so much buzz."

"Hang on—"

"That's right," Chloe snapped. "I had the lead, before production decided I wasn't good enough and begged you to sign on instead."

Could that be true? My mind raced back to the first conversation I'd had with production. It was true that I hadn't auditioned and that they had approached me. They'd given me the pitch and were thrilled when I accepted. Then they'd said something, something I hadn't registered at the time. Something about being relieved to have an "actual" professional on board for the role.

"Oh, shit."

"Shit is right. I was late for a handful of meetings and made one single fuss about my storyline and they axed me. I spent years trying to break into the industry after that first bit part when I was little. And when I finally achieved my dream, I had it snatched away from me the day after my family threw me a huge congratulations party." Her hands curled around the arm of the chair like claws. "It made me. So. Angry."

"I'm sorry. This industry is the absolute worst." At least I could agree with her on that.

"But hey." Chloe's face brightened. "It was a chance to work with my idol again, so I figured maybe it wouldn't be so bad. But then day after day, as we got closer to filming, I became more and more disappointed. I'd been so close to my dream. But I still tried to be nice to you the first day. And you were nothing . . . but a huge . . . bitch."

"I've been nothing but nice to you! I let you eat lunch with me. We went to get coffee!"

"Oh, and it's such a privilege to be allowed to eat lunch with you."

"That's not what I meant! I—"

"Can we stay on task, please?" Teddy asked, sounding pained.

"Anyway." Chloe tossed her head. "I thought maybe I'd been wrong all those years. You weren't my idol. You were fake, and now you were standing in my way. We'd only done one day of filming. If something happened to you,"—she mimed holding a knife and dragging it across her throat—"it'd be so easy to put me back in the role. We'd have to reshoot what, one scene? A scene that wasn't even that great, thanks to that one over there." She motioned to Teddy.

"He wasn't that bad," I insisted. "Better than you." Teddy glanced at me, grateful, and I gave him a small smile.

"Please." Chloe laughed. "I knew that if I got rid of you, we could start over like nothing happened. I wouldn't have to tell my family I'd fucked up the one opportunity I'd had in almost twenty years. My career would be back on track! So I decided to take matters into my own hands." She frowned. "Too bad that PA looked so much like you in the dark."

"You didn't mean to kill Trevor?"

Chloe shrugged. "It was an accident. I just wanted to hurt you, bad enough that you'd have to quit the film and I could take your place. I'd seen you walking around base camp earlier that night so I hid behind a trailer and waited for you. Bad luck for Trevor that he walked by first."

I gaped, shocked at her lack of remorse. "And Brent?"

"More collateral damage." Chloe rolled her eyes. "When Brent started raving at the bar about you suspecting him, I knew you were doing exactly what I needed you not to do: poking your nose in my business. I had to stop you."

"Brent stealing my lunch was just a coincidence?"

Chloe's eyes filled with tears. "I'd saved some peanuts from craft services in case I found the chance to slip you some. And then catering left the food unattended, giving me the perfect chance! So I planted the peanuts, satisfied that they would get you once and for all." She choked back a sob. "Until he decided to be a jackass."

There was still one thing I wasn't clear on. "What about Audrey? Why did you attack her that day?"

"Oh, her. Walking onto set that first day, I knew I recognized her. Something about her face, and her voice. And then I finally put my finger on it! She was in that terrible movie a few years back. God, it was bad. I just told her I knew who she was and she freaked out."

"That's all?"

"Well. After Brent died, she also saw me coming out of the

food tent holding the EpiPen I'd swiped from the first-aid kit. She asked me about it later and I told her if she told anyone, I'd blow her cover and tell everyone who she really was."

"What about Trevor's friendship bracelet?"

"I took it on a whim and gave it to Audrey as a sign of our 'friendship.' Wouldn't do very well for me to hang on to it, would it?"

"You're a psychopath."

Chloe shrugged. "Call me what you like."

Seething, I looked around the room, just to have something else to look at besides her. It was grotesque, the posters with my face in various expressions of horror staring down at me. Maybe I should have been scared, as scared as I looked in those photos. But all I felt was rage.

"What's all this for then? If you hate me so much?" I nodded my head toward the memorabilia, which—I suddenly noticed—included Jacques, my beloved stuffed raven, down on the floor near my feet.

Chloe looked confused. "What do you mean?"

"All these posters! And this stuff you stole from my trailer! Why hang it up and put it all down here if you can't stand me?"

"I . . . I don't know."

I forced a laugh. "You're pathetic. You're just an obsessed fan having a tantrum that you're not getting your way."

"I'm no fan of yours," she spat. "I despise you."

I shrugged. "Call it what you like."

She glared at me. "You have no idea what it's like, trying to make it in Hollywood."

"I have no idea what it's like? I've been making movies since

I was eight! And now I'm quitting—did you know that? Because I know exactly how hard it is for women like me and you and Audrey. It's soul-sucking."

"Please. You didn't even have to try to get your first role. It all fell in your lap."

I opened my mouth to retort, but then snapped it closed. She wasn't exactly wrong.

"I've been struggling for almost two decades!" Chloe spat. "Do you know how mean casting directors can be? I've gotten rejected because my ear lobes were too flabby. My ear lobes!" Rising from the chair, she pointed at the side of her head. "I had surgery to pin them back, and I still couldn't book jobs."

"I'm sorry." She wasn't wrong. I did have it easy getting jobs. And casting directors could be assholes. Once one told me that in order to book a lead, I had to swear I wouldn't eat carbs for the duration of filming. Bizarre. "No one deserves that."

"No. No one does. And now, I finally get to have my revenge." Chloe raised the gun. "Teddy will just be more collateral damage."

# Chapter Thirty-five

They say your life flashes before your eyes before you die. In my case, that wasn't true. What flashed before my eyes were my regrets.

I regretted not being honest with my dad sooner.

I regretted not believing Teddy when he told me he didn't leak the photo.

I regretted not figuring out it was Chloe sooner, especially when my dad had the answer in his cabin the whole time.

And as I stared at her pointing that gun at me, convinced I had mere moments left to live, I regretted letting my fear get in the way of me feeling everything I had to feel for Teddy.

I turned to look at him, wanting his gorgeous face and that adorable flop of hair to be the last thing I saw in this world. This was my last chance to say what I needed to say. I wouldn't keep making the same mistake.

"I'm falling in love with you." I whispered the words, not

wanting Chloe to overhear. I didn't want her to be part of this moment.

"What?" Teddy leaned closer. Well, as much as his bindings would allow.

"I'm falling in love with you!" I repeated, louder this time.

"Quinn, I can't hear you!"

Ugh, goddamnit. "I said I love you! And . . ." I closed my eyes, taking a deep breath. "I'm sorry. For, you know, everything."

Teddy's eyes lit up. "Really?"

"Very really." Something like peace swelled in my chest, the satisfaction that if I was about to die, at least I wouldn't have to add not telling Teddy how I felt about him to my list of regrets.

"Oh, gross." Chloe cocked the gun. "Enough of this crap."

But then, a banging sound echoed from above. A noise like a door slamming against a wall.

My heart leapt. The police.

"What the hell?" Chloe tipped her head to the ceiling. "I'll be right back. Neither of you move." She laughed to herself as she climbed up the stairs. "Not like you could."

I waited until I heard her reach the top of the stairs.

"Start screaming," I instructed Teddy. "Mara's outside and called the police. I think that's them up there."

"Did you guys make up?"

"I think so."

Teddy beamed. "Aww! I knew you two would work it out."

"Thank you, but we need to start making noise!"

"Oh, right."

The two of us took deep breaths and yelled as loud as we could, for as long as we could. I screamed until my throat was searing and my stomach hurt; Teddy yelled even louder and longer. But still, no one came.

"I don't think this is working." I stared at the door at the top of the stairs. "I still don't think they can hear us."

Teddy's head fell back in exhaustion. "Damn."

My mind whirred. "I have a new plan." I slouched in my chair, reaching down toward the floor where Jacques lay nearby. "When she gets back, let me do all the talking." I paused, noticing the way his eyes still managed to shine in the dim light. "I really am sorry, by the way." I bit my lip, wishing I could list all the ways I'd screwed up and all the things I wished I'd done differently.

Teddy sighed. "I know. We'll talk later." His eyes drifted upward, where Chloe was pacing above us. "I think she's coming."

"Shoot." I strained as hard as I could, buying me another inch or two as I stretched to reach the stuffed bird. "Trust me, ok?"

"I believe in you." It was a simple statement. Confident. My heart ached. He had no reason to be that confident in me. But as I reached a millimeter further, feeling like surely my wrist was going to break, my fingers finally brushed feathers. I gripped the bird with my fingertips, and with a few more maneuvers, I had it securely in my hand. Another click and I detached the leg, holding it like a dagger as the rest of the bird flopped to the floor.

Footsteps down the stairs.

"We're good. A very funny thing happened, though. The police showed up. Something about looking for a killer." Chloe hopped off the last step and went to retrieve her gun from the shelf. "Luckily, they bought my story that I had definitely seen the killer too, and they had definitely just run out of the house and into the woods! Maybe I am a good actress." She chuckled. "Now, where were we?"

"Wait! Before you kill me, I want to know one more thing." Careful not to draw her attention, I tightened my grip on the dagger. "Why kill me now? The film's been cancelled. They won't reshoot it with you in the lead."

"I already told you." Irritation flickered across her face. "This is about revenge now."

I wiggled the blade against the ropes binding my wrists, making slow but steady progress. "Wouldn't it be more satisfying to let me go and become more successful than me? Make me watch as you beat me for roles?"

Chloe looked dubious. "I don't think so. I think I really want to watch you die." She cocked the pistol.

"Wait! Uh . . ." A few strands of the rope broke beneath my fingers. Many more to go. "I could use my influence to help you get roles. We were friends. We could forget this whole thing ever happened."

"Hmm, no. After the two of you die, do you understand how infamous this movie will be? How famous I will be?"

Another flick of my wrist, and the blade set my wrists free. Triumph lit up my brain and I jumped to my feet.

There was just one problem. I'd forgotten my ankles were still bound together.

I crashed to the ground, sending the chair I was still attached to tumbling after me. It smacked me against the back of my head, sending stars sparkling across my vision.

Ow.

"God, you're stupid." Chloe raised the gun again. "Are you trying to make this easier for me?"

"Never." Now positioned conveniently at her feet, I grabbed her around the ankles and yanked her to the ground next to me.

"Shit!" The gun flew out of her hand as she went down, clattering across the floor and firing, the bullet hitting the wall. I grabbed for the dagger and sawed through the ties binding my ankles. But Chloe rebounded quicker than I expected, hopping up and running after the gun.

"Drop the knife." She pointed the gun at me, legs spread as she took aim. "Now."

"Not a chance, bitch."

"Fine. Say goodnight, Quinn."

The door at the top of the stairs flew open. "Drop the gun, ma'am!" There, silhouetted in the doorway, was Larry the cop.

"I already told you that the killer left," Chloe whined.

"I said drop it!" Larry ran down the stairs, followed by half a dozen of his colleagues. As they filed down the stairs, they revealed Mara, standing triumphantly in the doorway.

"Little did Chloe know I was here to refute her bullshit story." She sighed. "Thank God you have me around."

My heart squeezed. As soon as I got out of that basement, I was going to owe Mara the biggest thank you present.

"Ok, ok. You don't have to be so mean. Ouch!" Chloe cried as Larry slapped handcuffs on her. "I didn't do it." She squinted a few times until tears bloomed in her eyes. "I swear I didn't."

I rolled my eyes. "She admitted everything to me, like, fifteen minutes ago."

"Did you record it?"

"She had my hands tied behind my back, how on earth would I have done that?" I paused for a moment, thinking. "I do have several envelopes licked by her, though. DNA evidence."

Chloe's eyes dried instantly. "Fine, I did do it!" Her eyes roamed the room. "Hey, where's the press? Don't they cover things like this?"

"Ma'am, you're coming with us." Larry turned to Teddy and me. "Will you be able to meet us at the station for a statement?"

We nodded.

"Good." He motioned to the other cops. "Alright, boys, let's go."

Satisfied the police had things under control, I wasted no more time, rushing over to Teddy.

In the long seconds it took for me to close the space between us, I planned to apologize. To tell him all the ways that I'd been wrong, and to tell him how sorry I was that I hadn't believed him, and that I'd assumed the worst in him, and that I'd left him to be abducted by a deranged killer. I'd planned to tell him all of those things, as many times as I needed to, until he believed me. And if it still wasn't enough for him to forgive me, I'd have to live with my consequences.

But by the time I finally reached him, all I could do was frantically untie his wrists before straddling his lap and kissing him, murmuring my sorries in the moments I paused to take a breath.

And he kissed me back—thank God, he kissed me back—between telling me that it was ok and that he forgave me.

*

When we finally left the house, it was still dark but the horizon had a hint of the sunrise to come. Chloe had yammered on and on as Larry escorted her to the police car, asking once again when the media was going to show up to get her side of the story. Larry didn't bother to answer before slamming the door.

"Alright, you two." Larry approached Teddy and me, pulling a notebook out of his pocket. "You know the drill."

Nodding wearily, Teddy and I each made a statement, filling him in on everything we knew. Finally satisfied, Larry promised he'd call us with anything else they needed. Then he left and got into his police car, driving off with Chloe staring moodily out the back window.

As the car disappeared, Mara yawned. "As much as I enjoyed this, I need to go back to the hotel. I feel dead on my feet."

"Yes, go! Oh, right." I rubbed my temples, realizing how foggy my head had gotten. "I need to drive."

"No, that cop over there said he'd give me a ride." She waved to the man waiting by the remaining car. "He's cute, don't you think?"

"Oh my God, Mara."

"What? The best way to get over a guy is to get under another." She winked and held out her arms for a hug. "Come here."

I hurried over, holding her tight as another wave of regret washed over me. "I'm really sorry," I whispered. "I owe you big time."

"It's fine." She pulled away, grinning. "You can pay me back by giving me all the details of you guys' make-up sex."

Teddy's eyebrows flew up in alarm. "What?"

"Nothing." She smiled innocently and blew us a kiss before getting into the car, leaving Teddy and me alone. We sank onto the porch, Teddy wrapping an arm around me and pulling me close. I leaned my head against his shoulder with a sigh, exhaustion creeping up on me, too.

"I'm really, really sorry," I whispered. "I should have believed you when you said you didn't leak those photos. I should have given you the benefit of the doubt."

Teddy shrugged. "I understand why you didn't. It looked pretty shady."

"Still, I shouldn't have reacted like that. Even if we never find out—"

"Oh, I found out."

"Really?" I pulled away in surprise. "What happened?"

Teddy's eyes darkened. "I was trying to think when someone could have gotten a hold of my phone. Even if someone grabbed it during filming, they wouldn't have had my passcode. Then I remembered. The day after we took that selfie, Natasha asked to borrow my phone for a call. Afterward, I caught her tapping around on it. She must have emailed it to herself and then sent it to the tabloid. Wouldn't be surprised if she was the one who took the photo at the field, too."

"How pathetic." At least we hadn't been totally off base about Natasha—she might not have committed murder, but she'd certainly been willing to stoop pretty low to get publicity for the movie. "How would she have even known the photo was on your phone?"

Teddy's cheeks flushed pink. "I may have set it as my background."

Warmth spread through my chest, and I snuggled back under his arm, wrapping my arms around his waist. "You're the cutest."

Teddy pulled me closer, squeezing me tight. "I meant what I said the other night. That you mean the world to me. That I'm falling in love with you."

"I know," I breathed.

"But I also understand you're not looking to get involved, so—"

"I am," I interjected.

"Hmm?"

"Looking to get involved. I mean, with you. Not anyone else."

"Oh? And how does that feel?"

I pulled away so I could look up into his eyes. "Like I trust you. Like I know you wouldn't hurt me." I took a deep breath. "I'm in love with you, too. I want to be with you."

A smile bloomed on Teddy's face, so pure and bright it made my heart ache. "I think I could make that work."

"And if you're still going on that reality show, that's ok, too. We can figure it out."

"About that . . . I want you to know—"

"It's ok." I held up a hand to stop him. "You don't have to explain. It's your career. Your choice."

"No, it's important that you know that I haven't been going on these shows or this movie for fame. I couldn't care less about being famous. I'd rather not be, actually." He absentmindedly ran his thumb along my knee. "It's for the money. Which I know sounds bad! But I need the money to give to my mom."

"Oh." The air went out of me with a whoosh.

"She lost her job last year, and she's been able to make ends meet with a couple of part-time jobs, but I know she's tired. And she's been working so hard for so long, ever since my dad died. I just want her to be able to rest."

"Wow, I'm an asshole."

"You didn't know." He pressed his lips to the top of my head. "And I understand why you have trouble trusting people. I just hope you trust me now. And I won't go on the show. Not when it would be compromising what we have."

I tipped my face up to look at him. "I think you should do it."

"Um, how?" Teddy leaned in close to my ear. "Do you know what happens on those shows? Let me tell you—"

I held up a hand. "I don't need to hear. I just want you to know that I trust you. If you go."

Teddy shifted so he could hold my face in his hands. "You're amazing."

Then he pulled me into a kiss, his lips tender and velvet, and for the first time, I let myself feel everything: how good it felt, how much he made me feel like the best version of me, and how much I wanted him to swallow me up and never let me go.

"One thing," he said, pulling away just enough to form the words.

"What's that?"

"Please cross detective off your list of possible careers."

# Epilogue

## Two years later

The woman tore down the hall of the film studio, scanning the nameplates of each room as she passed. Her feet thudded against the linoleum, the flickering fluorescent lights overhead lighting her way through the dark hallway.

She was looking for a specific person: the CEO who not only made his workplace a living hell but also helped the devil himself steal the souls of his lead actresses. Turning a corner, she spotted it. She'd made it to the right place.

"Come out, come out wherever you are," she called, coming to a stop outside of his office.

She threw open the door. The camera didn't follow her. Instead, it caught their silhouettes as she crept across the room, startling him where he sat at his desk. He leapt up, ready to flee, but it was too late—she tore out his throat, sending blood splattering onto the opposite wall as his screams cried out before fizzling to nothing.

"And cut!" I stood up behind the camera. "That's a wrap, people!"

The actress came out of the room, breathing hard but beaming.

"Did we really get it in one take?" she asked, wiping the sweat from her brow.

"We sure did. You killed it." I chuckled at my own pun.

"Hell yeah." She gave me a high five before leaving set to change out of her now-bloody costume. I took a deep breath, savoring the feeling of wrapping my first film—the first one I'd directed, that is.

The media frenzy after Chloe was identified as the mastermind behind the *House of Reckoning* killings was intense. At first, production considered moving forward with the film, thinking all the buzz might translate into big bucks at the box office. But it soon became clear that the public wouldn't react kindly to the studio profiting from murder, and the production stayed scrapped.

Natasha, predictably, did not react well. She started speaking to any media outlet that would have her, bemoaning the failure of the movie and blaming scaredy-cat execs for not releasing the film. When she let it slip in one interview that she'd resorted to leaking photos of her own cast to try to boost publicity, her lawyer quickly forbade her from talking to the press any further.

She responded by having a very public meltdown and quitting the industry altogether.

Chloe also loved speaking to the press, trying to build her image as a poor little girl from Alabama who had wanted to be a star and was brainwashed by all the sin of Hollywood. The trial was a lengthy process, during which Teddy, Mara, and I all had to testify.

Eventually, she was found guilty on all counts and sentenced to life in prison. She even wrote a memoir about the ordeal, titled *Mother, May I Flirt with Fame?* I immediately pre-ordered it.

Teddy went on to star in the reality show as planned, but not as a contestant. His name had so much buzz attached to it that the producers didn't bat an eye when he requested to appear as the show's bartender instead. He was in every episode, doling out relationship advice that none of the contestants took as he served them gallons of margaritas, which they did take.

As for me, I took a long, hard look at my life once the chaotic aftermath died down. Perhaps unsurprisingly, I didn't feel sad that the movie wasn't going to see the light of day. But I realized that I would miss creating stories and bringing characters to life, even if I wouldn't miss the stress and scrutiny of being in front of the camera myself.

So I started writing. At first, I didn't know what, exactly. But I spent the next month in a fever, writing the first draft of what would become the script for *Soul to Keep*. It took a while to iron out its edges, to figure out what I was trying to say. But when I finally typed "The End" on the final draft, it had morphed into a story about the lengths people will go to for fame—and what it costs us in the process.

When I called to ask Chloe's permission to base one of my characters on her, she agreed as long as I promised to use her real name.

Now, I climbed the stairs to the apartment that Teddy and I

shared, weary but satisfied with the day's work. I slipped the key into the hole and opened the door, trying to decide which pajama pants I would grab once I got inside. Definitely the plaid flannel, I thought.

Opening the door, I was met with softly flickering candlelight and the smell of something delicious simmering on the stove. Teddy poked his head out of the kitchen.

"How'd it go?" he yelled.

"Perfect." I kicked off my shoes and tossed my bag to the ground. "It's officially a wrap."

"That's amazing!" He emerged from the kitchen, wearing an apron with the nude torso of a beer-bellied man on the front. "I have something for you."

"Oh yeah?" I expected him to be making a sexual innuendo, which I wouldn't have complained about, but instead he was holding a small statue.

"Here you go. Congratulations on wrapping your first movie!"

It was a small, shiny, faux-bronze statue of a baseball player, the type given to seven-year-olds after their first season of the game. At the base was a small plate engraved with the words "World's Best Director."

"Oh my gosh, thank you!" I wrapped an arm around his shoulders and pressed a kiss to his cheek. "I love it."

"I wanted to get you something that looked more like an Oscar," he explained sheepishly. "But they were out."

"That's ok. I love it." I couldn't take my eyes off it. It was random and silly and so, so thoughtful—just like Teddy. My heart swelled and I thought there surely wasn't enough room in my body to fit the love I had for him.

He paused, watching me closely. After a few moments, I got the feeling he was waiting for a reaction I wasn't giving him.

"Um, what?"

"Quinn, did you look at it closely?"

I frowned, looking down. "Yes, of course. It's a super cute little baseball man, like the night we spent on the field! I love him!"

He sighed, crossing his arms. "Maybe look a little closer."

I held it up to my face, unsure what I was supposed to be looking for. I knew my eyesight was bad, but surely there was nothing I could be missing? But then I saw it—looped around the baseball player's bat was a ring. Specifically, a white gold band with a large solitaire diamond flanked by two smaller, but equally perfect, white stones.

The noise I emitted could only be described as a shriek.

"Do you like it?" Teddy asked, clearly pleased with my reaction.

"What is this? What is this?! What does it mean?!"

Teddy gingerly took the statue from my hands and removed the ring. And then, like something out of an honest-to-God romantic comedy, sank down onto his knees. My heart hammered in my chest, and I started fanning my face like a Regency romance heroine. I couldn't believe this was happening.

Fanning. My. Face. Ridiculous.

"Quinn. From that first day on set, I knew there was something special about you. Yes, even as you stormed up to me and told me I was a selfish asshole."

My cheeks burned. "Sorry about that."

"I knew that there was something in you that ignited a feeling in me that I'd never felt before. Because even when you were insulting me right to my face, all I could think about was how pretty and charming you were. And then you went on to prove to me, time and time again, that I would never meet another person like you. That I never wanted to meet another person like you. Romantically, that is."

I gulped.

"And then, like the heroine of some goddamn superhero movie, you came and saved me right when I needed you."

I smiled, thankful that he was generous enough not to mention that I had been the very reason he was captured in the first place.

"The last two years have been amazing, more amazing than anything I could have dreamed for. Even when you elbow me in the ribs when I start to snore. I can't imagine living without you. Will you marry me?"

"Yes!" I jumped into his arms as he rose to his feet, wrapping my legs around his waist in a move I'd only ever seen on *The Bachelor* but which it turned out can work in real life too. "I do. I mean, I will."

Teddy grinned under my kiss and slipped the ring onto my finger. Somehow, he'd bought a ring that fit me perfectly on the first try.

But that was also just like him: fitting me perfectly, even without trying.

# *Acknowledgments*

Getting this book to publication has been a wild ride, and I'm beyond thankful to my amazing agent Tanera Simons for making my lifelong dream a reality. Thank you for plucking me out of your slush pile and giving me a chance! More thank yous to Laura Heathfield, Mary Darby, and the team at Darley Anderson for additional support along the way.

Every writer dreams of finding an editor that instantly clicks with them and their book, and I was so lucky to find that in Katherine Burdon. Thank you so much for taking a chance on me, Quinn, and Teddy – and for sharing a deep admiration for Adam Driver. Additional thanks to the broader Quercus team for helping this book come to fruition!

Writing can be lonely and painful and exhausting, so a million thank yous to the Slack – I love you all dearly and couldn't hack it in this industry without you. A special thank you to Piper, LC, Chandra, Siana, Lani, and Sami for reading early drafts of this manuscript. Your encouragement (and gentle roasting) is the only reason this book exists!

More special thank yous to my husband Dann, who is a real-life romance hero; my son Felix, who is the only person I want to impress; and my dad, who's always been the most supportive parent I could ask for, even when I had pie-in-the-sky, perhaps-unrealistic dreams of becoming a writer. Thank you to my mom and Grandma Dexter, for a million things but also for giving me my love of reading.

And finally, thank you to my brother for thirty-four years of memories. You would have been mortified to be mentioned in a romance novel. (Sorry about that.)